THE KATRINA CONTRACT

by

Larry Nocella

The Katrina Contract is a work of fiction.

Copyright © 2013 Larry Nocella

Cover photos "Drowning duck in blue water" by viperagp
and "Gun With Bullet Holes And Blood" by PiXXart
Licensed through BigStockPhoto.com

CreateSpace file ver 2.0 edition prepared October 2013
CreateSpace file ver 3.2 edition prepared July 2014

QECE publishing
www.LarryNocella.com

ISBN-13: 978-0615910383

ISBN-10: 0615910386

All rights reserved.

Other works by Larry Nocella

NOVELS

Loser's Memorial

Where Did This Come From?

SHORT STORY

It Never Goes Away

THE KATRINA CONTRACT

by

Larry Nocella

PART 1

CUSTOMER SERVICE

1

In a cubicle in a dark room somewhere, a young woman pushed a blinking amber button on her desk phone. She forced herself to smile as she adjusted her headset microphone. She spoke English with the bouncing lilt of an Indian accent.

"Customer service agent twenty-five sixty-one. How may I help you?"

"Guns," the caller urgently whispered. "They've got guns!"

He said something more but the words were obscured by a muted scuffling, as if he was stuffing his phone in his pocket.

Then silence.

The operator scribbled three words on her notepad.

Old. Male. American?

"Hello?" the operator said. "Hello, sir. How may I assist you today?"

A whoosh filled her ears, as the caller's mouthpiece was uncovered. The caller was mid-sentence.

"-not sure how to use this thing. Is anyone there? Is this working?"

"Hello? Sir?" the operator said. "I will be glad to be of assisting today. The connection seems to breaking. Can you get-"

"They're storming the ship," the man said, interrupting. "Men in masks. They're taking hostages. Come get me. Now!"

"I will be glad to provide you excellent customer service today. However, I will be requiring your account number before I am able to process any request."

The operator winced as a woman near the caller screamed.

"Oh, my God! They've got guns!"

"I told her that," the man barked. "Hello? You there? Come get me right now!"

"Sir," the operator said, "I am sorry but I need-"

The woman on the caller's end screeched again, unleashing a sustained piercing squeal. The operator's headset earphones peaked and ruptured into static. When the electronic equipment recovered, the woman on the caller's end was yelling.

"-such a cheap ass! We just had to do it like this. You could have bought your own boat. You could have bought your own plane! You see what happens? You see!"

"Shut up!" the man yelled back. "I'm calling for help!"

"Sir," the operator said, her eye on the script tacked to the fabric walls of her cubicle. "I want to provide you with exceptional customer service, but I am sorry and cannot hear you. Can you move someplace with more silence?"

"It's my damn wife," the caller said. "Are you coming to get me or what?"

"Sir, this is a private line," the operator said calmly. "We require your account information. If you do not provide it, I will sadly be necessity to terminate this call so I may excellently serve other customers."

"Don't you dare hang up on me, you curry-munching cow-kisser. I'll buy your whole damn village and burn it to the ground."

The operator felt her cheeks burn as she ran her finger down her operator tip sheet, stopping at the line that said, 'Customers may be angry, but you can always be respectful.'

"Sir, I am trying to provide you with top quality serv-"

The woman on the line screamed again, this time further away from the caller. "They're shooting! They're shooting!"

"Damn it, lady," the man yelled into the phone. "Don't you know who I am? I could buy and sell you a million times. Can't you see the number I'm calling from?"

"Mister, it is possibly you are using a stolen phone. Provide your account number, please."

"Hide in the closet!" the woman on the caller's end said. "In the closet!"

The operator endured several seconds of scratching and grunting noises. Her eye caught the digital timer on her phone's display flashing as it passed fifty seconds. The note taped next to the timer read, "Over one minute equals failure."

"Sir," she said, "your account number."

"This is ridiculous! For how much I'm paying, you should-"

"Sir, without your account number-"

"Fine. Let me find it. I can barely see. Wait. Here it is. Seven nine seven six two one. Now stop messing around and get me out of here. This is deadly serious. Life and death."

The operator punched the numbers into her computer. The screen responded with a friendly window that said simply, "Verified. Confirm password."

"I am pleased to tell to you that your account number has passed confirmation," she said. "Now I will be needing your password."

"More questions? Just send help. Do it now!"

"They're close!" the woman on the calling end whimpered. "I think they're on our deck. Oh, no! No! No!"

"Will you shut up? They're going to hear you."

"Your password. Sir?"

"Oh, let me think, it's-"

A loud bang obliterated his words.

"I'm sorry sir," the operator said, frowning at the phone timer, now well over one minute.

"There was a background noise. I couldn't quite hearing you."

"Sweetheart! It's sweetheart!" he yelled before quickly dropping his voice to a whisper. "Please hurry. They're here. They're breaking in next door."

The woman on the calling end was sobbing.

The operator typed in the password. Her computer screen responded with a form, most of the fields already were populated.

"Thank you, Mister Sinclair," the operator said. "Your account has been activated. Now please can you give me details on your situation?"

"I'm on a cruise ship," the man whispered. "The Sunset Mist. Terrorists are taking over. Guys with guns and ski masks. Now get me off this damn boat!"

"Our system has confirming your approximate locale via satellite GPS through your cell phone. Now I ask that you to do the needful and get to a safe pla-"

The line crackled and was silent.

"Sir? Hello? Sir?"

She waited.

Silence.

The operator grumbled to herself as she completed the computer form and then pressed enter to submit it.

"What a jerk," she mumbled to herself. "I hope they find him in that closet."

As soon as the words left her mouth, she noticed a tiny, blinking red dot in the corner of her computer screen next to the words "Call Recording."

She flicked off her phone and looked over her shoulder as she slouched a little lower in her seat.

2

Nothing was going to save him. Nothing. He was going to die here.

They were trapped. The zip crack of a bullet exploded in his ear. He could hear his squad yelling to each other, but he couldn't make out the words. He could hear the enemy, speaking in their gruff language, and they were much, much closer. Rod crouched behind the rock and looked up to the moon.

It was full and beautiful.

"Probably the last time," he said to himself. The bullets were cracking closer now. He could barely hear anything but their whipping sound.

Running from cover was almost certain death, but staying until he was overrun was absolutely certain.

He chose almost over absolutely and launched himself down the rocky mountainside. Lines of light speared the dark as tracers arced past him in both directions, coming from his comrades and his enemies.

"Keep moving!" he yelled to himself.

Suddenly all the noise stopped. In the silence he heard a squeak. Like someone stepping on a dog's toy.

He was in the sun, dripping sweat, strolling a crowded market, when a woman wearing a black burqa walked toward him and stopped. That was strange, he thought. They never stopped. They always kept walking.

He saw the flash of silver as the blade drove for his chest. He reacted on instinct, grabbing her wrist, twisting it until it cracked and she screamed. He bent her broken arm back with both hands and stabbed her in the neck with her own knife.

She opened her mouth to scream, but only the rubber toy squeak sound emerged.

The boy, he had to be a boy, a face that young, that smooth, could only be a boy, not a man.

The boy tore open his vest, like a superhero. Underneath, instead of a colorful uniform, he was a mass of wires and explosives. The boy pointed at Rod, cursing in a language Rod didn't understand. People around the boy scattered, but Rod knew there was no time to run. He curled, twisted, holding his forearm over his head. It was the only protection he could reach in time. From the corner of his eye, he saw the boy disappear in a white flash.

The explosion sounded like a rubber duck squeak.

"Help us!" voices cried in the darkness, between the explosions. *"Help us!"*
Rod couldn't find them. His night vision goggles had been torn off. He stepped in something slippery that made a terrible moaning sound. He was in Hell. He was never going to get out. He was going to die horribly, like everyone around him. Nothing could save-

Squeak!

"Hayger!" North screamed. He could hear the horror in his own trembling voice. "Guys! Hayger's down. It's bad. Hayger. Come on, buddy!" North looked down at his friend, the man's uniform darkened with blood the blood all over his chest. Hayger's eyes were lightly closed, his mouth opening and closing, no sound coming out but a dry breathing-

Squeak!

Hayger was gone. North was alone, ducking between rocks, trying in vain to not kick up dust. The enemy was out there, stalking him. Nothing was going to save him. He was going to die. Die in this-

Squeak!

What the hell was that squeaking noise in the middle of this burning hot barren moonscape dump of a country?

"Daddy?" a young boy's voice said.
Rod shook his head.
"Daddy?"
Squeak!
Rod opened his eyes.
The memories of blood and mayhem were gone. He was staring at himself in his bathroom mirror, scars crisscrossing his chest, water dripping from him, a towel around his waist. The steam in the air was clearing.
"Daddy? Are you okay?"
Rod looked down. His son Toby was at his side, tugging gently at the towel.
Why is Toby here? Rod wondered.
His son reached out and touched Rod's massive fist with his finger.

"What are you doing to Mister Duck-Duck?" Toby asked.

Rod opened his left fist. The squashed rubber yellow duck toy let out an airy gasp, as if breathing a sigh of relief.

Toby took it from him and cradled the toy in his cupped hands until the rubber popped out to its normal shape. Then he threw his arms around Rod.

The horror in Rod's mind dissolved. The blood and the dust, the stench, the tension and the fear melted away. They were all powerless against Toby's feeble grasp and the supernatural powers of Mister Duck-Duck.

Rod knelt and hugged his son.

"Daddy," Toby sighed.

"Hey, buddy," Rod said. "I love you. Don't know what I'd do without you."

"I love you too, Daddy."

He hugged his son, pressing his face into the boy's neck.

If you only knew, kid.

When Rod could feel Toby squirming, he released him.

"How did you get in, buddy?"

"Mommy."

Footsteps sounded on the carpeted stairs. Rod frowned. He stood and turned.

"Hey," Carol said, abruptly.

"Hey," Rod answered, just as terse.

"Why are you up so early?"

"Guy Barra's on vacation," he said. "I'm covering for him."

"Real vacation," she said, "or," she made quotation marks with her fingers, "Special Vacation?"

"I don't know," Rod said.

Carol rolled her eyes.

"Barra. He the short one? Olive skin, dark bushy hair?"

"That's him."

"He's kind of cute."

Rod didn't respond.

Toby sat on the floor and tossed Mister Duck-Duck from hand to hand.

"I let us in," Carol said, "because I didn't think you'd be up."

"How did you get in?"

"I still have a key."

"Oh."

"You want it back?"

"I just didn't know you had one."

"Here," she said, pulling the key from her key ring. "Take it." She slapped the key on the sink counter.

"So, can you pick him up, too?" Carol said.

"Yeah, I got him."

"Daddy," Toby said. "Mommy said I can stay over."

"Of course you can, buddy."

"Yay! That will be the best!"

Carol pressed her lips together tightly. Rod smirked.

"All right, Toby," Carol said, "Mommy's going now."

"Bye, Mommy."

"Aren't you going to give me a hug?"

Toby looked up at Rod. Rod met his gaze but didn't say anything. He looked at Carol and shrugged.

"Come here," Carol said, kneeling. "Give mommy a hug."

Toby walked toward her, head down. He put his arms around her limply.

"You love mommy, don't you," Carol said, rubbing his back. "You love her, right?"

"Yes," Toby muttered.

"All right," Carol said, standing. "I'm out. Don't forget to pick him up, okay? I've got plans for tonight."

"Sure," Rod said. "You'll have to let yourself out."

"Oh I'm good at that," she said, laughing. Her cell phone chirped. She picked it up and was talking as she descended the stairs.

"Yeah," she said, "I can do it. Is everyone going to be there? Just dropped the kid off. Freedom for one beautiful night." She chuckled, slamming the door shut behind her.

Rod turned to Toby. "Hey, buddy, you want to go play while I get ready?"

"Yeah."

Toby didn't move.

"What's up? Why do you look sad?"

"Daddy, can I stay with you?"

"Sure. You're staying over tonight."

"I mean, forever."

"Don't you like staying with Mommy?"

"She has friends over. They get loud. I can't sleep. And they smoke. It stinks."

Rod knelt by his son.

"Hey, I'll talk to Mommy about that. Right now, we're together. So let's have fun before I take you to school, okay?"

"Okay!"

"And tonight, it's nothing but pizza and movies."

"Promise?"

"You got it."

3

The worldwide headquarters of Redfire Advanced Security Solutions was a tinted-windowed monolith rising from a grassy field. The building and its manicured grounds appeared to have been assembled by extracting a skyscraper from the nearest city and dropping it into the middle of a golf course.

An enormous version of Redfire's corporate emblem decorated the outside corner of the top floor. When the sun struck the polished silver stylized flame, the logo seemed to burn.

The even-cut grass at the base of the thirty-story tower was surrounded by a ten-foot fence topped with barbed wire. Regularly spaced along a paved walking path inside the fence were tall metal poles capped with flood lights and cameras.

Rod North steered his car away from the main entrance where four lanes of cars had backed up at the security booths, waiting to check in. He drove along a smaller road, following the "Security Employees Only" signs. The queue at this checkpoint was much shorter.

"I'm telling you, he's complaining that he can't sleep!" Rod yelled into his cell phone.

"Oh, that's crap, Rod," Carol said from the other end. "You're still bitter because my lawyer kicked your lawyer's ass."

"You say that every time Toby complains to me. I don't bring up the fact that you're bitter because you didn't get as much child support as you wanted."

"I can always try again."

Rod felt a pain developing above his right eye. "Carol, can you think of someone else first for once? Especially our son? He said you smoke and you have friends over late and it keeps him awake. I'm not telling you what to do, I'm telling you to tone it down when he's with you, okay?"

"When I see him, I'll ask him how he feels about it."

"He's obviously afraid to tell you. Do you know why that is?"

"He's just shy."

"I think he's afraid you'll yell at him."

"He needs to lighten up. Where do you think he got that from?"

"Carol! He's a kid! A child, okay?"

"Well, he's got to grow up sometime. Are you sure you can pick him up tonight?"

"Yes. For the tenth time."

"Good. Because I have plans. With the girls, and maybe someone else."

"Well, I hope he's patient."

"Oh, he is," she said, dragging out her words slowly.

"Are you trying to sound sexy? If you're hoping to make me jealous, it's not working at all."

"Just letting you know that I'm having fun."

"All I'm asking is that you take it easy when our son is around, okay? We're not in our twenties or thirties anymore. You can still have fun, but Toby comes first."

"Sure, Rod. Whatever you say. Always be good. Do the right thing."

"Sorry I'm that way. I guess to you it's a flaw."

"Damn right it is, that's why you were never any fun."

"I'm at work now, Carol. Gotta go."

Rod hurled his phone onto the empty passenger seat. It bounced up against the window, ricocheted into the dashboard and fell to the floor.

He pulled up to a barrier and held his company badge under the scanning laser.

"Hey, Rod," the armed guard in the booth said, "how's it going?"

North didn't answer. The gate lifted and his car jerked forward with a squeal as he sped through.

* * *

After parking, North walked to the nearest entrance and swiped his ID badge across a small black panel. The panel chirped and the magnetic bolts behind the door released with a loud clack. He pushed through and waited for the door to latch behind him.

His steps echoed in the long unpainted concrete hall as he walked under a ceiling that alternated between fluorescent lights and black hemispheres hiding cameras.

He stopped at a door blocking his path and looked to his right through the reinforced glass. The guard on duty looked up at the clock.

"Hey, North. You're early. Way early."

"Yeah," Rod said, opening the door. "Don't remind me. I'm filling in for Barra."

"I hear the line out there's already backed up. Had a few call outs."

"Great."

The door buzzed as it unlocked.

* * *

Rod entered a small room lined with ten heavy-duty metal lockers on either side, a wooden bench down the middle. He opened his locker and stored his lunch, removing his automatic pistol. He checked the ammo and the safety before holstering the weapon at his hip.

He rested his right hand on the weapon and tapped the two photos on the back of his locker door. The largest was of him and Toby, arms around each other, at a baseball game. Toby's cap was too big for his head and sliding down to the side. He held his plastic bat tucked under his elbow and a giant foam 'We're number one' hand aloft.

Underneath that photo was a picture of the six men in Rod's old military unit. Each of the muscular men were dressed in desert camouflage and posing with their heavy rifles. 'Afghanistan Class of 2002. Iraq Class of 2004. Your Mom Class of 2006, sucker!' was painted on the side of the helicopter they were leaning against.

Rod pulled a silver necklace from his locker. A small pendant the size of a quarter dangled from the end. Inside was a picture of him and Toby smiling into the camera.

This photo was less staged than the other. Toby was sitting in the tub, his lower body obscured by a layer of soap. He was looking up, his large brown eyes round, his skin wet, as if he was newly born. The smile on his face made Rod's heart stutter. Toby held both hands above his head, palms up as if making an offering of the object resting on his fingers, his son's favorite toy, Mister Duck-Duck.

Rod clenched the necklace in his fist and pressed his fist to his lips.

Rod felt his neck muscles loosen, the memory of Carol's scraping voice dissolved.

He closed his eyes and inhaled deeply. He held his breath, then exhaled.

He put the necklace on, tucked the pendant under his shirt then slammed his locker shut.

* * *

Back in the hall, he walked a hundred more steps to another door, used his ID to pass through and exited the drab grey into a colorful mixture of rainforest and shining black marble.

The lobby of Redfire Advanced Security Solutions' global corporate headquarters was split down the middle. Revolving doors connecting to the outside were separated from the elevators leading up into the building by a security desk and three metal detectors. Visitors were funneled toward the metal detection gates by the gentle curves of a low retaining wall that held the soil for a lush indoor forest. The air was kept humid to nurture the exotic ferns and flowers. The organic smell helped warm the coldness of the marble floor and walls.

An elderly woman sold coffee and pastries from a cart to employees waiting to pass through the security checkpoint. The ample foliage on either side of the large security desk served a dual purpose: it kept the atmosphere relaxing and the air refreshing, but its main purpose was obscuring the bulletproof floor-to-ceiling concrete and steel barrier behind it.

Except for security team members, who came in through the side doorway, anyone entering the building had to pass through this gauntlet to reach the elevators and the inside of Redfire World Headquarters.

The morning rush was on. Two queues extended back from the desk, each at least twenty heads deep. Five security employees were checking people in. This involved scanning their badges, stiff laminated cards that hung around their necks or were clipped to their suits. Security confirmed the photo on the ID matched the picture on the computer and the person presenting it, then beckoned them through the two active metal detectors.

The third metal detector was unused, closed off by a rolling gate.

The lines moved slowly. Rod sat behind the security desk, quickly glancing over a bank of black and white screens. From here he could see what every camera on the Redfire campus was seeing. Each screen held its image for ten seconds before automatically switching to another. A digital stamp in the lower right corner indicated the camera's location as well as the time and date.

"Hey, Rod," an older security guard called out. His nametag read 'Phelps.' He took an ID from a young executive in a custom-fit suit and held the laminated barcode under a red laser. Phelps handed the ID back after the scanner sounded a friendly beep.

"Harold," North said.

"You're late," Harold Phelps answered, scanning another ID.

"I'm filling in."

"Yeah, well, me too. And I'm staying past quitting time. Barra is always on time when he picks up from my shift. And I'm never late when I take over from you."

"Sorry," North said.

"Sorry? Yeah, right. Then why does it always happen?" Phelps continued to scan badges as he spoke. "You're never sorry. Of all the managers in the rotation, you're the only one ever late."

North stared at the camera monitors. The executives passing through were silent, watching back and forth as Phelps berated North.

"Come on, get up," Phelps said. "You and I can take the third gate and make another line."

North pushed himself up and began taking badges while Phelps powered up the metal detector and rolled the gate aside.

Suits started breaking off the other lines, moving to the newly opened entrance.

"You guys really need to have more gates," the first executive in line said as he handed North his ID.

North grunted.

The suit chatted with Phelps.

"Working late, Harold?"

"Late for me, early for you."

"You look busy as always."

"Those acting lessons are paying off."

The suit laughed and passed through the gate.

The next one was equally cheerful.

"How's it going, Phelps?"

"Same old. Keeping trained monkeys out of a job."

"Yeah, you and me both."

North rubbed his hand over his face, fighting back a yawn. He took the next ID, scanned it and handed it back. The queue to their metal detector formed against the front of the desk as the suits continued to banter with Phelps. North glanced up. One of the suits met his gaze, blinked rapidly and stepped back, looking away.

No photograph failed to match its owner. No one carried or wore any items that set off the metal detectors. The ritual was choreographed and well-rehearsed and entirely unsurprising to anyone.

* * *

At 9:30 a.m. the rush ended and the lobby was quiet again.

"All right, fellas, I'm out of here," Phelps said to the security team. "North is in charge."

He walked briskly to the security exit and went through without another word, slamming the door behind him.

North was sitting at the bank of screens, watching them cycle through their different viewpoints. He stayed apart from the four other security guards as they joked among themselves.

"Some of these corporate chicks should have been models. I swear to. Mm."

"If I was only a few years younger."

"You'd still be too old for them."

"Hey, where it counts, I'm still twenty-one."

"I didn't need to know that. Besides, your boyfriend said that's not true."

"I'd take those corporate chicks two at a time."

"Yeah, right. You'd die of a heart attack."

"Women today are like men. Get in, get out."

"That's just fine with me, honey."

"You need a spanking!"

They all guffawed.

"Guys!" North yelled at them. "Come on. A little lower. Sound echoes in here."

"Sorry, boss," one of them grumbled. They whispered to each other.

"Besides," North said, "it's time to make your rounds."

"Barra doesn't make us go until ten."

"Barra's not here. I am. It's almost ten anyway."

The four shuffled out of the lobby to patrol the perimeter of the building. North stayed alone at the desk, checking a form on a clipboard as he confirmed through the cameras that each guard had arrived at his checkpoint and given the thumbs up through the video feed.

He had the radio on, the volume low, hearing but not paying any attention to the news.

* * *

North glanced at the clock. It was almost noon. The team would be finishing their rounds soon and then taking lunch two at a time.

One of the security screens caught North's eye. The stamp indicated it was a roof camera, but the screen was washed out as dust blew against the lens. North held down a button to prevent the image from cycling to the next camera's view.

The whiteout faded to show a helicopter, its rotors slowing. Two suits rushed forward to greet a third who descended from the chopper. They were all frowning, walking briskly, heads down. North couldn't hear what they were saying, but their hand gestures were urgent and quick.

"Hm," North mumbled. "Something's going on."

* * *

The security team returned from their rounds. North was about to tell them to pick lunch times when a woman spoke from behind him.

"Are you Roderick North?"

North turned to see a young lady, dressed in a dark business blazer and skirt. She had short black hair, her features vaguely Chinese. Rod guessed she couldn't have been older than twenty-five.

Harold Phelps was standing with her. He looked pissed off.

"Yes," North said. "I'm Rod North."

"I'm here with your replacement," she said. "I'm supposed to take you upstairs."

"Oh," North said. "Sure."

"I'll give you a moment to switch out," the young woman said.

Phelps stepped to the bank of screens and checked the clipboard.

North grabbed his cell phone and signed off on the papers, logging out of the system by scanning his badge.

Phelps grumbled out loud. "I had just gotten home and took my shoes off when I get the call to come back. They said I was needed to work another shift because no other supervisors are available. At the end of this, I'll be pulling over 24 hours."

"Now, Harold," the young woman said. "Human resources is working on getting you some help as soon as-"

"Save it, young lady. So what gives, Rod?"

North didn't reply.

Phelps persisted. "They said you were needed for something else."

"I don't know what this is about."

"I think you do," Phelps said, looking over his shoulder. The young woman was walking across the lobby toward the elevators, but he whispered anyway. "I was pretty sure about Barra, but I never thought you were ex-Special Forces. You're big, but I think I could take you."

North said nothing. The older man was blocking his way from the desk.

"Come on, North, you can tell me. I know what's going on. I've been working here long enough to notice some guys get," he made quotation marks with his fingers, "vacation."

"I really should go, Phelps."

"This is just your holding place, right? That's why you don't give a crap. Barra just does a better job of faking that he cares. He's a stand-up guy. But this work is beneath you, is that it?"

"Phelps, let me past. I know you're pissed about the shift, but that's not my fault."

"You work here until they need you for something else. A different kind of security. Bodyguards mostly, but I've heard rumors about the more sinister stuff, like knocking off a guy. Am I right? I might not be in your special club, but I'm not stupid. I notice things."

"Goodbye, Harold."

They brushed shoulders as North pushed past.

"I'll take your silence as proof that I'm right," Phelps said. He yelled across the lobby, "Tell me, North, what's the quickest way to kill a man?"

North let the question bounce off his back. He caught up with the young woman, who was holding an elevator for him.

"Right this way, Mister North," she said.

When he stepped into the elevator, she turned a key in the control console and pushed one of the buttons surrounded by a gold frame engraved with the words "Senior Executive Team Levels."

"Scan I.D., please," a pre-recorded voice said. The young woman leaned forward and swiped her badge across the control panel.

"Thank you," the voice said.

The elevator ascended.

4

"I'm Ashley," the young lady said, shaking North's hand.
"Nice to meet you," he said. "I'm Rod North. Call me North."
"Of course, Mister North."
"I'm guessing they haven't told you anything other than to come get me?"
"That's right."
"So you have no idea what I'm going to be doing? Not a clue?"
"I don't really even know what this is for."
"Who's your boss?"
"Mister Addison."
"Addison? Never heard of him."
"Everyone on my floor is relatively new."
"Seems to work that way up there. Lots of turnover."
"If he tells me to send an email, I do it. If he tells me to go pick people up, I do it. I don't need to know the details. I just do my job. No questions asked."
"A good survival strategy."
"When I get to his level, that's how I want my people to be. Just do what you're told. If they need to know, I'll tell them."
"Or not. Because you're the boss."
Ashley chuckled uneasily. "I know, right?"
She looked around the elevator, avoiding his eyes. The ride continued in silence until the doors opened with a ping.
North followed her down the maroon-carpeted hall and into a small room with drab tan walls. Two office chairs faced each other across a table. There were no windows and no other furniture.
"Mister Addison wanted you to wait in here," Ashley said.
"I know the drill. I've done this plenty of times. Ever notice this looks like an interrogation room?"
"Uh... I think it's just supposed to be like private, that's all. You can, um, have a seat. Mister Addison will be with you shortly."
Rod sat down.
Ashley left and closed the door behind her. A key rattled in the doorknob from the other side. After the sound stopped, North tested the door handle and laughed.
She had locked him in.
"Like that would stop me," he mumbled.

He checked his cell phone. No signal. A camera peeked at him from the corner of the ceiling. He waved to it.

"Real private," he grumbled.

5

North moved to the other seat so he was facing the exit. He drummed his fingers on the table for only a few seconds before the doorknob rattled again.

A man wearing a dark pin-striped suit stepped in and locked the door behind him. His jacket's gold buttons and cufflinks twinkled in the fluorescent light. He was carrying an unmarked manila folder. His face was tanned an unnatural orange-bronze that accented his blue eyes and manicured eyebrows. His gelled hair reminded North of the models from Carol's fashion magazines.

The newcomer tested the doorknob to make sure it was locked. Then he finally turned and looked North in the eyes.

"Hello, Mister North," he said. "I'm Redfire Account Executive Clarence Addison."

North waited for him to say 'Nice to meet you,' but he didn't.

"Okay," North said.

Addison extended his hand over the table. North shook it, making Addison struggle a few seconds before releasing him.

"So, what's this all about?" North asked. Addison unbuttoned his jacket and sat down. He pressed his fingertips together and leaned back in the chair, resting his right foot on his left knee. His shoes glistened in the harsh light.

"You'll know what you need to when you need to."

"All right," North said.

"Your file indicates you've gone through this before."

"Lots of times."

"Some of the things I'm about to say you've undoubtedly heard, but I will be going over everything for the purpose of our records. Please note we are being recorded." He nodded to the camera in the corner of the ceiling.

"Got to keep the lawyers happy," North said.

Addison held up his hand. "This will go faster without interruptions."

"I was just-"

"Time is critical. Now, I need you to confirm you're aware this entire conversation is being recorded."

North leaned back in his chair and folded his arms. "I am."

"And are you aware this recorded conversation will be used in legal proceedings against you should you deviate from the contractual obligations of your employment?"

"I am."

"And do you acknowledge that your employment contract with Redfire Advanced Security Solutions, Special Projects Division, stipulates that you will on occasion be promptly dispatched on highly secretive assignments that exploit your special talents?" Addison took a deep breath after he finished.

"I do," North said.

"You're an old pro."

"I've been with Redfire for a while."

Addison held up his hand. "Small talk is not necessary."

"But you-"

"Mister North, may I continue?"

North stared at him.

"Or do you want to keep wasting company time?"

Addison pointed toward the camera as a reminder. "May I go on?" he said to North. "Is that okay with you?"

North's eyes narrowed.

Addison continued. "This is your verbal notification that Redfire Advanced Security Solutions wishes to activate the portion of your employment contract relevant to clandestine activities. Pursuant to that end, only a select few Redfire employees, their identities known only to myself, are aware of this as yet unspecified task. For the purposes of extreme privacy for our customers, our executive team, excluding myself, but up to and including our chief executive officer, has not been and will not be notified of this task until it is complete or confirmed aborted or failed. Have you understood everything I've said so far?"

"Yes."

"Sign."

Addison slipped a stapled collection of paper from the folder and spun it around to face North. He pushed a gold-trimmed pen across the table.

"Careful with that pen," he said. "It's worth a lot."

North leafed through the stack, not bothering to read the tiny single-spaced text. He flipped through the pages, signing next to the small red stickers.

"Wait a second," North said, closing the packet. "You're supposed to be explaining what I'm signing."

"Waivers," Addison said.

"And exactly what am I waiving?"

"As a veteran you should know."

"I know you have to say it out loud if I ask," North said, smiling slightly. "It's part of my contract."

"I'm trying to save time."

North shrugged. "Remember we're being recorded."

Addison pressed his lips together tightly and exhaled through his nose.

"Fine," he said. "You are waiving your right to hold Redfire and its representatives or stockholders or board of directors responsible for any damages or injuries, up to and including death, that you may sustain during your assignment. You also agree not to disclose any details of the assignment to any person or media entity. This includes immediate family, spouses and/or children. The contract you are signing is primarily concerning terms you've already agreed to as conditions of your employment. We're simply getting another signature. To be sure."

North resumed flipping through the pages. "Next you're supposed to tell me what happens if I don't sign. Come on now." He set the pack of papers down again and smirked.

Addison frowned. He spoke fast and low, like a disclaimer at the end of a used car lot's radio ad. "If you choose not to sign, your employment with Redfire will be terminated immediately and you will be sued for breach of contract. Redfire will seek all your back wages plus additional damages caused by your deceptive business practices."

"Wow. You're good. Some guys use a script."

"Anything else?"

"Aren't you going to inform me of my next of kin's rights?"

"No," Addison said abruptly. "That's no longer part of the process. Now sign."

North signed the last page and slid the packet across the table. Addison slipped the stack into the manila folder.

"Congratulations, Mister North," he said. "You've been activated."

"Am I still allowed one call?"

"Pen," Addison said, his hand out, palm up, across the table.

"What pen?" North raised both hands. They were empty.

"Pen." Addison said more firmly.

North grinned. He flicked his wrist and suddenly he was holding the pen. Using both hands, he placed it in Addison's palm with exaggerated care.

"Technically," Addison said, "because of the need for secrecy and efficiency, the phone call is at the account executive's discretion. But I will allow it."

He pulled a mobile phone out of his pocket.

"Only Redfire phones work up here against the signal blocking. Push the green button. You will have five minutes from the moment the first call connects until the phone is automatically deactivated."

"Are you sure you want me to do this?" North said. "That's five whole minutes of company time gone forever."

"Remember," Addison said, "no discussions of your assignment."

North pushed the green button and held the phone to his ear. He looked up at Addison.

"Some privacy, please? Even people who are arrested get one call."

Addison stood and unlocked the door.

"People who are arrested have more freedom. And they don't get paid. Consider yourself lucky I'm letting you have this much."

"Five whole minutes," North said. "Oh, thank God."

"You're welcome."

Addison closed and locked the door behind him.

6

Carol answered her desk phone.

"Hello. You've reached Carol Nor- ah, Carol Webster's desk. How may I help you?"

Rod winced at the sound of her voice.

"It's me," he said. "I'm glad I caught you."

"I'm at work. What's up?"

"I only have five minutes." He took a deep breath. "Look, you'll have to get Toby from day care. Something came up at work."

She was silent for a moment.

"Shit," she said. "Not that. Rod, I have plans."

"I can't help it, Carol. This is my job."

"What about your son?"

"Our son."

"Rod, I've been planning this weekend for at least a month. Do you know how hard it is to get everyone together with their schedules?"

"All I'm asking is-"

"When will you be back?"

"I don't know that, Carol. I can't know."

"That's not helpful, Rod. What if I did the same thing? What if one day I just up and took off because it was part of my job? Damn it."

"Carol, don't be so selfish."

"Me? Selfish? I'm not the one who is bailing out."

"I'm not bailing out. I'm going to work."

"Like Toby knows the difference."

"Carol."

"Rod," she said, mocking his tone.

"You know I have to do this."

"What? Go kill somebody? Can't someone else do it? Can't they just drop a bomb on whoever the guy is?"

"I don't have much time."

"You might not come back, right?"

"That's right."

"Well, excuse me if I don't cry."

"Carol. I don't even know what to say to that."

"Toby's going to be heartbroken."

"I'm doing this for him."

"That's what you told me too, way back when. 'I'm making the world a better place.' It never ends, Rod. You know what that means?"

"What?"

"You suck at making things better."

She hung up.

Rod dialed the daycare.

"Hello, and thank you for calling-"

"Hi, this is Rod North. Toby North's father. I need to speak with him. It's very important and I don't have much time."

"It's nap time, do you want me to wake him up?"

"Yes. Please. Hurry."

"All right. Hold on."

Rod watched the timer on the phone's display count up. It was at three minutes, thirty seconds.

Thirty-one.

Thirty-two.

Thirty-three.

"Come on," Rod said out loud, putting the phone back to his ear.

"Daddy?" Toby sounded slow, groggy.

"Hey, kid. You having fun?"

"I was sleeping. It was nap time."

"Listen, buddy, I won't be able to get you. Mommy's going to pick you up."

"What?"

"Mommy is going to get you, okay?"

"Why? Where are you going?"

"I have to do something for work."

"What do you have to do?"

"Important stuff."

"Like what?"

"Adult stuff."

"If mommy gets me, can I see you for pizza and movie night?"

"I don't think I'll be home by then, buddy. We'll do it later, okay? Some other time."

"When?"

"When I get back."

"When will that be?"

"Toby-"

The phone clicked off.

"Time expired," was flashing on the screen.

"Hell," he said. He dropped the phone on the table and pinched the bridge of his nose in a vain attempt to fight off a sudden migraine.

He rubbed his eyes on his shirt sleeve just as the door opened.

"Time's up," Addison said.

North was staring at the floor. He didn't move.

"Come on, North."

"I just said goodbye to my son," North said without looking up. "Give me a second."

"I thought you were an old pro at this."

North slammed his hands on the table and sprang up. He brushed against Addison as he stepped through the doorway.

Addison closed the door behind him and jogged ahead, leading down the hall. He spoke as he walked, not bothering to look back.

"You signed on for this, North, so drop the attitude. It's time to earn that huge paycheck of yours. Your son will thank you later."

Addison stopped, blocking the hall. He turned and held out his hand. "By the way, you owe me a phone."

North held the phone before him and clenched his fist. A snapping noise spat from between his fingers. He rotated his hand and dropped the device into Addison's palm.

Addison looked down at the darkened and cracked screen.

"Did you just crush my phone?"

"Come on," North said, walking past him. "You said time is critical."

"You broke it."

"You said it was done after five minutes. Now it's done."

Addison dropped the phone into his pocket. "It's a violation of your contract to damage company property."

"Then you better shut your goddamn mouth and keep moving."

"You threatening me? I'll make a note of that."

"Please do."

7

They continued walking on in silence. North followed Addison past several closed doors under the ever-present security cameras, hidden behind black hemispheres embedded in the ceiling.

They turned a corner, passing the door that led back to the elevators. Ashley was standing there, her hands behind her back as she blocked the door. She stiffened when she saw them.

"Hi, Ashley," North said as he passed.

She bowed her head, avoiding his eyes.

"Come on, North," Addison said. "There's no going back now."

Hearing Addison's words, Ashley leaned back, pressing her body against the door, stepping sideways to block the handle. She looked up at North, her cheeks pale, eyes wide. Her lips were trembling.

North shrugged and walked through the door at the other end of the hall. Addison locked it behind them.

"If I wanted to cut and run," North said, "do you really think she could have stopped me?"

"We're short on people. We use who we have."

"I'll try not to take that personally."

North let him pass and followed him down a short hall that opened into a conference room.

A laptop computer and a projector rested at one end of a dark polished wood table. Twelve chairs were available but only two were occupied, one by a man and one by a woman. North didn't recognize either of them.

"Sit," Addison said harshly, as if commanding a dog.

North glared at him for a second before taking a seat across from the others. Addison stood at the head of the table near the projector.

"I'm Rod North," North said.

"Elizabeth Holland," the young woman answered, her thin lips neither smiling nor frowning. She met his gaze with icy gray eyes. Her short auburn hair was cut in a bob at an angle to match her sharp jawbone. She was wearing a black sleeveless button-down business top, showing off her tan, well-toned arms.

"David Jeffers," the man seated near her said. "Just call me Jeffers." He greeted North with an informal salute. His hair was tied back, ample gray in the blonde ponytail. His face was weathered and covered in gray stubble. He was dressed in a pink polo shirt and khakis. His rumpled appearance struck North as better suited for a beachside pub than an office building.

"Nice to meet you both," North said.

"Likewise," Jeffers said.

Holland inclined her chin.

"Great," Addison said. "You've all met. Congratulations. You're a team now."

Holland, North and Jeffers all exchanged quick glances.

"Moving on," Addison said, clapping his hands together. "I don't like to repeat myself, so pay attention. You've all gone through the official orientation, and endured the legal crap I'm required to say. Now I am in full control. Everything from here on out runs my way. There's no Redfire anymore. There's just me."

The three team members were silent.

"I have only one rule: Do what I say and don't screw up. Got it?"

He waited a second.

"Isn't that two rules?" Jeffers asked.

"If I say it's one, it's one. Now, quiet," Addison said. He powered up his laptop. The projector glowed, but no image appeared on the far wall. Addison tapped on his computer, cursed, then banged on the projector. The fan inside whined. He pounded on his keyboard angrily. Still nothing.

North looked at Jeffers, who smirked and shook his head.

Finally with a flash, the far wall lit up with a huge version of a page torn from a magazine. A brief article was crowded alongside a large photo of an elderly groom in a tuxedo and his much younger and taller bride walking across a red carpet. Her gown was sparkling and sheer, her ample breasts threatening to pop loose.

"Tell me what you see," Addison said.

"Looks like a page from a tabloid," Holland answered. She read the first line of the photo's caption. "The Billionaire's Buxom Bride."

"Focus on the photo."

"Sure. I'll start with the old guy. Bald. Spotty and wrinkled. Leaning on a cane. Wearing bifocals. Has to be at least eighty. His tuxedo fits well. The lady on his arm seems at least forty years younger. He definitely comes from money."

"North," Addison said. "Why don't you break down the sugar baby? Tell me what you see."

"Sure," North said. "She looks like a model, maybe a porn star. Looks like she's had a top-notch boob job. Not that I notice those things."

"You didn't mention her see-through gown," Holland said.

"I didn't notice," North answered. "It's see-through."

"Easy, kids," Addison said. "Ever hear the name Danforth Percy Sinclair?"

"No," North said, "but I'm guessing he's the old rich guy?"

"Would Redfire work with a poor client? Yes, that's him," Addison said. "Worth more than you or I ever will be. More than all four of us put together over a dozen times."

"What's the story with the girl?"

"The story is she's out of your league, North. That's Sinclair's wife. Her name is Yvonne Windstorm. The singer. You know." He sang without enthusiasm, in barely melodic tones, "Do it to me, do it do it. Oh baby, do it to me like you do. Ever hear it?"

"No," North said, "but let me say your rendition was outstanding."

Jeffers snorted, holding back his laugh. Holland didn't show any emotion.

North continued. "I've heard of her, but that's about it."

"I'm sure you have. She's been in most of the soft-core yank mags. Anyway, she's irrelevant to the mission. The old guy is the target."

"Target?" North repeated, raising his eyebrows and leaning forward.

"Down, boy," Addison said. "Target as in objective. Purpose. Mister Sinclair recently placed an activation call to our Premium

Services Account line. During the call he reported he was on a cruise ship that was being hijacked."

"I listen to the news all day," Jeffers said. "I didn't hear anything about a hijacking."

"Oh, hello, Jeffers. I thought you'd fallen asleep. To address your comment, the media probably doesn't know yet. But they will soon. Now look at this."

Addison pressed a key on his laptop and the tabloid page was replaced by a photograph.

Three men in black ski masks, each one brandishing an AK-47 rifle, were gathered on the white top deck of a cruise ship. "Sunset Mist" was painted on the bow in a flowing pink script. The men were standing under a mast flying a black and green flag at its top. Raised below it was an upside-down American flag, torn and partially burned.

"The black and green flag is a modification of the national Kariqistan flag," Addison said.

"How did you get these pictures?" North asked.

"From one of Redfire's assets onboard the Coast Guard vessel the Bonnie Jane, already en route. The captain sent his helicopter ahead to scout. They got these pictures but pulled back when she started taking fire."

"So, did the Coast Guard bring out a negotiator?"

"Possibly. Probably."

"You mean there's something you don't know?"

"Wrong," Addison said, holding up his index finger. "As far as you're concerned, I know everything. Is a negotiator on the scene? It is more accurate to say I don't care. And since I don't care, you don't care. Mister Sinclair has secured the resources of Redfire. He's our one and only concern."

"And the service we're providing him is what?" North asked.

"The service we are providing him," Addison repeated loudly, "which is what I would tell you if you stopped asking questions, is this: get him off the boat alive as soon as possible. That's it."

"A Katrina contract," Holland said.

"We prefer not to use that term," Addison said. "The official name is a Private Rapid Response Extraction Service. And let me remind you, they're extremely confidential."

"They're public knowledge," Holland said, her cheeks blushing slightly. "It's in Redfire's annual report."

Jeffers snorted.

"Something funny?" Holland asked.

Jeffers shook his head. "I didn't think anyone read those things." Addison continued.

"Yes," he said, "This is a Katrina contract. Redfire's top-selling product since 2005. Next time you cash your paycheck, say a prayer of thanks for government incompetence. Now we need to prepare to leave."

"Wait a minute," North interrupted. "This is all the intel you have? Didn't Sinclair say anything else?"

"He did mention we should hurry up," Addison said.

"Well, excuse me for asking, but I like to know as much as I can when I'm about to enter a hostile environment," he said, glancing at his teammates. "So, is there any more information?"

"How much do you need?" Addison said. "I'm not going to hold your hand. Besides, I've given you all we have. That photo of three men with AK's. Probably a few more on board. Terminate them or don't as necessary. Just get Sinclair free as quickly as possible so he can go back to counting his money."

"But the Coast Guard is already there."

"Maybe you weren't listening. What was my one rule? Do what I say. And I say get Sinclair and bring him home. I don't care about anything else."

North shrugged, his arms extended.

"All the other Redfire assignments I've been on were combat-related," he said. "This is a rescue mission. Not military support, not recon, or anything else. There's huge potential for collateral damage here. These jobs might be a hot product for Redfire, but they're new to me. I've heard of them, but never been on one. So forgive me asking for some more info before I put my ass out there."

Addison leaned forward, both hands flat on the table. "Yes, North. I've seen your record. I'm impressed. I understand you've historically had more of a wet work focus, but you're making it harder than it needs to be. Sinclair calls us and we go get him. That's it. Rules of engagement are up to you. Whatever is holding him back, natural or man-made, he's paying us so he doesn't have to deal with it. He doesn't have to wait for an incompetent or non-existent federal rescue, a protracted negotiation or a clumsy assault by a bunch of rent-a-cops playing commando."

"Isn't that what we are?" Jeffers said.

"You're supposed to be professionals," Addison said. "This is a huge opportunity. A chance to show other potential customers we're the best private armed services provider. These Katrina contracts, they're the wave of the future."

"But if they're so secret," Jeffers said, "how will other customers-"

Addison cut him off, raising his voice. "Word will get around at the country club. Now, do you have any questions relevant to the mission?"

The room was silent except for the whirring sound of the projector's fan.

"There's nothing else you can tell us about what to expect?" North asked. "Any clue as to the hijackers' motivations? Demands?"

"No. And we don't care. I'm hoping the three of you, with your years of experience, can handle a bunch of ignorant desert rats in the middle of the ocean."

Addison paused a moment.

"I'll take that silence to mean you're done with the bellyaching. Based on your skill sets, I've chosen your assignments. North and Holland are the infiltration team. Jeffers will be operating a four-seat micro-submarine to bring you in and get you out."

"Four seats?" North said. "What if he's got his wife with him?"

"Mr. Sinclair's contract stipulates that it applies to him and only him. She's inconsequential," Addison said.

"Does Mrs. Windstorm-Sinclair know she's inconsequential?"

"All that matters is that you know it. Sinclair's contract is for himself only. I'm sure he considered his wife might be with him when he activated his account, but we don't do this for free. You are to rescue only him."

"What if he won't leave without her?"

"You are authorized to restrain him and even render him unconscious in order to fulfill Redfire's end of the contract. His consent was implied when he activated the account. That's the agreement he signed. I'm sure the army of lawyers he can afford goes over every word of every contract the guy signs, so it's time for you to stop worrying about him and focus on the task."

"That's what I'm doing."

"Then you won't mind getting started," Addison said, slamming shut his laptop. "The helicopter is waiting on the roof to take you to our boat near the scene. We'll drop the micro-sub as far out as possible and you'll take it from there. Any questions?"

Addison paused for one second.
"No. Good."

PART 2

TO THE RESCUE

1

U.S. Coast Guard Patrol Vessel Bonnie Jane bounced over the calm ocean, its engines rumbling at full throttle. Sunlight pierced through spotty cloud cover, scattering tiny sunbursts on a sea unbroken by land in all directions.

The Bonnie Jane's crew had just completed tethering her helicopter to its landing platform on the aft deck of the ship. Captain Edgar Dunn was examining the chopper's metal skin with the pilot.

"I stayed as long as I could, sir," the young pilot said, his voice warbling slightly. "But with that many guys shooting, I knew it was only a matter of time before we went down. I did get some pictures, though. Only three. I think."

Captain Dunn poked his finger in one of the several still-warm bullet holes.

The pilot shivered. "They sprang up on me, Captain. I thought I was dead. I don't think it's in a terrorist's nature to fire warning shots. Thank God their aim was terrible."

Dunn turned to the much younger man, clasped his shoulder and looked into his watering eyes. The pilot's lips quivered.

"Son," the captain said, "I've been a sailor long enough to know you don't think about good luck for too long, you just accept it. You got us some visuals, and you got back safe. That's what counts."

The pilot cleared his throat. "Thank you, sir. She's still air-worthy if we need her. Rotors weren't hit. Neither was-"

"We'll talk about that later. Let the mechanics look her over. For now, get some rest. Know you did well."

"I did? Thanks. I mean, thanks, sir. I mean, aye, sir. Aye. Captain."

The young man's face was regaining color. He saluted crisply. Dunn clapped the pilot on his back and turned away, heading toward the fore deck.

Dunn removed his baseball cap and scratched his bald head vigorously. He replaced the hat tightly and sighed as he watched the man standing at the bow leaning forward into the wind.

Nelson Goodkin removed his wire-framed glasses with both hands, wiping water drops off the lenses with the sweatshirt he was wearing under his windbreaker. His slicker hung low and long for his skinny frame. He snapped his left hand to the railing as the ship hit a swell. With his free hand, he slid his glasses onto his nose just in time to be hit in the face with spray.

"Damn it," Goodkin said.

Captain Dunn noticed the Sunset Mist cruise ship was coming into view on the hazy horizon. From this distance, the ship was the size of a rice kernel but growing fast.

Dunn yelled over the roaring wind as he approached Goodkin. "Doing all right, Mister Goodkin?"

"I'm fine," Goodkin yelled back, leaning forward to keep his balance. "Did your pilot secure any imagery?"

"He's a little shaken, but he's a tough kid."

"What about the photos? Did he get them?"

"He said he got three."

"Only three?"

"You didn't say how many you needed."

"It should be obvious I'll need as many as I can get. The high ground in this engagement belongs to whoever has the superior quality information."

"I ordered him to fall back if he started taking fire. The bird was hit several times. We're not trained or equipped for combat. We're a rescue vessel. You ask me, the boy performed bravely."

"But only three photos?" Goodkin said, looking sideways at Dunn.

Dunn didn't respond. He kept his eyes on the horizon and the growing Sunset Mist cruise ship.

"Three will have to do, then," Goodkin said. He followed Dunn's gaze. "What data can you provide me about this cruise liner?"

"She's not one of those behemoth ships," Dunn said, "one of those floating resort types that hold more people than some of the island villages they dock at. She's much smaller. They call her a cherub-class. The passenger manifest indicates they left port with only around 200 people. Most cruisers carry at least ten times that."

"How big would you say it is, compared to your ship?"

Dunn turned around and pointed to the cabin roof of the Bonnie Jane. Goodkin turned awkwardly, still clutching the railing.

"See the top of my girl here? That's thirty feet from the water line. She's also around fifty feet long. I'd say the Sunset Mist is about a hundred feet tall, and maybe three hundred feet from bow to aft."

"So roughly three times as tall, six times as long."

"Sounds about right," Dunn said.

They both turned to face the Sunset Mist cruiser again. Goodkin squinted up at the sun. "This had to happen on a beautiful day, didn't it?"

"Every day is a beautiful day out on the ocean."

"It's cold, it's wet and it smells like a swamp. And there's nothing to see. What's so great about it?"

Dunn leaned forward, resting his forearms on the railing. "It never stops moving. It's invigorating. Keeps me awake and keeps me young. Even the rough days have a charm. There's nothing like it."

"You can have it. I'm going inside to do some research."

"You remember where my office is? Through the lounge area and in the back. I'm going to make my rounds and I'll meet you there."

"Grab the pilot's photos too," Goodkin said. "All three of them," he added, shaking his head.

"Will do," the captain said.

Goodkin retreated from the fore, pulling himself along the railing hand over hand. He entered the main cabin, letting the door slam shut behind him. Inside, two crew members were playing cards on a small table. In the corner, a television's static-laced picture showed a basketball game. The two sailors looked up at Goodkin and then back to their cards.

Goodkin ignored them as he pulled a tablet PC from an inner pocket of his windbreaker. He pressed a wireless earplug into his ear, and positioned the attached microphone bulb against his jaw. He balanced the tablet on his left hand, sliding his fingers under a small holding strap on the PC's back, while using his right hand to tap, slide and pinch the screen on the other side. He walked toward Captain Dunn's office, bent over the computer.

"Hey," one of the card-playing sailors said. "That's the captain's quarters. No one else allowed."

Goodkin didn't look up. "I've got special permission."

"I don't care what you have," the sailor said, standing. "No one goes in there. Captain's orders."

Goodkin remained hunched over his tablet, tapping and stroking as he spoke.

"Really?" he said, "And when was the last time you had breakfast with the president?"

"Huh?"

"Precisely," Goodkin said. He kept walking and still didn't look up.

"Let him go," the other sailor said. "Captain said he's a V.I.P. so he's probably got the okay. Besides, you're just trying to see my cards."

"I'm not. That guy's a jerk."

"Yeah, and so's your mom. Come on."

Goodkin entered the captain's quarters.

2

The door sprung shut behind Goodkin. He jolted and wiped his glasses again, glancing around Captain Dunn's sparsely decorated office. A framed commendation from a Florida senator hung on the wall next to a photo of the Captain with his arm around a young woman who appeared to be his daughter. Tucked into the frame was a wallet-sized photo of Dunn smiling, holding an infant wrapped in a pink blanket.

The rest of the wall space was covered with intricate maps of the sea, crisscrossed by lines, symbols and numbers. On the maps Goodkin was used to, land was the focus and water was represented as a featureless solid blue. This map was the opposite. All the detail was in the sea, the land indicated by unmarked pale green shapes.

"Keep it," Goodkin said out loud. "You can have it."

He sat at the captain's computer and double-clicked an audio file on the desktop.

A narrator introduced the clip: "Cruise vessel Sunset Mist departed Miami en route to Bermuda at oh seven hundred hours. This call was received at Miami port command at oh nine hundred hours."

A beep followed, then the actual call. A persistent hiss sounded behind the gasping voice. "S.O.S.! S.O.S.! This is Captain Karl Vernon of the luxury liner Sunset Mist calling out to anyone who can hear. We're being overrun by terrorists. Lock that door! That one, too. Block it with something! Men in masks, they've got guns. Look like AKs. I don't know what nationality. Uh, it looks like they're taking hostages. I don't know how many or where they came from. Ah, just guessing now. Maybe seven? Eight men? They may have been among the passengers. Oh, shit-"

The sound of muffled machine gun fire crackled in the background, obscuring a barrage of cursing from the men near Captain Vernon.

"Warning shots. They were just warning shots, thank God. Looks like they're herding everyone into the ballroom. No visible casualties. Block that goddamn-"

A enormous bang obliterated whatever he said next.

"-in! They're storming the bridge-"

A scraping noise was followed by a voice that sounded only part human. It reminded Goodkin of a computer-synthesized voice, or a throat cancer survivor wearing an artificial larynx.

"Hands up," the robotic voice said.

"We surrender," Vernon yelled. "Crew! Hands in the air! Now!" His voice faded as he moved from the microphone. The crew's protests diminished. The next sound was the unmistakable crack of slapped flesh.

"I said we surrender!" Vernon cried.

"On your knees!" the robotic voice answered. "All of you. If you have a cell phone, throw it down now. If later we find you kept one, we will kill you! Do it n-"

The sound stopped with a solid click.

"Transmission ceases there," the narrator said.

Goodkin emailed the file to his tablet. Using the captain's mouse he opened a second audio file.

"This call was received at Miami port at oh nine thirty hours," the same narrator said. The hissing background noise returned, and this time the digitized throat-cancer-survivor voice spoke up close.

"Attention all of you stinking pigs and rabid dogs who inhabit the evil nation of the U.S.A. We are the Children of Kariqistan. Listen very carefully or every one of your countrymen aboard this ship will die. Here is what we require: all multinational corporations must leave Kariqistan. All Western forces must withdraw from our nation and all Muslim nations worldwide. Finally, the sum of fifty million dollars shall be delivered to me in cash. Fail to fulfill these demands and the Americans on this ship will never be seen alive again. I will allow only one boat in our vicinity for communication and delivery of these demands, but that is all. Any more will be considered a hostile act. Do not challenge us."

"Transmission ceases there," the narrator said.

Goodkin rested his tablet on the captain's desk so he could use both hands, tapping and swiping his computer's screen.

The door opened and Captain Dunn poked his head around the corner. "Mister Goodkin?"

"Some quiet, please?" Goodkin said. "I'm making notes. Transmitting them back to the nerve center."

Dunn entered the office carrying rolled up sheets of office paper. He stood over Goodkin and waited a moment.

"May I have my seat?" the captain asked.

Goodkin looked around, surprised.

"Oh, of course." He stood to let Dunn behind the desk and took the chair on the other side.

Dunn pointed to Goodkin's tablet. "The lives of all those people on that boat rely on that little thing?"

"This little thing," Goodkin said, still hunched over and tapping on the screen, "is cutting-edge tech. It keeps me jacked in with an enormous diplomatic, media, advisory and research network."

"So you're just the tip of the iceberg."

"If it helps you to conceptualize my organization using ocean-based metaphors, then yes, I am, in more ways than one. This negotiation is part of an experimental program. We're testing scalable models on how to address these crises in the future. I helped design this approach."

"Hm," Dunn said. "Probably is cheaper to send just one guy."

"And more efficient. Conceivably, we could have multiple incidents at once. Our adversaries could attempt to overload our preparedness, a denial of service attack, if you will. Better to have a central command staffed with psychological profilers, negotiation experts, linguists, et cetera, with a single representative in the field, wired into everyone. We don't need to expend resources shipping a herd of people along just to talk."

"Nothing wrong with saving money," the captain said. "Just seems like a heck of a thing to experiment around."

"Someone has to lead when we're developing new paradigms." Goodkin rocked his head back and forth and from side to side, stretching his neck. "Now, if you don't mind, I need some of your files."

The captain raised his eyebrows and hesitated as if he was thinking of something to say. Finally he chose silence and slipped on a pair of bifocals. He leaned his head back slightly while looking at the screen.

"You're going to make me use this thing, aren't you?"

"I was going to do it for you, but you wanted your seat."

"Well, I could use the practice." Dunn slid the mouse around, mumbling to himself while Goodkin fidgeted. "What is it you need?"

"I was wondering if you heard from your sources about any pre-event orbital perspective imagery."

Dunn stared at him.

"Did you hear back from the satellite people?" Goodkin said. "You said they promised to email you."

"That's right. They should have."

After far more mouse clicks than could have possibly been necessary to open one email, Dunn spoke again.

"Looks like we got a response. Here goes. Captain Dunn, satellite shows nothing unusual. Only the target vessel. No unusual movement on deck. Tracking indicates no external ship-to-ship transfer. Full spectral analysis indicates no hull penetration by subsurface vehicles."

Goodkin tapped away on his PC while he talked. "So that indicates a strong probability the terrorists were commingled with the civilians when the ship embarked. Does the email say anything about the passenger list?"

Dunn kept reading. "Let's see. Passenger list has been sent for investigation. Will call with results and email negotiation team at address provided by federal agent Goodkin. That's all it says."

Goodkin checked his screen. "Hm. No messages yet," he said.

"You want to see the pictures my chopper pilot took?" Dunn asked.

"Sure. That won't take long."

"I told you he was taking fire."

"Of course."

Dunn grabbed the papers he had brought and laid all three out on the table.

"Printouts?" Goodkin said. "Paper?"

"Yeah," Dunn said. "One of the guys in the tech center printed them for me."

"Can you just do a wireless transfer, or give me the chopper's memory stick?"

Dunn paused. "Um, I can have someone-"

"Never mind," Goodkin said, "I'll take a picture and transfer."

He held his tablet out, using the camera built into the back to snap a shot of each color printout.

The first photo was of a man dressed completely in black, including gloves and a ski mask. The only place his bronze skin showed was in the eye and mouth holes of the mask. He was holding a pole with an American flag on the end. Flames curled around the flag's blackened edge.

Goodkin snapped a picture of the next image.

The second photo showed the charred remains of the American flag hoisted on the ship's main mast, underneath another flag comprising two thick stripes, one black and one green.

"I didn't immediately recognize the flag," Dunn said.

"Looks like a permutation of the internationally-recognized Kariqistan flag. Before you ask where Kariqistan is, it's in that region that borders the south of Russia."

"Ah," the captain said, "Genghis Khan territory."

"That's right. All his inbred children surrounded by mountain ranges and well-armed. After the Commies went out of business, dozens of tiny landlocked countries no one ever heard of and no one can pronounce showed up in there. Profile is primitive yet volatile."

"Well, if their borders don't touch the sea, I'm probably not going to know about them," Dunn said. "Still, I could probably brush up on geography."

"Don't bother," Goodkin said. "The country itself doesn't know where it begins and ends. Before you picked me up, we tried to call the Kariqistan ambassador. Problem was, there was no consensus from their embassy on who that might be. Several factions claim legitimate governance. One ambassador was out to eat, the other was at a strip club. Whichever one responds first is the one the home team will deal with, but that's their action item, not mine."

"It's just not natural for people to live that far away from water," the captain said. "I think it messes with their heads. But I guess you're not here for my opinion."

"No. I'm not."

Goodkin held his tablet over the third photo and snapped a picture. Three terrorists had their upper bodies obscured by muzzle flashes as they fired at the helicopter.

"No explanation needed for this one," Goodkin said. Both men were silent for a moment. The only sounds were Goodkin's gentle tapping on his tablet's screen and the constant hum of the ship's engine.

"My commanders haven't told me much," Captain Dunn said, "other than to ferry you out there."

"Mm," Goodkin said, not looking up.

"I know you're probably not at liberty to say, but some of my crew are a little nervous. Could these Kariqistanis be body bombers? Maybe they're planning to destroy the boat even if their demands are met."

"It's not a suicide mission." Goodkin still didn't look up.

"Why do you say that?"

"They're disguising their voices."

"That robot sound?"

"Yes. Why change your voice if you're just going to kill yourself?"

Dunn thought about it. "Makes sense. And why hide behind a mask?"

"You got it. The psychology of their actions indicates they want to live."

"Hm," Dunn said. "Makes perfect sense."

"Good."

"No. That's bad."

Goodkin finally looked up. "How so?"

"I'm a sailor. Always have been. The sea is unpredictable. It does strange things to people. It's taught me to always account for madness. I'm suspicious of anything that makes sense in a nice, neat way. Maybe it is a suicide mission, or there's some other reason their voices are changed that we're not considering. Maybe they're protecting their families back home. Maybe they're just nuts."

Goodkin rested his chin on his folded hands and smiled gently.

"Captain, for as long as you've been at sea, I've been studying the pathology of individuals in high-tension, high-stakes interpersonal communication. So let's make a deal. I'll leave the boat captaining to you. You leave the analysis to me."

Dunn shrugged. "Fine. What do I know?"

"Exactly."

3

North, Jeffers and Holland were all naked. Their business clothes were draped over the chairs in the small storage room that led to the rooftop landing pad. They were changing into all-black wetsuits Addison had provided.

"Remember to remove anything that could identify you," Addison said. "Jewelry, watches, earrings, anything. I'll keep it safe here. I'm going to step out for a minute and go get your weapons. Jeffers, you're the oldest, make sure everyone behaves."

North zipped up his wetsuit, politely looking away from the others.

He was startled when Holland stepped before him. Her suit was pulled up only to her waist, leaving her small, pointed breasts exposed. She stared at North's chest and poked him in his sternum.

"You wearing something under there?"

"No."

"Addison said remove anything that identifies you."

"I did."

"No, you didn't. I saw you have something on under there. Unzip your top." Holland zipped hers up.

"Whoa," Jeffers said from across the room. "This isn't a strip joint, people. Good thing, too. Because, if Addison got naked..." he shivered, then chuckled.

"North's got some kind of necklace on and I want him to take it off," Holland said. North stared into her grey eyes. She didn't flinch.

"Take it off," she said.

"Get away from me," North said. "You're not the mission commander."

"No, I'm not, but the guy who is just said no personal items."

"Well, he won't know unless someone tells him. It's something my son made, a good luck charm."

"It could identify you and therefore Redfire if you end up K.I.A."

"It's a picture of me and my kid."

"Don't worry about it, Holland," Jeffers said. "Let's stay a happy family."

"Screw that," Holland said. "This guy is already breaking the rules of engagement."

They were all quiet for a moment.

"So, how much money do you think this Sinclair guy has?" North said.

"Trying to change the subject?" Holland said.

"Damn, you're observant. You must have been in psy-ops."

"Good guess," she said, winking. "You going to remove that necklace?"

"How much money?" Jeffers said quickly. "Enough to retain the services of Redfire, all this hardware and logistical support? I'd say the guy is damn well off."

"You think we could ask for a tip?" North said. "What's the gratuity for saving someone's life? Eighteen percent of a billion doesn't seem like too much."

Holland turned away and tightened her suit.

Addison returned with two metal briefcases. He slammed them down in front of Holland and North. They snapped open the case latches, revealing dull black guns resting in gray molded foam.

"Custom," Addison said. "Water-resistant nine mil with silencer. Thirteen shots per clip. No serial numbers on the gun or the ammo. You're welcome."

North slipped his hand around the grip and lifted the weapon, pointing it into an empty corner of the room.

"Impressive," he said. "It's light. The balance offset of the silencer is barely noticeable."

Holland tested her weapon in the same manner. "Very sexy."

"Where's my toy?" Jeffers asked.

"The micro-sub is waiting for you when you all stop dicking around."

"Is that your way of telling us to hurry up?"

"That's why I left you in charge, Jeffers," Addison said. "Because you're so damn smart. You all ready?"

"All except for North, sir," Holland said. "He's wearing a necklace."

Addison turned to North and said, "I said no personal stuff."

"I don't know what she's talking about." North unzipped his suit. His chest was bare. No locket hung from his neck.

"Is this some stupid game?" Addison said. "I don't have time for this crap."

"I know you still have it," Holland said to North. "You just hid it."

"Could I really move that fast?" North asked, offering her a quick wink as she had to him. "Am I really that good?"

Her cheeks flushed.

"Speed is everything here, people," Addison said, raising his voice. "North, are you clean?"

"Sure am."

"All right, then," Addison said. He turned to Holland. "A little trust, all right?"

"So why don't you trust what I'm telling you?" she asked. "Because I'm a woman?"

"And here I thought you were just part of the team. I'm trusting North because he has much more experience, okay? You might not even be here if we weren't so short-staffed. Now, let's get something other than bickering done."

Holland glared at North. He smiled and shrugged.

"If we're going to be a team," he said, "We'll have to work together, all right? Truce?" He offered to shake hands.

"Yeah, whatever," she said, turning away.

4

On the Bonnie Jane, the intercom in Captain Dunn's office beeped. Startled, Goodkin dropped his tablet PC. As he bent over to retrieve it, his glasses clattered to the deck. He cursed and slid out of his chair to gather both items.

"Bridge to Captain Dunn," the intercom said.

Dunn turned in his chair and pushed a button on the wall next to the speaker. "Dunn here. Go ahead, bridge."

"We're almost there, captain. I'm slowing her down to keep our distance. Since they opened fire on the bird, I don't want to get too close."

"Wise move, bridge. I'll be up. Dunn out." He looked at Goodkin, who was kneeling on the floor. "You all right?"

Goodkin put his glasses on. "I'm fine."

"Need help?"

"I said I'm fine."

"Follow me, then." The captain started for the door and grabbed the handle, then paused and let his hand drop. "Actually, something is on my mind."

"Is this urgent?" Goodkin asked, rising to his feet.

"I got the call for this task from as high up as my chain of command goes," Dunn said. "I'm supposed to take care of you and give you anything you want. I'm a good sailor, so I'll follow orders, but man to man, just between us, do you mind if I ask you a question?"

"We're short on time," Goodkin said.

Dunn was blocking the door. He didn't move. "Off the record, Mister Goodkin, it will only take a second."

"Fine, then. What?" Goodkin bent over his tablet and began tapping the screen.

"No disrespect to your profession," Dunn said, "but what is the point of talking to these barbarians? If someone was holding a gun to the head of my granddaughter, I wouldn't talk to him. I'd just be thinking about whether to cut his throat left to right or right to left. These people we're dealing with are savages. So why talk? I've seen enough drunken sailors to know some people don't want to listen and you're best off not trying. Sometimes you just have to kick their ass."

Goodkin looked up from his screen. "It's not for the hostage-taker that I do what I do, Captain. It's for the hostages. If the belligerents didn't have those human shields, I might agree with you, but that's their strategy, to prevent an obvious assault. So we defeat them in a different way."

"I suppose..."

"Everyone can be negotiated with. You just have to find out what matters to them and then threaten to take it away. It's what they're doing to us, it's what I'll do to them, if you ever let me out of here."

"Hm. Put that way, you make talking sound like an act of war."

"Exactly," Goodkin said. He smiled thinly, lips closed. He reached past Dunn, striking the captain's side as he grabbed the door handle.

"Now we need to go."

* * *

When they emerged onto the deck, a section of the horizon was blocked by the bright white hull of the Sunset Mist. The cruise vessel towered over them, her decks and walkways empty as if she were completely abandoned.

From the lower perspective of the Bonnie Jane, they couldn't see the top deck except for the flag mast. The upside-down and charred American flag flapped in the gentle breeze under the large green and black flag representing the Children of Kariqistan.

"Looks like a ghost ship," Goodkin said.

He followed Captain Dunn up the cramped metal stairs along the outside of the cabin onto the second floor that housed the small glassed-in bridge.

The first mate was behind the wheel of the ship. Two other sailors were watching screens built into the metal console that surrounded the interior.

"Captain on bridge," the first mate shouted when Dunn entered. The sailors straightened up and saluted.

Dunn waved them off. "As you were."

"Aye, sir."

"Captain," Goodkin said, looking around at the other men. "Some privacy?"

"This is my bridge," Dunn answered. "I will vouch for these men. They know-"

"Are they absolutely essential?" Goodkin interrupted.

"Everyone on my crew is essential."

"I don't agree."

Dunn put his hand on the wheel of the ship. "First Mate Smith and crew," he said, "you are relieved."

"Aye, sir," the crew responded.

"Keep everyone at the ready," Dunn said, "but no one enters the bridge. Buzz me only if there's an emergency. First Mate Smith, I'm counting on you to convey that order."

"Aye, sir," Smith said, exiting the bridge behind the other two sailors. The door's spring-hinges pulled it shut.

Goodkin was examining the communications panel.

"This looks self-explanatory," he said, lifting a red telephone handset and setting it down again. The ship's intercom squealed and popped. "Whoops," he said. He ran his fingers over the switches nearby.

"Careful there," Dunn said. "What you see is what you get. You can broadcast through our ship's intercom, from ship-to-ship with loudspeaker and from ship-to-ship on standard CB frequencies. You can also have the calls routed to the speakers and microphones in here so you don't have to stay attached to the phone."

"Perfect," Goodkin said.

"That com-panel is all yours," Dunn said. "I'm going to stay with the wheel as protocol dictates. I'll make sure we don't drift into our neighbor. I don't want to drop anchor now in case we need to move fast."

"You have any binoculars?"

"Top drawer in front of you."

Goodkin fished them out and scanned the Sunset Mist. Dunn pulled open a drawer and used his own pair of binoculars, keeping one hand on the wheel.

Goodkin tapped his tablet screen and narrated what he saw. "From this angle, I can't see the whole top deck. Looks like everyone is inside. I can barely catch some shadows moving about on their bridge, but that's about it. No signs of violence." He paused before adding, "Yet."

He selected the video camera application and held his tablet before him, scanning sideways, filming a panoramic view of the quiet cruise ship.

"Transferring video imagery," he said, tapping the screen. "Give it a second, signal out here is less than optimal."

Dunn hung his binoculars around his neck and checked the dials and digital readouts on the wheel's console. His attention was drawn away when he heard Goodkin mumbling to himself.

The negotiator had bowed his head and closed his eyes tightly. His arms were outstretched, the tablet still in his right hand, facing the sky. A droning noise resonated in his chest.

"Ommmmm..."

He breathed in and out loudly, ten times, then opened his eyes and rolled his shoulders, exhaling forcefully several times. The ritual reminded Dunn of the breathing exercises he and his wife did before their first daughter was born.

The captain shook his head.

Goodkin tapped the wired microphone bulb at his chin and said, "Implementing verbal contact. Audio recording and transfer on." He flicked the switch on the console labeled "Outside Loudspeaker." A popping noise bounced off the cruise ship. He lifted the Bonnie Jane's handset and spoke slowly so his booming voice would not be distorted by the echo.

"To the people in control of the cruise ship Sunset Mist. This is Federal Agent Nelson Goodkin of the United States Department of Homeland Security. I am here to discuss your demands. Please contact me on the ship-to-ship CB frequency. Let's work together so we can conclude this situation peacefully and in a way that is acceptable to everyone."

He released the button and set the handset down. Another pop bounced between the ships.

Goodkin spoke into his tablet PC. "Contact initiated."

He clipped the tablet to his belt, leaned against the communications panel and folded his arms, facing the cruise ship, his back to Captain Dunn.

5

The helicopter was roaring fast and low across the ocean, leaving the coast of Florida behind. The chopper was so close to the water's surface, it left a trail of spray in its wake.

"Speed is critical," Addison yelled into his headset's microphone over the thundering rotors. "So I've ordered the Redfire supply ship to move forward without us. Jeffers, your micro-sub will be waiting for you there."

North, Holland and Jeffers were crammed onto the back bench of the helicopter, Jeffers in the middle. Each small jolt of the helicopter caused their knees, elbows, or earphones to knock against the others. When they shifted to adjust, they collided again. The entire trip in the back bench seat was an uncomfortable three-person dance.

Addison and pilot were snug in their front row bucket seats. Addison had never introduced the pilot. He was silent, concentrating on flying the helicopter.

"I just thought of something," North said into his mic.

"The first time's always difficult," Addison said. He was checking his cell phone and didn't look back.

"What if Sinclair is dead?" North asked. "He made the call but since then they've killed him?"

"Then you leave the body, come home and we're all done," Addison said.

"Any other backup plans?"

"Backup plans are too expensive."

"This guy's a billionaire and you don't have a backup? It seems common sense if the guy is buying a Katrina contract to have some insurance."

"We are the insurance."

"He's right, North," Holland said. "Who ever heard of insurance for insurance?"

"Insurance insurance? Might not be a bad business venture," Jeffers mumbled. "And then maybe insurance for that."

"I'm talking about a backup, that's all," North said. "What if we run into trouble?"

"Don't," Addison answered.

"What if trouble comes looking for us?"

Addison turned in his seat to face backwards and look North in the eye. "There's no backup, North. Deal with it. From your special ops and wetwork experience, you should be used to that. More people involved increases the profile of the mission and endangers secrecy. Redfire sells itself on being discreet."

"None of this seems well-thought-out," North grumbled.

"When I picked you off the roster," Addison said, "did I make a bad choice?"

North met his gaze. "Maybe."

"Well, there weren't a lot of options. Everyone else was busy."

"Nice to know we're second-stringers," North said.

"There won't be any trouble, sir," Holland said. "We'll take care of it."

Addison turned forward again. "I appreciate that, Holland. A can-do attitude does a lot for morale. Pay attention to her, North."

"A can-do attitude sometimes means people aren't being realistic," Jeffers added.

Holland turned to face him.

"I'm not saying that's the case here," Jeffers said quickly, his voice trailing off.

* * *

No one spoke again until they could see the aft of the boat racing away from them at full speed, a wake of white foam marking its path. Once they saw the ship, it grew quickly as the helicopter closed in. They were close enough now to see the crew pointing and running about the deck.

The pilot spoke to the ship's captain through his headset.

"On approach. Keep her straight. Steady. That's good. Good. Hold it. Hold it."

The ship's bridge was elevated on a tower rising above the low, flat fishing area in the back. The deck had been cleared so the chopper could land.

"She doesn't look designed for holding a helicopter," the pilot said.

"Sometimes you have to improvise," Addison said.

"Are we really in this much of a hurry? She's not going to stop?"

"Just get us down there."

"This is crazy."

The ship bounced across the water with the helicopter chasing it, descending gently through a thickening cloud of grey exhaust.

"Tell them to at least slow down," the pilot said.

"No," Addison answered, "that would waste time."

"I can barely see."

"Then concentrate on flying and not bitching."

North and Holland crammed themselves against the side of the helicopter. Jeffers leaned backward as hard as he could. Being in the middle, he grabbed a knee of each person on either side of him. No one complained.

The helicopter was vibrating, buffeted by the draft swirling around the bridge tower as the ship plowed forward. Spray dotted the lower part of the cockpit windows, crawling upwards as the helicopter edged closer.

The chopper suddenly surged forward, rotors slicing close to the antennas on top of the bridge. Everyone in the cockpit but the pilot splayed out their hands to brace for impact. The pilot grabbed the control stick with both hands, trying to steady the chopper inside the draft-free zone just behind the bridge tower. If the helicopter moved too far forward it would collide with the ship. If it fell too far back, the air rushing around the boat would push them away.

Two sailors stood on the ship's deck, well clear of the landing zone, signaling the alignment of the chopper's skids with hand gestures.

"This is nuts," the pilot yelled. "Tell them to stop. We'll lose ten minutes max."

"Not good enough," Addison answered, his voice quivering. He was gripping the chopper's frame tightly, his face pale.

Hovering, the helicopter swung to the port side, over the water, then back over the deck. Then it fell behind over the churning wake, then forward, to almost strike the tower again. The pilot's hands were shaking on the stick, fighting the competing forces.

Jeffers put his hands over his face. Holland closed her eyes and turned away. North ground his teeth.

The chopper drifted backwards, away from the tower. The pilot flicked a switch, cutting all power to his craft. North's stomach churned as they dropped to the deck with a crunch and bounced, tilting backward.

The view inside the cockpit rotated skyward as the helicopter rolled backwards. Equipment tumbled all about the cabin. Those inside watched with silent horror as the ship's tower dropped from view until all they could see was sky.

The view froze for a very long second.

The helicopter tilted forward as they crashed down with a second crunch. The sailors moved quickly, pulling tight on cables looped through the landing skids.

Everyone caught their breath as the bird was secured at multiple points. Each new anchor reduced the chopper's shaking until it was bouncing over the water as one with the boat.

The quiet in the cockpit was broken when the pilot spun in his seat, stabbing his finger at Addison's face.

"Don't you ever! Ever! Make me do that again."

Addison firmly pushed down the pilot's hand.

"Do not talk to me like that. Not if you want to keep your job. And your finger."

"All this risk for one frickin' guy," the pilot mumbled. He tore his headset off and threw it against the cockpit window.

6

The captain ran across the deck to meet them as they stumbled out of the helicopter.

"Mister Addison, I got your message," he said. "I've calculated the nautical miles distant from where we think it's safest to drop the sub and kept our speed at-"

"Just give me an E.T.A."

"About a half-hour until we get there."

"A half-hour? Our client isn't supposed to be kept waiting."

The captain took a step backwards as if slapped. "I just let you land on my boat without stopping. Do you know how insane that is? There's no way we could do better."

"Well, then, I have to be honest. Your best sucks."

"Are you kidding me? Who's the client? The damn president?"

"Think richer and more powerful."

"Well, you said this was top secret, so fine, I don't want to know. I'm just trying to tell you that thanks to your landing stunt that we're close enough that if the Coasties have a bird in the air, they probably saw you coming."

"Their chopper is grounded."

"How do you know?"

"I just do. Besides, I'm counting on them being preoccupied and not caring once we turn around."

"What about the micro-sub?"

"Too small to notice on radar."

"You've got an answer for everything."

"I'm sure if you keep asking questions you'll find one I don't."

"Fine. This is your show."

"Damn right," Addison said. "Now where's the micro-sub?"

"Right this way, your highness."

"That's better," Addison said as he walked next to the captain. Jeffers, Holland and North followed.

"I feel better," North said, "now that I see Addison's a jerk to everyone, and not just us. I won't take it so personally."

"I don't think that's accurate," Jeffers mumbled. "He's not a jerk. He's an asshole."

"Maybe so," Holland said, "but assholes get results. If you were this rich guy Sinclair, wouldn't you want someone like Addison working your account?"

"If I was rich as Sinclair, I would have bought my own yacht," North said.

"Maybe he's a rich man because he cuts so many corners," Holland said.

"Then I would have paid for someone to protect me."

"He did. Us."

"You've got an answer for everything. Just like Addison," North said. "Let's hope that's all you have in common."

Holland didn't reply.

* * *

The captain led them to the front of the ship, where a crane held the micro-sub aloft. The small craft was shaped like a dull grey bullet twelve feet long and six feet in diameter. Its rounded tip was a thick hemispherical window secured to the main body with hexagonal bolts two inches wide. Four portholes lined its middle for viewing up, down, starboard and port. The porthole on top was larger than the others to double as exit and entry. The back of the sub tapered off to an exposed propeller engine between four stabilizer fins.

Jeffers slid his hand over the sub's smooth metal surface.

"Very nice," he said.

"If a torpedo and a short bus ever mated," Addison said, "this would be their first child. North would be their second."

North didn't react.

"I think I'm in love," Jeffers said, still stroking the micro-sub.

"Should we leave you two alone?" Holland asked.

"Let me show you how it works," the captain said. He flipped open a latch that was flush with the sub's body, exposing a small recessed wheel. With both hands he spun the wheel, releasing the top porthole. He climbed a ladder and dropped into the sub, Jeffers following. From outside, looking through the bulbous window at the fore, the others could see them hunched over the pilot's controls.

North and Holland peered through the mid-section portholes.

"Looks cramped," she said.

"Seats four and only four," Addison said.

"No markings?" Holland looked down the length of the sub.

"No markings. I don't know you and neither does anyone else."

"We are the insurance plan," Holland said.

"At least one of you listens to me," Addison answered, glancing sideways at North.

The captain and Jeffers emerged from the sub. Jeffers rubbed his hands together.

"Can't wait to try her out. When do we leave?"

The captain started to answer but Addison cut him off. "Fifteen minutes. Captain, I need some time alone with my team, and I don't want to be disturbed."

"My pleasure." The captain walked away.

"All right, kids," Addison said, "this is your final briefing. Find Danforth Percy Sinclair and get him off the boat. Stick him in your sub, come back to this vicinity, and we'll find you. Jeffers, the captain gave you the rendezvous coordinates?"

"He did."

"All right, here's your earpieces and microphones. I take it you all know how to use a throat mic? It's not secure, so keep the chatter light."

Addison held out his hand, palm up. Holland, Jeffers, and North each took an earpiece and fitted it into their right ear, then snapped the throat microphones around their necks.

Addison kept talking. "If the area around the rendezvous point isn't clear, get somewhere close and we'll pick up your signal. There's a tracker on the sub, but it's encoded so only I can read it. You've all got your weapons and gear, so any final remarks? This is the last time we'll talk until you get back."

Holland, Jeffers, and North looked at each other. No one spoke.

"Excellent," Addison said. "Don't screw up."

He turned and walked toward the bridge.

* * *

The sub slid beneath the surface, the interior darkening except for the faint green glow from the instrument panel.

"I love this thing," Jeffers said, hunched over the controls. "This guy has got to be loaded for Redfire to dispatch prime hardware like this."

The hull creaked as the sub dived.

North and Holland were practically forced to embrace in the sub's cramped interior. They were sitting on square benches, facing each other and looking out the portholes opposite. North's left shoulder was crammed against the back of Jeffers' chair.

"We're supposed to get a fourth guy in this can?" North asked. "The three of us can barely fit."

Jeffers laughed. "Us old guys don't take up much room. Just fold him up. Continuing dive."

The sub descended further. North looked up through the hatch window above him. The sun shrank from a disc to a point.

"How deep are we going?" Holland asked.

"You always ask the men in your life that?" Jeffers said.

"Sure do. But today I'm making an exception. I'm asking you."

Jeffers guffawed. "We're going deep enough," he said. "So if anyone looks down from the cruise ship, they won't see us."

Holland shifted and accidentally knocked her head against North's.

"Damn it," she said. "We sit any closer we'll have to get married."

"No thanks," North said. "Never again."

"Aw, did some girl break your heart?"

"I don't blame you," Jeffers cut in, "I can't stand arguing. When my girl starts yelling, I just want to go back to the field. I'd even rather face live fire. Anything other than endless nagging any day."

"Damn," Holland said, "if I knew this was going to be girls' night out, I would have worn my dress."

They all chuckled and fell quiet a moment, listening to the engine whir. The only evidence they were moving were the bubbles floating by the portholes.

North looked through the hatch above. The sun was a small hazy blur. "Seems like we should wait until dark," he said.

"That defeats the purpose of a Katrina Contract," Holland said. "Besides, who cares? It's hit and run. Emphasis on run. Grab the package and get the hell out."

North laughed. "You sound like a guy I know. He works for Redfire, too."

"Yeah? What's his name?"

"Guy Barra. Every hear of him?"

"Big guy? Kind of an oaf?"

"Sounds about right."

"Don't know him. That describes almost everyone I work with. Male and goofy. Present company included. I swear Redfire should skip the private contracts and start selling sausage."

"You sound like him," North chuckled, "that's all. Have a similar who-cares attitude. We were in the same unit back when I was military. Then we both went private and joined Redfire."

"So, what's your history, Holland?" Jeffers said. "What's a not-so-nice girl like you doing in a place like this?"

"What do you mean?"

"I mean, North and I have talked a little, what's the deal with you?"

"Deal with me?"

"I'm just trying to be social. I just met you a few hours ago. If it's going to be this tough then forget it. I was just wondering what service you did before Redfire."

"I've worked in the private sector my whole career."

"Doing what?" North said.

"It's private," she said.

"I thought you said you were in psy-ops."

"I never said that."

"Come on."

"I've spent a lot of time doing the things you military types want done, but don't want to do, because some politician is afraid he'll get caught. That's what I like about the private sector. Fewer rules."

"They're called laws," North said.

Holland smirked.

"So are you going to share anything about yourself? You know, build camaraderie?" North asked.

"Nope," Holland said. "Knowledge is power."

Jeffers laughed. "Well, chalk that up to another one of my failed attempts to be conversational."

* * *

Holland was gently knocking her knees against North's. "Hey, wake up, grandpa. Other grandpa says we're almost there."

"You ready, North?" Jeffers asked. "You were really out."

"I'm good," North said, rubbing his eyes.

"You sure, old man?"

North didn't answer.

"All right, game time," Jeffers said. "We're under and alongside the cruise ship right now. Call me when you're onboard and then again when you've got our guy. No communication unless there's an emergency. Ready?"

North tapped the pistol on his right thigh and knife on his left. He touched his earpiece and throat microphone. "I've got all I need."

"Holland?"

She tapped herself exactly as North had done. "I'm good."

"Let's rock and roll," Jeffers said. "Surfacing now."

7

The red phone on the Bonne Jane's communication console rang. A light flashed on the handset.

"That's the ship-to-ship line," Captain Dunn said to Goodkin. "I'm guessing it's for you."

"Receiving call," Goodkin said into his PC's microphone bud. He rolled his shoulders and reached for the red phone with his right hand, balancing his tablet in his left.

Dunn held the steering wheel steady. "I'll be as quiet as a ship rat."

"Be quieter," Goodkin said. He let the phone ring once more before answering. "This is Nelson Goodkin speaking."

"Mister Goodkin," the caller said. The voice was digitized exactly as it had been on the recording of the terrorists' demands. "Greetings. I would talk with you."

Goodkin activated his sound recorder app with his thumb and pressed the back of his hand on a switch labeled "Speaker Phone." A pop sounded inside the bridge as he returned the handset to its cradle.

"Go ahead," Goodkin said aloud, stepping to the windows, holding his tablet flat before him, his free hand hovering over the screen. He gazed across the bow of the ship toward the horizon. "To whom am I speaking?"

The robotic voice came from the bridge speakers this time. "You will know me as Hussein."

"All right, Hussein. And who do you represent?"

"We are the Children of Kariqistan."

Goodkin looked down at his tablet. A window popped open with a map and list of bullet points. He scanned the information. "Research team info: Kariqistan. Obscure former Soviet Republic in South Asia.

Primarily Islamic. Very poor, but rich in oil and rare earth minerals. Constant civil war. Gathering data on Children of Kariqistan. Nothing yet, but there are many factions inside the country."

"All right," Goodkin said, "And what, may I ask-"

"Stop," Hussein said. "I talk first."

"Of course, but eventually I will need to reply. Go ahead, Hussein."

"Who do you represent, Goodkin?"

"I am a Federal Agent with the United States Department of Homeland Security."

"So, the pigs sent a lap dog."

"Hussein, let's not talk about me. You have hostages. They are my first concern. Let's talk about them and what we can do to make sure they are returned unharmed."

"Yes. The hostages. And for holding them you think us evil, yes?"

"What I think isn't important, Hussein. What matters is that innocent-"

"Let me tell you about hostages, Goodkin. Let me tell you about innocents."

"All right."

"When I was a young boy, my village was attacked by bandits. After they had murdered the men and taken the women out to their trucks to rape them, they gathered the children together. One by one they made them run across a field. Escape and you are free, they were told. But the bandits shot them. One by one. Fleeing across an open field, children were shot in the back by monsters and cowards. Only one child survived. He pretended to be dead, a bullet in his shoulder, lying next to the corpse of his sister."

"That's terrible, Hussein. But the people-"

"I am that survivor, Goodkin. Shot at five years old. The bodies of my friends, my brothers, my sisters, my father, all were left there to be feasted on by birds and scavenging dogs. I never found my mother. She was taken away with the others, for rape, for sale, or worse. So let me ask you, Goodkin, have you ever seen a field of dead children, half eaten by animals?"

"No, Hussein, I have not. That's-"

"The men who did this were mercenaries, sponsored by the United States government. Your politicians thought they could buy off one of the countless gangs of thugs in my country. Ah, but you do not know us Kariqistani. They took your money, they killed for you, and when you asked them to do something, they ignored you. You see what your money went to, yes? The killing of the children. This is why we are the Children of Kariqistan."

Goodkin rocked his head from side to side, stretching his neck, twirling his finger in a "hurry up" motion. He interrupted quickly as Hussein paused.

"That's a horrific story, Hussein. No one would blame you for being angry. However, just like those children, the hostages you are holding are innocent. You have the power to release them, to prove yourself better than those who attacked your village. The people you are holding have nothing to do with the problems of your country."

The speakers crackled as Hussein made a noise of disgust. "Ah! This is what you Westerners always say! Democracy is wonderful, people have choice, they control their destiny. Yet somehow you are also always free of blame. No one is at fault because it is always someone else who did it, yes? And did my family have anything to do with the evils of the corrupt government in my fatherland? Or the corrupt government in your land that armed them? Or the petroleum and mining multinationals that control your military and plunder my country?"

"No, Hussein. No, they did not."

"So they did not deserve to die."

A flashing message popped up on Goodkin's tablet: "Psych team advisory: Do not get bogged down in debate."

Goodkin tapped on the message to delete it.

"They did not deserve to die," he said. "Neither do the people on that boat."

"But my guests reap the benefits of this corruption. All around me here on this ship I see nothing but luxury. I would love for these pampered fools to live one day in Kariqistan. They would be broken by nightfall, when they realized their servants had run off with their food. Soon enough they would join me. Perhaps yet I may convert some."

His digitized dry chuckle sounded like a computer error alert.

"Hussein, they are human beings like you, and like any child from Kariqistan. What is it you want? What can I do for you? What can I do so you will let them go?"

"Ah, Goodkin. Now we come to what is important. Here is what we must have. All American forces, official and unofficial, meaning your mercenaries, must leave Kariqistan. We want all resource-thieving multinationals out as well and we want fifty million dollars in cash. The money must be provided in untraceable American bills. If you do not deliver, we will return our guests one body at a time."

"Hussein, you sound like an honorable man. There's no need to hurt anyone, but I'll need to make some calls about those requests, all right?"

"They are demands. Not requests. And no hostile actions, Goodkin. For each one of my men harmed, I will kill twenty Americans. I have plenty to spare."

"I'm working with you, Hussein. There's no need for violence."

"I am generous and patient, Goodkin, but do not disappoint me. For now our talking is complete. Do not bring any other vessels into this area and make no aggression."

"No hostile action will be taken against you. I will be in touch soon."

Goodkin flipped the switch on the console. The sound in the bridge cut off with a sharp click. Goodkin adjusted his mic bulb and began tapping his tablet.

"You get all that?" he said. "Any progress on finding the Kariqistan ambassador? Yeah. I know. Good luck with that one. I never heard of them either. It's probably a new terror group, that place grows them like weeds. Or poppies. Right. Let me know. Thanks."

Goodkin sat down on a stool and closed his eyes.

"So," Captain Dunn said, "you're all right doing this whole thing alone?"

"I'm not alone at all," Goodkin said, holding up his tablet. "The team's right here. Besides, most of them are needed to handle optics and relations."

"Optics and relations?"

"The media."

"I know the type," Dunn said. "From my days in the marines. You do the work, guys on shore get all the credit since it's their face on the news. It's a great way to kick-start a career without having to do anything. You create the impression you helped when all you really did was announce that something got done. But it-"

"My tablet is still transmitting, Captain. They can hear everything we say."

Dunn clamped his lips shut, his cheeks flushed.

Goodkin stood with his back to the captain, hands clasped behind him, the rectangular screen of the tablet reflecting Dunn's scowling face.

The captain looked away. "So. Uh, now what?" he asked. "Is the guy going to get his money?"

"Not a chance. Official policy is we don't negotiate with terrorists. We let them think they might have their demands met, but we're really just waiting them out."

"Oh," Dunn said. "Well, what if they-"

"Just pilot the boat," Goodkin said, cutting him off. "That's all I need from you."

Dunn didn't reply. With his right hand clamped on the wheel, he raised his binoculars with his left and scanned the decks of the Sunset Mist. Other than the shadows moving behind the tinted bridge windows, she seemed completely abandoned.

He lowered his binoculars and shook off a chill.

8

North's ears popped as the micro-sub rose toward the surface. The vessel's hull creaked, relaxing against the weakening pressure.

"Almost there," Jeffers called out. "We're visible from above by now."

"I'll go first," Holland said.

North nodded. "Works for me."

They both pulled their ski masks over their heads, leaving only their mouths, eyes and nostrils exposed. North grabbed the release wheel near the top porthole.

The interior brightened as the sub broke into sunlight, bobbing on the water like a discarded bottle.

"We're up," Jeffers said, his tone calm but crisp. "Go."

North spun the lock wheel as fast as he could. The top hatch came loose with a hiss. He braced his feet against the machinery inside the sub and pushed open the small round door, setting it down quietly on the outer metal skin of the sub.

When he stood, the rim of the porthole was at his waist. The white hull of the Sunset Mist loomed above him, open walkways bounded by railings rising all along its side. The nearest railing was several feet above, the hall ending in a service door on one side, a dead end on the other.

North quickly scanned the ship for movement.

Nothing.

He reached down into the sub and signaled Holland with a thumbs-up. She slapped a three-pronged grappling hook into his palm. North pulled, drawing out slack from the cable. He spun the hook over his head once before releasing. It caught the bottom rail with a clang.

North pulled with all his strength on the cable, hand over hand, dragging the sub toward the cruise ship until it gently banged against the much larger ship's hull. He dropped into the sub.

"Good to go," he said. Holland was twisting the cable around a metal brace.

Jeffers had spun his chair around and was looking on.

"I've got that, Holland," he said. "You go."

Holland leapt up through the porthole, grabbed the cable and climbed up, hanging down, going hand over hand until she could grab the railing. She twisted her grip, pulled herself up and vaulted over. She landed on her feet crouched like a cat, her pistol out, watching the nearby service door.

North followed up the cable in the same manner, landing on the metal walkway with a thud. As soon as his boots hit the deck, Jeffers let out the cable until the hook fell loose. North tossed the hook into the water and Jeffers pulled it in.

North took a second to confirm the hall to their back ended in a dead end. He turned and faced the door, gun drawn.

Inside the micro-sub, Jeffers was furiously spinning the wheel to seal the top porthole. He gave a thumbs-up through the glass and retreated to the control panel. The sub quietly sank under the water, until it was gone in the darkness.

Jeffers' voice sounded in their ears. "Test. Test. Can you hear me?" he said, the volume fading.

North pinched his neck with thumb and index finger, activating the throat mic. "We hear you," he said, looking to Holland.

She activated her mic. "I'm here, too."

"We're all good," North said. "See you soon."

"Happy hunting," Jeffers said.

Holland was checking the door. She tugged on the handle twice while North kept watch out on the open sea. Without warning, Holland stepped back and pointed her gun at the lock. The silencer kept the shots quiet, but the bullets hit the metal with an echoing clang.

She tested the handle again. The door held.

"God damn it," North said. "Keep it down. Use your knife."

Holland turned around to say something, but her gaze shot past him.

"Company! Coming around!"

North turned and saw the angular gray shape of a small military vessel in the distance. A white wake spread out from either side. She was approaching fast.

"Down!" Holland yelled.

The railing they had climbed over consisted of three thick pipes with open air between them to prevent the ship from taking on water. Broad, solid supports were spaced every ten feet.

Holland and North crouched together behind one of the supports just wide enough to hide them both.

"Did they see us?" North asked.

Bullets pinged over their heads, sparking on the hull above them. A burning smell filled the air.

"I'm going to say yes," Holland said.

North peeked from their cover. The dull gray vessel was closing fast. Muzzle flashes erupted as riflemen on the deck shot at them.

North leapt up and threw his weight against the door. The metal bent with a squeal but held. He dove back to cover as gunfire peppered the door, flinging sparks.

"If they get much closer, we're done," he yelled. "Get your knife."

Holland unsheathed her combat knife.

"Go when I fire," North said.

He leapt up, fired two shots and dropped. The return fire hit the hull above him. With their attackers distracted, Holland rushed the door, jamming her knife into the space between the handle and the lock. She wiggled the blade but the door didn't budge.

"Come back!" North yelled. "Jump back!"

Holland's knife bent, and the door gave, flinging open with a bang. She dove in, bullets lancing over her hunched back and into the ship's interior. North kept low and leapt in after her.

On their knees inside, they slammed the door shut. Bullets ricocheted off the door but failed to penetrate. The firing outside stopped.

They caught their breath in the darkness, creeping backwards, weapons trained on the door.

The sound of the engine grew louder as the ship came closer, idling just a few yards away. They heard men yelling, but couldn't make out the words.

The engine sound roared, then slowed, then stopped.

Holland stood up. "Not the most elegant entrance, but–"

North grabbed her and pulled her down. He held a finger to his lips. They waited, listening to the waves gently slap the cruise ship's hull.

"Come on, they're gone," Holland said.

"They only revved the engine," North whispered. "They're trying to trick us."

"Let me peek."

"No," North held her with one hand, gun still aimed at the door. She struggled but North held on.

"Patience," he said.

Holland stopped squirming.

They waited, listening.

Waves calmly brushed against the cruise ship.

Suddenly, the quiet was destroyed by an engine roaring to life. This time it faded away. North let go of Holland's arm.

She moved to the door and peeked out where her knife had made a slight indentation.

"All clear," she said, rising from her crouch. "Some of your old Special Forces buddies out there?"

"If they are, we'll be getting to our target just as this whole thing ends."

"Then we better hustle," Holland said. "I don't want them to get all the kills."

9

Dunn and Goodkin looked up as they heard the clear cracking sound of gunfire. Out on deck, the Bonnie Jane's crew dove into cover, hiding behind the ship's equipment.

"Who's shooting?" Goodkin yelled.

Keeping his right hand on the wheel, Dunn snatched up his binoculars with his left and scanned the Sunset Mist.

"I don't see anyone on the cruise ship, and it sure isn't coming from my boat. Not without my order," he said.

The red ship-to-ship phone rang. Goodkin answered it by switching on the bridge speakers.

Hussein's metallic voice rattled over the intercom.

"So, Goodkin! This is how you deal with us? This is how you establish trust? You bring men with guns? You open fire? You must want these hostages to die!"

"No! Stop! Hussein!" Goodkin yelled back. He paused to lower his tone. "I don't know where those shots are coming from. I did not give the order."

"You bastard dog liar!"

"There!" Dunn called out, pointing.

Goodkin turned. Another boat was rounding the fore of the cruise ship. The new vessel was smaller and bulkier than the Bonnie Jane. She was colored the uniform gray of a Navy ship, a drab contrast to the white and orange of the Coast Guard vessel and the pastel colors of the Sunset Mist. Men on the deck of the newcomer had their rifles trained up at the walkways of the cruise ship.

"What the hell?" Goodkin said. "Who is that?"

Dunn scanned the ship's hull markings. "Looks like the U.S. Navy. If I had to guess, I'd say the SEALs are here."

"I didn't appeal for military support," Goodkin yelled. "They'll just make the situation more volatile. Why were they shooting? Why didn't they announce their approach?"

"I don't know."

"I'm not talking to you," Goodkin said, "I'm talking to them." He pointed at his tablet.

"Oh, sorry," Dunn said.

"What do you mean you didn't know? Well, find out!"

Goodkin turned to Captain Dunn. "Captain, tell them to stop immediately."

"I'll try, but they don't take orders from me."

"Tell them I said so."

Dunn hesitated. "Well, all right," he said. "Let's see if that works."

Captain Dunn grabbed the ship-to-ship com. It looked exactly like a CB handset. He pressed a button on the side. "U.S. Navy vessel G.F.9.5., this is Captain Edgar Dunn of the U.S. Coast Guard patrol boat Bonnie Jane. Request that you cease all fire immediately."

"Don't request. Demand," Goodkin said to Dunn. "Why didn't you give me a heads up? I should have been told they were coming."

"You expelled my entire crew from the bridge. I can't watch all the instruments."

"Didn't your crew think it was important enough to let you know?"

"I'll find out," Dunn flicked a switch on the console. "First Mate Smith," he barked. "Report to bridge. Now."

Goodkin tapped his tablet and spoke. "I am. Gathering unexpected situational data now. I expect you to do the same. Yes. Do that. All of it. Stand by."

The first mate was on the bridge in seconds.

"Aye, Captain Dunn," Smith said. "You wanted to see-"

"Why didn't you tell me another ship was coming?" Goodkin yelled. "People could have been killed. This whole situation is delicate. And who are they?" He flailed his hand in the direction of the Navy ship as it drifted closer.

The first mate kept his eyes on Captain Dunn as if Goodkin wasn't even there.

"First mate," Dunn said, keeping his voice low. "Explain."

"Aye, sir. The naval vessel radioed ahead to let us know they would be providing support. Bridge proceedings were not interrupted, since it was not an emergency. As ordered." Smith slid his eyes toward Goodkin, then back to Dunn. "Sir."

Goodkin stepped up to the first mate, the tip of his nose grazing Smith's ear.

"My situational awareness is your top priority," Goodkin said. "I need to know everything. Every. Thing. If a bird craps on the deck, someone better tell me, understand? Now I know that might require some thinking, but you need to adapt."

Smith didn't react.

Dunn removed his cap and scratched his bald head vigorously. His scalp was flushed deep red. He replaced his cap and spoke calmly to First Mate Smith.

"Keep us posted, sailor. Dismissed."

"Aye, sir." The first mate saluted and quickly stepped off the bridge.

An unfamiliar voice spoke over the intercom. "This is Captain Robert Burnett of the United States Navy Special Forces vessel Gunfish 95. Say again, who is giving me orders on this frequency?"

Captain Dunn reached for the handset but Goodkin waved him off and flicked a switch, activating the bridge speaker phone.

"This is federal negotiator Nelson Goodkin from the Department of Homeland Security. We have a hostage situation here. Cease all small arms fire immediately."

"We already have," Burnett answered.

"Great. Now proceed to vacate the area."

"I want to make it clear," Burnett said. "We have not stopped shooting because of you, Goodkin. The targets we had acquired simply moved out of sight."

"Targets?"

"My spotters said they saw two bandits along the walkway on the opposite side of that cruise ship. They had no hostages with them, but they were armed and wearing masks, so I gave the order to open fire. You almost had two less bad guys."

Goodkin pressed his fists against the sides of his head and squeezed his eyes shut. "You idiot!" he roared. "They've promised to kill dozens of hostages in retaliation if any of their team is harmed. I demand you stop all shooting unless I give the okay! Is that understood?"

"We are responding to the Sunset Mist distress call as appropriate."

"You are to follow the orders of the Incident Area Commander as designated by Multi-Agency Emergency Management and Response Protocol."

"Now, son, I have no idea what you just said."

"I'll make it simple then, Burnett. You listen to me."

"I take orders from the American people, not bureaucrats. This whole thing could be over in an hour. I've got a squad of Navy SEALs here and they'd just love to-"

"Captain Burnett, this is Captain Dunn," Dunn interrupted. "This is not a secure channel. Our friends on the Sunset Mist can hear everything we say. Why don't you come on board my boat and we'll discuss this?"

"On my way."

Goodkin shut off the bridge mic. "Who the hell is this cowboy?" he said.

"No idea," Dunn said.

Goodkin tapped his tablet. "I wasn't talking to you."

Dunn shook his head and watched as the Navy ship moved closer, turning to align herself side-to-side with the Bonnie Jane. He activated the intercom. "Crew, this is Captain Dunn. We're going to have guests from our friends in the Navy. Play nice and be respectful as you would with any other group of ladies, all right?"

The Navy vessel Gunfish 95 swerved as the two crews dropped rubber barriers between the ships and threw lines to their counterparts.

In minutes, the boats were tethered together.

10

Dunn was quiet, watching as his crew and the Navy crew called to each other and lashed their ships together. Their voices were muted on the closed bridge. Goodkin furiously tapped his tablet's screen. Dunn craned his neck to look over Goodkin's shoulder, but before he could see anything Hussein's distorted voice boomed over the speakers.

"Goodkin! Do you want blood on your hands? Send that Navy ship away or I will kill seven hostages, throw their bodies in the sea and hang their heads from the deck!"

"Hussein," Goodkin answered, activating the bridge mic. "Hussein, please be patient. We're trying to figure out-"

"Do it now. How dare you come to me with words of peace and then fire on my ship! You Americans cannot be trusted! You are an evil people!"

"Hussein, be reasonable. I didn't know they were going to be here. Sometimes orders get confused. Surely you understand that."

"Enough games, Goodkin. Enough sweet words. The second ship must go immediately."

"I agree, Hussein, I'm caring for that now. There's no reason to hurt anyone. We are working on your request, but it takes time."

"One boat, Goodkin. Or Americans will die and their families will blame you. I grant you ten minutes."

The bridge speakers popped as Hussein disconnected.

"Hussein? I can't guarantee- Hussein! Damn it!"

He punched the bridge mic switch, shutting it off.

A deep, unfamiliar voice behind Goodkin growled, "Let me guess. You're the crybaby negotiator."

Goodkin turned to face a man a full head taller than him wearing a deep blue Navy captain's uniform. The man's jacket stretched tightly around his ample belly. His hair, what of it that could be seen below his cap, was crew-cut and white. His grey eyes stared out sharply from his sagging, pale face. A cell phone's hands-free transceiver clung to his ear, the blue light blinking slowly.

The man's name patch read "Captain Burnett."

Burnett saluted toward Dunn and muttered, "Captain."

Dunn saluted back.

Behind Burnett were two other men dressed entirely in black. They were holding rifles almost as long as they were tall. Burnett snapped his head to the side.

"Snipers," he barked, "take positions!"

"Aye, captain," the men replied. They quickly exited the bridge.

"Whoa, whoa," Goodkin said. "Wait a minute. Come back." The snipers were already gone, one moving to the fore and the other to the aft of the Bonnie Jane.

"Bring them back," Goodkin said.

Burnett stared down at him. "Now, why would I do that, son? I understand you've got some bad guys that need killing and that's my crew's specialty. Now, exactly who the hell are you?"

"I'm Nelson Goodkin, federal negotiator with the Department of Homeland Security and this incident's Area Commander. Who the hell are you?"

"Captain Robert Burnett of U.S. Navy Special Forces transport Gunfish 95. Now, why are you protecting these terrorists?"

"I'm protecting hostages. This is a delicate situation. Your boat has to clear out. If you don't, they're going to start executing people."

"Why does this boat get to stay?" Burnett said. "My vessel is equipped for assault."

"Are you serious?" Goodkin asked.

"The Gunfish crew is ready for anything. We've got better equipment and better training than these weekend wetbacks."

Dunn raised his eyebrows but said nothing.

"Seven minutes, Mister Goodkin," Hussein's voice crackled over the speaker. "If that ship does not leave, Americans will die."

"Ah," Burnett said. "That must be the bad guy. Why does he sound like a robot?"

"Burnett, please, there's no time." Goodkin said.

"Call me Captain Burnett."

"Captain Burnett, that was my contact among the kidnappers. He wants only one boat nearby. I told him we would honor that. Now you're breaking my promise. You have to get your ship out of here."

"You made promises to a terrorist? Some negotiator. Let me talk to him. Hey!" Burnett yelled at the speaker, "Hey, robot!"

"Stop!" Goodkin said. "We will formalize the engagement parameters later. For now, just move your ship."

Goodkin turned to Dunn and said, "A little help here?"

"Burnett," Dunn said slowly, "one captain to another, we're respectfully requesting that you withdraw your vessel. We'll give you a full briefing, but you have to move her first. Fair enough?"

Burnett's eyes narrowed. He stared at Dunn, then Goodkin, then back at Dunn. "All right," Burnett said, "but if things get hairy, I'm calling her back."

"Fine," Dunn said.

"Four minutes, Goodkin," Hussein said over the speakers. "Blood will flow. Do not make me do this. It is all up to you."

"That bastard," Burnett said.

"Burnett!" Goodkin screamed. "Order your ship out of here!"

"Don't talk to me like that, son. I'll wipe this deck with your bare ass."

"Captain Burnett," Dunn said, "please hurry."

"You're running out of time, Goodkin," Hussein said. "Would you like a dead man or a dead woman? How about a child? Or all three? I can't decide, so I'll, how do you say, cover all the bases, yes?"

Burnett scowled but tapped his earpiece and spoke aloud. "Gunfish, this is Captain Burnett. I'm going to stay aboard the Bonnie Jane with my snipers, but I need you to clear the area. First mate, you have command. Fall out of visual range, but stay at the ready to return ASAP. Do it quickly. Burnett out."

"Crew," Dunn said over the intercom, "turn the Navy ship loose. Double-time."

Gunfish 95 choked white exhaust across the deck of the Bonnie Jane as its engine revved, the crews of each boat undoing the knots and hurling the ropes across the widening gap. The Navy ship pulled away and turned from the Sunset Mist, heading toward the horizon.

Goodkin closed his eyes and sighed heavily, squeezing his forehead with his right hand, his tablet dangling along his left side. He pressed a button on the console and spoke.

"Hussein, look. They're leaving. As promised."

Goodkin activated his tablet PC camera, and snapped a quick shot of the Gunfish, capturing her identification numbers. He transmitted the photo along with a quickly-typed message: "On scene. Need data."

"You are late, Mister Goodkin," Hussein said. "You took too long. How many did I say I would kill again? Give me the number."

"Hussein," Goodkin said, "we did what you wanted as quickly as possible."

"I am not convinced you take me seriously, Goodkin."

"I do. We do. Please, there is no need to harm people." Goodkin leaned on the console, his eyes closed tight.

"Wait," Hussein said. The speakers clicked off.

"Oh, hell," Goodkin said. "Damn it."

Dunn and Goodkin scanned the Sunset Mist with their binoculars. Burnett fished out his own from his pants pocket. They could only see the railing for the top deck, but there was no one there.

The Bonnie Jane bobbed on the water as her crew waited. The only sound was the gentle brush of waves and the receding engine of Gunfish 95.

"Is he killing them now?" Burnett said. "I swear-"

"Quiet!" Goodkin barked.

They waited. A minute felt like an hour.

The bridge speakers popped abruptly. All three men jumped.

"I am a generous man," Hussein said.

Goodkin exhaled loudly.

"But my patience is limited," Hussein said. "Next time you are slow to fulfill my demands, people will die."

"Yes, Hussein," Goodkin said. "Of course. Thank you."

"I must admit I am disappointed. I had really hoped to kill some Americans. Perhaps later. Regardless, I will call you when the second vessel is far enough away."

Goodkin bowed his head, leaning it against the Bonnie Jane's window. Dunn removed his cap and wiped the sweat from his scalp.

"That damn bastard," Burnett said. "Are you going to let him bully you?"

Goodkin, his cheeks bright red, spun violently to face Burnett.

"You moron! You almost got people killed with your tough guy act!" He crossed the bridge, stabbing his finger with each step. "If you want to help, you do what I say. I'm trying to resolve this peacefully!"

Burnett held his ground, staring at the smaller, thinner man for a moment. "Then we agree," he said. "I'm all in favor of resolving this peacefully. The bad guys rest in peace, the good guys live in peace. All you're doing is playing Hussein's little bitch."

"I don't give a crap about Hussein! I'm trying to help the hostages. What about that simple concept don't you get? If you kill terrorists, they kill the captives."

"Not if we kill bad guys fast enough."

"Are you an idiot?"

Burnett spat on the deck at Goodkin's feet.

"Excuse me," Captain Dunn said.

Burnett snarled. "You're just another pampered college kid, Goodkin. I bet you never had to-"

"Boys!" Dunn yelled. "You're both on the Bonnie Jane. And on my vessel I'm the captain. Not you," he pointed to Goodkin, "or you," he pointed to Burnett. "Got it? Now, stand down."

Goodkin turned away. Burnett shrugged and folded his arms.

Dunn grumbled. "Good enough. Now, Goodkin. If you'd be so kind as to brief Captain Burnett on the situation."

Goodkin was across the cabin from Burnett, as far away from the other man as he could go and still remain on the bridge. He removed his glasses and pinched between his eyes.

"All right," he said. "Fine. We've been-"

Burnett cut him off. "The SEALs I'm ferrying can have that boat cleaned of bandits in no time. Those hostages to be on their way to whatever overpriced mosquito farm they're going to real quick. They could be firing up their joints, visiting the local whores and getting their pockets picked by nightfall."

Goodkin's face reddened. Dunn and he locked gazes. Dunn held up a hand, warning him to stay calm.

"Burnett," Goodkin said. "Captain Burnett. Listen. Just please listen. I'm sure your crew is the best at what they do, but let's, ah. Hm. Look at it this way. We can always kill them later. If we attempt a raid, chances are greater that innocent Americans die in the process. It makes sense to try talking first."

Captain Dunn spoke. "You have to admit, Burnett, the man's making sense. Best to take the safe way first."

Burnett squinted. "Sounds more like he's insulting the job my men would do."

"No," Dunn said, "not at all."

"Either that or he's using his psy-ops voodoo on us."

Dunn shrugged. "I prefer to just call it logic."

"That means it's working on you."

"I never said I was in psy-ops," Goodkin said.

"That means you probably were," Burnett answered.

Goodkin threw his hands in the air and let them slap down at his sides. He brushed the screen of his tablet with his shirt. "Look, a more peaceful approach might save some of your precious crew from getting killed, all right? It might save your SEALs."

Burnett turned his back to them and paused a long time, thinking. Finally he shook himself and stood up straight.

"All right, Goodkin," he said, turning. "Damn your negotiation skills."

"I hope it shows you that I'm good at what I do."

"Not really. It only shows I can't trust you. For now, we play it your way, but when you realize terrorists need more than a stern talking to, let me know. I'll speak a language they understand."

"Deal," Goodkin said. "Until then, no shooting. And one boat."

"You don't have to repeat it. So what's the status of the hostages?"

"I was getting to that before you showed up." Goodkin picked up the com. "By the way, you should know every single word of this conversation is being recorded." He pointed to his tablet.

"Record away. I'm fine if everyone knows who let those monsters live."

"Burnett," Dunn said. "Please. We were making progress."

"Every word, Burnett," Goodkin repeated. "Recorded and sent live to my superiors in Homeland Security."

"Works for me," Burnett said, folding his arms. "My superiors in the Navy will want to speak with them. I'll play nice out of respect for Captain Dunn, since you're his dead weight to carry. And I'll give you right of way as first on the scene. But by all means, have your people call my people. My only regret is I won't be able to hear your folks get chewed up and spit out."

"You can't just show up and take over," Goodkin said. "How did you even know this was happening?"

"Bad news travels. Word gets around."

"So, what were your specific orders?"

"I don't have to tell you anything." Burnett said.

"Ah, so you didn't have orders. Am I right?"

Burnett said nothing.

"You just heard about this incident, somehow. So you came here on your own, or were passing by and heard the distress call. Or someone knew about your ambition and wanted to help you grab a bonus. Whatever the method, the result is you don't have formal orders at this moment, correct?"

"A captain is permitted by naval rules of engagement to respond to contingencies. It's why the Navy employs men," Burnett said. "Not computers." He looked down at Goodkin's tablet PC.

"Well, then," Goodkin said. "Until I hear otherwise, I'm the commander. And Dunn agrees. And until you can prove you've received orders otherwise, those are your operational constraints. Understood?"

Burnett looked at Dunn.

"Sounds about right," Dunn said. "Seems like we have an agreement. Goodkin is Incident Area Commander. Burnett, if you want, call your bosses and let them issue new orders to Goodkin's people. Everyone agree?"

"I'm good," Burnett said. "I can't wait to see how this goes down. I really do hope you're recording."

"Finally," Goodkin said. "Now I need some fresh air."

* * *

Goodkin held the microphone bulb to mouth as he exited the bridge. Before the door closed, Dunn heard him whisper, "You getting all this? Find out everything you can. Did you get the image? Good. Yes, Captain Burnett, U.S. Navy. And find who is leaking information. No one should know yet."

The door slammed shut.

Burnett tapped his earpiece. "Burnett here. Tell the SEAL team to get ready. They are going to be boarding that cruise ship soon if it kills me." He waited. "I don't care, tell them." He paused. "Including that. All the toys. Burnett out."

Burnett turned to Dunn, extending his hand. "I'm not sure we were properly introduced."

Keeping his left hand on the boat's steering wheel, Dunn stretched out and shook Burnett's hand.

Burnett chuckled, "Are you glued to that wheel?"

"Protocol," Dunn said. "Hands on the wheel at all times."

"No wonder you get along so well with college-boy. You both have a very rigid interpretation of procedure," Burnett said. "You're going to dislocate your elbow if I ask you to shake hands again."

"Each captain has his way."

"Ain't that the truth. I know I wouldn't tolerate that punk on my ship."

Dunn shrugged.

"Orders," he said.

Goodkin returned to the bridge and adjusted his glasses. Burnett took his place on the opposite side of the cabin, leaving Dunn in the middle at the ship's wheel.

"Any word from Hussein?" Goodkin asked.

"None," Dunn said.

"Good. Now I'd like to get back to work."

He flicked on the com.

"Hussein, are you there? Hussein?"

11

"I am here, Mister Goodkin. I am waiting for that Navy ship to be removed from my sight. And I am losing patience."

"You can see she's retreating, Hussein. I am a man of my word."

"Are you, Goodkin? There are levels of trust. You haven't impressed me so far."

Burnett snickered. Goodkin turned his back to him and continued talking. "You can trust me, Hussein. I moved the ship for you as a sign of good faith. Now you've got to give me something. Show me that the people you're holding hostage are alive and well-cared for."

"Ah, Mister Goodkin, so greedy. Why don't you tell me about how my demands from your corrupt nation are proceeding?"

"The balls on this guy!" Burnett hissed. Dunn waved at him to be quiet.

Goodkin continued, undistracted. "I've spoken to my superiors and told them your demands. They will be more likely to comply if they see you are being reasonable. Show me the hostages. Alive. Or we go no further."

Goodkin slid his finger across the tablet's screen.

"I thought we shared mutual respect," Hussein said. "Now you need proof? Don't you trust me?"

"I know you are an honorable man, but there are others who do not believe me."

"Are those the ones shooting?"

Burnett fidgeted.

"Yes," Goodkin said, turning to face Burnett. "Prove to them my faith in you is not misguided. Show them that they have been foolish in thinking the Kariqistani only understand violence. That's the only way I can help you get what you want. I'm having trouble holding off those who would rather barge in and kill you."

"Damn right," Burnett muttered.

"Last warning, Captain," Dunn said softly, "or I'll have you removed from the bridge."

Burnett folded his arms and turned his back to Dunn.

Hussein continued. "What you are saying, Goodkin, sounds a lot like good cop bad cop. I see this in your American movies, yes? Bad cop wants to kill me. This is your Navy vessel. Good cop, that is you, wants to assist. I am supposed to run to you and beg for protection from bad cop. Good cop is the real power. Am I right?"

"Hussein, all I want is to make sure the people you are holding are safe. Their families are worried sick. This is a fair thing to ask for."

"One moment, Goodkin." The speaker popped and the bridge was silent.

Goodkin, Dunn and Burnett waited, saying nothing, avoiding each other's eyes.

Goodkin tapped and pinched his tablet screen while whispering. "Base, are you building a psych profile? Let me know what you find. I've got my tablet crunching the personality metrics as well. Goodkin out."

Hussein's voice came back without warning. "I am considering your request but while you are waiting, make no hostile action. The hostages will die if even one of my men is harmed or any further aggression is made toward us."

"Move quickly, Hussein. We must make sure those people are being treated properly." Goodkin made eye contact with Burnett while he continued speaking to Hussein. "You have my word none of your men will be harmed."

"I have your word, Goodkin," Hussein said, "for what it is worth."

PART 3

VOLUNTEERS NEEDED

1

The Sunset Mist's main banquet hall was crowded far beyond its capacity. Two dozen tables and hundreds of chairs had been hurled into broken piles in the corners of the ballroom. The remaining floor space was so completely covered by seated passengers that the carpet's purple and red pattern was nearly obscured. Thick gold curtains covered the windows so the only light in the room came from several crystal chandeliers.

Nearly 200 captives, dressed for relaxing in the sun, were restrained by plastic ties around their ankles and wrists. Their hands were bound behind their backs to more fully incapacitate them. Some hostages were sleeping, leaning against their neighbors or the walls. Some had tipped over and were curled on the floor. Most stayed seated, rocking and shifting to prevent their legs from cramping. Their eyes darted toward any movement while they kept their heads down.

The only standing people in the room were the three masked men blocking the exits. One stood by a single door that led to the kitchen and the other two by the double doors that connected to the ship's main interior hallway. The men were dressed completely in black, from their heavy rubber-soled boots to their gloves. Only their eyes, nostrils and mouths were exposed. They did not seem bothered by the stale heat.

Periodically, one of the men, presumably their leader, strolled among the captives, slowly meandering about the room, the barrel of his AK-47 assault rifle sweeping across the crowd.

"You're doing good," the masked man said, his voice electronically distorted by a small cylinder attached to his neck. "Stay quiet and you'll get through this just fine."

The other two terrorists did not speak at all.

"Please," a captive said. "Please let us go."

"Quiet! Not one word," the lone speaking terrorist bellowed. His words ruptured into static as his vocal distortion device was pushed beyond its limit.

Several prisoners gasped. Some bowed their heads and cried.

Life inside the ballroom had been this way for hours.

Any talking among the captives was silenced by angry electronic yelling. Even the young children captives (their hands and ankles bound with plastic ties as well) had stopped whining and instead opted for sleep, their small heads rolling back on their parents' thighs, mouths slack.

"Excuse me," a voice called from the crowd. "May I go to the bathroom?"

Several other captives hushed the speaker.

The masked man replied, "Of course you may."

"May I use the restroom?"

"No."

Across the room, someone sneezed.

"Bless you," a voice called out. A round of hushing rippled throughout the room.

"Quiet!" the terrorist yelled.

Some captives still held conversations. They did so by looking down, careful not to move their lips, speaking as softly as they possibly could.

"I'm glad there's no clock in here."

"I wish there was. I could count the number of minutes I have left."

"Don't talk like that. We're still alive. We'll make it."

"Nothing is more dangerous than hope."

"The Lord will see us through. Gotta believe in Jesus."

"Try shutting up."

"Believe in the power of the Almighty, and all things are possible."

"Don't start that crap. The Almighty made these pricks."

"The Lord works in mysterious ways."

"How convenient."

"I said shut up," the terrorist yelled.

Except for those brief exchanges and the occasional cough, sniffle or sob, the room was silent until the quiet was pierced by the staccato popping sound of machine gun fire. The noise was faint but unmistakable. The masked men crouched down, raising their guns.

The prisoners gasped and immediately hushed each other, tipping themselves over to duck.

As quickly as it began, the shooting noise stopped.

Dozens of the passengers were crying. Dozens more shushed them.

The terrorist leader peeked through the crack between the double doors and signaled to the other two. All three bolted from the room, the last one out locked the doors behind him.

The prisoners were alone.

2

Couples leaned their heads together and whispered prayers or words of love. Some simply touched, eyes closed, resigned. Others struggled against their bonds with no success. Groups that were separated called to each other in an impossible combination of a yell and a whisper.

"I love you."

"Keep praying."

"Don't give up hope."

The talking grew louder as each person tried to be heard over those nearby.

"What if that shooting was them killing some other passengers?"

"You saw the terrorists, they looked surprised. Scared, too."

"Shut up! They said not to talk."

"They're not here, jackass."

"They have cameras in each corner of the ceiling, idiot."

"Desert monkeys don't know how to use cameras."

"How long have they been gone?"

"Shush!"

"Did he lock the door? Check the door."

"You do it."

"I'd check it but you're closer."

"I'm tied up."

"Well, so am I!"

"Will you please shut up?"

"The marines are here, don't worry about it."

"Not the marines, the Green Berets."

"No, the SEALs. That's who was shooting. I hope."

"Who cares?"

"You think this is it?"

"Could be!"

"If it was so important for us to be quiet, why didn't they gag us?"

"You're going to get us all killed!"

"Does anyone still have their cell phone, or did they take them all?"

"Would they really bring a few hundred gags?"

"Do you think the government is trying to work something out with them?"

"The USA doesn't negotiate with terrorists."

"That always sounded totally bad ass. Now, not so much."

"Yeah. Kinda sucks when you're the hostage."

"Why do you care? We're getting out of here!"
"You don't know that."
"What do they want anyway?"
"Money, probably. It always comes down to money."
"Why doesn't the rich guy pay?"
"Who?"
"The rich guy."
"Yeah. Why doesn't he pay the terrorists?"
"If we're not being rescued, that's a good backup plan."

The idea spread across the room quickly, preempting several conversations.

"Hey, where's the rich guy?"
"What? Who?"
"The husband of that singer lady."
"The billionaire. He could pay them off!"
"Where is he?"
"Is he really on board?"
"I thought that was just a rumor."
"Oh yeah. He's here. He was on the Penthouse deck. I saw him walking around up there a couple times."
"You were just watching his wife."
"Hell yeah, I was. But I saw him too."
"So where did he get to?"
"Yo, buddy! Sinclair!"
"Mr. Sinclair!"
"Paging Danforth Percy Sinclair. Your limo is here."
"Come on. This is serious."
"Right here. Sinclair is right here," someone said, nodding towards a hunched and gaunt elderly man. His legs were bent up and he was resting his head sideways on his knees, eyes closed.

The information rippled across the ballroom.

"Over there, he's over there! He's with us. Near the corner." The entire room was swept into the discussion, heads turning, bodies shifting, all to face the corner where Sinclair was sleeping.

"Hey, old man, you awake?"

Sinclair didn't move.

"Looks like he's taking a nap."
"Leave him alone."
"It doesn't matter anymore, people. We're being rescued."
"We don't know that for sure."

"He'll be our insurance plan."
"He can't pay ransom for all of us."
"Why not?"
"He's got the money to spare."
"What do you say, old man?"

Sinclair shifted, turning his head the opposite direction, away from those calling him. He kept his eyes closed.

"Sinclair! Wake up!"
"We need you to buy off the terrorists."
"Then we can all go home."
"Yeah, you can afford it."
"No negotiating, just bribe them."
"They would just use that money to sponsor more terrorism."
"So? Right now, the only terrorism I care about is the one I'm caught up in."
"I just want to go home."
"Let's take a vote."
"If we don't pay them we might not live through today."
"How do you know they want money?"
"As long as it gets me out of here alive, I'm up for anything."
"Yeah, you are. Because it's not your money."
"Who cares? He's got plenty."
"Forget it, let's rush these fools. There's two hundred of us."
"There's only a few of them."
"But they have guns. We don't."
"Have you noticed we're all tied up and the door's locked?"
"We might be killed."
"We might get killed anyway."
"Why is everyone freaking out? This is over."
"Why don't we hear what the old man has to say?"
"What will it be, chief?"
"Old man, what do you think?"
"Sinclair! Wake up!"
"If those gunshots aren't a rescue party, what are you going to do?"
"You going to pay our ransom?"
"Will you be a hero or a jackass?"
"Don't put it like that."
"I can't believe this."
"Everyone quiet! Let the old dude speak."

All eyes turned to Sinclair. He was wearing a Hawaiian shirt, pleated Navy blue shorts and black socks with sandals. He curled his bony frame into a tighter ball, the last remnants of his white hair sagging over his knees. He looked like an insect stricken by repellent, curling up to die.

His wife, Yvonne Windstorm was seated nearby. She shifted, vainly trying to shield him from the crowd. She was at least forty years younger than him, wearing a black bikini over her large breasts. A white mesh tank top and tight yellow shorts clung to her every curve.

Sinclair leaned away from her.

"He doesn't owe you anything," Windstorm said, her long bleached hair tumbling over her shoulder.

"Fine. We can all die, then."

"Why can't he pay? He won't miss it."

"Is he asleep?"

"You don't speak for him."

"I'm his wife."

"Yeah, his third."

Several individual voices calling to Sinclair at once clashed, becoming indistinguishable. The noise was met with an equal amount of shushing.

"I'm sorry," Windstorm said, "I wish there was a way I could make this better."

"Shut up, lady."

"Take off your top. That'll make me feel better," someone called out, setting off a spatter of uneasy chuckles.

"I can't believe people are joking at a time like this."

"Quiet, people! They said be quiet!"

"If we get out of here alive, this will be one crazy story."

"Yeah. If."

"All of you, please," Windstorm said, her eyes welling up. "Just pray."

Sinclair stirred. He lifted his head and turned toward his wife. His face was a bright red.

"Be quiet!" he yelled, his head vibrating from the effort.

Windstorm snapped her mouth shut, her eyes watered and her lips trembled.

"Just stop!" Sinclair said, "This is bad enough without you arguing with them."

The room continued to buzz.

"Hey, the old man's awake."
"Did he answer our question?"
"Is he going to buy us out of this?"
"Where are the terrorists?"
"Maybe they got 'em."
"They got 'em?"
"Someone said they got 'em!"
"Awesome!"
"U.S.A.! U.S.A.!" The chant caught on and obliterated all other discussions.
"Why is everyone chanting?"
"It's over! The special forces killed the terrorists!"
"We're going home!"
"Praise Jesus!"
"But Jesus didn't kill the terrorists!"
"Who cares? U.S.A.! U.S.A.! U.S.-"

The ballroom doors crashed open. Except for a few shouts and yelps of surprise, the room fell silent as the three terrorists returned. They strode among their captives, guns lowered, assuming their previous positions: one by the kitchen door, two blocking the doors to the main hall.

"I said quiet!" the leader yelled. "You are being watched!" Keeping one hand on his rifle, finger on the trigger, he pointed to the four corners of the ceiling, one after the other. In each nook hung a small black sphere hiding a security camera.

"Next person that opens their mouth," he said, "will be taken out and shot."

The captives bowed their heads and were still.

"Now," the leader said, "we need six people to come with us."

A chorus of horrified gasps filled the room.

The lead terrorist strolled among the crowd. The other two gunmen kept their weapons pointed in his direction, covering him. Each prisoner averted their eyes as the masked man walked past. He walked randomly among his captives, dodging hands and feet. He stopped in the center of the room, turning around, looking down on those seated around him.

"You," he said, "stand up." He reached down and grabbed the bindings around a woman's wrists, lifting her to her feet. She squealed as the plastic bit into her skin.

"No! No! No! I have a family," she cried. "Please."

"Quiet!" the terrorist yelled, shaking her.

"Stop!" a man seated nearby yelled. "She's my wife. Take me instead." He was wearing the same pink polo shirt and brown shorts as the woman. The man struggled to his knees, colliding with the people around him.

"Take me," he said.

"Shut up," the terrorist said, pushing the woman toward the exit. She waddled as fast as she could, her steps restrained by the bindings around her ankles.

"You said you needed six," the husband pleaded. "Take me, too!"

"No, Martin," the woman yelled across the room. "Don't!"

"I won't leave you, Gwen," he said, moving toward her by scraping his knees across the rug in tiny steps. Several hostages sniffled back tears.

The lead terrorist guided the woman to the double doors.

"Stay here," he said and then moved to the kneeling husband.

"You want to find out where she's going?" the captor asked, his computerized voice cold. He raised his rifle.

"Martin! Sit down!" the woman screamed.

The man clenched his eyes shut as the terrorist poked his gun barrel into Martin's belly, finger on the trigger.

"I'm her husband," Martin said, swallowing hard. "Whatever you have planned for her, I'll face it, too. Please."

"Martin, don't," the woman said. "Our kids."

"I'm doing it, Gwen," Martin yelled. He leaned to the side to look around the terrorist. "I'm coming with you. No matter what. I love you."

"I love you, Martin," Gwen yelled back, her voice wet and rupturing.

More hostages began crying.

"Right," the terrorist said. He slung his rifle over his back and grabbed Martin's elbow, lifting him, dragging him to his wife.

He pushed them both together, then turned toward the center of the room and spoke.

"I need four more. Any other volunteers?"

While he scanned across the room with one of the silent terrorists, the third one kept his rifle pointed at the captives, Martin and Gwen. The couple pressed against each other, rubbing their heads together like two affectionate cats.

The other prisoners were sobbing and whimpering, one girl far louder than anyone. Her crying pulsed as she hyperventilated.

The lead terrorist moved toward her. As he came closer, she screeched louder. "Ohhh no! No! No!"

The terrorist reached down and grabbed her arm. Her scream was so loud and shrill, the artificial larynx the terrorist was wearing caught the noise and squealed a computerized harmony to her caterwaul.

"Quiet! Stop shouting!" he said, shaking her as he lifted her to her feet. She was wearing white shorts and a blue bikini top. Her straight white-blonde hair flailed in the terrorist's face as she thrashed.

"Yo, punk! Let her go," someone yelled.

Everyone looked toward where the voice had come from.

A bronze-skinned young man was leaning against the ballroom wall as he struggled to stand. His bindings cut red lines on his wrists and ankles. He was wearing a basketball jersey that came down to his mid-thighs, nearly obscuring his shorts. The name "Zachary" was written across the back of his shirt above the number 18. He was wearing a baseball cap with the visor askew.

Feet together, he hopped toward the blonde girl and terrorist, gold chains around his neck clanking as they flapped. He tripped against the other prisoners, flailing to stay up.

"Hey! Watch it!"

"What are you doing?"

"Sit down, kid! Get down!"

The boy fell, tumbling onto other captives. His frantic twisting kept him going as he staggered forward, determined.

The masked man stepped away from the struggling girl and raised his gun.

"Don't touch her," the boy yelled as he bounced across the human terrain. He was getting closer. The hostages closed their eyes, screamed, looked away.

The terrorist spun his machine gun and raised it, ready to bring the butt smashing down on the boy's head.

"Zack! No!" the girl screamed.

The boy landed on his knees before the terrorist and turned his head to the side, eyes clenched shut.

"She wit' me, yo," Zack said, gasping. "Take me instead, homes. Take me."

"Za... ah... ack," the girl stuttered as she wailed. Tears were streaming down her face, forming dark lines through dried sunscreen.

"Brittany, you my girl," Zack yelled. "I ain't leavin' you."

"Shut up," the terrorist said. "We'll take you both."

Brittany and Zack were pushed toward the exit to stand with Gwen and Martin. Brittany leaned her head on Zack's shoulder.

"I... just... want... this... to... end..." she cried, gasping each word.

The third terrorist kept his gun aimed at the four selected captives.

"Shush, girl," Zack said. "I'm here now, aight? Z-dawg here."

"Two more, any volunteers? Another couple, perhaps?" the leader asked. His distorted voice echoed across the silent room.

"Take me!" someone yelled.

Everyone looked toward the voice.

The elderly Danforth Sinclair was stretching his neck, rocking side to side. "Take me!" he croaked. "Over here!"

The lead terrorist watched for a moment.

Sinclair yelled again, his voice hoarse. "Come get me! I volunteer!"

"Fine," the leader said. He turned to his comrade. "Get him. We'll watch these four."

The masked man began stepping over bodies, heading across the room.

"Quiet, old man," someone near Sinclair whispered.

"What are you doing?"

"Damn geezer."

"Are you nuts? You're going to get shot."

With the speed of a striking snake, Sinclair whipped his head around toward where the question had come from. "I'd rather that," he hissed, his eyes bulged, his teeth bared. "I'd rather die then use one cent of my money to save you parasites."

Before anyone could reply, the terrorist had reached him.

"Why so eager, old man?" he asked. "You don't know what this is for."

"I don't care. I need to get out of here."

"Hey," someone nearby called out, "do you know who that is?"

"Shut up!" the terrorist leader yelled from across the room. "Don't make me say it again!"

"He's ri-" the man started to say, but the rest of his words were lost as the nearby terrorist kicked him in the stomach.

Several hostages screamed.

"You heard him! Quiet!" the terrorist yelled. He kicked the hostage again. The prone man curled up.

The terrorist lifted Sinclair.

"Wait!" a woman cried out. "Me too! I'm his wife."
Yvonne Windstorm was volunteering.
"Be quiet," those around her whispered.
"Don't do it, lady!"
"She's nuts."
"Another couple?" the leader asked. "Fine, take her, too."
The masked man dragged Sinclair toward Windstorm, then lifted her from behind with his hands in her armpits.
"Danny," she whined. "Aren't you going to tell me no? Try to talk me out of this?"
Sinclair looked away and said nothing.
"Danny?"
The terrorist slung his rifle over his shoulder and pulled them both toward the double doors, one hand on each of them, inside their elbows.

Gwen and Martin were resting their heads on each others' shoulders. Zack was whispering into Brittany's ear, her long hair falling over his neck.

Sinclair and Windstorm stood apart, not touching. His face was stony. Watery black lines trailed down Windstorm's cheeks.

The chosen six were pushed out into the hall. Two terrorists left with them, guns aimed at the captives' backs. The doors closed behind them. The ballroom immediately erupted into crying, praying and whispering.

"Quiet!" the lone terrorist yelled. He fired several shots into the ceiling. The hostages screamed as plaster and chandelier fragments rained on them. The room fell silent except for the soft sound of panicked breathing.

The terrorist kept his gun level, finger on the trigger. He swept the barrel across the entire room and back again.

One man held nearly 200 captives motionless with fear.

3

North knelt and pressed his ear against the door to the outside walkway, listening for the Navy ship.

"Sounds like they've gone around to the other side," he said.

"Yeah," Holland said. "I already pointed that out. What's wrong? Don't believe me?"

North opened the bullet-ridden door and looked out on an empty horizon. The Navy ship was gone. He stepped back inside, making sure the damaged lock latched shut.

Holland was guarding the doorway into the ship.

The vessel's interior was made entirely of metal. Giant steel cylinders were fastened to the hull with enormous hexagonal bolts as large as North's head. Clusters of pipes trailed everywhere, as numerous and as tangled as vines in a jungle. The space was starkly painted in gray and white.

"Why do you think they left?" Holland said. She was examining dusty cardboard boxes on metal shelves, pushing them aside, reading the labels.

"I don't know," North said. "Why would they consider us worth killing then just take off? Good question. They must have gotten called away. What are you doing?"

"Looking for passenger brochures. Maps." She pulled two pamphlets out of a box and handed one to North.

In the cover photo, the Sunset Mist rested on glass-like water under a cloudless sky. Palm trees waved from the sandy beach in the background. The pamphlet read, "Guest guide map to The Sunset Mist, your paradise away from home."

"Where do you think they all are?" Holland asked, paging through the map.

"I'd guess near the bridge," North said. "That way they can operate the ship and communicate. The prisoners are probably somewhere nearby and more toward the interior."

"The Plaza del Sol," Holland said, pointing at the map. "That's the deck with the control room, same level as the bridge. And the main ballroom is nearby. A perfect place to store hundreds of people."

"Looks like we're on this bottom level. The utility deck."

"We'll have to go through the engine room to get to the staircases. Go straight up and then kick some ass."

"Not quite," North said. "Looks like there's stairs at either end. They alternate."

Holland checked the map. "That's a weird way to design a ship. I'm surprised that's even allowed."

"I guess that's why they usually register them with some banana republic," North said. "No rules. No regulations. No laws. Squeeze in as many rooms as possible. Pack people in like sardines."

"Sounds about right," Holland said. "Not very efficient if you're trying to get anywhere, but in an emergency, everyone heads outward, so no harm done. And if they get hurt, hey, there's no regulations, so who cares? Who's going to sue you for breaking a non-existent law?"

"I just love your attitude," North said.

"Thanks. So how do you feel about taking the elevator?"

North shook his head. "Too vulnerable to ambush, and it will probably ding to announce we're coming. If they haven't shut it down. But they can't shut down stairs."

"Wow. You're pretty smart for a grunt."

"I try," North said. "I vote standard two-man move-and-cover scheme. I lead."

"Fine," Holland said. "I'd probably move too fast for you."

"Keep thinking that."

Pressed to the wall, North crept down the corridor, his boots squeaking lightly on the metal floor. Holland pointed her gun behind him, watching the doors he passed. At the turn in the hall, he waved to her.

She rushed forward and joined him. He pointed to a door labeled with stenciled black letters, "Engine Room. Authorized Personnel Only."

North kicked open the door and pointed his gun left, staying low, using the door as cover. Holland aimed her gun over him, snapping to the right.

"Clear."

"Clear."

They swept the room, aiming into vast spaces between the cylindrical banks that housed the cruise ship's massive engine.

"Looks empty."

"Quiet, too. Engine's off."

"So making a quick run somewhere isn't part of their plan. They must be cooking up something else."

"Hell yeah, they are. Look."

Holland turned to see where North was pointing.

A pile of brown bricks stacked waist-high lay on the floor. Each brick was wrapped in clear plastic with a warning label that read "Caution! Explosive!" in several languages. A web of wires connected the stacks to each other and small black metal boxes in between. A flashing red light blinked from each box. The entire pile leaned against a large fuel tank jutting up from the deck and rising to the two-story high ceiling.

"Holy shit," Holland hissed.

"This is a lot of boom," North said. "Looks like they want to sink this ship and sink it fast."

"Or send it into orbit."

"I think it's fair to say we can expect the hostiles to be fanatical. Suicidal even."

"Probably," Holland said. "Know anything about defusing?"

"Not enough that makes me want to take a chance on that. Hey, look at this," North said, pointing to a box with an antenna. "I'll bet someone on the bridge has a remote detonator."

Holland stepped backwards, away from the bomb. "We should get going."

"Hang on," North said. "I'll alert the negotiator."

"What? This isn't our problem. The bandits might overhear us and learn our position. Then they'll blow themselves up sooner. I don't know about you, but my goal is to make this a suicide mission for them only."

"But the feds should know what they're dealing with. We can make it an anonymous communication."

Holland shook her head. "No. They know they're dealing with maniacs. You and I, we need to stay focused."

"This is crucial intel. They could help us by slowing the terrorists down, keep them talking-"

"The other people on this boat didn't pay us."

North stared at her for a moment before speaking. "You're serious."

Holland continued. "We're here to save one person, not a bunch of hostages, not even this ship. If we get a chance, after we have our guy, sure. We can call whoever you want and share our information. For now, we move like ghosts."

North rubbed his chin. "This stuff could kill everyone on board. Including us."

"All the more reason to get moving."

North stared at her.

"Don't look at me like that," Holland said. "Now come on. Staircase to the Oceanview deck is that way. Let's get our man first, then handle the charity work."

"I don't like it," North said. "I've done ops before but never with civilians involved. This feels wrong, not helping our team," North said.

"There is no team. We're on our own side," Holland said. "Besides, paradigms change. Gotta change with 'em."

"What the hell is a paradigm?"

"Forget it. Lead on."

4

Hooded and gagged, their wrists and ankles still bound, the six chosen hostages were dragged out through the bridge doorway and into the sun. They were tethered by rope, their casual beach clothes flapping in the breeze.

A terrorist tugged on the line attached to the first person, leading the shuffling train to the edge of the Sunset Mist's top outdoor deck. He pushed them against the safety railing so it pressed against their bellies. The captives tried to back away, but the terrorist held them in place, jabbing their backs with his gun. The six stood on display, a hundred feet above the sea.

* * *

On the Bonnie Jane, Burnett, Dunn and Goodkin watched the sad parade, each through his own binoculars.

"I don't think this was the conga line they expected," Captain Burnett said.

In addition to the terrorist nearest the hostages, two other masked men followed further back, machine guns pointed at the captives.

Goodkin alternated between looking through his binoculars and snapping pictures by holding the back of his tablet to face the cruise ship. He spoke aloud after each photo.

"Six hostages. One appears to be a couple. I say that because of the matching outfits. It's obvious one is male and the other female."

"Could be a fruit and his sister," Burnett said.

Goodkin continued to describe the scene aloud.

"Also present are two young people. Early twenties. Male is wearing a basketball jersey, I don't know which team. Wearing large gold necklaces. Possibly Latino ethnicity? That's just a guess based on skin tone. The young girl is wearing a blue bikini top and white shorts.

Looks like white-blonde hair poking out from under her hood. Caucasian."

"Mm-hm," Burnett mumbled.

"One more male and one more female. Both appear older. Male is elderly, based on posture, white arm hair. He's wearing plaid shorts, Hawaiian shirt. Seventy years old at least. Final hostage is middle-age. Female."

"Definitely," Burnett said. "Look at them knockers."

Dunn lowered his binoculars and glared at his fellow captain. Burnett didn't notice.

Goodkin continued. "She's wearing a white top, black swimsuit underneath, yellow shorts. Speculating, was she once some kind of model?"

Hussein's voice crackled over the speakers. "Are you satisfied, Goodkin? You see we take good care of our guests."

Goodkin did not respond. He held the microphone bud close to his mouth. "All hostages appear tired but well. No obvious signs of injury."

"My snipers could drop those bastards from here," Burnett whispered. "Say the word, and the world has three less savages."

Goodkin lifted the com and flicked the switch for the outside speakers. "Attention, hostages," he said. His words boomed across the sea and echoed against the cruise ship.

"This is United States federal agent Nelson Goodkin from the Department of Homeland Security. We are working to get you off the boat as soon as possible. We want to make sure you are being treated well. Please nod your heads yes if you have access to drinking water."

None of them moved. The old man bobbed his head yes, the others shook their heads no.

"Mixed signals on the water question," Goodkin said to his tablet. "Majority says no water."

He pressed the button for the loudspeaker again and said, "To your knowledge, has anyone been injured?"

All six shook their heads from side to side. No.

"Do their responses really matter?" Burnett asked. "They could have been prompted, and they have bad guys with guns all around them. It doesn't take a load of common sense to know they shouldn't tattle in front of their captors."

"Five of them just did with the water," Dunn said.

"Quiet," Goodkin said.

"You see, Mister Goodkin?" Hussein said. "We are providing them with excellent care. They might not even notice their cruise is off schedule. We will gladly return them once our simple requests are fulfilled. We are working with you, now all that I ask is that you work with us."

"Would you like us to bring over water, Hussein?" Goodkin said. "I'm not convinced they are getting as much as they need."

"You can imagine how difficult coordinating visits to the restroom would be for me, Goodkin, so we are saving the water. It would not be an issue if you pursued my demands as quickly as you claim you are."

"Hussein, make sure you give them water. It's an easy thing to do. Your quarrel is with our government, not these people."

"No, Goodkin, these people support your government by allowing it to exist. As do you."

"They still should have water."

"Fulfill my demands, then we will talk about water."

"Keep them well, Hussein. The worse off they are, the harder it will be for me to help you."

"Oh, I think you'll be fine. Your country has many people. Perhaps too many. For now, let me instruct my men to return our guests to their quarters. Then we will speak again."

"Of course, Hussein."

Goodkin disconnected by pressing a button on the console.

The lead terrorist yanked the rope and led the shuffling hostages away from the railing. The line disappeared from view.

"That made me sick," Burnett said. "Do you need to be so polite to that monster?"

Goodkin was tapping and stroking his touch screen. He didn't look up as he spoke. "It's all part of the game," he said. "What I say has to be believed. It doesn't have to be sincere," he paused a moment, then added, "captain."

Burnett squinted and turned to Dunn. "Did he just insult me?"

Dunn shrugged. Goodkin lifted the microphone bulb to his mouth and stepped outside onto the walkway around the bridge.

Before the door closed, Dunn and Burnett heard him say, "You got all that? Good. Yeah. I was thinking that too."

5

North led, walking briskly in a tense crouch, gun out. Holland, poised the same, followed behind, turning to watch their backs every few steps.

The walls and ceiling were painted a light pink. Red and gold patterns swirled in the thinly cushioned rug over the metal floor. Each hall was lined with several numbered doors on either side. Only the occasional gentle rocking of the sea reminded them they were on a cruise ship and not inside a hotel.

Beach towels and the contents of burst suitcases littered the floor.

"It's quiet," North whispered. "They definitely collected everyone."

"Or they're all dead," Holland said.

"No blood. That's a good sign."

"No blood yet."

North sighed.

"What?" Holland said. "I'm just observing."

"How about you observe more with your eyes and less with your mouth?"

The hall ended at a restaurant, where a panic had obviously taken place. Wicker chairs were tipped over and crushed. The remains of shattered martini glasses and broken plates were everywhere. Fake palm trees lay on their sides.

Food was still waiting at a buffet table. A large, clear plastic bowl was tilted awkwardly in the ice it was resting on, shrimp spilling out of it and across the floor, as if they too had been trying to escape.

North and Holland crept around the perimeter of the room, one on either side, their boots crunching on the broken glass. Slowly they scanned, guns out, eyes sliding steadily left and right. They met again at the opposite side of the restaurant.

"All clear," Holland said, "except for the smell of rotting seafood."

"Yep," North said. "Everyone must be on the higher decks like we thought."

They relaxed their postures.

The doorway was blocked by a tipped-over podium. Its sharp wooden edge had dug a gash into the fake bamboo paneling. The "Wait Here to be Seated" sign hung crookedly by a single tack.

"Check this out," North said, pulling a clipboard from underneath the stand. "It's a list of passengers. Danforth Sinclair. Here he is. Looks like he was staying in the penthouse suite."

"Where else?" Holland unfolded her deck map. "Top deck, of course, above the bridge. No way we're getting there without going through bad guys. Not that I'm complaining about whacking some bandits."

"Whacking some bandits?" North repeated, raising an eyebrow. "Is this an action movie?"

"Oh, sorry," Holland said, "I meant neutralizing hostiles."

"That's better," North said. "Let's keep heading up."

Just past the tipped podium, they came to a metal staircase. The names of the decks were carved into a wooden sign on the wall, a smiling dolphin alongside each level pointing the traveler in the proper direction. The dolphins next to Breezeway, Crystal Beach, Skyline Vista and Plaza del Sol all pointed up. Only the Utility Deck dolphin pointed down. A waving dolphin's cartoon speech balloon said, "You are on the Oceanview deck!"

"Same formation?" North asked.

"Works for me," Holland said.

North led with his gun before him. He took the seven stairs slowly to the landing then took the final seven, doubling back up to the next level. There was no movement in the hallway, no signs of life, just more burst luggage cluttering the floor.

Holland waited at the bottom of the stairs as North continued on to the Breezeway level. She started up after him, but immediately froze. North was holding his left fist in the air, quietly alerting Holland to stop. He walked backwards down the stairs, back down the landing to the Oceanview deck.

"Security cameras," he whispered.

He peeked into the deserted restaurant they came from and punched his fist into his hand. "Damn it!" he hissed.

"What?"

"Look up. We just walked across the whole restaurant without noticing the cameras. How could we have both missed them?"

Holland poked her head into the restaurant and scanned the corners.

"Huh," she said.

"That's it? Nothing else to say?"

"What should I say?"

"That was a dumb rookie move. By both of us."

"Why beat yourself up over it? Who cares?" she said. "Maybe we caught a break. If they had seen us, we'd have a lot of guests right now.

Since we don't that's some good intel, and I know you love your intel. This means they're not watching the cameras closely, or at all."

"Probably," North said.

"We should keep moving. That way, even if they saw us, we've cleared the area. It's not a mistake unless something goes wrong."

"Yeah, I guess. Hey, what are you–"

Holland bounded up to the stair landing, aimed her gun with both hands and fired. The silencer muffled the shot, but to North it still sounded like thunder. The camera above him exploded, raining debris on him at the bottom of the stairs.

"Damn it!" he growled.

Holland looked down at him, signaling him to follow. "Problem solved."

North's face burned red. "Or made worse. I hope they didn't see that. Or hear it."

"If they didn't see us in the restaurant, they probably aren't watching. How were we going to get past it anyway?"

"Most systems sound an alarm when a camera malfunctions. It's to prevent intruders doing exactly what you just did."

"I don't hear anything."

"At the control station. That's where the alarm is."

"Where we've already proved no bandits are there to hear it."

North was climbing the stairs. Where the camera had been was now just a black burn in the ceiling, a jutting mechanical arm spitting sparks.

"We don't want to draw attention to ourselves, all right?" he said. "You start knocking out cameras, they'll know we're here and start killing hostages. Leave the cameras up, but move more cautiously. Try to stay hidden."

"I've got a better idea. Let's move faster."

"Fine, you want to lead?"

"No," she said, "I'm good."

Holland smiled and held out her hand as North passed her. "Welcome to the Breezeway deck. Right this way, captain."

6

None of the six hostages could see where they were going. They were guided through the darkness by the tug on their wrist bindings, with only an occasional verbal command from the computerized voices. With each constrained step the bindings bit their ankles. Some of them were sobbing, some hyperventilating from the effort and panic.

When the sun left their skin and the breeze died, they knew they had been returned to the ship's interior. They marched along to the lonely sounds of breathing and shuffling footsteps.

"Down. Sit down," one of the captors commanded. He was standing so close, the hostages could hear his real voice an instant before the robotic distortion took over. Strong hands pushed on the captives' shoulders, forcing them to the floor. The rope that held them all together was removed, but their hands and feet remained bound.

Their hoods were yanked off, leaving the three couples blinking. They were seated in a small dining lounge across the hall from the main ballroom. A mural painted on the wall was intended to give the illusion that the room was high in a tropical forest. "The Jungle Canopy" was spelled out in cartoon bamboo sticks. Tables, chairs and a small snack cart had been pushed into the corner of the room, opening up the floor space.

The six hostages sat looking up at their masked captors.

Two of the terrorists stepped aside, machine guns lowered.

The third masked man approached them, his machine gun hanging over his shoulder by its leather strap.

"Thank you for your cooperation," his garbled voice said. "That went well. We showed your government that we people of Kariqistan are not the vicious killers you make us out to be. Now we will show that we are also merciful." He nodded to the other two men.

The captors held their breath, watching over their shoulders as the men walked behind them to the snack cart, retrieving bottles of water.

Like baby birds being fed by their mother, each hostage looked to the ceiling and opened his or her mouth. The captors poured water directly down their throats, stopping only when the mouth slapped shut to swallow.

After each hostage was given water, the leader turned to one of his silent assistants and said, "Do it."

The leader walked out with one man, leaving the last one behind. The lone remaining terrorist flipped a latch on his gun and spoke to the hostages.

"Please turn your heads."

Before they could comply or beg for mercy, the masked man fired his automatic machine gun into a couch that had been pushed against the wall. The relentless cracking sound tore at their eardrums.

As quickly as he had started shooting, the terrorist stopped.

A fog of gunpowder, dust and vaporized foam filled the air. Brittany shrieked and shook as she tried to restrain her crying. Zack shushed her gently. The other four hostages were stunned into silence, their heads bowed. Martin and Gwen leaned against each other.

A great wailing floated to them from the ballroom across the hall.

"Shut up!" the captors in the other room yelled. The mournful cries slowly quieted.

The gunman turned his back on the six captives and left, closing and locking the door behind him.

* * *

Gwen and Martin Marigold kissed furiously. Gwen trembled as she and her husband pressed their heads against the other, their eyes closed.

"It's okay," Martin whispered. "It's okay. We're alive. We're together."

The young couple in their early twenties were both crying. They kissed deeply with open mouths, their tongues writhing together.

"I love you, Zack," Brittany choked out.

"You my all, B." Zack whispered to her. His tone changed as he growled, "When I get da chance, I'm gone waste dem bitches."

The third couple did not attempt to embrace or even touch each other. Yvonne Windstorm sat alone, frowning, a single tear sliding down her face. She looked to her husband, Danforth Percy Sinclair.

"Oh, Danny," she said. "Look at them. That's how we should be."

Sinclair barely moved. He stared ahead and growled. "This whole thing is wasting my damned time."

"I thought we were dead out there," Brittany cried, her tears smudging her eyeliner. "I thought they were going to push us overboard."

"What's wit dat punk?" Zack asked. "Why he shoot up da couch?"

"Must have been just trying to scare us," Martin Marigold said, pressing his cheek against the nape of his wife's neck. "You heard all that screaming? Everyone in the other room must think we're dead."

"So maybe they're not so bad," Brittany said, her voice high-pitched, hysterical. "Maybe they just wanted to make a point. To scare us. Terrorist means scare, right? It doesn't mean you have to kill anyone."

Martin lifted his head. "Hey, kid, do what you can to calm your girlfriend. Sounds like she's well on her way to Stockholm Syndrome."

"Stock-who-wha?" Zack said.

Still staring straight ahead, Sinclair snapped. "Just tell her to calm down. Or at least shut the hell up."

"Danny!" Windstorm said. She turned to Brittany. "He didn't mean that, sweetie. He's scared too. He just shows it differently."

"I'm not scared. I'm pissed," Sinclair mumbled.

Gwen Marigold kept her eyes closed, nuzzling against her husband. "The man outside said he was a federal negotiator. So the world must know what's going on. This will probably be over soon. I hope."

"If I could get to our room, it would be over a whole lot sooner," Martin said.

Gwen lifted her head, her eyes wide, mouth dropping open. "Martin. No," she said, "Say you didn't."

Zack pulled his tongue out of Brittany's mouth. "What magic you workin', G? You got a piece?"

"I do," Martin answered.

He turned to look his wife in the eyes. "I'm an American citizen and it's my right. I'm allowed to be prepared."

"Oh, God, Martin," Gwen said, leaning away from him. "If you were so prepared, why is it in our room?"

"I don't carry it with me when I sunbathe."

"You never told me. How could you?"

"I'm only twenty years old," Brittany wailed, stuttering her words out. "I don't want to die. I wish I never came on this trip. I mean, it was great meeting a real celebrity, Miss Windstorm, but-"

"Oh, thank you, honey," Yvonne Windstorm said. "See, Danny? At least the little girl appreciates me."

"Then she can pay your bills."

"Right now," Brittany said, "I just want to go home."

"Look," Martin said, "we have to come up with a plan in case the negotiation fails. We have to work to escape on our own."

"Hell yeah," Zack said. "Fuck the negotiation. Let's rule these punks."

"Can you keep it down?" Gwen said. "If they hear us, they'll come in and gag us. Or worse."

"My bad, yo."

"All right," Martin said. "Let's get to know each other. My name is Martin Marigold and this is my wife, Gwen."

"Hello, everybody," Gwen said. She chuckled uneasily. "How are you?"

"Yo, my name is Zack and this my home girl, Brittany."

"Hi," Brittany said. "Um. Like. Nice to meet everyone."

They all turned. "I guess you all know me, right?" Yvonne Windstorm said.

"I take it you're famous somehow?" Gwen said.

"You don't know her?" Brittany asked, her mouth hanging open.

"I heard something about a celebrity on board," Gwen said. "But who are you?"

"That's Yvonne Windstorm!" Brittany said.

"The one and only," Windstorm said.

"Oh, maybe I've heard of you," Gwen said. "It's nice to meet you."

"I thought you looked familiar," Martin said. "The singer, right?"

"And actress," Windstorm said.

"Right. Do it to me, do it, do it. That's you?"

"It's me," she said brightly. She smiled, arching her back slightly, her breasts lifting her mesh shirt to expose her pierced belly button. She dropped her high-pitched voice. "And this is my husband, Danforth Sinclair. Say hello, Danny."

Sinclair grunted, and kept staring straight ahead.

"The billionaire?" Martin said.

"That's him," Windstorm said, her voice high-pitched again.

"Yo, money bags," Zack said, "why don't you toss these punks some dead prez? All us roll up on outta here first class?"

"That's not a bad idea, Mr. Sinclair," Gwen said. "Can you offer them money? You've got millions to spare."

Sinclair replied without looking at them. "I have that money because I never give it away, even when people threaten me. So the answer is no."

"But our lives are at stake. Yours too."

"Now, honey, wait," Martin said. "If they find out who he is, that would slow down our release even more. They would increase whatever ransom they're asking for. It would complicate things. We should be glad those dumb savages don't know who he is."

"The man knows his business," Sinclair said. He curled up his legs up and rested his head on his knees, closing his eyes.

"Well, thank you, sir," Martin said. "It's a pleasure to meet you."

"Besides," Sinclair muttered, "this will all be over soon."

"Dang, Grandpa Wall Street is no use," Zack said. He turned to Martin, "What now, Cap'n Commando? How we gon' score your gun? Where da crib?"

"Right now, we're on the Plaza del Sol Deck. My room is just two levels down. Room 446 on the Crystal Beach level."

"Dat close, yo," Zack said. "Let's get-"

"Wait a minute," Gwen interrupted. "Even if we get loose and can get out of this room, which I think they locked, even if you got your gun, what are you going to do?"

"Easy," Martin said. "We kill one of them, then we've got two guns. We kill one more, then three."

"Then we got a revolution, yo. We waste all dem pricks," Zack said, raising his voice again.

Brittany shushed him.

"Can't we just let the professionals talk us out of this?" Gwen said.

"Honey," Martin said, "why should we wait for them? What if they can't help us?" He turned to Zack. "What do you say, kid? You want to help me break loose so I can get my gun?"

"Hell yeah," he said, nudging Brittany with his elbow.

"Uh, sure, whatever." she said.

"Everyone in?"

Windstorm added, "Don't forget me." She leaned onto Sinclair. "Danny, wake up!"

Sinclair didn't open his eyes. "I'm awake, damn it. I'm just resting. And no. I'm not helping with any ridiculous schemes. That will just get you killed. But if you want to, feel free."

Gwen looked to her husband. "He's right, Martin. Just relax. They're talking this out. They'll let us go. How long can they last on a boat with no supplies? We'll be out in no time. They'll talk it out."

"That's what they said on September 11th."

"What do you think they're going to do? Crash the ship into a building?"

"I don't know, honey, maybe detonate it in a harbor? Point is, why wait? Look, these Kariqistani bastards probably laid out some demands. If those demands aren't met, they'll start killing people to show they're serious. Starting with us."

"Then why didn't they kill us already? Why shoot the couch? They've got tons of hostages."

"Gwen, this is exactly why I didn't tell you I was bringing the gun."

"Because I ask questions?"

The Marigolds glared at each other.

Gwen looked away first. "All right, I'll help," she said, "I know there's no talking you out of this. But I think it's a terrible idea. I'm only going along so I can save you from yourselves."

"Straight up, generalissimo," Zack said. "We got us a crew. What next?"

"First thing, we get out of these bindings. Any ideas? Anyone?"

They were silent for a moment, looking around the room.

"Can someone get over to the snack cart and look for a knife?" Windstorm said. "Then we can cut ourselves free."

"Yo, I'm down," Zack said.

"No," Brittany squealed. "What if they come back in?"

"We'll just say he had to pee and he wanted some privacy," Martin said. "Zack, can you get over there? When you get there take a piss, or spill something and we'll call it piss. If they come in, that's our story. Just in case. Everyone got that?"

"Martin, please. Stop this," Gwen begged. "He's just a boy."

"Yo, lady," Zack said, "I'm all man. Just ask my girl. And you can't stop me, I'm already gone." He bounced on his buttocks, moving across the floor toward the snack cart. "All that old-school break-dancing is payin' out."

"Just do it fast," Gwen said. "And try to be quiet."

Brittany stared after him, swooning, pale. Gwen wriggled to her side and leaned against her. "It's going to be okay. We're going to get out of this. We just have to keep the men from being totally stupid. Tough job, right?"

Brittany nodded, a weak smile crossing her face. "Yeah. He's always trying to help, but sometimes... urgh."

Gwen shook her head. "Believe me, I know exactly how you feel," she said, watching her husband whip his gaze from Zack to the door and back again.

Zack continued to slink across the floor towards the snack cart.

Windstorm turned toward her husband. Sinclair was still curled, legs bent, head resting on his knees, eyes closed. He snored softly, making a faint rattling sound when he exhaled.

LARRY NOCELLA

PART 4

UNWANTED VISITORS

1

Shielding his eyes from the sun as he paced the deck, Goodkin spoke loudly so his mic could pick up his voice over the wind.

"I thought they looked fine, too. Uncomfortable but unharmed. Sure. Hussein is definitely media savvy. We're in a lull period now except for this Navy jackass cowboy-wannabe. Have you gotten in touch with his commanders? Well, make sure to escalate that. What about him? I'd appreciate any details. Especially the dirty kind. I'll wait."

Goodkin stared up at the lifeless cruise ship until he heard the voice in his ear again.

"Yeah, I'm still here," he said. "Really? Well, that's juicy. I knew it. He is exhibiting standard compensation behavior. Yeah. Stay in touch. The live transmission working okay? Yeah, I'm getting a few breakups in the signal, but overall, it's decent. All right, I'm heading back inside."

Goodkin stepped onto the bridge. Dunn was chewing tobacco, rocking the steering wheel back and forth gently. Burnett was talking aloud, his back turned.

"Any time one of them comes out, you line him up," he said. "The order to fire may come quickly and I want us to take advantage before anyone goes chicken. The only obstacle is this pea-brained bureaucrat I'm dealing with. Out."

Burnett tapped his earpiece. He turned and jolted slightly when he noticed Goodkin had returned. Dunn stopped chewing.

"Something to say, Goodkin?" Burnett said.

"Not at all," Goodkin answered.

The bridge speaker crackled. "Captain Dunn. This is First Mate Smith."

Dunn pushed a button. "This is Dunn. Go ahead."

"We have multiple signals on radar coming toward us, moving fast."

"Identify friend or foe," Burnett said. Both he and Goodkin used their binoculars to scan the horizon.

"Say again, Captain? What was that?" the first mate said.

"Nothing," Dunn said, glancing at the radar screen. "I see them. Have they identified themselves?"

"They're moving quick," Goodkin said, peeking over Dunn's shoulder.

"Helicopters, sir," the first mate said. "Four of them. We have established radio contact with one."

"And?"

"It's the news media, sir."

"Aw, hell," Dunn said, he leaned back and looked up.

"Any orders, Captain?" Smith asked.

Goodkin squinted at Burnett. "The news media? Burnett, did you call them?"

Burnett puffed out his chest. "Me? Call those parasites? The only people I've talked to are my crew and my commander. I asked him to confirm I was doing the right thing waiting for your coffee klatch to end."

He smirked.

Goodkin gripped his tablet with both hands. "Burnett, until I hear otherwise, I expect you to cooperate."

"If my admiral confirms you're the man in charge," Burnett said, "I'll be the good sailor I always am and continue to follow orders."

Goodkin turned to Captain Dunn. "Did he call the media while I was off the bridge?"

"I'm not getting in this," Dunn said. "You two work it out."

"You're awfully paranoid, college boy," Burnett said. "I already told you I didn't."

"I don't believe you. Rogue behavior fits your profile."

"I've got a profile?"

"We all do. As for you, it's clear you want to compensate for something. It must hurt having to ferry the SEALs around all the time, never being a part of the fighting. A long career but no combat. All because of that back injury. Or was there some other problem with your spine?"

Burnett folded his arms. "Well, I'll be damned. Did you do a background check on me? Is that why you were out there on the deck, talking to your little toy?"

"I didn't have to. It's easy to see what motivates you. I draw conclusions from your actions."

"I think you're drawing them out of your ass."

"Am I? Then why do you seem so angry? So eager to fight? Was my ass accurate?"

Goodkin moved his mic closer to his lips. "I wasn't talking to you. No. Nothing. Never mind. Forget it."

"Maybe I should tell you what I see in you, Goodkin," Burnett said.

"Go ahead," Goodkin said, opening his arms wide. "What do you see in me?"

"You don't want to know, college boy."

"I just said I did."

"Sir?" First Mate Smith's voice broke over the bridge. "Captain Dunn? You still there? Awaiting orders, sir."

Captain Dunn's face burned deep red. He took a deep breath, then calmly said, "Smith, tell them to keep their distance. Dunn out."

He punched a switch. The speakers popped.

"Fellas," Dunn said, his voice a low growl. "I don't care how bad you hate each other, but don't ever. Ever! Make my bridge sound like it's beyond my control. Got that?"

Goodkin and Burnett glared at each other.

Burnett's earpiece blinked. He tapped it. "Burnett. Go. Yes, I'm aware of the bogies. It's the media. Stand by. Out."

"Don't order anything rash," Goodkin said. "Don't order anything unless I say. We need to keep this environment and everyone in it free from any escalation catalysts."

They watched the circular sweep of the line on the radar screen. Four dots representing the news helicopters closed toward the center that represented the Bonnie Jane. Dunn tapped his fingers. Goodkin stroked his tablet and Burnett clenched and released his fists.

"Captain," the speakers crackled, "this is First Mate Smith again. I radioed as you requested. They did not indicate a desire to slow down or keep away. Will await your further orders. Smith out."

"They're racing each other," Goodkin said to his mic. He held his tablet in front of the radar screen, so his camera could transmit what he was seeing. "Can you see that? Look, they keep trading off the front position. Damn it. How could they have known so quickly? Well, someone told them."

Goodkin turned to Dunn. "Is there a TV on this bridge?"

Dunn pointed to a screen built into the console and lifted the com handset.

"Inbound helicopters, this is Captain Dunn of Coast Guard rescue vessel Bonnie Jane. I would like to repeat the message of my first mate. Break off. Do not come any closer."

"Contact!" Burnett yelled, pointing out the windows of the bridge. Four black dots appeared against the pale blue sky.

The television showed a weather report for eastern Florida.

"How do I change the channel?" Goodkin asked.

Dunn pointed to the TV controls among the field of buttons. "Right there."

"Need help?" Burnett chuckled.

Goodkin tuned the TV until he found a channel showing the ocean rushing by, a cruise ship in the distance. The text crawl across the bottom of the screen described the footage: "Live video from MCSBN news chopper."

Outside, the helicopters, each painted with the colorful logos of the major news networks, roared over the Bonnie Jane and spread out above the Sunset Mist.

A few seconds later, the television showed the same scene from the perspective of the choppers, the top deck of the Sunset Mist rotating into view. The panic of the terrorist takeover had left a mess that Goodkin and the others were seeing for the first time. Towels, beach chairs, handbags and duffel bags were scattered across the deck, several floating in the pool. A large grill was tipped over, ejecting a smudge of charcoal across the white deck.

A reporter spoke over the images. "You are watching live footage of our long-range news chopper in the air above the hijacked cruise ship, the Sunset Mist. The vessel was taken hostage by Kariqistani terrorists early this morning and is now anchored several dozen miles from the Florida coast. As you can see, there is a Coast Guard vessel here and a Navy ship off in the distance. On the mast, there seems to be some type of flag hoisted above a damaged American flag."

"Oh, my goodness," the studio newsreader said. "It looks like the American flag has been shredded and burned. Is that what I'm seeing?"

"Yes it is. A very disturbing sign. All else appears quiet here. No signs of any movement."

"And the fate of the passengers?"

"At this time, we just don't know."

Goodkin stepped away from the television, colliding with Burnett. Both men stumbled backwards. Neither apologized. Goodkin moved around the larger man and stared up at the choppers through the bridge windows.

"We need to get them out of here," Goodkin said to his mic.

Hussein's distorted voice echoed through the cabin. "Mister Goodkin?"

Goodkin spoke immediately. "I'm sorry, Hussein. No need to worry. Just give me a few minutes. I'll have them removed."

Hussein chuckled. "I appreciate your appearance of concern. However, I must decline your generous offer. The media may stay as long as they like, provided they do not come any closer than your boat. Some of them may not be the news outlets they appear to be, yes?"

"Aw, hell," Dunn grumbled. "This was enough of a circus already."

"Hussein," Goodkin said, "I am going to tell them they must leave."

A woman's voice cut in over the bridge speakers. "You can tell us all you want, but we won't. The American people deserve to know what's going on."

"And who the hell are you?" Goodkin said.

"This is Fran Amaretto of CNB news. We're here to cover a story, as our nation's laws allow, so that's what we're going to do."

Goodkin's voice cracked. "These terrorists have already threatened to kill hostages just for having two boats in the area. You and your colleagues must evacuate. Just by being here you are endangering-"

"Nonsense, Goodkin," Hussein interrupted. "I am glad to have you, Miss Amaretto. Please be sure to film our primary mast. See the American flag in ruin. See the true Kariqistani flag flying above it, proudly defiant of all empires. Show your people."

"Thank you, sir. And to whom am I speaking?"

"Call me Hussein."

"Pleased to meet you, Hussein. And what is your agenda here? Why are you taking these people hostage?"

"Wait a minute," Goodkin said. "Miss Amaretto, I order you to stop broadcasting on this channel. You are impeding our rescue efforts and endangering national security. This area is under US federal government control."

"Correction, Mister Goodkin," Hussein said. "This area is under my control. If you want to save lives then you will let me speak to whomever I wish, yes? This is a simple thing. Deny me and I will become agitated."

Goodkin replied through clenched teeth. "Remember, Hussein. I am the one fulfilling your demands. They're just using you."

"You are trying to get me to surrender. Miss Amaretto is trying to get my message out. It seems wiser to talk with her."

"I'd like to speak with you next, Sir Hussein, sir," an unfamiliar male voice said. "This is Hector Ortiz of the UBS Network."

"No!" Goodkin barked. "This is ridiculous!"

"But it is what I desire," Hussein said. "Yes, Mister Goodkin? And since you are so concerned with what I want, I say Mister Ortiz shall have his turn next."

Goodkin pressed the mute button on the console while the other two networks introduced themselves to Hussein.

"How the hell are they intercepting this channel?" Goodkin asked Dunn.

"There's nothing to intercept. It's basically a CB. Anyone can get on it."

Goodkin kicked the metal console, drew his foot back and winced. Hussein and Fran Amaretto were talking, their conversation coming over the bridge speakers of the Bonnie Jane.

"We represent not just the Kariqistani people," Hussein said, "but also the future of our great nation. The children. Since the USA will not listen to us, we will not stop killing Americans until their government and multinational proxies stop raping the people and the natural wealth of Kariqistan."

Goodkin was limping in circles, favoring his injured foot.

Burnett clapped him on the shoulder. "Looks like we're on the same side now, college boy," he said. "I haven't heard from my admiral yet, and since this is your area of control, if you feel that the presence of these vultures is impeding your ability to save hostages, why, I would have no choice but to act on your order to remove them."

He winked at Goodkin.

Hussein was still talking, his mechanical tone rambling on about returning Kariqistan to its former glory.

Goodkin twisted away from Burnett, turned down the volume on the bridge speakers and clipped his PC tablet to his belt. He closed his eyes and rubbed his temples with his thumbs. He looked out at the four news choppers bobbing in the air above the Sunset Mist.

"What do you have in mind?" Goodkin grumbled.

"Just a warning shot," Burnett said, grinning.

"Forget it. Let me try again."

He tapped the Bonnie Jane's microphone button and spoke over Hussein.

"Attention, all American media. You are in violation of federal law simply by being here. Evacuate now or you will be prosecuted resulting in a prison term of up to twenty years. Do I make myself clear?"

The airwaves were silent for only a few seconds.

"What do you think, Hector?" Fran Amaretto said. "Think he could make that charge stick?"

Hector Ortiz chuckled. "I think the UBS defense lawyers would love the opportunity to knock that softball case out of the park."

"No doubt," Fran said. "Same with my pals at CNB. Go ahead, Hussein. You were saying?"

Hussein continued, "I was reminding you that the people of Kariqistan-"

"Damn it!" Goodkin kicked the console again.

"Enough!" Dunn yelled. "This is my boat. You will respect her."

"Sorry," Goodkin said, hobbling toward the windows facing the Sunset Mist.

He rested his forehead on the glass, watching the helicopters float in slow, lazy circles above the cruise ship.

He adjusted his mic and said, "Team, this is Goodkin. The media's here. All four majors. Hussein is taking interviews with them instead of negotiating with me." He paused. "I tried that. They're not responding to threats of prosecution. Got anything else? Well, that's why you're there. I don't care who. Their bosses, their wives, their lovers. Yeah. I'll try. Well, come up with something. Great. Thanks for nothing."

Goodkin was quiet for a long time.

Finally, he sighed loudly and pushed off the windows.

"All right, Burnett," he said, "let's talk about that warning shot."

"You guys keep that conversation to yourselves," Dunn said.

"Right, let's leave the good captain to his television." Burnett said, beckoning Goodkin to join him at the bridge windows.

They whispered to each other while Dunn turned his attention to the news broadcast. He flicked the channel to CNB and turned up the volume to make sure he couldn't hear what Goodkin and Burnett were plotting.

* * *

"Now for CNB breaking news off the coast of Florida. A small cruise ship, the Sunset Mist, en route from Miami to the Bahamas, has been taken hostage by Kariqistani terrorists. Our reporter Fran Amaretto is on the scene in our news helicopter. Fran, what's the situation out there?"

Text appeared at the bottom of the screen: "Voice of Fran Amaretto, reporting live for CNB." The words floated over a map of Florida, a large X in the sea indicating the location of the cruise ship. A smaller box showed the video taken from the news helicopter of the towels and chairs scattered across the Sunset Mist's top deck.

"It's a beautiful day outside," Fran said, "But there is nothing attractive here. Look at this disturbing image. See the main mast? Focus in on that, please. There we go. That's the Kariqistan national flag, or I should say, a variation of it, flying above the charred remains of the American flag hanging upside down."

The camera zoomed in on the flag mast, capturing the two flags calmly twisting in the wind, one clean and whole, the other burnt and torn. The image was held with a moment of silence before the camera zoomed out again.

"That definitely gives one pause," the studio reporter said.

"I spoke with the leader of the captors," Amaretto continued, "a man going by the name of Hussein. He was charming, intelligent and very well-spoken. He is using some kind of electronic distortion to disguise his voice and claims to be a member of a group called The Children of Kariqistan. Hussein had a list of demands which included the immediate removal of all multinational from Kariqistan, for all Western military forces to withdraw from all Muslim countries, and fifty million dollars. He said they are, and I quote, ready to kill and ready to die to have those demands met. I recorded some of our conversation. Can you play that back in the studio?"

The recording played with subtitles over the zoomed-in footage showing only the two flags.

"So, Mister Hussein," Amaretto said, "why are you doing this? Why have you taken a ship hostage and threatened to kill innocent American people?"

The digitized voice of Hussein replied as the words spelled out over the image of an electronic sound wave. "We are here to end the exploitation of our homeland, Kariqistan. The military proxies of the USA have entered our borders and sown chaos by supporting corrupt warlords. We demand that the invaders who rape our land leave. If this simple request is not met, we will be forced to take action. No one in the USA is innocent. I want to make that clear. Kariqistanis are victims of your cruelty. Every American is a murderer and we will not stop killing Americans until they leave us in peace!"

The image switched back to the bird's-eye-view of the Sunset Mist.

"As you can tell," Amaretto concluded, "Hussein is very angry, very determined. Note his chilling message that they will not stop killing Americans. That is definitely a threat the federal negotiator on the scene here will want to take seriously."

"How many hostages do they have?" the studio reporter asked. "Have you seen them?"

"I haven't seen them. Hussein assures me they are well-cared for, but there is no proof of that nor how many captives there are. He did tell me, however, and I haven't confirmed this yet, but he claims that at the request of the negotiator, he brought out six hostages to show they were safe. That's all I have on that for now. Back to you."

* * *

Burnett and Goodkin had finished their talk. They approached the control console.

"You two done scheming?" Dunn asked.

Neither Burnett nor Goodkin answered. They simply turned to watch the TV. The CNB report was concluding.

"From all of us back in the studio, thank you, Fran. Be safe out there. Our thoughts and prayers are with the hostages. We turn now to CNB geopolitical analyst Professor Brian K. Romero. Thank you for taking the time, Doctor Romero."

"Oh, God," Burnett said, "here we go with the blowhards."

"Quiet!" Goodkin snapped. "I want to hear this."

"Thank you for having me," Doctor Romero said, sitting in front of a bookshelf.

The CNB news anchor asked, "What should we take away from what little we have learned so far?"

Doctor Romero cleared his throat before speaking. "Kariqistan is part of the former Soviet Union. One of those countries absorbed by the Russian Revolution that didn't exist again until the U.S.S.R. broke up in the early nineteen-nineties. Most Americans probably couldn't find it on a map. It's primarily Muslim, landlocked, extremely rich in resources, but poorly managed. That's partly due to a corrupt government and partly because of the civil war that has been raging there ever since the Russians pulled out. Everyone wants to control the wealth of resources, so that leads to constant strife."

"And what do you make of the leader of the terrorists, this man who calls himself Hussein? What do you draw from his statement that, quote, we will not stop killing Americans, unquote? Do you think our government will have any kind of response?"

"I think absolutely they will. You can't just say you're going to kill Americans, while holding hundreds of them hostage, their fates unknown, and not expect some kind of response. No government in the world tolerates that kind of talk without action. Wars have been started over much less."

"A war? Are you expecting some sort of military reprisal?"

"Kariqistan is ruled by warlords who respect strength and force. The rule of law comes in a distant second, if at all. The civilized world and neighboring nations could use the natural wealth. I'm just speculating, but I'd be surprised if there is not a decisive application of military power sometime soon."

"Sobering thoughts, professor."

"Now I've also written a book on the subject-"

"We thank you for your time, I'm sure we'll be talking with you more as this situation unfolds. Back after this."

Dunn muted the television as it switched to a commercial for paper towels.

"So," Burnett said to Goodkin, "you're the quarterback. What's the play?"

"I need to think," Goodkin said, pinching the bridge of his nose to ward off a headache.

Dunn rocked the Bonnie Jane's steering wheel and glanced at the clock.

2

"What do you think?" North asked as he stepped around an overturned hammock.

Holland was looking up, sliding her hand over the several bullet holes in the faux-bamboo walls of the Breezeway deck's lounge.

"Looks like standard automatic weapon fire," she said, "probably AK."

North looked across the floor. "There's no blood, and those holes are high. Probably shot above their heads as a warning."

"That's what I was thinking," Holland said. "Collect them alive and show up at the table with more chips."

"And by chips you mean lives."

"Same thing."

"Unless you're one of the chips."

Holland sighed. "Do I have to explain metaphors to you?"

She turned and raised her gun. North ducked as she fired into the corner of the ceiling, destroying a security camera. She rotated and aimed for the camera in the opposite corner. Her gun spat again and the second camera exploded, spraying sparks.

"Damn it!" North yelled, rising from his crouch, "I said not to do that."

Holland slid the gun back into her thigh holster.

"That's why I did it. I'm making it clear you're not the commander."

"What the-" North stood there, his mouth hanging open. "We have to work together."

"Sure." She exited the lounge and waited in the stairwell. "But you don't have to like how I do things."

"I do when you're acting like an idiot rookie. When your actions endanger me and the mission."

Holland ignored him. She was examining the wooden sign and comparing it to her deck map.

North followed, rolling his head in a circle to release the tension in his neck.

"Says we're on the Breezeway," Holland said. "Next up is Crystal Beach. I want to see how many levels to go before I get to start popping bad guys instead of electronics. After Crystal Beach is Skyline Vista and then Plaza del Sol where the bridge-"

North jolted, grabbing her wrist and pulling her underneath the higher half of the split-level stairwell. With his free hand, he placed a finger to his lips.

They both listened, holding their breath.

Holland shrugged. *I don't hear anything.*

North held a finger in the air. *One above us.*

The sound was faint but grew until it was unmistakable: booted footsteps. The gentle thud changed to a clomp as the person walked off the thin carpet to the top of the metal stairs.

The footsteps stopped. Holland raised her gun. North shook his head no.

"Crystal Beach aft," a robotic voice said, "all clear."

The footsteps faded back down the hall.

North moved quickly, Holland one step behind. They tip-toed up to the landing. The target was walking away. He was dressed all in black, a mask over his head. North saw the barrel of a machine gun jutting out past his elbow.

North pointed to himself. *I'll take him.*

Holland nodded, her lips tight, the color draining from her face.

North crept to the top of the stairs and Holland followed, aiming down the hallway as the target continued away from them.

North followed, pressing his body into the recessed door frames of the closed rooms. The slight cover of a door jamb was better than no cover at all.

The guard arrived at an intersection and paused, looking left and right.

Step by step, each footfall silent, North closed in. His prey registered no movement, even when North was directly behind him, close enough to touch.

With one swift motion, North's huge left hand clamped over the man's mouth and nose, squeezing them shut. His right arm slid underneath the man's chin and crushed against his windpipe.

Behind the mask, the man's eyes flew wide as he clawed for his gun.

North dragged him backwards, tearing the rifle loose with his left hand and hurling it down the hall. His prey tried to scream, but with his throat crushed, only wheezed. His eyes bulged, the whites turning pink, then red.

He reached backward for North's face, trying to scratch his eyes, pull at his ears. North leaned back. Realizing his arms couldn't reach, the victim fought with his legs. He stomped on North's foot, trying in vain to break his toes. The boots Addison had supplied were protected by a steel tip. The victim kicked North's shin with his heel, again striking only boot.

North bent his arm against his own chest, leveraging all his weight into the man's neck. The target began to thrash, running his legs backward, ramming North against the wall. The crash echoed through the hall. North's vision flashed black. The terrorist gathered his strength and rammed backwards again. This time a doorknob dug into North's lower back. His grip dislodged for an instant and he heard the sharp intake of breath.

North crashed backwards again, the doorknob gouging him. The terrorist pulled in another sharp breath. Holland was at his side, gun out.

"Stop letting him breathe!" she said.

"I'm not letting him," North gasped.

"I'll shoot him."

"No! You'll hit me!"

North lost his balance and fell to the deck, his victim on top of him. Working against gravity and North was too much. The terrorist's flailing became weaker, less accurate, then useless. North could feel the pulse in the man's neck dissolve into a light tapping, then nothing.

North released his grip, the dead weight resting on him.

Holland was standing over him as he looked up at her from under the corpse.

"I thought he was going to buck loose," she said, grabbing the dead man's wet suit and rolling him off North.

She wiped her hand on her thigh rapidly, then rubbed it on the wall, as if trying to clean off dirt.

North watched her while he gasped, his breath returning to normal.

"Took you long enough," she said. "You're supposed to be good."

North rose to his knees.

"Just help me hide thi-"

North heard the familiar spitting sound of a silencer shot. He threw himself to the deck next to the body.

Holland pointed: the security camera at the stairwell sparked, hanging by a wire.

"Now we don't have to hide anything."

North stared at her as he caught his breath. "Holland," he said slowly, deliberately, "I really wish you would stop doing that."

"And I really wish you wouldn't act like you're the only one on this mission."

"We're supposed to be a team."

"A camera that's out could be anything. A short, a malfunction, an unfocused lens, debris blocking the view. But a camera that shows us can only indicate one thing: us."

North stared at her.

"I can see the sparks flying in your brain like the ones in that busted camera," she said. "Just admit I'm right."

"We could also just sneak past the cameras. You keep shooting them, the control board will light up, maybe sound an alarm. You're just as likely to draw attention to us. Hell, forget it. I'm not here to argue. Just help me hide this body."

"We don't have to," Holland said. "They won't see it."

"They might come by again," North snapped. "Can you just help me?" He turned the body over and lifted the man's legs.

"Fine," Holland said. She grabbed the body by the wrists and looked away. With North walking backwards, they carried the still warm, still flexible corpse to the base of the stairs. A small storage closet there contained several stacked boxes labeled simply as "paper products." They pushed the body in the corner and arranged the boxes so anyone opening the door would not see him immediately.

North began patting down the body.

"What are you doing?" Holland asked. "We took out the garbage. We're done."

North continued to search. "Once we're clear, we can hand off any intel we pick up to the negotiating team."

"You're sidetracking our mission."

"Just shut up and hang on a second."

"We need to go," Holland said.

"If these guys are Kariqistani," North said, "why aren't they wearing any emblems?"

"Since when did terrorists wear colors? Ragheads can't afford them."

"If they can't afford them, how did they afford this thing around his neck that distorts his voice? And why would he want his voice distorted at all?"

"Who cares? They're bad guys. The thing they do best is die." She kicked the corpse's boot. "Good job, buddy."

"Hey," North said, "you don't have to be disrespectful." He passed his hand over the dead man's eyes, closing his eyelids.

"Don't do that," Holland said. "Screw him. He would have killed you."

"I'm taking his headset," North said, yanking the wire from behind the body's head. "We can listen in on what they're saying. This guy was speaking English. What do you make of that? I didn't even notice an accent."

"I did. He sounded like a computer."

"Your smart-ass routine is getting old."

"Old as you? Fine. It's easy to explain. They're mercenaries. That's how they got the tech, that's why they speak English. Or some rich Kariqistani prick paid for this mission. Ever hear of Occam's Razor? The simplest solution is usually the correct one."

"Sounds like someone who never got out in the real world. I thought you just said these ragheads can't afford colors. Now suddenly you think they're mercs."

"And I thought you just said we can't shoot cameras because it's better if we move faster, but you take the time to loot this guy's corpse.

I don't have all the answers, North. Just the solution." She tapped her gun.

"No, you have squat. I'm learning about them. I know they've got prime hardware. That means chances are they are well-trained and organized."

"So some Kariqi warlord or oil brat financed them. Who cares? Does that change anything we're going to do?"

North scowled as he fitted the headset to his ear. "I'm ready now."

"Good. Crystal Beach deck is next. Sounds like a fun place."

3

Goodkin flipped through the channels on the Bonnie Jane's television. Every one of the major networks represented by the helicopters outside was reporting on the Sunset Mist hijacking. ACB, MCSBN, CNB and even upstart network UBS each showed an aerial view of the deserted top deck accompanied by audio and transcripts of Hussein's distorted threats. Only by noting the ghostly logo in the lower corner of the screen could Goodkin distinguish which network he had tuned to.

He muted the volume.

"This is ridiculous," he said.

"I can always fire a warning shot," Burnett said. He sat on a stool and leaned back, hands behind his head as if he was relaxing in a recliner. "But you want me to wait and you're the boss for now, so I'll wait." He kicked up his boots and rested them on the console.

"Captain Burnett," Dunn said, "please respect my boat."

Burnett let his feet drop.

Goodkin flicked a switch.

Hussein's voice filled the bridge. "-and that is why. We have no mission further than that."

The four reporters barked questions over each other.

"Please," Hussein said. "We have agreed to take turns. It is the only way. Miss Amaretto, I believe I have taken a question from each person so I am now back to you."

"Thank you, Hussein," Fran Amaretto of the CNB news network said. "I want to follow up to the question from Mister Ortiz about your intentions here. Do you feel the international community will come to your aid? That taking hostages will win you sympathy?"

Goodkin turned to Dunn, talking over Hussein's reply. "Can you believe this? He's hosting a press conference."

Dunn shrugged. "What do you want me to do?"

"The media is to terrorism what oxygen is to a fire, I always say," Burnett said. "People can't be scared of what they don't know about."

Goodkin pointed his tablet's camera at the television. He held it there while speaking into the mic bud.

"Can you do something about these reporters? Well, try again, damn it. Talk to the boss of the boss. Then go up the ladder. We're looking really bad out here."

"No kidding," Burnett chuckled.

Goodkin activated the Bonnie Jane com.

"Hussein," he said. "This is Goodkin. I know I'm interrupting, but we cannot tolerate you using hostages to host a talk show. The Geneva Convention classifies such an act as a war crime, and a crime against humanity. We are going to clear the area so our negotiations may continue."

The reporter from ACB broke in on the line. "Who the hell are you? We have a right to be here. I don't buy this war crime crap. We're the media, for heaven's sake. Ever hear of the first amendment?"

"Ever hear of shouting fire in a crowded theater?"

"Isn't that just like a bureaucrat. Worrying about fire with all this water around."

"Listen to me. I'm a federal negotiator. We're trying to get the hostages released. All you're doing is trying to get a story."

"Mister Goodkin," Hussein said, "how are you progressing toward fulfilling my reasonable requests?"

"Hussein-"

The MCSBN reporter spoke up. "Mister Hussein, we were wondering if you care to speak about your vision for the future of Kariqistan."

"Hey," Fran Amaretto said. "He wasn't done answering my question yet."

The other reporters all spoke at once.

"Hussein, do you have ambitions to rule your homeland?"

"What would you say directly to the American people?"

"Are you at all concerned about a military response against your country?"

"Hussein!" Goodkin yelled, his voice one of many.

"One at a time, please," Hussein said. "I do not know who of you asked, but yes, an American military strike on Kariqistan will not deter our mission. We fear no empire."

Goodkin flicked off the com.

"I can't get through," he yelled.

Burnett shook his head. "All a guy has to do is take a few hostages and he's suddenly worth listening to." He looked at Goodkin, "Or talking to."

Goodkin ran his hands over the console's buttons. "Damn it, there's too many controls here. How do I shut the speakers off? How do I make it stop?" Dunn leaned over and flicked a switch. The bridge was suddenly quiet except for the sound of rotors buzzing as the helicopters outside jockeyed for the best camera angle.

Goodkin looked up as if staring through the roof of the Bonnie Jane, looking to the heavens for answers.

"We need to get them out of here," he said. "We have to."

"Just say the word," Burnett said.

Goodkin pressed his forehead against a window. He squeezed his eyes closed and was silent a moment.

"The warning shot," he mumbled.

"Declare the area unsafe," Burnett whispered in his ear, "and I'll have my directive to clear them out. Say it's to prevent loss of life. I can only act if I feel my ship is in direct danger, or it has received fire, or the man in charge says so. That's you as of now. Say the word and I'll have my boys scare the piss out of them."

Goodkin turned to Dunn. "What do you think?"

Dunn raised a hand defensively. "I think I can't wait until this mess is over."

"Are we within our legal rights?" Goodkin asked.

"How the hell would I know?"

Goodkin turned away from him.

"Of course," Dunn said. "You're not talking to me. Again."

"My call?" Goodkin said to his mic, "I'm consulting you, as consultants. Hell, you're no help." He gently banged his head against the window.

"Why the hesitation, Goodkin?" Burnett said. "Who's going to hold it against you that you pushed some parasites out of the way to save hostages?"

Goodkin mumbled to himself. He looked out at the bobbing helicopters, then pushed himself off the window.

"Dunn, can you bring me back on the com?"

"Are you sure you're talking to me now?" Dunn said.

Goodkin blinked at him. "I don't understand."

"That's the problem," Dunn said, as he flicked a switch. Hussein's voice erupted onto the bridge.

"Attention, all media helicopters," Goodkin bellowed. "You must leave this area immediately."

The conversation stopped.

"This is Fran Amaretto of CNB news. I want to remind-"

Goodkin cut her off. "You are impeding a federal negotiation and are putting lives at risk. Plus you're providing these terrorists with a free media platform. Indirectly, you are encouraging copycat actions."

"I say they stay, Goodkin," Hussein said.

"Hussein, if we are to have a serious talk, I will not compete with people who are using you and your captives to boost their own careers."

"I want them to stay. This will make sure you do not try any-"

"My only concern is the safety of the hostages," Goodkin barked. "I am ordering these helicopters to move and cease communication," he took a deep breath, "or we will make them."

Hector Ortiz of UBS spoke. "You're talking awfully tough with a man who holds over two hundred lives in the balance, Goodkin. What about their family members? Don't you think they want news of what's happening?"

"Their families want to see them again alive. My goal is to make that happen and you are preventing me. Now, if you do not clear this area, the nearby naval vessel will shoot you down. You have five minutes and not one second more."

"Goodkin," Hussein began, "I told you I would not permit a second ship here."

"And I told you I would not tolerate you exploiting the people you are holding captive."

The speakers crackled with the reporters protesting all at once.

"Dunn," Goodkin said, "can you shut them off? I don't care what they say."

Dunn shut off the speakers.

Goodkin tapped furiously on his tablet, talking to his mic as he did so.

"I know it's dangerous. Well, you're taking too long. You left me no choice, we need to start a cascade of reactions here. Nothing happens if the press keeps interrupting. Shut up. Of course I'm bluffing."

"I'm not," Captain Burnett mumbled.

Still tapping, stroking and pinching the screen, Goodkin turned toward him.

"Burnett, bring your ship in. Stay as far as you can to minimize Hussein's objections, but stay in range so you can fire that warning shot. We need to show these vultures we're serious."

Burnett turned to Dunn. "Captain, you might want to check your supply hold. Looks like college boy here just helped himself to some balls."

Burnett tapped his earpiece.

"Gunfish, this is Captain Burnett. We've got our orders. Finally."

4

North crept down the halls of the Crystal Beach deck. Holland followed, watching their backs.

"So," she said, whispering, "are the bad guys saying anything?"

"Sure are," North said. "They're saying Holland can't admit she was wrong."

He took off the terrorist's headset and held it out for her.

"They're not chatty. They just do an occasional check-in, like the guy we heard. Smart move. Too much talk and we might learn their movements, their numbers."

Holland took the headset and listened. They were halfway down the hall when she was startled by a computerized voice in her ear.

"All clear Crystal Beach fore."

"Take this back," she said, removing the headset. "It's distracting. One of them just checked in. He said Crystal Beach fore was all clear."

North took the headset back and slid it on.

"I'm still wondering why they're speaking in English." he said.

"Could be they're western-educated."

"But they say they're Kariqistani. Why speak English?"

"Maybe so they could talk with the negotiator? Who cares? Besides you?"

"Just gathering intel, since Addison gave us so little."

"Some intel."

"Why pass up on any? Besides, they just gave away that at least one of them is on this level in the fore, so we've got a decision. Do we take him out now or keep going for our target?"

"Finally," she said, "you're focusing on action."

"I have been all along. Smart action requires thinking. Thinking requires facts. Facts come from intel."

"Enough," she said. "Are you going to listen to me? Or just lecture me like you do every time I blast a camera."

"I asked your opinion. I'm listening, okay?"

"That's a first."

"Don't make me regret it."

"Good," she said. "Here's how I see it. If we ignore the bandit, he might be down here to meet us when we leave with our guest. Or he might come up behind us."

"And both of those are bad."

"Extremely bad," she said, "but if we chase him, we're just wasting more time. I say we stay on our target."

"But how are we going to move with a third-" North stopped speaking abruptly and held his finger up. One of the terrorists was speaking in his headset.

"Picking up external noise," the digital voice said. "Sounds like a chopper."

Another garbled voice replied. "News birds in the air. Boss is talking to the media. All going well. No mission change yet."

"Got it. Out."

"What did they say?" Holland said.

"I count at least four bandits now," North said. "Two guys were just talking, they mentioned a boss, and there's the fourth one on this level to the fore."

"You can tell their voices apart with that sound effect?"

"Barely. Bottom line is, expect at least four."

"Only four?"

North rolled his eyes. "Why would you want more?"

"The more of them there are, the more impressive it looks on my record."

"I'll remember you said that when they start shooting at us. This is all just a big career move for you, isn't it?"

"Sure. Isn't that what's in it for you?"

"I thought we were helping people. My mistake."

5

Goodkin watched the Navy ship Gunfish 95 glide closer to the Bonnie Jane.

"It looks like she's not even moving," he said.

"My mate knows what he's doing," Burnett said. "He's being careful not to create a wake. Doesn't want to make it too obvious."

"Perfect. Unanticipated positional dynamism is bound to cause disengagement."

"What?"

Goodkin sighed. "Just let me know when they're in range."

"Will do. I have to say, college boy, I underestimated you. This takes balls, firing on the media."

"I think he's bluffing," Dunn said. "You are bluffing, aren't you, Goodkin?"

Goodkin didn't answer. He was pinching his tablet's screen.

"Well, I'm not," Burnett said.

"Everyone there okay with this?" Goodkin said. "What about legal? Well, do I at least have a majority vote? Good. Well, I don't care. If we have a majority that means we are all in agreement. Understand? We are all on board with this. I agree. We need to get them out of there. It's a risky bluff, but our only one."

"Who's bluffing?" Burnett said.

"Not funny," Goodkin said.

Burnett shrugged.

The Gunfish turned to the side and pulled up behind the Bonnie Jane. The two ships were roughly the same size. They lined up fore to aft in single file, parallel with the much taller and longer Sunset Mist.

"No complaints from Hussein yet," Burnett said, "and there's no mistaking how close my boat is now."

Goodkin checked the television. Aerial footage of the Sunset Mist was still showing.

"Excellent," he said into his mic, "the media hasn't drawn attention to the Navy vessel. Optics still benign."

The television's speakers were on mute. Text on the screen read, "Poll: Should the USA use deadly force to resolve the hijacking of the Sunset Mist cruise ship by Kariqistani terrorists? Results: 97% Yes, 3% No."

Burnett's earpiece blinked. He tapped it.

"Burnett. Go." He listened for a few seconds. "Excellent work, first mate. Be ready to fire on my signal, not before or after."

He turned to Goodkin. "It's your show now. My first mate confirms the vultures are within range."

Goodkin flipped a switch on the console. Hussein was still speaking.

"-why we fight should be obvious to anyone. We defy the United States. We defy Europe. We defy China and Russia. We are not afraid-"

"Attention, all helicopters," Goodkin said, "you are ordered to evacuate the airspace around the Sunset Mist and cease all communication with those on board. Hostage negotiations will continue immediately. Leave the area or you will be extracted by force."

A long silence followed until Hussein spoke. "Goodkin, must we do this again?"

"Yes, Hussein. We must. Do you want to discuss your demands and the people you've kidnapped? Or do you want to be a television star? You can't have both."

Hussein did not reply.

"This is Hector Ortiz of the UBS Network. You can't be serious."

"You are putting lives in jeopardy, Mr. Ortiz," Goodkin said. "Now vacate the area immediately."

"You don't understand," Ortiz said. "If one of us leaves, then the others will get the story and our network will look stupid. We all have to stay, or we all have to agree to leave all at once. And that's not going to happen."

"We could always fly off a ways and keep talking to Hussein," said an unfamiliar voice from one of the other networks.

"No you can't," Goodkin said. "You can film from a distance, but you will have no communication with Hussein and no hovering in this vicinity. You have five seconds, starting now. Five, four, three, two, one."

No one responded. The helicopters did not move.

"I am not joking," Goodkin said. He pressed the mute button and nodded grimly to Burnett.

"Make sure they miss," he said.

"You got it, college- I mean, Goodkin. Sir."

Dunn snatched up his phone. "This is Captain Dunn. Spread the word the Navy ship is going to fire some warning shots."

Burnett tapped his earpiece. "Attention, Gunfish 95. This is Captain Burnett. Civilian choppers are not permitted in the airspace above the cruise ship by order of the federal negotiator. Send off a warning shot far enough to miss but close enough to scare them. Single air burst launch on your command, first mate."

The cannons of the Gunfish lifted and rotated, emitting an ominous buzzing sound as they turned.

The three men on the Bonnie Jane's bridge turned to face the Sunset Mist.

"Navy ship preparing to fire," Goodkin whispered. A drop of sweat fell onto his tablet's screen. He wiped it off quickly.

The helicopters bobbed in the clear blue sky.

Suddenly a black cloud appeared in the air among them. An instant later the thumping sound of the rocket launch and the boom of its explosion rattled the Bonnie Jane's windows.

"Sorry, old girl," Captain Dunn whispered.

The speakers burst with all the reporters cursing at once. The helicopters shivered in the air and scattered, almost colliding. They separated like a frightened flock of birds, then came together again in the air. Once they stabilized, they retreated to the far side of the Sunset Mist, using the cruise vessel as a barrier between them and the Gunfish.

"Goodkin!" Hussein yelled, "What are you doing? I'm going to kill someone if you do not stop!"

"Hussein," Goodkin said firmly, "I have encountered extreme difficulty getting your ransom. I assure you it will be impossible to convince anyone to entertain your demands if you harm even one single person! Even one!"

"Is that true?" Burnett whispered. "Or another bluff?"

Goodkin waved at him to be quiet.

The detonation cloud above the Sunset Mist was dispersing slowly, dropping ash on the top deck. Goodkin cleared his throat and spoke evenly.

"Attention, news media. You must clear out to at least a one-nautical-mile distance from the Sunset Mist in any direction. We are extremely serious."

Only Hussein replied. "Goodkin, I told you to get that Navy ship out of here! American lives will be forfeit!"

"Hussein, show me you are serious about negotiating. Show me you care about Kariqistan more than your own fame. Tell these people to leave."

Goodkin pressed the mute button on the ship-to-ship com.

"Chase them," he said to Burnett.

Burnett tapped his earpiece. "First mate," he said, "bring the Gunfish around the cruise vessel to establish another firing angle on the birds."

The Gunfish engines roared as they churned the water.

Goodkin released the mute button. "Hussein, are you there? Hussein?"

No answer.

"Hell," Dunn said, grumbling, twisting his fists as he gripped the rudder wheel.

"Hussein," Goodkin said, his voice cracking slightly. "Talk to me."

The ship's speakers offered no reply but the hiss of dead air. Goodkin tapped his fingers as the Gunfish chugged around the fore of the Sunset Mist.

"Navy vessel is repositioning," Goodkin said to his mic, "for better angle of attack on the interlopers."

"My first mate says the birds are still there," Burnett said, finger pressed against his earpiece.

"Fire another warning shot," Goodkin ordered.

"Will do. Gunfish, another warning shot. At will."

Once more the black cloud bloomed in the sky a moment before the sound hit them. The helicopters retreated over the Sunset Mist again, collecting in the sky above the Bonnie Jane.

Goodkin yelled into the com. "Damn it! Media outlet helicopters, this is not a game of tag! Remove yourself from this airspace or you will be shot down!"

Burnett held his finger against his earpiece. "Gunfish 95, if they don't back off, you are ordered to shoot them out of the sky." He paused. "I am fully aware. Yes, I know they are Americans but they are violating the law. You are ordered to shoot down the media. Burnett out."

"Hell yeah," Burnett said. "That felt good."

Goodkin's tablet made a ringing noise. He squeezed his microphone bud. "I know, I know. I was about to address that with him."

"Burnett, hold on a minute," Goodkin said. He switched off the ship-to-ship com. "Give them more time. You can't kill the press. We just want to scare them."

"They're calling your bluff, college-boy. It's time to get serious."

"We need to give them time."

"Time? In a helicopter? How much time do they need?"

"I forbid you from shooting down the media. As your commander. That's an order."

"What if none of those cameras showed up? What would these Kariqistani scumbags do? The media is helping the enemy reach any deranged idiot and their supporters. How many copycats are we going to have? Remember September 11th? How many people would have been terrorized if that wasn't broadcast like some holiday special?"

"Burnett. No."

Hussein's voice crackled over the speaker.

"Goodkin! Stop this madness!"

"Burnett, I think Goodkin's right," Dunn said. "With those helicopters leap-frogging the ship and the Navy boat zooming around and firing, someone is going to get hurt."

"I guess both of you are on their side," Burnett said, flicking his hand toward the cruise ship.

Dunn shrugged. "I'm not shooting at anyone."

"Gunfish," Burnett said, "see if you can angle yourself perpendicular to the cruiser. That way the fore and aft guns have a line of sight down her sides. Then those damn mosquitoes won't have any place to hide."

Goodkin activated the com. "Hussein, tell them to leave. Or you get nothing."

"We're not leaving, no matter who tells us," one of the reporters said. "We're calling your bluff, and we're filming every moment of this reckless endangerment of the press."

"It's called trying to save lives. Enforcing the law," Burnett yelled into the com. Dunn waved him away.

"Hussein," Goodkin said, "I know you think you are using the media, but they're using you. You don't really think they will tell your story the way you want, do you?"

"Stick it to 'em, college boy," Burnett said.

"Hussein, the media are pawns of the capitalist imperial system," Goodkin said. "Anything you say will be twisted, turned into lies. Your words will be used as justification for the murder of Kariqistani children. Even now the American public is advocating violence against you. They think you're a madman, they say your culture is backward, violent, that your nation should be bombed back to the Stone Age. Prove them wrong, Hussein. Now's your chance."

"Damn, you got a silver tongue," Burnett said.

"Quiet!" Goodkin hissed. "Hussein?" he said. "Are you going to tell the media to leave, or are you just like them? Another tool of the system? Hello? Hussein?"

"This is Fran Amaretto of CNB news. Did I just hear a federal negotiator siding with a terrorist? And advocating the censorship of the media?"

"Fran, this is Hector. You did. It's incredible. Did you get that on tape?"

"Sure did."

"Me too. Looks like we hit the jackpot. I'm definitely not leaving if it's going to be this good."

"Me neither."

Goodkin's cheeks burned. "Then record this, too!" he yelled. "You are committing a felony by impeding negotiations. Any deaths will be on your hands." He turned to Burnett. "Order them to fire again!"

"Gunfish. Burnett. Another warning shot. Make 'em sweat."

A low boom filled the air. One of the reporters screamed over the speakers as the cloud of ash dissolved in the sky and the helicopters retreated from it. "That one was too damn close!"

"Do not make me say it again!" Goodkin yelled. "All media must clear this area or, for the safety of American lives, you will be shot down!"

Much calmer, he said, "Hussein. Are you there?"

Hussein didn't answer.

"He's probably enjoying the show," Dunn said.

"But what would he gain from that?" Burnett said. "It might be fun for him, but it gets him further from his goal."

"I don't claim to know the man's motives, but that doesn't mean I'm wrong."

Burnett touched his earpiece. "Gunfish is ready for another shot."

"Fire another," Goodkin said. "Even closer."

"First mate, take the hairs off their heads."

The Gunfish aft cannon fired.

The black cloud appeared low over the Sunset Mist's bridge. Voices screamed over the speaker.

"They almost hit us!"

"That was too close. We're bailing out."

The ACB and MCSBN news helicopters rose and roared back towards the coast. Only the CNB and UBS news choppers remained hovering over the Sunset Mist, retreating to her aft, but staying close.

"Finally," Goodkin said. "Some progress."

"Hussein?" he said into the com. "Are you there? Hussein? Contact me so we may continue our discussions. Hussein?"

"You still have two more," Burnett said.

"Remove them," Goodkin snapped.

"You got it." Burnett tapped his earpiece. "Nice shooting, Gunfish. Make this next one so close they drop more crap in the sea than a flock of geese."

6

In the UBS network helicopter, Hector Ortiz laughed into his headset. "Look at those minor-leaguers run, Fran! It's just us now."

Fran Amaretto of CNB News chuckled back at him through his earphones. "You don't want to play chicken with me, Hector."

"The hell I don't."

Another black cloud erupted in the sky before them, spraying particles over the windscreens of their choppers.

"We are not leaving!" Amaretto yelled into her microphone. "Hussein, we want to tell your story. Please come back on the line."

"Navy vessel," Ortiz said, "we ask that you stop firing in our vicinity, we are American news media, trying to get a story. We are civilians exercising our first amendment rights."

Goodkin cut in. "This is Federal agent Goodkin. The firing will not stop until you clear the area."

The UBS chopper lurched. The pilot and the three passengers (Hector Ortiz, his soundman and cameraman) grabbed for handholds as another black cloud burst nearby. The sound of the explosion buckled their eardrums and deafened them for a few seconds. The helicopter glided backwards, away from the Sunset Mist until they were moving out across the ocean.

"Why are we leaving?" Ortiz said. "What are you doing?"

The UBS helicopter pilot chuckled. "What am I doing? I'm backing off. In case you haven't noticed, they're shooting at us. First we got the verbal warning, now the warning shots. Each one a little closer. You know what comes after warning shots."

"Where are you going, Hector?" Amaretto taunted him with the sing-song voice of a grade school bully. "Oh, Hector, what's the matter? Are you scared?"

Ortiz shut off his mic and faced his pilot. "They're bluffing," he said.

"They're bluffing?" the pilot said. "Cannon fire doesn't bluff. Look at our windscreen."

Ortiz took a moment. The windshield wipers were leaving black scratches as they tried to brush free the shrapnel fragments and ash. "They're not going to shoot us," he said. "We're American civilians. We're the media."

"You're pushing your luck," the pilot said. "Our luck."

"Come on, they're not serious."

"This isn't a tank, Hector. If those shots come any closer we could take enough damage to cripple the bird. Then we'll go down, we'll need rescue and then you'll get nothing. No story."

Ortiz banged his fist on the helicopter control panel. "Do you know how many times I've been told I'm going to be shot if I keep after a story? It's never for real."

"Oh, Hector," Amaretto said in his ear, "I think you've lost your edge. That's okay. You can catch the news on my broadcast. In case you forgot, it's CNB. The network with exclusive coverage of the Sunset Mist hijacking."

Ortiz looked over his shoulder to his cameraman. "Hello, back in the studio. I should inform you that we have been told by the military that we are impeding the progress of the negotiations, but we are staying in close to make sure you get the full story." He then turned to face the pilot. "We will not give in to censorship."

The pilot sighed and gently nudged the control stick. The helicopter hovered just beyond the aft of the cruise ship.

"I'll stop here. Is this close enough?"

"Move back to where we were over the deck. The U.S. military is not going to shoot down civilians."

Ortiz reached over and pushed the chopper's control stick forward. The pilot smacked his hand away. The helicopter rocked in the air.

"Touch my controls again and you'll lose that hand."

"I said do it," Ortiz yelled. "Now!"

He reached out again and slammed the control stick forward with all his weight, unaware that at the same instant, Gunfish 95 fired.

* * *

The UBS chopper shot forward, directly into the path of the cannon fire.

The black cloud of the exploding shell engulfed them. The helicopter listed and began to spin.

"We're hit!" the pilot screamed, grabbing the control stick with both hands and leaning back. "We're hit!"

Lights on the control panel flashed and died. Needles bounced back and forth wildly. Alarms buzzed. Video equipment tumbled across the cramped cabin, as the chopper whirled, pivoting around its failing main rotor.

Ortiz yelled into his microphone. "We're hit! The U.S. Navy shot us. Fired on civilians! On the media!"

The helicopter tilted downward.

"I can't control her!" the pilot screamed. "She's not responding!"

Everyone in the cabin was pressed against the sides of the chopper as the force of the rotation tried to hurl them outward.

"Oh, God!" Ortiz yelled. "Oh, dear mother of God!"

"We're going down!" the pilot yelled. "Going down! Mayday! Mayday!"

* * *

The crew of the Bonnie Jane watched it all happen.

First, rockets exploded between the two helicopters with precision, coming closer and closer. The UBS and CNB helicopters held their positions while the ACB and MCSBN choppers cleared out, retreating to a safe distance. The UBS chopper slid from side to side in the air, as if it was undecided where to go. It drifted backward, then rocketed forward, directly into the space where the warning shots were detonating in the air.

If the two helicopters had stayed apart, the shot would have exploded between them, but the UBS chopper moved into the space and took the direct hit.

The helicopter spun out of control, flames shooting from below its fuel tank. The spinning craft wobbled as it fought to stay aloft, but a spiral descent took hold.

The chopper slammed into the side of the Sunset Mist and hung there for a moment, bent and broken like a swatted fly. Then it exploded in a billowing fireball.

Burning debris fell into the water below.

"God damn!" Burnett yelled. "Now that's getting close to your story."

"No! No!" Goodkin screamed. "No, no, no! What happened? What happened?"

Pieces of the UBS helicopter and the bodies of those within tumbled to the water's surface. A huge dark gray ball of smoke hung in the air where it had struck the ship. The Sunset Mist's once-pristine white hull bore an ugly black smudge at the point of impact.

The remaining helicopter from the CNB network, carrying Fran Amaretto and her crew, tilted and rocketed away to join the other two media helicopters in the distance.

"Ha!" Burnett yelled. "Now they'll run!"

Hussein's digitized voice crackled over the Bonnie Jane's intercom.

"Ah, Mister Goodkin. I see you and your military are not quite the defenders of life that you profess to be, yes?"

Goodkin yanked the bud out of his ear and set down his tablet PC. He could hear tiny voices screaming from the speaker as he buried his face in his hands.

7

Holland and North were halfway up the stairs between the Crystal Beach and Skyline Vista decks when a light vibration shook the boat. A muffled boom echoed through the metal. They retreated backwards, slamming into cover behind the doorway at the bottom of the stairs. North scanned up the staircase as Holland checked down the hall.

"All clear," North said.

"Clear this way."

A second boom sounded.

"What is that?" Holland asked. "It sounds like cannon fire."

"Maybe our Navy friends are putting on a demonstration," North said.

"With hostages around, would they really fire this close to the ship? I prefer the direct approach, but I don't see the Navy doing it that way."

"Hopefully it's just a show of force, nothing real."

The ship was rocked by another boom.

"What the hell?" Holland said.

North held up his hand, signaling for quiet. He pushed in his earpiece.

"All units," a distorted voice said. "Rocket fire you hear is not directed at us. No immediate danger. Continue rounds as normal."

"What are they saying?" Holland asked.

North headed up the stairs to the Skyline Vista deck. "They told their team not to worry about it."

"Why not worry? Who would the Navy be firing on? Unless it's not the Navy shooting?"

"Maybe it's—"

North spun and pressed his back against the wall next to the doorway at the top of the stairs. Holland was on the landing below. North pushed his palm toward the floor. She retreated backwards.

Down the hall on North's level, a terrorist was approaching. North waited and listened. He tightened his grip on his gun.

Another boom, this one much louder, shook the ship. The vibration was followed by the unmistakable screech of metal scraping on metal. North's skin crawled. Something had hit the ship and slid off.

The terrorist looked back and forth quickly before turning and bolting down the hall away from them. Holland sprang up the stairs and dropped to one knee, aiming her gun with both hands.

"Wait," North hissed.

Holland's silenced pistol kicked with an abrupt spitting noise. Shot in the back, the masked man tumbled forward, his assault rifle flying loose, clacking down the hall ahead of him.

"He was retreating!" North said. "He didn't even see us!"

"He's an enemy," Holland said, her voice monotone.

The terrorist was crawling away from them, groaning.

"Hell, he's still alive," North said.

"All part of the plan," Holland said.

The bleeding man continued to crawl toward his weapon as she walked slowly toward him.

North followed, guarding their backs.

"He's probably still armed, watch it," he called as loud as he dared.

"I'm not stupid," Holland said. She kicked the terrorist in the side, rolling him over with her foot. North leapt over him and snatched up the loose rifle.

The man's eyes were huge behind his mask. His mouth opened and closed reflexively, trying to grab breaths that wouldn't come. He coughed through the vocal distortion box, making sounds like a computer faltering.

North watched Holland.

She swallowed hard. Her eyes darted up at him, then down to the terrorist. She kicked the prone man in the ribs again.

"How many?" she said. "How many of you are there?"

The terrorist's eyes lost their focus.

"He's gone," North said.

"Not yet," Holland pressed her gun to the man's forehead and rested her knee on his chest. He grunted.

"I'll finish you if you don't tell me a number," she said. "How many?"

The man's lips trembled. Blood oozed out the corner of his mouth as his eyes rolled up. Holland holstered her gun and wiped her hands on his vest.

"You could have let him go," North said.

"So he could have a better chance to kill us?"

"If we keep taking them out, they're going to know we're here."

"Yeah, just in time to realize they're all dead."

North shook his head. "Talking with you is pointless. Let's hide the body and keep going."

"Works for me. And you."

As they had done before, they dragged the corpse down the hall to a supply closet at the base of the stairs. A trail of black blood traced their path all the way back to where the man had died on the deck above.

"Look at this damn mess," North said.

"Relax," Holland said. "If you hadn't been hogging the earphones, I wouldn't have had to go get my own." She yanked the headset and mic off the corpse and wrapped the wire around her ear. She kicked the closet door closed.

"Look," North said, "if I tell you not to shoot, it's not a matter of me bossing you around. It's us acting like a team."

"So if we're a team, why are you telling me what to do? Where's my vote?"

North ground his teeth. "Just watch my back."

"Can I shoot someone if they come up behind us? Or should I ask you first?"

North ignored her.

8

Goodkin was standing on the deck outside the Bonnie Jane's bridge, yelling into his mic bud. He held his tablet at his side in his left hand, while he ran his right through his hair. He was pacing and gesturing furiously.

Dunn was on his phone inside the bridge. "I don't think there are any survivors but keep looking. The terrorists don't want us anywhere near the boat, so if you don't see anyone who could be saved, we'll just have to fish out the remains later. Captain out."

Burnett's earpiece blinked. "Oh, Lord, here it comes," he said, touching the blue light. "Sir. Yes, sir. I was instructed by the federal agent in charge to fire a warning shot. I was just following orders, sir."

Burnett listened a long time. "That is the chain of command as I understand it. I'm still waiting to hear differently. I couldn't agree more, sir. Goodbye." He looked up at the black smudge on the Sunset Mist hull.

"Just following orders, Burnett?" Dunn said.

Burnett smirked. "Sometimes you just go with what works."

* * *

Goodkin slammed the door open as he stomped back onto the bridge. He tuned the television to the local UBS affiliate station. The newsreaders were visibly stunned, their eyes red, makeup streaked by tears.

Footage from inside the UBS helicopter during its final moments played silently. Sky, sea and hull flashed by in the background. Limbs and faces and equipment jumbled about in the foreground until the screen turned to static.

"In case you're just joining us," one newsreader said, her voice croaking. "We have some devastating news. We here at UBS have lost four beloved colleagues, among them Hector Ortiz, longtime network reporter, winner of dozens of awards, respect..."

She choked and cleared her throat.

"Respected co-worker and dear friend. His helicopter crashed while he was covering the still-unfolding story of the Sunset Mist cruise ship hijacking. Other networks say that the helicopter was fired upon by the U.S. Navy. We are- ahem, excuse me, we are mourning and demanding answers."

Goodkin changed the channel to CNB. The newsreaders wore serious faces and spoke urgently. "We are receiving word from our chopper in the area that the U.S. Navy ship fired on and destroyed a competing network's helicopter. It appears there were at least three casualties. Our heart goes out to the families of those lost. We now go live to Fran Amaretto on the scene. Fran, can you tell us what happened?"

"I can. It all began when the federal negotiator and the U.S. Navy alerted us to clear the area."

"And how did you respond?"

"What viewers need to understand is that journalists are constantly told to clear an area by authorities. If we always immediately complied, we would never get the information our viewers want. Hector, um, I mean, the other network's helicopter was in the same area we were. We're lucky to be alive."

"And, did they give you any warning before shooting down the helicopter? Allegedly?"

"Yes. Yes, they did. They were firing warning shots."

"I know these are difficult circumstances, Fran, but there has been some speculation that the U.S. Navy intentionally shot down the helicopter. Any truth to that?"

"I think I'd best not say. This will no doubt come under legal investigation."

"All right, well, thank you, Fran. Stay safe," the newsreader said. "We'll go to commercial and come right back. You're watching CNB Network News."

Goodkin switched back to the UBS Network. The screen showed a black and white high school graduation photo of a young Hector Ortiz.

"Hector was with our network for a long time," the sniffling newsreader said, "so we've opened up a comment line for people to share their fondest memories or a friend gone too soon. Caller, go ahead."

"Yeah, am I on?"

"Yes. Hello, you're on the air. You want to express some thoughts about Hector Ortiz?"

"Yeah. Yeah, I do. I don't know about anyone else out there, but if my daughter was hostage on that ship and the media was buzzing around, distracting the negotiator and agitating the terrorists, I sure as hell wouldn't mind if they were shot down."

The male newsreader buried his face in his hands. The female's voice shook as she spoke. "But caller, you wouldn't have even known about the situation if they weren't reporting on it."

"Reporting is one thing, but I support our troops."

"No one is saying anything against the troops."

"You are. The whole damn media is. You're saying they killed civilians."

"A respected colleague of ours, a reporter, was covering a story. He was unarmed. And he was killed. That warrants an investigation."

"Well, he shouldn't have jeopardized a delicate mission. The terrorists probably got paranoid."

"Sir, according to other networks it was not the terror-"

"You media people are always pushing your luck. You don't respect-"

"Cut him off!" the male newsreader had emerged from behind his hands, revealing his bloodshot eyes. "Hang up!" he yelled. "Now!"

He stormed off camera and yelled, "Asshole!"

The call disconnected with a pop.

"We apologize to our viewers," the female newsreader said, looking sideways towards her partner's empty seat. "We will do a better job of screening our calls. We're all, as you might imagine, very upset and off balance here."

"How about that caller?" Burnett said, pointing at the television.

Dunn looked away. Goodkin was staring at his tablet and didn't respond.

"Ah, let's see," the newsreader said. "Let's go directly to some emails we've received. This first one is from Nancy. She writes, 'This is the terrorists' fault. If they weren't there, Mr. Ortiz would still be alive. I don't buy that the Navy shot down a news helicopter. My prayers are with the Ortiz family. And God bless our men and women in uniform.'"

"Thank you, Nancy. We'll have more of your emails later. Can we go to commercial, now?"

The screen cut to the colored bars of the test pattern for a few seconds, then to an ad for shaving cream.

Goodkin spoke into his mic. "No, of course the optics are terrible, but so far, public opinion seems to be on our side. Get the hostages out, hell with the media." He paused. "Well, I don't care what you think. It's worth a lot. We've got to move forward somehow."

9

Burnett tapped his earpiece.

"Burnett. Go."

He paused.

"Well, tell him to be a man. More than one? Christ. Take them down to the infirmary and have the doctors knock them out. See if they can surgically attach some balls, too. Over."

He turned to Dunn and shook his head.

"Damn rookies are bawling over that stupid chopper. Hell, accidents happen. People die."

"Especially when you're shooting at them," Dunn said.

Goodkin was pinching the bridge of his nose and clamping his eyes shut. He was speaking to his tablet.

"Setbacks are inevitable, but we're completely defensible. Yes. We fired warning shots. Yes, we begged them to leave. It's all recorded. Then watch it again. Yes. The other media caught it, too. Fine. I'm going to re-establish communication. Back on track. Yes. I will. Yes. Can I go now?"

He clipped the tablet to his belt and took several deep breaths before activating the Bonnie Jane's com.

"Hussein. Are you there? This is Goodkin. Hello, Hussein?"

No reply.

"Hussein, what happened was a tragic accident, but we need to keep to the business at hand."

He waited.

"Goodkin," Hussein said slowly. "You are a negotiator, are you not? Yet you could not come up with a better way to remove the media than to kill them. This does not impress me."

"What happened was not of my doing, or of my choosing, Hussein."

"It never is," Burnett grumbled. Goodkin ignored him.

Hussein responded.

"Onward, then. I will gladly discuss terms with you if and only if you permit the remaining news helicopters to come back. A compromise. You get to talk with me, and I get what I want, which is for the world to see what America has driven the oppressed people of Kariqistan to do. Seems fair, yes? You get something, I get something."

"Hussein, I can't do that."

"Negotiate with me, then. How about two helicopters?"

"No. Hussein. None."

"How about one? Someone must tell our story or else what is the point of this exercise?"

"See?" Burnett said, turning to Captain Dunn. "I told you! Terrorists need the media."

Hussein was still talking. "Do you want more blood on your hands? If so, I will gladly supply it. That will not be your fault either, I presume."

Goodkin pressed his fist to his forehead.

"All right," he said. "Fine. One. Only one. That's a fair compromise. But they are not allowed to interfere with our negotiations. No interruptions."

"That is a fair request. I would like Miss Amaretto of the CNB network to return."

"I'll see what I can do," Goodkin said.

"I will not speak to you again until her aircraft returns, and that Navy ship has moved out of firing range. Is that clear? Goodbye, Goodkin. Don't disappoint me."

The speakers popped. Goodkin muted the bridge microphone.

"You heard the man," he said to Burnett.

"Why don't you just get in touch with his agent?"

"It's only one media outlet. I can live with it. It's not ideal, but it's something."

"You just got out-negotiated."

"Burnett. Please. Just move your ship. And be quiet."

"Damn, college boy. I thought we were friends."

10

Goodkin activated the com.

"Calling Fran Amaretto," he said. "CNB network helicopter, can you hear me? Miss Amaretto? Hello? This is federal negotiator Nelson Goodkin."

"This is Fran Amaretto of CNB speaking. Go ahead."

"We, ah, have an interesting situation here. I have decided to permit one and only one media helicopter in the vicinity of the Sunset Mist, provided there is no interference with my communications. Can you please bring your helicopter closer to the coast guard vessel, the Bonnie Jane?"

An angry male voice cut in, "What about us? Why is the federal government negotiating with only one network? If there are new developments, all of us need to know."

"Shut up, Harold," Amaretto said. "You're just jealous because ACB is a sucky network and your show is unwatchable."

"Oh, right, Fran. And your cleavage has nothing to do with your ratings."

"If you had anything to flaunt, I'm sure you would."

"We all just heard their exchange. This Goodkin clown didn't work out a damn thing. Hussein asked for you. Are you the official network of terrorists now?"

"Can I get some private conversation here?" Goodkin bellowed. "Miss Amaretto, tell your pilot he has permission to approach the Bonnie Jane. To any other media helicopters who can hear this, you are warned to stay back and not talk on this channel."

"If we do," a female voice interrupted, "are you going to fire another so-called warning shot?" She paused to let the sarcasm sting. "We're going to run with this, Fran. At best you're state media. At worst, terrorist-sanctioned."

"Fine. Make me the story. That's some good journalism," Amaretto said. "Goodkin, let's talk on my cell." She recited her number over the air. Goodkin entered it into his tablet. "Anyone else listening, don't bother calling."

Goodkin hung up the com. He activated his tablet's telephone app and dialed the number.

"I can't believe this," Burnett said. "We just got them out of here, now you're bringing them back?"

* * *

The CNB helicopter glided slowly toward the Bonnie Jane. The remaining two network choppers from ACB and MCSBN edged closer but stopped.

Amaretto's phone was ringing. When she answered, Goodkin was already yelling, "Burnett! Tell your ship to stand down!" Much more calmly, he said, "Miss Amaretto? Are you there?"

"It's me," Fran said. "That Navy ship isn't moving." She turned to her pilot and said, "Hold here." The pilot nodded. The helicopter stopped in mid-air.

"Looks like a setup to me. I wouldn't go any closer," one of the left-out reporters said over the Bonnie Jane's speakers.

Fran listened to the discussion on Goodkin's end.

"Burnett, the Gunfish has to move," he said.

"Let me talk to the nice reporter lady," Burnett said. "I'll put her at ease."

"No, Burnett. You said you would do as I instructed."

"Who's that in the background?" Amaretto asked. "The Navy captain? I'm fine talking with him. I want assurance that we won't be fired on. Not even warning shots."

"Hang on," Goodkin said. "Let me set up for collaboration. I'm going to put you on my speaker phone. I've got Captain Dunn of the Bonnie Jane, Captain Burnett of Navy Gunfish 95 and my whole team back on land listening. This conversation is being recorded."

He tapped the screen and set the tablet on the console.

"We're on conference call."

"Hello, everyone. This is Fran Amaretto of CNB news."

"Okay," Goodkin said. "As you know, this situation is extremely delicate. You heard my discussion with Hussein. He wants the media in close. I don't like the idea because it's impossible to negotiate if he's putting on a show."

"Right," Amaretto said. "You want to keep me out, but he wants me in. Remind me again if our country has freedom of the press?"

"Before I let you in," Goodkin said, "I need to know that you'll play by my rules. You can listen, but no talking. If you break silence, I'll tell Hussein you can't be involved and he'll have to choose another network. Then we're all back to the beginning."

"Goodkin, I recognize your authority here, and I appreciate your assurance," Amaretto said. "But I need the okay from the Navy captain."

"Captain Burnett here," Burnett said. "Look, miss, if it were up to me, all of you media types would be gone. I'm against giving in to Hussein's demands. I say we stop talking and just kill him."

"See, Goodkin?" Fran said. "This is what I was afraid of. You give me the okay, but the man with the guns isn't so soothing. Tell you what, Captain Burnett. If you let me closer, I'll see what I can do about telling your side of the story regarding the late Hector Ortiz and the UBS network chopper. Killing clearly identified non-combatants is a war crime, isn't it? You could really be screwed, depending on how that incident is framed in public opinion. The other two networks still here, they're not happy at all. It would be bad for you if the press was unanimous in condemning you."

"You don't scare me."

"Then you're as dumb as you sound."

"Think what you want, lady. You just talked me out of letting you in the zone."

"Wait, Burnett, wait," Goodkin said.

"No, Goodkin. If she's going to threaten me, I'm not letting her in."

"I'm in command! It's already been decided."

"Between you and Hussein. I didn't approve. Have him pick another network."

"You said you'd defer to my judgment. You can't be serious."

"Okay, look," Amaretto said. "What if we brought one of your men on board?"

Burnett was silent.

"It's win-win," she continued. "You get a man in the air for recon. We get closer to Hussein, who is the key to our story. And we also get to interview a man in uniform while Goodkin negotiates. That gives me something to fill the dead air. Everyone's happy."

"No," Goodkin said. "This is ridiculous."

"Hm," Burnett said, "I think I like it. She's a better negotiator than you."

"No. No, no, no."

"You're in far much more trouble than I am over that downed chopper, Goodkin. Probably more," Burnett said. "You were the one who gave the order to clear the area. You were the one who insisted on being in charge."

Goodkin ground his teeth while everyone waited for him to choose.

As though speaking through extreme exhaustion, he finally sighed, "All right. Amaretto, have your chopper come to the Bonnie Jane. Burnett, call your man."

Goodkin tapped on his tablet and stepped away.

"You heard that plan?" he said into his mic. "I'm improvising, okay? It's raining egos out here."

Burnett touched his earpiece. "Savant! Report to the bridge."

"I don't like it either," Goodkin said to his tablet. "No. I've made the decision. It's part of our program, the front line has situational adjustment authority. Improvisation is required during times of operational dysfunction. No. All right, fine."

Goodkin turned to Burnett and spoke slowly. "Captain Burnett. My base team is expressing some reservations. We don't know how Hussein will react if you've got a man in the helicopter."

"Tell those desk commandos and pencil pilots that he knows we've got snipers watching him and he hasn't said a word. Why would one of them in a chopper make him nervous? He's got to assume we've been lining him up the whole time."

"All right, but if he says anything-"

"If Hussein complains we'll take my man down. But this is more of a strategic move than you realize." He winked at Goodkin. "Trust me on this one, college boy."

A man in a dark blue Navy uniform carrying a rifle crashed onto the bridge. He saluted sharply.

Dunn and Goodkin stared. The new arrival had been on the bridge earlier when the Gunfish first arrived, but so briefly they didn't get a good look at him. Now that they could observe him, they noticed just how awkward he appeared.

His buck-teeth were enormous. His eyes were set so close together they seemed crossed, the gray pupils bulging from beneath a unibrow as though he was glaring comically. Acne covered his cheeks. His uniform fit poorly over his bony frame.

"Savant," Burnett said, "I have a special mission for you. You're going on the news chopper. Keep scouting for shots but don't take any until you have my order."

"Yes, sir!" Savant bellowed, so loud that Goodkin and Dunn jolted.

"Now, go out on deck," Burnett said. "The civilians will pick you up."

"Yes, sir!" Savant yelled again.

"One more thing," Burnett said, lowering his voice. "Don't tell the media lady anything. Just yes, ma'am, no, ma'am. Nothing else."

"Yes, sir!" Savant bellowed, spraying Burnett with spittle.

"Damn," Goodkin said. "We're not deaf."

"We are now," Dunn mumbled, his finger in his ear.

Savant saluted and left.

Burnett watched him go, then turned to Goodkin and smiled.

"What?" Goodkin said.

"Freaky looking bastard, isn't he?"

"Since you asked, yes. But so what?"

"Trust me. That reporter thinks she's playing hardball? Squeezing us for a human interest angle? Wait until she learns who she's got there.

He's not what you'd call photogenic, but even more, he's not a talker. There's a reason we call him Savant."

"Not his real name?"

"No. That's just his nickname, but perfectly appropriate."

"You let someone who isn't right in the head carry a sniper rifle?" Dunn asked.

"All due respect, Captain," Burnett said. "But be careful how you judge him. He's ugly as sin and a social misfit for sure. But the way he handles a gun, he's a genius. Hell, an artist. He makes shots no one else makes, in the wind, through reduced visibility. At night. While running. He can do it all. That crazy-looking bastard is one of the highest rated marksmen in the Navy. And he follows orders to the letter. I mean literally. He just doesn't have it in him to do otherwise. That news lady thinks she's getting some philosopher warrior? I just wish I could see the look on her face."

He chuckled.

"The perfect soldier," Goodkin said. He smirked.

"Shoot," Burnett said. "I'm trying to help you out and you get all editorial."

He tapped his earpiece. "Listen up, Gunfish! Withdraw from the area of the Sunset Mist. We have an unusual situation here. You are to permit, repeat, permit the CNB chopper to fly where she pleases in the vicinity of the cruise ship. However, you are to prevent any other media helicopters from approaching. Savant will be on board the CNB chopper gathering intel."

"Aye, sir," the first mate said. "No firing on the CNB bird. Open season on the others if they go near the hot zone."

"You got it, Gunfish. Burnett out."

* * *

The water around the Bonnie Jane rippled outward in concentric circles as the CNB helicopter hovered above. A rope ladder fell from the chopper and Savant climbed up, rifle slung over his back. He pulled himself into the cockpit.

Hussein's voice broke over the intercom. "Putting a sniper on my helicopter, Mister Goodkin?"

Goodkin turned to Burnett: "I told you."

"Well, get to negotiating, college boy."

"Hussein," Goodkin said, "I'm just trying to keep everyone happy. Our Navy friends insisted. You get your media, they get a man on the helicopter."

"And you get nothing, yes, Mister Goodkin?"

"Hussein, all I want is to keep people from dying."

Hussein paused.

"I will accept this. For now. But if a single shot is fired, if anyone attempts to rappel from that helicopter to my ship, they will be killed instantly along with twenty of my guests. Understand?"

"I understand, Hussein," Goodkin said. "No one will shoot."

Burnett grunted.

The CNB helicopter lifted the rope ladder and drifted toward the Sunset Mist.

Dunn was at his place behind the steering wheel, Goodkin near the communications console, Burnett off to the starboard side of the bridge. They watched the helicopter bob in the wind, slowly rising above the lifeless cruise ship.

"This seems like an awful lot of work to satisfy a man who hasn't produced a single dead body," Burnett said.

Dunn and Goodkin turned to stare at him, their mouths hanging open.

"Don't look at me like that. I'm just making an observation. The guy says he's going to kill people if he doesn't get what he wants, but he hasn't set a deadline, he hasn't received anything, and still he hasn't killed anyone yet. Maybe he's bluffing."

Dunn shook his head. Goodkin poked his tablet.

Burnett rubbed his chin, narrowing his eyes.

"Or maybe he's chicken shit."

11

The CNB helicopter traced a wide oval pattern in the air above the Sunset Mist, floating from fore to aft and back again.

Fran Amaretto turned to the Navy sniper.

"I'm Fran Amaretto," she said, shaking Savant's hand.

"Yes, ma'am," he mumbled.

She squinted to read his name tag.

"You're Savant?"

"Yes, ma'am."

"Phil," she said to her cameraman, "see if you can capture him setting up."

Savant pulled out his seatbelt as loose as he could get it and strapped it around his waist. He opened the small back window on his side of the chopper, poking his rifle barrel outside.

"Do you mind if I ask you a few questions?" Amaretto said.

"No, ma'am."

Savant was turning dials along the rifle, flipping latches, squinting through the scope.

"Can you tell me what all those controls mean? Tell me a little about what you're doing?" she said. "How does the gun sight work? Is it like a camera lens?"

"Yes, ma'am."

"You can say more, you know. Elaborate."

Savant didn't reply.

"The studio is expecting an update now," Phil the cameraman said.

"Fine," Amaretto said. "Go."

"In three, two, one."

"This is Fran Amaretto of CNB news, off the coast of Florida, in the air above the hijacked cruise ship the Sunset Mist. What you're seeing here is exclusive footage not seen on any other station. Earlier there was an unfortunate accident involving a rival network. The authorities instructed all of us out here to keep our distance, but some did not and accidentally moved into the path of the Navy's warning shot. It was a tragedy for all involved, but I assure you, it was not the fault of the U.S. Navy or the brave men and women of our armed forces."

Phil signaled thumbs up.

She turned slightly in the cramped helicopter cockpit. "To give you further information on this situation, we have one of the Navy SEALs along with us. This is Corporal Savant."

Savant was sighting down the barrel of his rifle, one eye winking, his head turned away from the camera.

"Corporal Savant, can you share with us what you're doing?"

Savant continued to look down the barrel of his gun at the bridge of the Sunset Mist. He didn't acknowledge Amaretto or the camera.

"Uh, well, as you can see," she said, "he's busy with his rifle in case, well, in case he needs to act. I'm sure he'll give us more information soon and when he does, we'll pass it along."

She cleared her throat. Savant barely moved.

"Ahem. Okay," she said. "Ah, for now, let's look at the ship again. Below us, Phil, can you get that? Thank you. Viewers can see the top deck is strewn with towels, life jackets and chairs. There must have been a terrible panic when the terrorists took over the ship. The federal negotiator is ready to begin talking with the terrorists again soon. We'll keep you updated if anything changes."

"All right, Fran," the newsreaders in the studio said. "Is there anything new? Any new developments?"

"With the Navy's sniper riding along with us, we expect something to happen any moment now."

"All right, then, check back in when you have more. Be careful out there."

"We will. This is Fran Amaretto for CNB news."

The signal cut.

"Hell," she said, "it figures, we get an exclusive and the guy's shy."

Savant didn't respond.

"You know, Savant, you're supposed to talk. Did Burnett put you up to this? You can say more than yes or no. Hello?"

Savant's eye was pressed to the rifle scope, watching the deck.

"So you're not a talker, are you?"

"No, ma'am."

"You just shoot things, don't you?"

"Yes, ma'am."

"And by things, you mean people."

"Yes, ma'am."

"So, who is on that boat anyway?"

Savant didn't answer.

"Did you hear if it's anyone of significance? Did the terrorists choose that boat for a reason or was this just random? Did you hear anything from your captain?"

"No, ma'am." Savant's face was expressionless as he answered, his voice monotone.

"You don't have respect for the media, do you?"

"No, ma'am."

"But freedom of the press is one of the rights you defend by killing people."

"Yes, ma'am."

"You realize that doesn't make a lot of sense? You're... oh, never mind."

"Yes, ma'am."

PART 5

FREE FOR ALL

1

Zack made his way across the lounge. Though his ankles and wrists were bound, his hands behind his back, he still moved by a combination of slinking, rolling, and wriggling on his butt. He reached the wall and sat with his back against it, using it as leverage to rise to his feet.

"Go, kid, go," Martin said.

Zack took one hop and lost his balance. He hit the floor hard, slamming on his right side.

Brittany screamed.

Zack moaned, rocking on his shoulder.

"You okay, son?" Martin said, glancing toward the locked doors.

"Imma gone hafta inchworm this bitch," Zack said.

"What did he say?" Gwen said.

Zack rolled over onto his belly, arched his back upwards and squeezed his elbows and knees together, then lunged forward. His elbows thumped on the carpet. He pulled his knees forward and repeated the process.

A boom sounded outside the ship.

They all, except for Danforth Percy Sinclair, chattered nervously.

"What up with tha bang-bang?"

"What was that noise?"

"Sounded like a cannon."

"Do you think they're shooting at us?"

"Quiet," Martin said. "Everybody quiet."

Zack had stopped.

"Yo, cap'n, we still on?" he said.

"Just keep going," Martin said, rocking from side to side, rotating slightly with each motion until he was facing the doors.

"Still clear," he called out periodically. Gwen and Brittany watched Zack curl and lunge across the room, moving away from them toward the cart in the corner. Sinclair was still sleeping, head resting on his bent knees.

Yvonne Windstorm rocked on her buttocks to move closer to Brittany. "Hey, little girl, don't cry," she said. "It's going to be all right. You look sick."

"I just feel ill," Brittany said, wiping her running nose on her shoulder. "I'm so young. I haven't really lived. I'm so scared we're going to die here."

"Oh, you cute thing," Windstorm said. "You've got your whole life ahead of you. Someday you'll look back on this and laugh."

"I'm only twenty-one," Brittany sniffled. "If I had lived as long as you, I might feel better."

Another muffled boom vibrated the ship.

"I'm not that old," Windstorm said.

"Oh no. No. Oh, my God," Brittany said, "I didn't mean it like that. I mean, you've had such an exciting life. You're married to a rich man, you're famous. You've uh... been in movies."

"But look at me now," Windstorm said. "I'm in the same situation as you."

"You've lived, though. You've partied with rock stars."

"That's just for show, dear. It doesn't mean anything."

"You're beautiful."

"Money buys a lot." Windstorm winked and looked down at her breasts.

Brittany chuckled weakly.

Another boom thundered outside.

"What the hell is that?" Gwen asked. No one answered.

"Look at your boyfriend over there," Windstorm said. "He's trying to save us all, but most of all he wants to save you. He's risking his life. Honey, you have what's important. He loves you."

"Yeah," she said, chuckling to herself. "He's okay."

"He's better than that. I can't tell you how many times I've been with other couples and the man asks me to sleep with him, right in front of his wife. But your boy? He hasn't even looked at me. At least not in that way. It's sweet."

"That's my Zack." She had stopped sniffing.

"So you hang on to him. He's a good one."

"I guess I'll keep him."

Zack was nearing the snack cart.

"Of course," Windstorm said, "that might mean he's gay."

"What?"

"Oh, I'm just kidding, honey."

"Read between the lines, girlie," Sinclair barked, his eyes still closed. "She always acts nice when she's jealous. She wishes she was your age."

"Danny," Windstorm said, her voice suddenly shrill, "just shut up. You're much more pleasant when you're quiet. And asleep."

"Believe me, I prefer sleeping to hearing you act human, but you won't stop talking."

"I'm trying to comfort this girl."

"Of course you are."

Another muffled boom rumbled through the ship.

"Yo yo," Zack called from across the room. He had arrived at the snack cart. "Z is downtown, takin' it to the hole."

"All clear," Martin called back. "Go for it."

"Oh God, be careful," Gwen said.

Wedging himself between the cart and the wall, Zack wiggled to his feet. The cart rocked under his weight. He turned around so his bound hands could reach the drawer handles. He pulled the drawers open then spun around to examine their contents, repeating the process from the lowest drawer and working his way up.

"Anything good, kid?" Martin yelled. "Anything with a blade?"

"Lots of plastic spoons, yo. Loads of napkins, too. Hold up. I'm having trouble reaching this top drawer."

"You should have gone," Gwen said to her husband.

"I don't have his flexibility," Martin said.

"You're taller."

"Honey, please. What is this?"

"It's not safe. He's just a boy."

"So you would rather I went? I'm trying to manage our escape. What's the rich guy doing? He's taking a damn nap."

"He's useless," Windstorm said.

Sinclair kept his eyes closed. He didn't react.

"He's trying to rest," Gwen said. "Or at least pretending to. Maybe that's what we should all do. If they come in-"

Another muffled boom shook the boat.

"Pay dirt, yo!" Zack yelled. Facing away from the cart, he looked backwards over his shoulder. He grunted, stretching to reach inside the drawer. He jumped to get his hand in further, but when he came down he crashed against the cart, his wrist bending awkwardly. He yelped and fell face first into the wall, then tumbled backwards, knocking his head on the cart's icebox as he crashed to the floor.

Brittany yelped. "Zack!"

The cart rocked as if it was going to tip over.

Zack groaned.

"Sh!" Gwen hissed sharply. "The door!"

The door handle was shaking. Someone was unlocking it.

"Stay down, boy," Martin said. "Stay down."

"What's our story?" Windstorm asked. "What's our story?"

"Shhh!"

A head covered with a ski mask peeked in, assault rifle dangling by a strap around the man's shoulders. He scanned the room quickly, then paused a moment.

He stepped back, slammed the door and locked it, gone as fast as he had appeared.

"What the hell?" Gwen said.

"Seemed like he was in a hurry."

"Maybe he's looking into what those noises are."

"Oh, my God," Brittany cried, "I thought we were dead."

"Damn it, Martin," Gwen said. "Zack, get back here. Hurry. It's too dangerous. If they see you over there-"

"Gwen," Martin said. "Now is not the time."

"Zack! Come back! Now!" Brittany screamed.

"Shut up, girlie," Sinclair said, grumbling. "Or you're going to bring them running. Then they'll kill him right in front of you. Then I'll have to listen to you cry."

"Danny!" Windstorm said. "That's enough! Zack, honey, are you all right?"

Zack moaned. "My head is jacked up. But I got a screwdriver."

"Get back here now," Gwen said.

"A screwdriver?" Martin said. "I guess that will have to do."

Zack thrashed around on the floor, rolling onto his belly.

He worked his way back to the group, using his inchworm technique, wincing each time he landed on his elbows. He held the screwdriver between his hands, almost stabbing himself in the face a few times as he bounced along.

"Are you sure that's all there was?" Martin asked.

"Lay off," Gwen said.

Zack returned to the group and collapsed face down, the screwdriver rolling across the floor toward Martin.

"My skull," Zack moaned.

Brittany tipped herself over, resting her head on his back, sobbing.

Sinclair opened his eyes, saw the screwdriver and laughed. "That's not going to help at all," he said before curling up again, tighter than before.

Windstorm shook her head. "Danny, there's no need to be rude."

Gwen tried to elbow her husband. Instead, she just crashed against him, but Martin got the point.

"Uh. Hey, good job, kid," he said, frowning at the screwdriver.

"Yeah. Thanks."

The ship vibrated as a thundering crash several times louder than the others shook the floor.

"What the hell was that?"

"Felt like something hit the ship."

"That was a big one."

"Is someone attacking?"

"Are we sinking?"

They could hear screaming from the main ballroom abruptly cut off by the terrorists yelling.

"Whatever's going on," Martin said, "we need to get ourselves free as soon as possible."

"Why?" Gwen asked. "Maybe we're being rescued."

"We don't know that. So the smarter move would be to keep going. Now let's see if we can somehow use this screwdriver."

2

North was on his knees, using a bath towel to clean up the blood trail that led down the stairs and into the janitor's closet. Though the stain was fresh, he couldn't erase it completely. His efforts removed the dark red stripe, but left a pink smear.

"Not sure why we even bothered to hide the body," he muttered to himself, throwing the towel into the closet and closing the door.

Holland was consulting her deck map. When North finished she tapped the wooden sign on the wall. "Upstairs is Skyline Vista, last known location of our dead friend in the closet there. Level after that is the bridge and Plaza del Sol, where we think they're keeping everyone. You ready for this, gramps? We're almost there."

"I'm ready for this to be done."

"Hell yeah."

Holland was folding up her map when North stuck his hand in the middle of it. "Wait a second," he said, pointing to a small block on the Skyline Vista deck. "We're near the Main Security office."

"So?"

"We might be able to learn something from the security cameras. At least the ones you haven't shot out."

"You were dying to say that, weren't you?"

"Let's detour and see what they've got. That might give us some intel on how they're holding the hostages."

"You and your damn intel. More like a distraction."

"You want to charge in blind?"

"No, no, I'll go. I know how much it means to you. Plus I'm sick of arguing. You must drive your wife crazy."

"Ex-wife. And it turns out she went crazy all on her own."

"Believe what you want. I have a feeling she'd tell a different story."

They climbed the stairs, careful not to step in what remained of the blood. A sign at the top landing was decorated with smiling children on a beach and the words "Welcome to Skyline Vista" written across the sky in cloud-like lettering. Just beyond, in the middle of the hall, was the large blot where Holland had shot the terrorist.

North led, gun in one hand, map in the other. Following the signs toward the security office, he veered away from the usual course to the next staircase.

"Let's not waste too much time," Holland whispered, watching their backs.

"We'll just be a minute," North said.

He turned a corner. The gaudy carpeting abruptly ended in a gray rubber floor.

A plaque on the wall bore none of the beach-themed decor the other signage did. The metal plate read simply, "Main Security Office. No unauthorized personnel beyond this point."

The door to the office was cracked open. A robotic voice spoke in their ears through the headsets.

"Security Room, status." the voice said, "Any word on your inventory of Crystal Beach and Skyline Vista?"

A second digitized voice from inside the security room answered.

"I'm still short two. One from each of those decks. All other decks fine."

An instant later, the same words echoed inside Holland and North's stolen headsets. They scrambled backwards to an intersecting hall. Holland ducked into the ladies' restroom and North followed, peeking out the door.

"I'm looking at the monitor console," the second voice said. "We've got a couple cameras down in those zones."

"Think we have company?"

"Not sure. Could be a localized malfunction."

"We need to know. Mission parameters dictate we initiate final protocol if we're boarded or we lose anyone."

"Right. All units, report to bridge ASAP. We need a quick headcount. Crystal Beach and Skyline Vista teams, watch out. If we've got stowaways, they're probably near you."

A scraping noise came from the security room. It sounded like someone rising to their feet and pushing a chair back.

North let the restroom door close. He pressed his ear to the door.

"What's happening?" Holland whispered.

North pressed his finger to his lips.

The sound of footsteps passed by and moved away from them, fading into silence.

North slowly opened the door and crept from their hiding spot to the security room. He smoothly holstered his gun and drew out his knife. Holland followed, covering his back.

North peeked through the gap between the door and the frame of the security office. The room was empty. He entered, Holland close behind.

A bank of a dozen black and white monitors stared at them. The screens held a scene for several seconds before cutting to another view, automatically cycling through the cameras. In the bottom right of each screen was a digital stamp, identifying the deck and the time.

"Just like your placeholder job," Holland said.

"Look," North said, pointing to a screen that was solid black, except for digital text in the lower right corner. "Oceanview deck aft. That's one of the cameras you took out."

"Yeah. So?"

"I'm just showing you how easily they can track us."

"You're not letting this go, are you? If it's so easy track us, how come they haven't found us yet?"

"You're missing the point."

"Which is?"

North exhaled loudly. "Which is talking to you is a waste of time, apparently."

He scanned the control panel. "Since they're bringing everyone up to the bridge for a meeting, let's see if we can get a peek."

Holland kept her gun aimed at the door.

"Here they are." North pointed to a monitor showing hundreds of people sitting on the floor of a large ballroom. The three terrorists walking among them moved to the room's double doors and left.

"Plaza del Sol. Ballroom" was stamped on the image. North held down the button under the monitor, preventing the screen from cycling to another camera view. "Our guess was right."

"My guess," Holland said. "What about the bridge?"

North pointed to another monitor. It was stamped "Bridge" but was a solid black. "They're smarter than that."

"So you're saying taking out the cameras was smart," Holland said, smiling.

"I'm saying they knew enough to guard against a video intercept of the bridge. The enemy you underestimate is the enemy that kills you."

"That's funny," Holland said, "I don't feel dead. Come on, we know where our targets are."

"How are we going to get in there?"

"I'll distract them by killing them."

"But they're all up there now. So it's two versus what? At least six."

"So the odds are against them."

North's face burned red. "Can you cut the bravado for one second?" he barked. "Just one second?" Much quieter he added, "Damn, you're annoying."

"Fine," she said. "Here's what I'm thinking. If we wait here we're just waiting. If we follow them toward the bridge while they do their headcount, then hide nearby, we can move again when they've returned to their posts. There will be fewer of them around our target. Maybe we can even get a count as they come out."

North nodded, his face grim. "Not bad."

"See? I'm not just a smart ass. That's just an extra bonus."

"What do you make of this 'ultimate protocol' the terrorist mentioned?"

"It means we better haul ass. Sounds like they might blow the whole ship. Better to get up high then."

"That's what I was thinking, but something doesn't feel right."

"Well, I told you my plan. We can worry about your feelings later."

"Do you have the patience for your idea? Sneaking up behind them and waiting for them to return to their stations? You're not going to jump out and start shooting, are you?"

"Would I do something that foolish?" she smiled broadly.

North shook his head. "If it was the only way to prove yourself right, I think you would."

"You make it sound like I'm just about my career."

"Well, aren't you?"

"The more kills I get, the better it looks on my record. If these rats are going to blow themselves up anyway, who gives a damn? They get martyred, which is what they want. I get a notch on my record at Redfire, which is what I want."

North stared at her. She stared back.

"Now I know why I feel like I'm the only one who cares," North finally said.

"Correction," Holland said, "you're the only one who cares too much."

3

Goodkin's eyes were drawn to the ugly black burn on the side of the Sunset Mist. He tried to avoid it, put it out of his mind and move on, but that was impossible. Every time he looked up, there it was, a reminder that he had lost control. That's where the UBS news network helicopter had collided with the hull and exploded.

That's where three people had died.

Or was it four?

He didn't know.

"Quit daydreaming, college boy," Burnett said. "What now?"

"All this activity," Dunn said, "and we still have a boat load of hostages."

"I believe Burnett's question was directed to me, Captain Dunn," Goodkin said. He cleared his throat. "Now that everyone is done trying to exploit this situation, maybe I can get down to-"

"Goodkin!" Hussein said. "Goodkin. Answer me. This is urgent."

Goodkin activated the com. "Hello, Hussein. How can I help you?"

"I need to talk. There is a problem."

"Calm down, Hussein. What's wrong?"

"Two of my men are missing."

Goodkin did not immediately reply. He looked across the bridge to Burnett, who shrugged.

Goodkin pressed the mute button on the ship's com. "Do you know anything about this?" he said.

"Maybe I do," Burnett said, "maybe I don't."

"I have given this man my word," Goodkin said, his voice low, "that his men will not be harmed as long as they don't hurt anyone. If you have a team on board that ship, not only are you putting innocent lives at risk, but you are undermining the strategic initiatives of the federally authorized Incident Area Commander. Me."

Burnett shrugged again. "I promise you I haven't given any orders to storm the boat, but if one of my men goes rogue, sees an opportunity and takes out some bad guys on his own, well, I'd be sure to discipline him in public, but in private, I'd be slapping him on the butt for a job well done."

Dunn raised his eyebrows. "You'd slap another man on the butt in private? So it's true about you Navy guys."

"You know what I mean, puddle pirate."

"This is serious!" Goodkin yelled. "Do you have a squad on the boat?"

"Not to my knowledge," Burnett said. "What I'm trying to tell you is the best marines are the ones that know what the commander wants even if he hasn't told them. And they act on it. The only exception I know of is Savant, who needs everything spelled out, but he's up in the helicopter."

"All right, all right, quiet." Goodkin lifted his finger off the mute button. "Hussein, this is Goodkin. I have not ordered anyone onto the boat. Maybe your men are just lost."

"Absurd! You son of a dog. If we do not find them soon, my guests will suffer."

"Hussein, there's no need for threats. I'm sure there's an explanation. It's a big ship, maybe they're- Hussein? Hussein?"

No response.

Goodkin slapped his tablet on his thigh.

"Damn it, Burnett! I need to be certain that we have no one on that boat."

"I'm trying to tell you, I don't know myself. But I swear to you, I did not give any such order. And I know of no such order given by my crew."

Goodkin narrowed his eyes.

"I'm telling the truth. Why don't you ask Mr. Dunn over here if it's one of his?"

"Me?" Dunn said. "We're built for rescue, not assault."

"Goodkin, while we're having this heart-to-heart," Burnett said, "I should remind you that I'm only going to put up with taking orders from you for so long. When I get word from my commanders-"

"If you get word," Goodkin said.

"When," Burnett said, louder. "When I get word, I will be giving the order to assault the ship. Then the finest fighting men in the world will be all over that bloated, frilly excuse for a boat and Hussein won't be alive long enough to complain about it."

Goodkin flicked on the com.

"Hussein," he said, "please respond. And don't act rashly. I swear to you that there are no teams on that boat."

Goodkin watched the second hand on the bridge clock. It seemed to take several minutes to make a one minute cycle.

They were silent on the bridge, waiting.

Hussein finally replied. "Your words mean nothing, Goodkin. All I've gotten from you is deception. Swear on something important. Swear on the lives of your children."

"Hussein, we need to build trust. I've already told you-"

"This is how you build trust! Swear!"

Goodkin squeezed his forehead. "I swear on the lives of my children that there are no commandos on your vessel."

"On the lives of your children, yes? Hm, seeing how your nation treated the children of my country, I am not so sure I believe you even now. I must consult with my team. I will call you back within the hour."

The speakers popped as the connection broke.

"You think he's buying your promise?" Burnett asked.

"Should I buy yours?" Goodkin snapped.

"Probably, being as I'm not a terrorist."

"Just don't make me look like a liar to this guy. So help me."

"So help your children."

The Bonnie Jane internal phone rang. Dunn picked it up. "Go ahead, first mate. Yes. I will. You're sure it's authentic? Confirmed? Hold on." He put his hand over the mouthpiece.

"The Kariqistan ambassador wants to speak with the negotiator."

"That's odd," Goodkin said.

He tapped his tablet's screen. "Hey, team, why didn't any of you tell me the Kariqistan ambassador was calling?"

Goodkin pushed his earpiece in.

"Went through his own channels? You're supposed to be filtering all communication avenues. You've got a whole team of people there. Dialogue regulation is one of our core priorities. He should go through- oh, forget it. Let me take this. Yes, I'll broadcast it to you as I talk. But you guys have got to be more on the ball. You're supposed to be supporting me. So support, damn it."

Goodkin took the phone from Dunn.

"This is Nelson Goodkin, Federal Negotiator for the United States. Hello, Ambassador. Yes. Yes. But-. Sir, if I could just-. Sir, please. Please. Sir. I'm trying to tell you, but you keep talking. There are several things he- several. All multinationals removed from Kariqistani land. I know- No- Sir- western forces out of all Muslim countries. Sir- Mister Ambassador- Sir- fifty million dollars."

Dunn and Burnett could hear the Ambassador's yelling through the handset. Goodkin shifted his balance as he listened and waited for silence.

"Does that guy ever take a breath?" Burnett mumbled to Dunn.

Goodkin spoke. "Mister Ambassador, those are the- that's what I- those are the- same things that I want, sir. Only I don't- we don't- know them enough to know about their families. No, sir. I wouldn't suggest that even if we did. Because we don't kidnap innocent people. That would make us as bad as- Yes, sir."

Goodkin pinned the handset between his chin and shoulder. He balanced his tablet in his left hand, massaging his temple with his right thumb.

The ambassador kept yelling.

Goodkin shifted his stance.

The ambassador yelled some more.

"That bastard sounds good and mad," Dunn mumbled to Burnett.

Goodkin shifted his balance again, then interrupted the yelling by raising his voice.

"Mr. Ambassador, I certainly appreciate- I said appreciate we have your permission- Sir, that's not- Sir, we try to talk it out. We don't just kill everyone- There are hostages, they could- no, I was unaware Congress has been calling for that- I agree- a declaration of war is bad. No, I can't make it go away. Not even if we kill them all."

Goodkin rolled his eyes up and leaned his head back, letting his mouth pull open.

"Even if no hostages die. I know they don't - they don't speak for all Kariq- No, we can't just black out the media. I know what happened- Sir- Sir, that was an accident. I'm trying- Sir. Please. You're not- let me finish. I'm sure- I know- children will die if there is a war. I'm trying to avoid any violence, why- I am talking-"

Goodkin fell silent and listened. He shifted his posture several times. The ambassador continued ranting.

Finally, Goodkin yelled, "We can't just go in shooting!"

Burnett tilted his head and raised an eyebrow.

Goodkin turned his back to him. "We can't just sink the boat and blame it on the terrorists. We don't go in shooting. We talk first! No- no- It's not- I don't- no, I don't want to defy you, sir. I understand you are important, it's just that, if- if we- if- if- if we do, hostages might die. I understand it will likely be- sir- sir- sir- Oh, forget it."

Goodkin slammed the phone down.

He held his tablet up to his face and yelled at it. "Hello! Could someone out there run damage control for me? Make yourselves useful for once. And what's this rumor of an impending missile strike against Kariqistan? Or declaration of war? Well, find out!"

4

"Okay, on to the ballroom then," North said.

Holland laughed. "Are you asking me on a date or admitting my plan makes sense?"

"Oh, it makes sense, I just doubt you'll have the patience to execute it. We're supposed to sneak up behind them and hide until they return to their stations so there's less of them guarding the hostages. Good idea. Now why would I suspect you'll break cover and start shooting?"

"Because you've got a personal problem with me?"

"No."

"Because you have a problem with women in general?"

North ignored her, following the decorative wooden signs that guided them from the security monitoring room. Guns out, they jogged along, making sure their feet landed softly. North held up his fist to signal a stop. Holland halted, spinning to watch their backs.

North peeked around the corner.

"Clear," he whispered and moved forward.

"There's no way they would leave the hostages alone," Holland said.

"If they're doing a serious headcount, maybe they'd just lock the prisoners in."

"Or maybe they're amateurs."

"Or they're implementing the final protocol they were talking about. Whatever that is."

The hall ended in a staircase. A smiling mermaid carved into a wooden sign pointed up with her right hand. In her left she held a seashell that contained the words "Bridge and Plaza del Sol ballroom this way."

"Now we're getting serious," North said "You ready?"

"You don't ever have to ask."

North kept his gun aimed at the top of the stairs as he walked up to the next level. He passed another wooden sign welcoming him to the Plaza del Sol deck. Painted dolphins indicated all the destinations on this level. One pointed toward the bridge, one in the opposite direction for the ballroom. The others showed the way to the gym, the spa and the outside deck.

"Game time," Holland whispered.

North flattened himself against the wall and signaled all clear.

Holland moved past him to the next intersection.

Using this leap-frogging formation, they covered each other, passing lounges and bars identified with the names of Caribbean islands: the Jamaica room, the Caymans room, the Bahamas room.

North peeked around a corner. He ducked back and signaled for Holland to hold.

"What's up?" she whispered.

North didn't answer. He watched as a terrorist tested the door handles along the hall, making sure they were locked before heading down to another set of doors, checking them before heading off in the direction of the bridge.

Holland peeked around North.

"Let me take him out," she said.

"No," North whispered.

The terrorist was almost clear.

Holland stepped around North and into the hall, gun out. North smacked her hand aside.

The terrorist turned a corner. Holland darted back into cover. North grabbed her and pulled her into a nearby men's room. He closed the door and whirled on Holland.

"What the hell are you doing?"

"I wanted to kill him."

"Why? That would attract unnecessary attention."

"How can he pay attention if he's dead?"

"From his comrades, you idiot."

"Don't call me an idiot."

"I have a problem with killing when it's not absolutely necessary."

"Who cares? They're terrorists. Besides, it looks better for both of us."

"Looks better? What the hell?"

"Yeah. The mission is more impressive if there's casualties. And if the Navy SEALs are going to come in and kill them anyway, what's the difference?"

"Where are you getting this crap?"

"Addison told me I need more field experience to get ahead."

"Addison. I should have known. Never met the guy before and I hated him the first time I saw him this morning. How much field experience does he have?"

"I don't know."

"Exactly. He's probably the one putting that glass ceiling above you."

"But now he can't. I've got a kill."

"And he told you that you needed kills?"

"He didn't say as much."

"What did he say?"

"He said they were short staffed and this was a golden opportunity."

"So where was the rest of the staff?"

"I don't know. I doubt he even knew. It's all secret. How would he know?"

"Good point. I just don't want-"

Holland cut him off. "My resume and my education are as glowing as they can get. If I add field experience, they'll have to promote me next time there's an opening. They'll have to."

"Look," North said. "There's nothing more dangerous than someone with something to prove, okay? There's no I in team."

"And there's no team in I. Hit your head on the glass ceiling long enough and you'll learn that."

"All right. Look. No random killings, okay? If you want, I'll lie and say you killed as many as you want. That way we're both happy. All right?"

"I'll think about it."

"By the way. Are you and Addison a thing?"

"Why do you ask that?"

"That's a yes."

"You're confusing a thing with a trade. He probably is, too. Men. You say you want no strings attached, but then you always come back to the well."

"Hell, I can skip the editorial," North said. "Forget I asked."

"Girl's gotta do what a girl's gotta do. Aren't you military types the ones always talking about full-spectrum dominance?"

"I didn't realize the spectrum went into my crotch."

"Then maybe you should stop being a judgmental jerk about how I do things. I'm half your age and just as far in my career."

"Only in the private sector."

"Is there another one?"

They stared at each other for a while before North spoke.

"I vote we get moving now," he said, shaking his head.

"Please. Let's."

North crept out of the men's room, Holland close behind.

He slid forward pressed against the wall, gun raised and ready. At the ballroom's double doors he kneeled and peeked through the space between them. The room was quiet, except for the occasional cough and some whispered, tense conversation.

"Any bandits in there?" she swung her gun up and down the hall, covering North from both directions.

"Seems clear," North said. "But I can't see the corners of the-"

"Good enough."

Holland reached over him and grabbed both handles. She threw the doors wide, smashing them inward. The hostages yelped and tilted over, ducking as low as they could, curling themselves against the floor and screaming.

North was left crouched in the open doorway.

He had no choice but to enter the ballroom and scan for any bandits he might have missed. Holland strode in, gun sweeping across the room in her right hand, hushing the prisoners with her left index finger over her lips.

North cursed under his breath. He pulled the doors closed quietly behind him.

The hostages stared up at them, their eyes wide. Their gazes followed North and Holland's every move.

Whispers floated around the room.

"Are you here to save us?"

"They're not like the others, no voice-boxes."

"But they look similar."

"The good guys have arrived."

"Oh, thank God!"

"We're getting out of here!"

"Get me out of here!"
"Praise him! Praise the lord!"
"We're free!"
"Cut me loose."
"God bless America!"

Holland and North shushed them, but no one listened.

They tried again, but the murmur of excitement and elation grew louder.

"Shut up!" Holland said frantically, jabbing her gun at them.

The room quieted.

"Does anyone here know a Danforth Percy Sinclair?" she whispered.

The hostages looked around, heads swiveling.

Finally someone spoke up. "The rich guy? With the singer wife?"

North turned, looking in the general direction of the speaker. He couldn't make out exactly who was talking.

"That's him," North said. He pulled out a copy of the tabloid page Addison had given them and held it up. "This guy. Has anyone seen him?"

There were several replies, each talking over the other.

"One at a time," North said.

"He was here," a captive said. "They took him."

"Took him?"

Suddenly the prisoners were all talking at once again.

"Who cares about him?"

"Let us go!"

"They're going to be coming back soon."

"We have to get out of here!"

"Who are you people?"

"How many of them are there?" North asked.

"Let us out. You're here to rescue us, right?"

"Cut our binds!"

"Are you guys the Green Berets?"

"Quiet!" Holland yelled. The ballroom chatter fell to a low murmur. She swept her gun over the crowd, finally pointing it at the man nearest her. "You. Only you talk. How many of them are there?"

"You don't have to point the gun," he said, leaning backwards. "I'd say there's less than a dozen."

"Do you know where Sinclair is?" she pointed to the page North was holding.

"No. They took six people away. He was one of them. You've got to let us out."

"Where were they taken?"

"I don't know. They didn't say. We heard gunshots after they left."

"Let us go!" someone yelled and the room erupted into pleas again.

Holland yelled over them as she moved toward the door. "We'll be back for you," she said, "but first we have to go take care of these bad guys, all right?"

"They killed the others!"

"Just let us go!"

"We'll escape somehow."

"We'll swim."

"Cut us free!"

The entire room was loudly begging for release.

"Shut up!" Holland screamed, her demand drowned out by angry buzzing of the crowd.

"We need to leave now," North yelled. "He's not here."

"Help us! Help us! Help us!" the crowd started chanting in unison.

They darted back out into the hall. North closed the double doors gently, cutting off the sound.

"This whole adventure keeps getting weirder," North said. "We better find him and roll out quick. That bandit I saw, the one you wanted to kill, he was checking the doors along the other side of the hall here. If he's making sure they're locked, someone or something must be in there. Let's try them."

"But the hostages just said the ones that were taken out were killed."

"They don't know that. If they were killed, where are the bodies? Terrorism is part showmanship. Why not put them on display? If they didn't know who Sinclair was, why would they take him away but not kill him? If they knew he was rich, why not make a big deal about having him? Something is off here. Humor me, all right?"

"Maybe they don't-"

"Just stay focused!" North snapped. "I told you you've got nothing to prove to me. So stop arguing over everything. We need to confirm Sinclair's status, okay? Damn it, Holland. You're really pissing me off."

"Easy for you to say there's nothing to prove. I won't ever be denied a promotion because I didn't have enough in-mission kills. That's not going to happen ever again."

"Yes it will. They'll come up with some other B.S. excuse. Damn, if your attitude is the future of the company, then screw it, I might as well quit."

"Well, look at that. We agree on something."

5

"Just a screwdriver?" Martin asked Zack. "Is that all that was there? They had to have a knife or a box cutter. Something."

"The cupboard was bare, yo," Zack said. Brittany was napping, leaning her head on his shoulder. She sniffled as Zack rubbed his cheek against her scalp.

"Martin," Gwen said, "the boy was brave to go at all. Leave him alone. Let's try to make it work." She rocked on her buttocks until she was facing away from him. "Now, give me the screwdriver. Put the handle in my palm."

Back to back, they felt for each other's hands. Gwen held the screwdriver upright.

"Now I'll hold it tight," she said, "and you rub against it."

They paused for a moment. Yvonne Windstorm giggled. "If this wasn't so serious, that would have been a funny."

"If you say so," Gwen said, not smiling.

Martin lifted up his hands and felt for the tool's blade, pressing down so it slid between his wrists and the plastic tie. He leaned against the screwdriver with all his weight. Gwen could hold it for only a few seconds before she lost her grip.

"Keep trying," she said.

"There has to be a better way."

"There probably is, but until anyone thinks of it, we'll do this."

"All right. Hold it tight this time."

"I am."

They tried again.

"Is there anything I can do?" Yvonne Windstorm asked.

Martin's weight knocked the screwdriver out of Gwen's hands.

"Damn it," he said. "Hold it steady."

"When you put your weight behind it, it's too much."

Yvonne Windstorm giggled.

Martin and Gwen tried again.

Gwen shook, holding the screwdriver upright with all her strength. Martin reared up so he was squatting, back to back with his wife. The screwdriver caught his plastic tie and sharply bent it, but didn't break through. He shook, the blade pressed against the binding for a few seconds until he slipped. He fell hard, the screwdriver scraping his arm.

"Damn it!" he yelled.

Gwen looked over her shoulder and saw the screwdriver lying on the floor, drops of blood around it.

"You're bleeding."

"It cut my wrist. God damn it. You were holding it at an angle."

"I was holding it so you could get leverage."

Brittany awoke with a high-pitched yelp. Zack nuzzled against her as she blinked, and yawned.

"How's your head?" she said to Zack.

"A little sore, but you know me, girl, skull hard as rock, no doubt." He lifted his chin toward Martin. "Yo, G. You got clipped."

"I know. I know. It's not bad."

"All right," Gwen said. "Let's take a break. Try to stop the bleeding."

"Nothing is going to cut these bindings," Sinclair said. "Save yourself the trouble."

"Oh, now you're interested in helping," Gwen said.

"I didn't say I was helping, lady. I just don't want to hear any more complaining."

"Well, excuse us, your highness."

"Danny, shush," Windstorm added.

They were quiet as Martin pressed his wrists together.

Gwen broke the silence. "Mr. Sinclair, why don't you just buy them off? Pay them whatever ransom they want? You can afford it." She turned to Windstorm. "You're rich, too, right? Don't you have access to his money?"

"Sorry, lady," Sinclair said. "I'm not stupid. I made her sign a pre-nup."

"Gwen, that's not the right approach," Martin said. "Let's not turn on each other."

"I'm not turning on anyone. We're working together. We don't need your gun. We don't need anything but Lord Big Shot's checkbook."

Sinclair laughed. "I already went over this in the ballroom. Hell, this whole boat's infested with parasites. But since I must, I'll repeat myself. Like I told the others, if these thugs find out who I am, they'll want more money than whatever they're already asking for. Then it will take longer for you to get out of here and go back to your pathetic life."

"Bull. Whatever they're asking for, you can afford it."

Brittany wiped her nose on the shoulder of Zack's jersey. "That's not a bad idea, mister. Can you help?"

"Danny? Danny boo-boo?" Windstorm said. She tilted her head and pouted, "What do you say?"

"I say this is crap. I hate this stupid cruise and I have hated it since the second we boarded. I knew the rabble would be a problem, but you wanted your fame. They'll have cell phones, you said. It will go viral, you said. Whine. Whine. Whine."

"Bullshit, Danny," Windstorm said. "You agreed to this because it was cheap and there was a penthouse suite. That way you didn't have to interact with humanity. You never would have left your room if armed men hadn't dragged you out of there."

"Everyone, let's stay calm," Martin said. "No need to get hysterical. If he pays them to let us go, that money will fund terrorism. We need to speak their language. We need my gun."

"Your husband said it, lady," Sinclair said to Gwen. "Now be a good wife and listen to him."

"What if I turn you in?" she asked.

"What?"

"Gwen, stop it!" Martin said. "Stop it now."

She ignored him. "You heard me, Sinclair. Danny boo-boo. When they come back in here, what if I point you out? What if I say, 'You want to get really rich? Hold on to the shriveled turd over there.' Then maybe they'll let me go. I don't have one-tenth of your money. You can't spare a dime for me, but maybe you'll spare it for yourself."

"Oh, my God, honey," Martin said. "You sound like a socialist."

"Shut up, Martin. You don't even know what a socialist is."

"What it be like, moneybags?" Zack said. "Lady Spitfire here has more points than Jordan."

Sinclair struggled to sit up. "Someone translate what this hooligan is saying."

"Duh," Brittany said. "He's asking if you're, like, going to pay them. If you don't, we'll tell them you can. Then they'll let us go and just keep you."

"Gwen," Martin said, "look what you've done. You've brainwashed the children."

"Brains? No. Washed? Definitely not," Sinclair said.

Zack shrugged off Brittany. Wiggling, he moved himself next to Sinclair.

"What are you doing?" Sinclair said, just as Zack leaned back and head-butted the older man in the shoulder. Sinclair fell on his side with a thud.

"Yo, bitch!" Zack yelled. "Use your eye teeth and watch your tongue when you talk to my girl."

Sinclair stayed down, catching his breath.

"Oh, now I'm convinced," he said. "This goon physically assaults me and you expect me to help? That's great salesmanship." He righted himself and shifted away from Zack, who wriggled back to Brittany's side.

"Gwen, honey," Martin said, "we are not going to get out of here by buying our way out. Or by agitating the kids."

"Then how are we going free, Martin? Shooting our way out with a gun that's still in our room? Stabbing them with a screwdriver while we're all bound? Maybe we can all bite their ankles."

"What about those boom noises?" Windstorm said. "Wasn't that the army or something attacking?"

"Whatever it was, nothing more has come of it," Martin said. "We're on our own."

"Why don't we vote?" Brittany said.

"I don't like it," Martin said.

"Too bad," Gwen said. "All in favor of having Mister Sinclair offer up a fraction of his wealth, say aye."

"Doesn't matter," Sinclair said. "I'm not doing it."

"Then we'll turn you in. All in favor, say aye."

"Aye," Brittany said.

"Aye, you," Zack said.

"Aye," Gwen said.

"Nay," Martin said, "I'm not going to take part in the tyranny of the majority."

"I believe Mister Sinclair is a no," Gwen said. "So the vote is three to two in favor of turning our rich friend over to the terrorists. It's on you, Miss Windstorm. Do you want to pay these people a little bit of your husband's huge wealth, or stay here as prisoners and possibly be killed?"

"Well-"

"It's all you, girl," Zack said. "Stalemate or go."

"I just want this to end. Danny, I'm sorry."

"Vote how you like," Sinclair said. "I'm not doing it."

"Danny, we have to help these people. And ourselves."

"That reasoning is why it took you so long to get out of the trailer park," Sinclair said. He snorted. "And without me, you'd still be there."

Windstorm bowed her head and stared at the floor a long time. When she looked up, her eyes were watering.

"Count me in," she whispered.

"Majority rules," Gwen said. "Now, when they come in-"

Sinclair cut her off. "Fifty thousand. For your silence. No one says who I am. Fifty thousand."

"Oh damn," Zack said. "Fifty G? Each?"

"That's right, young man," Sinclair said. "More money than you'll ever see working at whatever fast food place is foolish enough to hire you."

"Mister Sinclair," Martin said, "let me apologize for my wife. She's just very stressed, as you can understand."

"This is assuming we live," Gwen said.

Sinclair smiled. "Of course."

"Only fifty-thousand?"

"Yo, do I get a bonus?" Zack said. "I got the screwdriver."

"I think you can do better, Sinclair," Gwen said. "One hundred thousand. For each one of us."

"Gwen!" Martin yelled.

She kept her eyes on Sinclair. "This is all peanuts to him," she said, "And he knows it. And you know it too."

"You're pushing your luck," Sinclair said.

"Christ, Danny," Windstorm said. "You're cheap even when it comes to saving your own life."

"Everyone stop it!" Brittany screamed the room into silence. "How can we talk like this? He's a person. We can't just send him to them." She sniffled. "You can keep your money, Mister Sinclair. I'm changing my vote. I won't say anything."

"Thank you," Sinclair said. "If only my wife was as loyal. You know, you remind me of her when she was much younger, much more innocent. Fresh. Unspoiled. Mmm... New." He narrowed his eyes at her.

"Yo, creepazoid," Zack said, sticking out his chest. "Stop droolin' or I head-butt you across the room this time."

Then he turned to Gwen. "Hold up. I'm lost, yo. Leader Lady, what the deal? We still on?"

"Votes are even now with your girlfriend backing off, but I don't care. Sinclair, does your offer stand? Even if it was me alone, I could say something."

"Gwen, now that's unfair," Martin said. "You lost the vote."

"No. It's tied. Anyone of us could blow his cover at any moment. That's why he made the deal for all of us, even you, even though you voted for him. Isn't that right, Sinclair?"

Sinclair said nothing.

"I'll take that as a yes. So, are we still on? One hundred thousand," she said. "For our silence. Right, Mr. Sinclair?"

"Right," Sinclair muttered.

"I didn't hear you."

"One. Hundred. Thousand. For. Everyone," Sinclair spat each word, his splotchy pale face turning purple. Jagged blue veins showed through his translucent skin. "As long as you keep your damn mouths shut. Starting now!"

6

"Hussein," Goodkin said, "this is all getting out of control. Let's talk about letting some hostages go. How about the women and children? Or the elderly? Just a few to start, to show your good intent. Hussein?"

"Goodkin." Hussein's voice crackled over the Bonnie Jane's speakers. "You will have to wait. I am checking on my comrades. Pray that none of them are missing."

"You're running out of time, Hussein. You won't have necessary food and water forever. Some of the older people probably need medicinal assistance."

"This I do not see as a problem. If you rush me, I can provide them as corpses."

"No. No. That won't be-"

"Then we have as much time as I say we have."

"Okay. Okay. Just, um, just call me when you're ready to talk."

"I will."

Goodkin hung up.

"Why are they keeping the lifeboats?" Burnett said. "Why haven't they cut them loose and pushed them away?"

"They know your snipers are out there," Goodkin said.

"True, but they have their human shields. If some of the hostages were to get free, they could escape in a lifeboat."

"After the news chopper, they're not sure if you'll shoot or not."

"So you're saying we did the right thing downing that chopper? That it's keeping them off guard?"

"Could be a suicide mission," Dunn said. "Maybe they figure, Why bother? Maybe everyone in there is already dead. Even the six we saw earlier."

"Good point," Burnett said.

"It's not a suicide mission," Goodkin said. "We've already investigated that contingency. It doesn't compute. They're disguising their voices so they must want to reintegrate into society somewhere. If this was a suicide mission, they would have killed the hostages and made a show of it. Or told us about a bomb. They haven't done any of that. There's got to be some other reason the boats are still there."

"What then?" Burnett said.

"I don't know."

"There's something college boy doesn't know?"

"I don't care to know. It's irrelevant."

"You don't know if they're suicidal and you consider that irrelevant?"

"Maybe they just forgot about the rafts," Dunn said. "Or overlooked it in all the excitement. But that's just my opinion. I call it how I see it."

"I'd appreciate it if you would both stop calling it at all," Goodkin said. "You're muddying the water."

"Maybe they intend to let some people off?" Dunn said.

Goodkin held up his palm. "Captain Dunn. Please stop. You too, Burnett. Okay? Just stop. No speculation. We deal only in known knowns."

Dunn shrugged.

"I say we make it a suicide mission for them anyway," Burnett said.

"Not yet," Goodkin said. "For now we wait."

His tablet emitted a chirping sound.

"Besides, I've got to check in," he lifted the mic bud to his mouth.

"I'll do the same," Burnett said, tapping his earpiece.

Both men exited the bridge, pacing the walkways on opposite sides of the boat.

Dunn was alone.

"I should lock the damn doors," he mumbled to himself.

7

The door handle rattled.

All six of the prisoners - Brittany, Zack, the Marigolds, Danforth Percy Sinclair and Yvonne Windstorm - looked up.

The handle kept rattling.

"Did they forget their key?" Gwen asked.

Her husband shushed her.

With a pop the door creaked open.

Brittany began whimpering as two masked figures entered, guns drawn. The others bowed their heads, watching the visitors' every move with their peripheral vision.

North and Holland led with their silenced pistols. They stepped into the room and quietly pressed closed the door. North moved along the right wall, Holland took the left.

The six hostages watched them quietly.

Holland reached the back of the room first.

"Clear," she said.

"Clear," North replied. He reached into the slit of his wet suit that functioned as a pocket. He stood above the six hostages and pulled out the tabloid page, examined it and pointed to Sinclair.

"You," he said. "What's your name?"

"Who wants to know?" Sinclair asked. "Are you with them?"

"Answer the question, sir. Your name?"

"Uh, Johnson. Why aren't you two wearing those things to distort your voices?"

"Is it really, sir?" North said. "Johnson?"

"Uh, yes," Sinclair said.

North stared down at him, then back to the picture.

Yvonne Windstorm spoke. "And I'm his wife. Uh, Sarah Johnson."

"Do you always have to think about what your name is?" Holland said. Then to North, "It's them."

North turned the page around, showing the hostages the photo from the tabloid that Addison had given them. "We're looking for the man in this picture, and this guy here looks a lot like him."

"I can see the resemblance," Gwen said. "But it's not him."

"And the woman in the picture looks like you," North said, pointing to Windstorm.

"We're impersonators," she said. "We pretend we're celebrities so the people have a good cruise."

"You're what?"

"Yeah," Zack said. "Riddle me this, yo. Why a rich guy like that be on a cruise with workin' peeps like us?"

Holland rolled her eyes. "Stop dicking around. It's him," she pulled out her knife. "I'll handle this."

The other hostages screamed and leaned away. Sinclair tried to scurry free, but only fell on his back, thrashing.

"Sir," Holland said. "We're here to help you."

"You are? Are you sure?"

"Yes. You know why we're here. You know who we work for. You called."

Sinclair stopped struggling.

"But you look just like the people holding us," Brittany said.

"Yeah," Windstorm said. "This is some kind of trick."

"Shut up, Yvonne," Sinclair said.

"I thought her name was Sarah," Holland said, smirking. "Mister Sinclair, if you'll let me near, I'll set you free."

Sinclair stuck his legs out.

Holland slid her knife between his ankles and sliced his bindings.

"Finally!" Sinclair said. "It's about damn time."

Holland moved behind him and cut the plastic ties around his wrists. She helped him to his feet.

"Oh, thank God! We're saved," Gwen Marigold cheered.

"You're the good guys," Martin said. "Superb! We finally caught a break."

"We still get paid, right, gramps?" Zack said. "We didn't tell. Word is bond."

"I was wondering when you were going to get here," Sinclair said to North and Holland. He rubbed his wrists where the bindings had left dark purple lines. "You sure took your time."

"We came as fast as possible," Holland said.

"But not nearly fast enough. When I get in touch with my account rep, I'm going to rip your whole damn company a new one."

"Customer?" Gwen asked.

"Mr. Sinclair, this is not the time for talking," North said. "We need you to do exactly as we say or your safety will be in jeopardy. If you have a complaint, you can contact customer service once we're clear. For now, come with us."

"Account rep? Customer service?" Gwen said. "What the hell is this? Aren't you going to free us?"

"We are here for Mr. Sinclair only," Holland said. "The Coast Guard is outside. They will take care of you."

"How come he gets special treatment?"

"Come with us, sir," North said, guiding Sinclair towards the door.

"What about us?" Brittany whined. "Are you coming back for us?"

"Yeah, we'll be back," Holland said. "In ah, just a few minutes. Sit tight and don't make a sound."

"You're lying!"

"Why don't we leave as a group? This is ridiculous." Gwen looked around at the other captives, her eyes watering.

"What about me? I'm his wife," Windstorm cried. "Please, what about me?"

"Only him, miss," Holland said.

"Yo, this is whack," Zack added.

"But we're married!" Windstorm said.

"You're wasting my time," Sinclair barked at North and Holland.

"The Coast Guard is coming for the rest of you," Holland said. "Please stay calm."

"Who the hell are you people?" Martin asked.

"You only paid for yourself, didn't you, Danny?" Windstorm said, whining. "You cheap asshole."

"Paid?" Martin said, "What the hell? We all pay taxes."

Sinclair, North and Holland were at the exit.

"Wait a minute," Gwen said. "Whoever you are. They've been coming in here and counting us. If one of us is gone, they'll think he escaped and they'll take it out on us."

"This is crazy," Brittany said. "Help us! Do something!"

"Yeah," Martin said. "Why don't you wait here and kill the terrorists when they come back?"

"We're not here for you and we're not here for them," Holland said.

"I didn't pay for a debate. I want to go now!" Sinclair said. North put his hand on the door handle. Holland drew her gun.

"What the hell kind of rescue is this?" Gwen said. "When I get home, my senator is going to get an earful. I'll go to the media."

"Go ahead," Holland said. "We're leaving."

"Holland will lead," North said to Sinclair. "Then you, then me. Got that?"

"Yes."

Yvonne Windstorm screeched across the room. "Danny, if you leave me here, I'm going to tell them what happened. I'm going to give the terrorists a description of you and tell them which way you went, so they'll find you. In fact, I might start screaming now."

"Help!" she screamed.

"Ignore her," Holland said. "Let's move out."

"Help!" Windstorm screamed, louder.

"Help us!" Brittany screamed.

"Help! Help!" Gwen joined in.

"Gwen, stop that," Martin said. "It's childish."

"Yo, terror freaks!" Zack bellowed. "We got commandos up inda club!"

North opened the door a crack. The hostages yelled louder. He quickly closed the door again.

"Damn it," he muttered.

"Help!" Brittany, Zack, Gwen and Windstorm cried out. They fell into a synchronized chant. "Help! Help! Help!"

"Stop it!" Martin yelled at them. "This isn't productive!"

They all quieted as Sinclair walked back to his wife, smiling tenderly. He kneeled before her, gently kissing the top of her head before cupping her face in his hands.

"Danny, baby," she said, crying. "You're going to leave me, aren't you?"

"Darling. They can only take one."

"But I'm your wife. Doesn't that mean anything?"

"Sir," Holland said. "You were just complaining about us going slow. Now you're holding us up."

"Honey? Danny?"

"Sugar Dimples," Sinclair said, his voice low and smooth. "When they rescue you, there's going to be lots of media. Hundreds of news people and their cameras. And they're all going to focus on you. Your fans will write letters of support. Your name will be all over the internet. When the world sees you emerging from here, you'll be wanted on every television show in the world. All for free."

Windstorm looked up at him, tears running down her cheeks. "Are you sure?" she whispered, sniffling.

"It will be publicity even I couldn't buy. I promise."

"Yo, money," Zack said. "If one's the limit, let your lady go and you stay. You're a punk leavin' your girl like this, ya lil bitch."

Sinclair didn't respond. He kept gazing into Windstorm's eyes. "When things get tough, just remember that light at the end of the tunnel is the flash of a thousand cameras. Okay, dear?"

She sniffled. "All right."

North peeked out the door. "It's all clear for now, Mr. Sinclair. We should go."

"Good luck, my dear. My sweetheart, my star among stars," Sinclair said. He kissed Windstorm's head once more as he rose.

"Don't just leave us here," Martin yelled out. "Can you at least get me my gun?"

"Look," North said. "I'm sorry it has to be like this."

"But it doesn't. You can help."

"I'm afraid it does," North said.

"My gun's in room 446. Crystal Beach level," Martin said, talking quickly. "Can you get it?"

"That's not too far," North said, hesitating.

"No, it's not."

"It's two levels down," Holland said. "Come on, North, don't get soft. Not now."

North strode over to Martin, pulling out his knife.

"Hold your hands out," he said. Martin did.

"More damn delays," Sinclair said.

North cut the plastic ties around Martin's wrists. Martin immediately started tugging at the bindings around his ankles.

"Martin, please," Gwen said. "Don't do anything stupid."

North arrived back at the door. "Ready," he said.

"What the hell?" Holland said. "If they get out, they're going to know we're here."

"No. Now they'll just think all six escaped."

"Excuse me," Sinclair said. "You're supposed to be focusing on me."

Holland pushed open the door.

North looked back at the hostages. Martin was pulling at the bindings around his wife's wrists.

"Good luck," North said. "Get off the boat as quickly as you can."

"Yeah, no kidding," Gwen said. "Thanks for nothing."

"I mean it, there's a bomb in the engine room."

"A what?"

The five remaining hostages yelled questions after him. North didn't answer. He was out the door, closing it gently behind him.

Out in the hall, Holland led, signaling for Sinclair to follow.

"Sorry we couldn't bring your wife, sir," North whispered.

Sinclair shrugged.

"Ah, forget it. It was time for a new one anyway."

8

"Now what, Goodkin?" Burnett said as he returned to the bridge. "This situation is running away from you fast."

"Well, at least no one has gotten killed yet," Goodkin said. He looked up from tapping his tablet screen. "Except by you."

"Nice try. You gave the order."

"For a warning shot. It was your crew that killed them. Are you saying you don't have full command of your vessel?"

"Don't mess with me, college boy."

"Fellas," Dunn said. "This is my ship and if I have to, I'm kicking you both off the bridge and locking you up in separate rooms."

"Goodkin!" Hussein's robotic voice ruptured through the speakers. "Goodkin! We have completed our head count. Two of my men are confirmed missing."

"Hussein, I assure you I don't know about that," Goodkin said. "Perhaps they're lost."

"No, Goodkin. No. We are certain. Two of my men are missing. Where are they?"

"Hussein, I have forbidden anyone from boarding the ship. I want this to end peacefully as much as you do."

"There will be severe consequences for my guests if those men are not found immediately."

"Hussein, all I care about is the safety of the hostages."

Fran Amaretto cut in. "Hussein, exactly what are you prepared to do if your men are not found?"

"Just be sure to keep filming," Hussein said slowly. "You will not be disappointed."

"Miss Amaretto," Goodkin said firmly, "do I need to bring in a more cooperative network? Do not communicate on this channel."

The line went silent.

"Hussein, I will be in touch." Goodkin hung up the com.

"I'm surprised," Dunn said. "The reporter lady actually listened to you."

Burnett grumbled. "I still think Hussein has jelly for a spine. I haven't seen him kill anyone."

"Anyone we know of," Goodkin said.

"Ask him to produce a dead body. Say you want to return it to the family."

"Why don't I call him a coward, too? He's taken over a ship with a small team. It makes total sense to question his courage and claim he's bluffing."

"Be sarcastic all you want," Burnett said. "But he keeps extending the deadline. Why hasn't he tossed out a corpse to prove he's serious?"

"Maybe he's not the monster you think he is," Dunn said.

"Maybe he's not the killer you both think he is."

"Why do I keep opening my damn mouth?"

"He keeps threatening," Burnett said, "but there's been no action. What do you make of that?"

Dunn answered. "That Mr. Goodkin here is good at his job?"

"Killing isn't as easy as civilians think. Maybe this Hussein guy has never actually done it and he's getting the jitters. I've seen it plenty of times. Guys study war in the classroom, they move pieces around on a table, but I think it's the smell that gets them. That's then we find out who the real men are."

"I've never killed anyone," Goodkin said. "And I think I'm a real man."

Burnett mumbled so only Dunn could hear. "Keep thinking that."

"Even so," Goodkin said. "You do raise a valid point. For once. For as angry as he's said he is, for all his threats, he does not appear to have killed anyone. If he had, why not show us a body? So far, it's just a burnt flag."

"Makes you wonder," Burnett said.

Goodkin hesitated. "A little."

"You know I'm right."

"It's not a bad observation."

"What if it's not a weakness?" Dunn said. "What if there's some other reason?"

No one answered him.

Goodkin spoke to the tablet. "Panel, did you hear that exchange? What do you guys think? Anything in Hussein's psychological profile that reveals he's got a weak stomach?"

9

In the CNB chopper above the Sunset Mist, Fran Amaretto pressed her cell phone hard against her ear.

"We've got a sniper with us, but the guy doesn't talk. I think he's retarded."

Savant betrayed no concern for her comment. He barely moved, his eye pressed to his rifle's scope, scanning the top deck.

"No, I didn't know that," Amaretto continued. "Interesting. I'll ask him. Are you sure? But why? He could buy a fleet of yachts."

She listened.

"He's really that cheap? She's really that desperate? I mean, they seem that way, but in real life? It's as if they're living out their own caricatures. You're sure?"

She scribbled notes on her pad.

"Hold off in the studio, okay? Let me do it. Of course I'll hurry. Who do you think you're talking to? I know, I'll get it out as soon as possible, but I want to see if I can use it to pry out a scoop. Just one call to the negotiator, okay? Relax. Then it's on the air. Promise."

She hung up.

"All right, I've got something," she said to Phil the cameraman.

"What's going on?"

"Count me down. Don't transmit it yet, though. Not until I say so."

Phil hefted his camera. "Got it. In three, two, one…"

"This is Fran Amaretto, still providing exclusive coverage on scene above the hijacked Sunset Mist cruise ship. CNB news has just learned that singer Yvonne Windstorm and her husband, billionaire Danforth Percy Sinclair, are among the hostages. Their fate remains unknown. Stay with us for updates. This is Fran Amaretto for CNB news. And cut."

"Nice," Phil said, lowering the camera. "Real nice."

"You like? Don't send it back to the studio yet. I want to call this Goodkin idiot. See if I can leverage this."

"Hey, Savant," she said as she dialed. "Looks like you're not the story anymore. Your fifteen minutes of fame were over in fifteen seconds. Are you upset?"

"No, ma'am," Savant said at the exact time Amaretto said it, mocking his monotone voice.

10

A telephone graphic blinked on Goodkin's tablet screen.

"Hold on," he said, interrupting the conversation with his advisory team. He checked the incoming call number.

"The CNB reporter is calling me. Yeah, her. I'm going to answer it and you guys should be able to hear everything. Here we go."

Goodkin tapped the phone icon.

"Miss Amaretto," he said, "this isn't a good time."

"I just learned you've got two high-profile people among the hostages."

"I appreciate you trying to get a story, but well, they're all equal in my eyes."

"I don't think so. These captives are a little more equal than others, as they say."

"You have five seconds before I hang up."

"I'm here to make a trade. You give me an exclusive, something the other networks can't possibly get, and I'll give you the names of the people."

"I don't use lives as bargaining chips."

"The hell you don't. That's your whole job."

Goodkin sighed. "You're already the official network of terrorists. What more do you want?"

"I want your Navy buddies to give me someone other than this dud, Savant. You deliver and I'll bury this story."

"So if I don't give you a more primetime-ready sniper, you'll make those two famous people's names known and put them in greater danger than they already are."

"A girl's got to make a living."

"The only thing I'm going to give you is advice. If you mention their names-"

"So, you know who they are?"

"I didn't say that."

"I think you do. You have to know."

"That's irrelevant. It could even be mistaken identity. Regardless, if you mention their names, and they are in fact captive on that ship, you will be tagging them for higher ransom, or possibly for a visible execution. Nothing good can come of you making those names public."

"All right, Goodkin, you had the power to stop this."

"You have the power to stop it!" he yelled. "Just don't broadcast it."

"If I don't, how long before one of the other networks does? Huh? Information like this doesn't stay secret long."

"Then you can all rot."

Goodkin hung up by jabbing the tablet's screen.

"You hear that?" he said. "The media is on to the VIPs we saw on the passenger list. Did you guys get a chance to confirm that yet? Or is some troll on the internet laughing?"

Goodkin paused.

"So it is him. And her. Yeah, I'd heard he was, but that much of a cheapskate? He could buy his own fleet."

Another pause.

"So she had an influence, I take it."

Pause.

"I realize it was only a matter of time, but it still pisses me off. You guys have got to distract them more. Unleash the talking heads, do some historical pieces on Kariqistan. The media is all over me. I'm getting my ass kicked out here."

"Ain't that the truth," Burnett said, hitting Dunn with his elbow. Dunn glared at him.

* * *

"Well, that went swimmingly," Amaretto said. "Screw it, send the footage in."

"Will do," her cameraman said.

Her phone rang. She answered and listened.

"They did? What channel?" Amaretto switched on the television, selecting the MCSBN network, their helicopter a dot in the sky far away. The screen showed a picture of Yvonne Windstorm and Danforth Percy Sinclair, with bold text above them, "Among the captured."

"Damn it, we got scooped," she said, punching the side of the helicopter.

"I wasn't delaying," she said into her phone, "I was trying to parlay that information into something more, but this negotiator guy is a pain in the ass. No, I wasn't getting greedy. Who cares? Just show it. This is a very fluid situation, so go back to your cushy chair and warm it up some more, all right? Air the damn thing."

She hung up.

"Footage has been sent," Phil the cameraman said.

"For what it's worth. We missed being first to the party."

She stared out the window, fuming. Finally she said, "This is your fault, Savant."

Without taking his eye away from his rifle's scope he replied. "Yes, ma'am."

11

Martin was scraping his wife's skin raw as he struggled to pull the plastic tie over her ankles.

"Hey, kid," he said to Zack, "you still watching the door for me?"

"Aye aye, cap'n, yo."

Gwen grunted as she pulled her feet toward her, pressing them together so Martin could fit his fingers inside the binding. At first he was working frantically, then he slowed, then stopped.

"What's wrong?" she asked. "It hurts, but I've got to get out."

"I should go alone."

"No. Please don't."

"I should. If you come with me, and we're caught, then they'll hold it against you too. I'll go alone, get my gun and find something to cut the plastic. I'll be right back."

He sat up.

Gwen was crying. "Martin, no. Please. No."

"One of us should be sure to survive," he said, blinking rapidly. "For our children."

"Yo, G," Zack whispered. "Party crashers."

The door handle to the room was shaking.

Martin kneeled, sitting on his ankles. He held his hands behind his back, pretending he was still bound.

"Remember your promises, everyone," Windstorm said. "Don't mention Danny, or no payday."

Two masked men burst into the room. They approached slowly, their AK-47s lowered. Each step was quiet and deliberate. The captives' eyes were drawn to the end of the barrels as they bobbed casually in the air before their faces.

"There were six of you," one of the terrorists said, his voice distorted. "Now there's five. Where's the other?"

The room was quiet. Each hostage could hear their own heartbeat.

"We're looking for a Danforth Sinclair," the second terrorist said. "We understand he's a wealthy man. Where did he go?"

"He was never here. It's only been us five," Windstorm said.

They turned to her. "You must be his wife. Now tell us. Or we'll take you."

"I think he's in the other room," Gwen said, "with all the other people."

"Shut up," the first one said, focusing on Windstorm, "I only want to hear from her. No one else talks. We know he was in here."

"I don't know where he is," Windstorm said.

The speaking terrorist lunged forward and grabbed Brittany by the hair.

"Zaaaack!" she screamed. Zack struggled forward, but the second terrorist kicked him in the belly, knocking him back. The terrorist rested his boot on Zack's chest.

"…can't…breathe…yo…"

Holding a clump of Brittany's white-blond hair, the terrorist dragged her roughly before Windstorm. Martin shifted, almost rising. Gwen caught his glance. She shook her head "no" in tiny, furious nods.

"There's two of them," she whispered.

The terrorist pushed Brittany's head to the floor, jabbing the barrel of his AK-47 against her temple. He released the safety on his weapon with a loud clack and looked up at Yvonne Windstorm.

"Tell me the truth, or this girl dies."

Brittany's face was bright red behind her scattered hair. Her eyes met Windstorm's.

"Please," her trembling lips formed.

Windstorm closed her eyes and turned her head. "I came on this trip alone," she whispered.

"What?" Brittany squealed.

"Lying," Zack coughed. "Bitch… be… lying… like… a… rug!" The terrorist leaned his weight on Zack, but the boy choked out the words with all his strength, his face turning purple with the effort. "Don't… waste… my… girl… homes… don't… bitch… be… lying."

The terrorist leaned off him. "Explain. Fast."

Gasping, Zack spat the words out. "Her man didn't sneak away. A dude that ancient could never get loose, aight? Two ninjas came in. Took him. Please, don't shoot."

Brittany was crying. She turned her head to look up at the terrorist, the barrel scratching a bright white line from her sunburned temple to just above her eyebrow. "Please," she said, "I'm a person. Just like you. I have parents. A sister. Please."

The terrorist lifted the gun off her and turned to his companion.

"What the boy says fits," he said.

They both backed up across the room and crashed out the door. The hinge pushed it closed, but there was no final click.

"It didn't latch," Martin said. "The others must have damaged the lock."

"Brittany?" Gwen said. "Are you all right?"

Brittany sobbed, still lying on the floor. Zack choked for air. Windstorm sniffled.

Martin started working on his wife's bindings again. "You're right, dear. We'll stay together. Look what they almost did to her."

He ran over to the snack cart.

"Where are you going?"

"I'm looking for anything useful."

He came running back with a jug of hand moisturizer.

"This should help get the bind off, or at least make it burn less."

Quietly, the Marigolds pulled and tugged at Gwen's bindings. Using the screwdriver for leverage and the moisturizer as lubricant, they were able to remove the plastic ties, scraping her skin raw and red as they pulled. Next they both set to work on Zack, who was still gathering his breath. With both of them tugging at the binding and Zack stretching, the tie came loose much quicker.

No one spoke. They all moved about sniffling.

All three then assisted Brittany. Zack held her hand and kissed her head. Once she was free, all four stood up, rubbing their wrists and ankles.

"What about me?" Windstorm asked. "Can't one of you help me?"

They ignored her.

"Hello? People?" she said. "Don't be mad at me. You made a promise. You swore not to say anything about Danny so you could get the money. That was the deal."

"Damn bitch!" Zack growled. He spun and kicked her in the chest with all his strength. Her breath flushed out of her lungs with a whooshing sound. She fell to the deck hard, her head snapping back.

"You almost got that girl killed," Gwen said. "Just to protect a man you clearly don't love and who obviously hates you, even as a trophy. That was lower than anything I've ever seen in my whole life."

Windstorm was gasping for air as Brittany stood over her and spit in her face. "When I get home, I'm deleting all your songs off my MP3 player!"

Martin hurled the screwdriver and moisturizer into a far corner of the room. They landed among a cluster of fake palm trees.

"Fetch," he said.

He then peeked out the door, gave the thumbs up and led the way, all four of them tip-toeing into the hall.

"They're escaping!" Windstorm called out weakly. "They're getting away."

When the door clicked closed, she wailed, all alone.

* * *

Martin led them away from the ballroom, beckoning them to the next hallway intersection.

"All clear," he whispered. "We need to get to the Crystal Beach deck. Our room is 446, in case we get separated."

"Yo, should we jailbreak the others?" Zack said, looking back to the ballroom's double doors. "Start a revolution?"

"We've got to take care of ourselves for now. Head for the stairs," Martin whispered, gently pushing the others past as he watched their backs.

"Yo, we bailin' on this bitch!" Zack said, throwing his arm around Brittany.

She barely reacted, instead shuddering and bowing her head.

Zack was the first down the stairs, leaping from landing to landing, his high-top sneakers slapping the metal.

"Quiet," Martin hissed.

They followed after him.

"Look," Gwen said. She pointed to the corner of the hall, where a shattered camera hung from its stand by a small wire.

"Daaaayyyyym," Zack said. "Eye in the sky got blanked by a nine."

"Keep moving," Martin said. "We don't need a play-by-play."

"Which crib, dawg? I forgot. Short term memory is baked, ya know?"

"Excuse me?"

"Four Four Six," Gwen said, speaking slowly. "Crystal Beach."

Zack bolted ahead, pointed to the correct door and kept running to the far intersection. He checked both directions and then returned to meet them at Room 446.

"All clear like a baby's rear."

Martin walked backwards down the hall.

"Looks good," he said. "No one is following us."

Gwen inserted her card key into the door and pushed it open slowly. The other three followed her in. Zack held the door open a crack, scanning up and down the hall.

"Just making sure we don't get our ass jumped like in the joint," he said.

"Stop acting like you're in an action movie," Gwen said. "This is real. You should see to your girlfriend. I think she's in shock." Zack came away from the door and sat on the bed next to Brittany. She was hunched over, shivering, her hands between her knees.

"My fingers are freezing," she said.

"Come on, baby, you all right, girl." Zack said, rubbing her back.

She sniffled, rubbing her arms. "I'm so cold."

"Yeah, you all right. My girl straight-up gangsta."

Gwen wrapped a blanket around Brittany and dabbed a warm, wet towel on the scrape the rifle barrel had left over her eyebrow. She handed the towel to Zack.

Martin was tearing through his suitcase, tossing clothes wildly.

"Where did you hide the gun?" Gwen asked, watching him. "Were you even going to tell me?"

"No, honey. I wasn't. I know how you feel about guns so I thought it was best you didn't know."

"What if they searched our luggage? What if I was carrying your bag when it was scanned? How did you get it through the metal detectors?"

"Money goes a long way."

"You didn't. Honey. My God."

"Here we go." Martin aimed the automatic pistol at the ceiling. He chambered the first round.

Zack bounced on the bed. "Aw, snap! Dat's da sound of payback in progress."

Brittany bowed her head. "Not so loud."

"They said there was a bomb on board," Gwen said. "What good is a gun?"

"It will help us clear a path out of here."

"To a lifeboat?"

"Good in theory, but when we're halfway to the Coast Guard ship, they'll just gun us down."

"Martin, if our kids were on a ship captured by terrorists, we would tell them to get the hell out of here, not play hero."

"That's because they're children. We're the adults, Gwen."

"That means we should know better."

"We taught them to take responsibility for themselves, not look for a handout."

"Man," Zack said, "I am going to wreck any mofo that tries stop us now. Come on, Master M, let's start wastin' these fools."

"Wait," Martin said. "My wife and I can swim, can you two?"

"Sure, dawg."

"Y-y-yes," Brittany said, her voice quivering.

"Maybe we swim for it."

"How is that different than taking a life raft?" Gwen said. "What about riding it out? Wait for the negotiation?"

"What about da bomb, yo?" Zack said.

"Zack," Martin said, "can you listen at the door while we discuss our options?"

Zack turned to Brittany and cupped her face in his hands. "Yo, baby doll, I'm gone lookout, you need anything call me, aight?"

He stood at the door, peeking out the eyehole.

"What if the bomb's a dirty bomb?" Martin said. "All the waiting, all the talking in the world won't help. We have to shut it down. Get one of them to disarm it."

"Disarm it? Coerce a terrorist?" Gwen said. "Martin, we should use what we know. And what we know is that there are people out there trying to rescue us, and people in here trying to kill us. We need to-"

"Yo!" Zack whispered. "Trouble in da hood!"

Brittany squeaked. Gwen leapt to her side, squeezing her shoulder with one hand, covering the younger girl's mouth with the other.

Martin crept to the door, gun before him.

"Only if necessary," Gwen said softly, nodding at the gun.

Martin didn't acknowledge her as he moved behind Zack.

They could all hear the footsteps, very close. Someone was moving quietly and purposefully.

Someone was hunting.

Brittany squinted and released a high-pitched whimper behind Gwen's hand.

12

Sinclair leaned against a wall and rolled his head back, gasping. His Adam's apple bobbed along his thin neck with each breath, his bony shoulders heaving. North held his arm out, ready to catch him if he collapsed.

Holland doubled back to meet them. "Sir, do you need help?"

Sinclair continued panting, sliding his gaze sideways at her.

"I'm not being sarcastic," she said.

"Maybe you should carry me," Sinclair said. "As compensation for making me wait." He coughed roughly. "Just make sure I get home alive."

"That's what I'm trying to do. But you're moving too slow. And you look ill."

"You make sure no one shoots me, and I'll get there."

"Sir," North said, "we need you to run. Or at least jog."

Sinclair turned to him. "I was assured that your service would be quick and professional. So far, it's neither. Unless you want me to complain to Redfire's board of directors, I suggest you and your partner start treating me like the premium customer I am."

"We're sorry, sir," North said. "Some men with guns held us up."

He was about to go on, but Holland cut him off. "Mr. Sinclair, we're trying to deliver those results right now. We need to keep the pace quick, all right?"

She bolted down the hall and turned a corner.

Sinclair limped after her. "That steroid bitch is pissing me off," he said.

"She's trying her best, sir," North said, following.

"Well, you're pissing me off too, for the record," Sinclair said. "Where are we going, anyway?"

"The bottom deck. We have a sub waiting for us. We jump down and we're gone."

"I'm not doing any jumping."

"It's not far."

"I refuse."

"I'll help you."

"I said no. Why didn't you bring a helicopter?"

"Mine was in the shop. You'll have to ask your account manager. A helicopter would be very high profile. Using a submarine, we can sneak away without being noticed."

North grabbed Sinclair's elbow, holding him back as they came to an intersection. North peeked around the corner where Holland had disappeared. She gave the thumbs-up from down the hall.

"I hope I didn't startle you," North said. "I had to make sure your way is clear. The engine room is at the bottom of the stairs ahead."

Sinclair leaned against the wall again. "I need a rest. No more stairs."

"We're almost there," North said.

Sinclair closed his eyes and didn't move.

"All right, then," North said. "This is as good a time as any to call for our pickup." He pinched the microphone around his throat. "Three, this is one and two. We have the package. Come in three. We're all ready."

North waited.

"Oh, my feet are killing me," Sinclair groaned.

North pressed his throat mic again. "Three, this is one and two. We're ready. Can you meet us?"

"Don't tell me I ran all this way for nothing," Sinclair said.

Holland came back around the end of the hall. "We don't have time to rest, North," she said.

"Just keep a lookout. I'm calling our ride."

She trotted back to the end of the hall.

North tried again. "Three? Are you there? We are ready."

He waited, listening, hearing only the sound of Sinclair gulping air.

"Let's keep going," he said. He touched Sinclair's shoulder.

Sinclair jerked away from him.

"I can walk!" he yelled.

North followed, covering their backs.

At the intersection Sinclair asked her, "Do you have any water?"

"Sorry," Holland said, "we don't."

"You came to rescue me and you don't have water? What about a first aid kit? What if I had been injured? What if I get shot?"

"You're right," she said. "We should have thought of that."

They descended the metal stairs among the giant steel cylinders that filled the engine room. Sinclair bent over, hands on his knees, catching his breath.

Holland moved ahead.

Sinclair noticed the clay bricks and wires arranged around the gas tank. He scanned the labels that warned, "Dangerous! Highly Flammable! Explosive!"

"Is that the bomb?" he asked.

"Yes," North said.

"Did you defuse it? Aren't you guys secret agents?"

"I'm ex-special forces, and she's, ah... neither of us possess the defusing skill set. We plan to get you far away very soon so this won't matter. To you."

"We've been sitting on a live bomb and you didn't move faster?" Sinclair said.

Holland was standing in the storage closet from which they made their entrance. "Three, this is one and two," she said, pinching her throat mic. "We have the package. Repeat, we have the package."

North and Sinclair arrived at her side.

"Anything yet?" Holland asked.

"I'm not getting-"

"This is three!" Jeffers shouted in their ears. "Lots of fish down here."

"We're ready," Holland said. "Pick us up."

"I can't. Too many blips."

"Too many what?"

"Other subs, damn it! Enemy subs. At least two. I caught one by surprise and sank it, but this thing only comes with two micro-torpedoes. The other sub is engaging. I'm playing cat and mouse now."

North and Holland exchanged tense glances.

"What's happening?" Sinclair said. "Can I hear?"

"They're firing!" Jeffers yelled. "Evading. Evading, come on... Whoa. That was close. So far, so good. Wait, here it comes ag-" A squeal sounded over their earphones, then static, then silence.

"That didn't sound good," Holland said.

"Someone fill me in," Sinclair said. "What the hell is going on?"

"The rules have changed, sir," North said. "We've, uh, we've encountered a unique contingency."

Sinclair's reply was obliterated as Jeffers screamed in their ears. "Mayday! I'm hit. Taking on water. Aban-"

His voice cut off abruptly. North and Holland stared at each other.

"Damn it," Sinclair said, stomping his foot. "Tell me what just happened."

Holland looked at North. "You tell him."

"Mr. Sinclair," North said, looking at the floor like a shamed schoolboy. "I believe we just lost our ride."

13

Hussein's angry voice crackled over the Bonnie Jane's speakers.

"Goodkin! I have learned there is a rich and famous passenger on my boat. Yet I cannot find him. I demand you tell me where he is!"

Goodkin answered. "I don't know what you're talking about, Hussein."

"I think you do. This information is on all your news networks, and it is taking away from the urgent message of the Kariqistani people. Have you ever heard the name Danforth Percy Sinclair?"

"I believe he is a wealthy man, but that's all I know."

"Be truthful, Goodkin, or I will become angry."

"Guaranteed he doesn't produce a dead body over this. You watch," Burnett said.

Goodkin swatted the air with his right hand, signaling for quiet.

"I'm telling you the guy's full of it," Burnett insisted.

Goodkin turned to the television news. Text reading "Among the hostages" was splashed above photos of Danforth Percy Sinclair and Yvonne Windstorm.

"Ah, crap," Goodkin muttered.

"Hussein, that's ridiculous," he said much louder. "A billionaire and a celebrity on a cruise ship? It's got to be a false rumor."

"If you insist," Hussein said. "I am going to look for this Sinclair myself. If I do not find him, there will be terrible consequences."

"Don't do anything rash, Hussein. I'm certain this is a mistake or a hoax. A billionaire would be on his own yacht."

"Reason? You speak of reason? There is no reason for the children of Kariqistan to die for multinational oil company profits, yet they do. When I return, I hope to have Mr. Sinclair. Then perhaps you will address our demands, since the wealthy mean everything to people in your country."

"Hussein, there has to be some other explanation."

Hussein didn't respond.

"Hussein. Are you there? Hussein?"

Goodkin hung up the com.

Burnett shook his head. "If he doesn't produce a body, I hope you'll agree it's time to turn my dogs loose."

Goodkin tapped on his tablet and stepped off the bridge. He stretched his back and shoulders as he spoke.

"Look, this guy's not budging," he said. "I'd like to try waiting him out, but he's becoming less stable. No. Don't do that. If you add any more attitudes to this jackass stew, things will go from worse to terrible. I'm spinning my wheels out here and that's all you've got? Yeah. Thanks for nothing."

14

The footsteps continued, fading away.

Zack gently pulled open the door. Martin stepped into the hall, his gun before him. Even holding it with both hands, the weapon shook.

The stranger was dressed exactly like the terrorists, all in black, wearing heavy rubber boots, a full body wetsuit and a mask. He didn't register any awareness that Martin was one step behind him.

Martin aimed at the center of the man's back, matching his footsteps, moving closer with each stride until he was close enough to touch.

"Stop," Martin barked.

The man halted and stiffened, rising slightly from his crouched position.

"I've got a gun on you," Martin said. "Drop your weapon."

The man didn't move.

Martin pressed the barrel against his spine. "Drop it. Now."

The man held his right hand up. He was holding a nine-millimeter, its barrel extended with a silencer. He splayed his fingers out and the pistol fell to the deck.

"Hands behind your back," Martin said.

The man did as told, slowly.

Zack emerged from their room with an electrical extension cord. He wrapped it around the man's wrists. When he pulled the final knot with all his strength, the prisoner grunted.

"You're done, bitch," Zack whispered in his ear. "Cooked meat."

"Get his weapon," Martin ordered.

Zack snatched up the gun and examined it.

"Firepower, straight up. Silencer, too. Nice piece, punk."

"You know how to use that thing?" Martin asked.

Zack scrunched up his face. "Please, G!"

"Then take the safety off."

"Right," Zack said, flipping the safety. "I knew dat, bro." He pointed the gun at the prisoner. Martin called over his shoulder.

"Get a chair and more cords. We're going to have a chat with our guest."

Gwen poked her head out of the door and disappeared back inside.

"Now we've got two guns on you," Martin said to the prisoner. "Don't try anything."

To Zack he said, "Get on the other side of him."

Zack ducked around the captive and pressed his gun against the man's chest. "Yo, now get a look at who busted yo dumb ass."

"Son, please," Martin said. "This is serious."

"Sorry, G."

"Okay. Now walk backwards. Slowly now."

Martin and the prisoner backed up with Zack following, facing them. Martin stopped when they were parallel with their room.

"Room four-four-six, on your left," Martin said. "Go in and sit down. Zack, you lead."

Zack turned and walked backward, guiding them into the room, keeping the gun against the prisoner's ribs. Brittany held the door open while Gwen stretched out three extension cords on the bureau. She had placed a chair in the center of the room between the two beds.

Brittany latched the door when everyone was inside.

The prisoner started to say something."You might want-"

"Shut up," Martin said, jabbing him in the back. "Sit down."

The prisoner dropped into the chair. Using the scavenged cords, Brittany and Gwen bound his ankles to the chair legs. They tied one around his neck, connecting it to the chair's back. His hands were still pinned behind him from the earlier binding Zack had applied in the hall.

When they were done, all four of them stood before him.

"Zack," Martin said. "You keep that gun pointed at him at all times. I'm going to unmask him."

"Right, boss."

Martin grabbed a handful of the mask and ripped upward.

The man had light brown hair shaved down to his tanned scalp. His cold and steady green-eyed gaze moved to each of his captors, one after the other.

Zack sat on the bed and pressed the silencer-equipped barrel of the man's automatic pistol against the side of its owner's head. He turned the gun sideways, Hollywood-style.

"I'm here to-" the prisoner said.

"I said shut up," Martin said.

The prisoner spoke quickly.

"I'm with the Navy SEALs. We're on the same side. My team and I are here to kill the terrorists who've been holding you hostage."

"Yo, do we look like hostages?" Zack said.

"Oh, thank God," Gwen said. "We're saved."

"Or he's lying," Martin answered.

"Hey," Brittany said. "He's got something in his ear."

Martin roughly stuck his finger in the prisoner's ear, knocking loose a piece of molded plastic colored to match the prisoner's olive skin.

The device was smaller than a quarter. Martin held it between his thumb and index finger.

"Communicating with your buddies?" he said. He flicked the tiny switch on the earpiece to shut it off before setting it on the dresser.

"I don't know who you people are," the prisoner said. "But I'm a scout for a Navy SEAL team that has infiltrated this vessel. You are putting American servicemen at risk by keeping me here."

The room was quiet as each of them thought about this.

"I don't know, dawg," Zack said. "Them bad guys spoke English, too. And dey all had tha same gear too."

"Quiet," Martin said. "Don't give him any information." He turned back to the prisoner. "We've learned there's a bomb on board. Where is it?"

"A bomb? Our orders were to neutralize terrorists. No one mentioned a bomb."

"Interesting," Martin said. "Because the commandos who set us free did know about it."

"I'm just being honest with you, sir. I don't know about a bomb. I have no clue who might have set you free. No idea what you're talking about. Maybe some of my team ran across you and let you go."

"Right. So you say you're not a terrorist, but you don't know about what the other good guys know. Which brings me back to the thought that you're lying."

Martin rubbed his chin and looked around the room.

"Gwen," he finally said. "Get the iron from the closet and heat it up."

She didn't move. "You can't be serious."

"I am. Now, please. Heat up the iron."

"I can't-"

"Do it!"

Gwen retreated to a corner of the room and folded her arms. She stared at her husband, her eyes glistening.

"Yo, B," Zack said. "Can you please heat up the iron for the commandant?"

Brittany looked at Gwen uneasily. "Um."

"Come on, girl," Zack said. "I'm askin' nice."

"Don't do it," Gwen said.

Brittany looked between her and Zack, back and forth.

"Fine," she finally said. She opened the closet, pushed aside the Marigolds' clothes and detached the iron from the wall. She went to the bathroom and plugged the iron in.

"We have to find that bomb," Martin said to the prisoner. "And you will tell us where it is and all about it. Is it a dirty bomb? Conventional? A bio-weapon?"

"I'm telling you, I don't know anything about a bomb. How about this? I know where my team is. I can lead you to them. If they shoot me, I'm a terrorist. All right?"

"Yo, bitch, we ain't stupid," Zack said.

Martin rested his hand on Zack's shoulder, quieting the boy.

"Martin, what are you going to do even if you learn where the bomb is?" Gwen said. "You don't know the first thing about explosives."

"She's right," the captive said, "and I don't either. You'd have to get help from my team. They might be able to deactivate it."

"Or detonate it," Martin said. "And we're not going to see your team, okay? Put that idea out of your head. Now excuse me a moment. Zack, keep watching him."

Martin moved toward Gwen in the corner. She squeezed her folded arms tighter. He tried to pull her close but she stepped back.

"Honey," he whispered, "we have to be united or he's going to play us off one another."

"What's there to play off? You've lost your mind."

"Stay quiet. That's all I ask."

"Fine. But I'm not taking part in this."

"I don't want you to."

He leaned down to kiss her but she turned away. He returned to his position before the prisoner.

"What do you want me to do to prove I'm a Navy SEAL?" the captive said.

"Tell us where the bomb is."

"Our intel did not mention a bomb."

"Then why did the other commandos know about it?"

"Who are you talking about?"

"The two who picked up Sinclair. A man and a woman."

"What? Who is Sinclair? There aren't any women on my team."

"If you're an American, how come you don't know Danforth Percy Sinclair?"

"The billionaire? I've heard of him. What's he got to do with any of this?"

"Two people came and picked him up, then they told us there was a bomb. They weren't terrorists. Why wouldn't you know about them? Who else would they be?"

"I don't know. Maybe passengers who got loose like you four?"

"Passengers dressed up like ninjas?" Zack asked.

Brittany stepped out of the bathroom holding the iron with a washcloth wrapped around the handle. Steam curled from the metal base.

"Um, this is ready," she said.

"Bring it here," Martin said. He took it from her, wrapping his hand around the towel.

"What are you doing?" the captive said. "Don't be stupid."

"Tell me where the bomb is," Martin said, moving closer, holding the smoking iron before him.

"I don't know anything about a-"

Martin slammed the iron onto the bound man's thigh. The prisoner screamed. The skin around the iron sizzled and hissed. The captive rocked the chair back and forth, trying to pull away. Gwen turned and covered her ears.

Martin lifted the iron. A black and bloody triangle smoldered on the prisoner's leg.

Brittany covered her mouth and retreated into the bathroom, cheeks bulging.

Zack shook his head. "Oh dayyymm."

Martin held the iron in front of the captive. "Tell me or I do it again."

The prisoner gasped. "Tell you what?"

"Where is the bomb?"

"I told you. I don't know." The prisoner ground his teeth. "I'm an American here to kill terrorists. A Navy SEAL."

"Bull to tha shit," Zack said.

"Brittany," Martin said, "bring a towel and gag him."

"Oh, uh, okay," she said weakly from the bathroom. She spat into the sink. "Just uh, let me like, clean up."

"Lady," the captive said, turning his head toward Gwen. "Lady in the corner, can you please talk some sense into them? I don't know where this bomb is or if there even is one. This guy has these two kids caught up like some kind of cult."

Gwen pressed her hands over her ears, harder than before.

"Shut up," Zack said, smacking the prisoner.

"Tell me where the bomb is," Martin said, holding the iron near the man's face. "Tell me."

"I don't know anything about a bomb. There is no bomb."

"Gag, please," Martin said.

"Don't," the prisoner said. "Don't do this."

Brittany spun the towel into a thick rope and flung it over the captive's face, pulling it through his mouth and tying it behind his head.

The prisoner was still talking into the gag when Martin pressed the iron onto his other leg, leaning his weight on it. The captive threw his head back and yelled. The scream was muffled, but it still filled the room.

Martin lifted off and sat down. The prisoner drooped forward, head down, breathing heavily and staring into the new wound on his thigh.

"Zack," Martin said. "If we're going to talk to this man, he needs a name. What would you like to call him?"

"Yo, you want me to name our pet?"

"Martin! Oh, my God!" Gwen yelled.

"Yes, Zack," Martin said, "Name him. It. Name it."

"Aw, G, I gots the perfect name, yo."

"Well, what should we call it?"

"Meat. As in dead, yo."

"Meat," Martin said, lifting the prisoner's head with two fingers under the man's chin.

He shushed the bound man's cries patiently, then whispered, "I like it. Meat it is."

Martin slammed the iron into Meat's belly.

Meat jolted backwards, almost tipping the chair. Zack grabbed the man's shoulders and pushed from behind. Meat stopped screaming and instead ground his teeth, his lips pulling back beyond his gums. Tears rushed out of his clenched-shut eyes, snot leaked down his upper lip.

Martin let up and stood over him, whispering as the prisoner coughed into the gag.

"This is what happens when people try to harm me or my wife. You brought this on yourself. And you have the power to stop it."

15

"What do you mean we just lost our ride?" Sinclair said. "I thought you were professionals."

"You're right, sir," Holland said, glaring at North. "Absolutely right, sir. We'll have this problem fixed in a moment."

Holland grabbed North and pulled him away from Sinclair.

"What are you doing telling a client there's a problem? That's bound to result in a low customer experience survey score."

"Sorry, but service isn't top of my list right now," North said. "I'm thinking of getting us out alive."

To Sinclair, he added, "We'll just grab a life raft, sir. Not a problem."

"I paid for private extraction because I like to keep a low profile," Sinclair said. "I'm not like my wife. She's supposed to lure the cameras away from me."

North and Holland ignored him.

"We get in a raft and they'll gun us down," she said.

"It's that or stay on the boat with the bomb," North said.

"Even if we make it and that bomb is powerful enough, we're still screwed."

"Possibly."

"What do you mean possibly?" Sinclair said.

"We can't stay here," North said. "Getting as far from this ship as we can is our best shot at survival. If we signal the Coasties, then the bandits might see a rescue boat coming in or us leaving. Better we grab a raft and just leave. Smaller footprint."

"This is ridiculous!" Sinclair said. "I'm going to demand a full refund."

"Mr. Sinclair," Holland said. "We're doing everything we can. Your satisfaction is our top priority."

"It sure doesn't seem like it."

"We should keep moving," North said. "At least get to the outside of the boat, for our ride, or to signal the Coasties. I'll lead."

He charged down the hall away from the engine room. He opened a door and stepped through to make sure the way was clear. The door's spring hinges automatically closed it behind him.

He turned to open it again when something heavy hit the back of his head.

North staggered against the wall, stars exploding in his fading vision. On the other side of the door he heard yelling in the digitized tones of the terrorists.

"Drop your gun! Get on the ground!"

Holland screamed something back.

North swooned.

"Don't go down," he mumbled to himself. "Stay up."

"Drop your weapon," the robotic voice on his side of the door said. "Drop it."

North pretended he was more stunned from the surprise blow than he was. He turned to face his attacker.

The shorter, stockier man was wearing a mask. He stepped back out of North's reach.

"Do it now, or die," the distorted voice said. The terrorist was aiming a pistol equipped with a silencer on him.

North pulled his gun out slowly and held it before him. He scanned the area. They were alone.

North leaned over.

"Drop it," the terrorist said.

North did.

As soon as his gun hit the deck he exploded forward, covering the ground between them in an instant and knocking his enemy's pistol upward. The gun spat two silenced rounds into the ceiling. North charged forward to ram his target's head against the bulkhead but the bandit twisted free, the gun flying loose.

North caught a hand chop in the side of his neck. Colorful dots flashed before blackness. It was a solid hit. Professional. North staggered backwards, part retreat, part possum.

The terrorist fell for it and lunged.

They grabbed each other and North got a look into the man's wild eyes. They whirled each other in a circle, trying to throw the other off balance. The terrorist was smaller than him but his balance and strength were equal.

No, North thought, he's stronger than me.

Panic bubbled up in North's chest as the bandit pushed him, ramming him against the pipes along the hallway. North let the momentum of the shove propel him away from his attacker. The distance gave him confidence, but the terrorist had time to pull free a knife. He swung in a horizontal arc, the blade hissing through the air.

North thought he had dodged the strike, but his wet suit shrank back along the cut, exposing a bleeding line. Pain streaked across North's chest, and a sensation much worse rattled loose inside.

Fear.

The terrorist was faster and at least as strong. North couldn't retreat through the door. Holland was silent on the other side, possibly dead.

Maybe North could surrender?

The bandit kicked him in the knee. The muscle and bone twisted, causing him to drop.

North cried out as he fell, his back thundering against the metal hull. Had he hesitated, or was his enemy that good?

The terrorist held North down, a boot pressing painfully into his solar plexus, cutting off his breath, knife poised to come down.

North stared up at the blazing eyes behind the mask.

"Make it quick, asshole," he growled.

Then he whispered, "I love you, Toby," and closed his eyes.

LARRY NOCELLA

PART 6

KNOW YOUR ENEMY

1

Carol was nuzzling against him, fading sunlight shining into their hotel room.

Through the open window they could hear the sound of the Caribbean surf. To Rod, it sounded as if the island was alive, breathing. They stroked their fingers together lightly, the thin curtain turning in the breeze that cooled their naked bodies.

"So," Rod said, "how do you feel about being Mrs. Roderick North?"

She smiled. "How do you feel about being Mr. Carol North?"

They kissed deeply. She rolled on top of him and he slid inside her. She smiled down at him with such tenderness, he bit his tongue so he wouldn't cry. She tucked her long auburn hair behind her right ear and began to grind against him slowly.

He ran his hands up her back as she dissolved.

* * *

North was sitting forward in the worn recliner he had owned since college.

His cousin and brother were on the sofa next to his father who had passed away two years earlier. Guy Barra was there, and even their friend, Chris Hayger, long deceased, killed-in-action. They were all crowded around the television, watching football. Barra and Hayger were pacing, too excited to sit.

Children played in the backyard and the women stood in the kitchen, their cheeks ruddy, each holding a full glass of wine, several empty bottles on the floor near the recycle bin. Their giggling had been getting louder and louder.

"Down to the wire, bro!" Barra said, slapping North a high-five.

"Everyone touch the lucky helmet!" North said.

They all reached forward from where they were sitting or standing and touched the plastic bowl shaped like a football helmet. The bowl held nothing but chip crumbs and dried stripes of dip.

The television roared with the noise of the crowd, the play-by-play announcer screaming to be heard. The women rushed into the room.

"Touch the helmet, ladies," Hayger yelled. "For good luck!"

Carol ran to the back door and called to the children.

"Hurry!" she said. "We need everyone to touch the lucky helmet!"

The children dropped their football and charged inside.

In seconds, the room was packed. Everyone at the party leaned forward and pressed against each other, just to make sure their fingertips grazed the plastic helmet.

The television volume was at its maximum.

"And it's the last play of the game," the announcer said, screaming over the thundering stadium. "They won't get another chance at this."

"Come on! You can do it," the bodies packed in around Rod shouted. He was utterly silent, concentrating.

"And there's the snap!" the announcer said. Football players on the field ran, collided.

"It's loose!"

"Recovery!"

"He's fading back!"

"Throws!"

The tiny man on the screen caught the ball and ran into the end zone.

The North family's living room exploded in celebration, along with the fifty thousand people in the stadium on TV. The cheering thundered from other apartments in the complex, a neighborhood erupting in joy.

"We win! We did it!"

The room was a riot of hugs and high-fives.

North, Barra and Hayger huddled together, arms around each other, leaping in drunken triumph.

"We did it! Champions! Champ-ee-yuns! Champ-ee-yuns!"

"We did it, Daddy! We did it!" Toby cheered as he rode Rod's shoulders.

"That's right, buddy! We did it!"

"I love you, Daddy! I love you more than anything in the world!"

All around them they were cheering, but Rod heard none of it. He was looking into Toby's eyes, his son's eyes, and Toby was looking into his. He coughed. Suddenly breathing had become a little difficult.

Someone slapped him on the back. Barra peeked over North's shoulder and stared into his face.

"Hey, bro, are you crying? Damn! Hayger get over here. North's crying!"

Hayger roughly grabbed Rod's face with both his hands, blasting alcohol-scented breath up his nose. North recoiled.

"Sheesh, dude," Hayger said. "It's just a championship." Then he yelled in North's face, "The national worldwide championship!"

Hayger threw his arm around Barra and the two marched off, cheering and chanting.

Rod clutched Toby to him and turned away from the crowd, wiping his eyes.

"I love you, too, buddy," he said. "More than anything."

* * *

As they walked the many rows of the graveyard, on the mild spring day, Toby clutched his father's finger in one hand and in the other he cradled his rubber duck toy, Mister Duck-Duck.

Rod pointed to a headstone.

"This is my and Mr. Guy's old friend," Rod said. "It says Christopher Tobias Hayger.

Toby's eyes widened. "He has the same name as me," Toby said.

"That's right, buddy. You were named after him."

Barra stood a few steps back, hands folded, staring at the ground.

"So why did he die?" Toby asked.

"He was trying to make the world a better place. Just like me and Mr. Guy. He always said he did tough things and fought bad people so the kids growing up don't have to."

Barra stepped closer.

"Don't listen to him, kid. Hayger and your Dad tried to make the world a better place. I did it just because I'm crazy."

He laughed then tickled Toby. The boy ran away, giggling. Barra gave chase, flailing his arms and roaring like a monster.

Rod watched them go.

"Sleep well," he said and placed his hand on the headstone.

* * *

The parade of memories wavered, like heat waves distorting Rod's vision. The green fields of the cemetery faded and vanished. Toby's giggling and the chirping birds went mute.

Then it all vanished.

Gone.

North was looking up to a metal ceiling, the terrorist standing over him.

The terrorist lowered his knife and pointed it at North's chest.

2

"What the hell?" the distorted voice of the terrorist yelled. "What the fuck?"

He made no attempt to attack. He just stood frozen, pointing with his knife at North's slashed open suit.

Rod looked down at his chest. A huge rip stretched across his wet suit from armpit to armpit, exposing where the blade had cut him. Blood oozed from the ragged arc. The medallion containing the photo of him and Toby and Mister Duck-Duck had saved a strip of flesh over his breastbone.

North didn't know what to say. He looked up at the terrorist as the man pulled his artificial larynx from his throat and lowered his knife.

"North!" he yelled. The voice sounded familiar.

"How do you know my name?"

"Wake up, you idiot."

Guy Barra was speaking from behind the terrorist's mask, but how could that be?

The terrorist kicked Rod in the boot.

"Snap to, bro!"

The terrorist tore off his mask. He was wearing Barra's face, too. The dark eyes, the bushy eyebrows, the wide nose and olive skin were identical. The face was his friend's, but how did the terrorist get it?

"North! What the hell are you doing here?"

North stared up at the terrorist body with his friend's face.

"Barra? Guy Barra?"

"Yeah, dumbass. I almost killed you, bro! What are you doing here?"

The fog in North's mind was slow to part.

"What? I- I don't get it."

Holland was shouting from behind the door. Barra stepped around North and opened it.

"Don't shoot!" he yelled. "Stand down! She's with Redfire!"

Sinclair was on the floor, curled in a fetal position, covering his head. Holland was struggling with the two masked men. Her nose was bleeding.

North pushed himself to his feet. His knee was aching where Barra had kicked it out. His chest wound burned. They all gathered on Holland's side of the door, gasping for breath.

"Take your masks and voice boxes off," Barra said. "We need to work this out."

The two men did as told.

Holland snatched her gun from one of them. "I'll take that." She pointed the gun at Barra. "What's going on?"

"Whoa, lady," Barra said, his hands up. "Chill. We all work for Redfire."

She looked at North. "It's true," he said.

"Okay, I'm lost."

"Put the gun down and we'll talk."

Holland lowered her gun.

Sinclair groaned. Holland helped him to his feet.

"Who's the old guy?" Barra asked.

"Don't tell him that," Holland said. "Mission confidentiality."

"It's okay, little girl," Barra said. "North and I go way back. Iraq. Afghanistan. Somalia. Hell, so far back, I think we met in Panama."

"Sounds romantic," Holland said.

"We're here to get him," North said, nodding towards Sinclair. "Private extraction."

"A Katrina contract," Barra said, rolling his eyes. "I've done a few of those."

"What about you?" North said. "Don't tell me you're working a false flag."

"You shouldn't tell him anything either," Holland said to Barra. "Even if we all work for Redfire. That's breaking confidentiality."

Barra dismissed her with a wave.

"What else would we be doing here? Of course it's a false flag. Take the ship, make it look like it was done by Kariqistanis, no casualties, get the hell out."

Holland pointed to Sinclair. "We've got a customer here. Can you stop talking about confidential Redfire activities?"

"Oh, please," Sinclair said. "You think I don't know about false flag ops? That's why I forbid my children or grandchildren from joining the military. War is for suckers."

"So you're the old guy everyone is talking about," Barra said.

"Who's talking about me?"

"Some reporter jackass got hold of the ship's passenger list. Word's getting around that you're on board. Are you really a millionaire?"

"Billionaire," Sinclair said. "With a B, as in broker. Speaking of, does anyone have a phone? If there's going to be a war with Kariqistan, I want to invest in crude. My so-called friends should have let me know ahead of time."

"Whoa, whoa," North said. "So what's your endgame, Barra? How do you succeed here?"

"Our orders are to scare the piss out of these hostages and put on a show for the media for 48 hours or until the USA launches military strikes on Kariqistan, whichever comes first. Then we take off."

"What if the US special forces attack instead?" Holland said. "You going to kill Americans?"

"They won't attack," Barra said. "They'll talk and talk and talk and we'll be long gone before anything happens. We used to work for them and that's always been the protocol. North, you remember that op in the Ukraine? They talked until the hijackers ran out of water and came staggering out thirsty as hell. Me, you and Hayger sat on our asses the whole time."

"You're breaking company policy," Holland said, "talking about your objective. You shouldn't even mention it in front of us, even though we're Redfire employees."

"North, where did you find her? She's into regs like a rookie."

Holland ground her teeth. North held his hand in front of her.

"She's all right, Barra. Lay off. How were you planning on escaping? Maybe we can hitch a ride."

"We've got a small sub waiting for us. Didn't you have a plan for yourself?"

"Our micro sub got taken out. I figured it was special forces scouting around. He said there were other subs down there. "

"We only brought one."

"I thought he said subs. Plural. Sounded that way but the signal was crap."

"So, problem solved," Holland said. "We'll just ride out on your sub."

"Doubtful. It barely fit the ten guys that came with me."

"Ah, crap," North said.

"What?" Barra asked. "Why are you making those faces?"

"Let's just say," Holland said, "you've got two extra seats."

"Aw, come on," Barra said. "My missing men. You took them out, didn't you? That's where they went."

North and Holland stared at the floor.

"God damn it," Barra said. "Those were good men."

"Not good enough," Holland said.

Everyone was quiet a moment.

"So," Holland said with fake brightness, "we just kill one more of your team and we've got room for all three of us."

Everyone looked at her.

"Was that in bad taste?" she said.

"How about we ice you, bitch," one of Barra's men said. "Then we don't need an extra seat."

"Try it, limp-dick."

"Holland, knock it off," North said.

"We're not doing this mission to kill anybody," Barra said. "Management wouldn't take the contract unless the risk was minimal. That way if we're found out, the P.R. damage is much more manageable. Blame it on some rogue employees. At least that's what our account exec said. You ask me, this whole thing is crazy. Then again, so am I."

"Who's your exec? You working with Addison?" Holland asked.

"No. The man's name is Deitz. Why?"

"Count your blessings," North said.

"Wait," Holland said. "If you haven't killed anyone, how have you been terrorizing the hostages?"

"We're not here to scare the captives. We're here to scare America and the media does most of it for us. They broadcast burning American flags, swarthy dudes in ski masks holding a bunch of white folks captive. No one needs to die to scare the crap out of people. That news chopper that went down wasn't even our fault."

"Does add some realism, though," one of Barra's men said.

"A news chopper went down?" North said.

"The Navy fired a Russian warning shot."

"What about the explosives? The bomb in the engine room?"

"All part of the theater. We haven't jettisoned the life rafts either. We're going to give people plenty of time to escape. Then we blow a hole in the ship, sneak away in our sub. Meanwhile, the media films the sinking of the Sunset Mist. Gives the people at home nightmares. They start calling Congress, crying for revenge. The marines go into Kariqistan, or the Navy shells the crap out of 'em. Sinclair and his country club buds get their crude oil pipeline compliments of the U.S. taxpayer, the wheels turn, the machine chugs, the status quo lives on and everyone's happy."

"Wrong," Sinclair said. "I'm not happy. I'm still waiting to be taken off this boat."

"No problem," Barra said. "I'll have Hussein, that's my terrorist name by the way, dump you and some other dinosaurs on a life raft for the Coast Guard. I'll say I'm releasing the elderly prisoners as a sign of good faith."

"That won't do. I paid Redfire for personalized treatment. That's what a Katrina contract is. I refuse to be sent over with the rabble."

"Dude," Barra said. "We don't have any other options."

"Come up with one."

"Get off the boat now in a life raft, or you wait with us and squeeze into our sub."

"I only wanted two things, quick service and privacy," Sinclair said. "I've received neither. You're telling me I have to wait or I can go over in a boat and let the media swarm all over me. What the hell did I pay you people for? Do you even know who I am? What I could do to your company?"

Barra pointed at Sinclair, but looked at Holland and North. "Is this guy for real?"

"Unfortunately," North said.

"Now I know all your plans," Sinclair said. "So if you send me over, before I even get to my money, I'll tell them what's going on. The Navy, the Coast Guard and the media. I'll screw your mission, screw your company and screw you all. I'll pull back the curtain on your puppet show."

"Damn it," Barra said.

"I told you not to talk about it in front of him," Holland said. "Guess I'm pretty smart for a rookie."

She winked at North. He smirked.

Sinclair folded his arms. "And I didn't get rich by not getting my way."

"Bro," Barra said to North, "you always did have a talent for causing trouble."

3

A digitized voice spoke over their headsets.

"Away team, come in. Come in, Away team. This is Home."

Barra adjusted the elastic band around his throat, snapping the distortion box back into place. He positioned his headset microphone on his cheek.

"Go ahead, Home. This is Away."

"The negotiator keeps trying to reach you. Says he has important news."

"Be right there. Away team out."

Barra pulled loose his voice digitizer and turned to the group.

"Let's go back up to the bridge and sort this out. I'll do some stalling."

"Won't their spotters or snipers see us?" North said.

"With your masks on, you look just like us. Our account execs probably got the gear from the same supply cabinet."

"What about me?" Sinclair said.

"You'll be our prisoner." Barra turned to his two men. "Tie his hands behind his back and walk with him."

"You will do no such thing."

"Fine," Barra said. "Stay here. You're not my responsibility."

"I'll stand near," Holland said. "So it looks like I'm guarding him. We'll be fine."

Barra led, followed by his two men, then Holland, Sinclair and North. Using a key, Barra opened a freight elevator. The six rode it directly to the bridge level, everyone staring ahead, alone in their thoughts.

"This is screwed up," North said. "What are the odds?"

"That a false flag and a Katrina contract happen to meet?" Barra asked. "Does seem freaky, but it was bound to happen eventually. Since Hurricane Katrina, private extractions have been the latest and greatest. They're perfect for Redfire. It's just like insurance. The customer pays but will probably never use it. It's practically free money."

"Nice racket," Sinclair said.

"You should know, rich guy," Barra said.

"I didn't mean that as an insult."

They got off the elevator and followed Barra past the ballroom where the hundreds of prisoners were bound and seated.

Barra stopped short of stepping onto the bridge and turned to Sinclair.

"Hey, old man, the captain has a small office in the corner, why don't you sit in there? That will keep you out of sight. Your girlfriend here can go with you."

"Fine," Sinclair said.

"Works for me," Holland said. "Minus the girlfriend part."

They stepped onto the bridge. The other masked men reached for their guns.

"Relax," Barra said, "they're with us. I'll give you the details later, but essentially, we've got two Redfire contracts going on at once here."

Barra picked up the ship's com microphone. "Quiet on the set."

He adjusted his voice box and flicked the switch.

"Goodkin," Barra said, his words now distorted. "You wanted to speak with me?"

Goodkin's voice filled the bridge. "Did you find your men, Hussein?"

"No, we have not. I suspect you imperial dogs are responsible."

"I hate to bring you bad news, Hussein, but the official word has come down. Our nation does not negotiate under duress nor give in to coercion. There will be no ransom payments. I tell you this not to make you angry, but so you understand your only option is to arrive at a peaceful solution."

Barra held the com near the console as he pounded his fist on the flat metal. "You think me not serious? You will see. The ocean will turn red!" He turned and winked at North.

"Hussein," Goodkin said. "Hussein, please. Don't do anything. Don't hurt anyone or your chances of a compromise will be gone forever. No matter what you do, the money is not coming. We need to find another way to come to terms. Hussein? Hussein?"

Barra shut off the com and pulled loose his vocal distortion box.

"I think he's getting tired of me. I need to ratchet up the terror a bit, but I'm running out of ideas."

"Throw a body overboard, set an example," North said.

"Where the hell am I going to get a body?"

"Use the old guy?"

"I heard that," Sinclair said from the captain's office.

"We've got corpses," Holland said. "The two North and I produced."

"Oh, crap," Barra said. He thought for a moment, hand on his chin as he stared at the floor.

"All right," he said. "Let's use them."

"Can't you just keep stalling?" North said. "Aren't the families going to want the bodies from Redfire?"

"Too bad," Barra said. "Look, bro, this negotiator dope may suck at playing hardball, but there's the Navy ship out there. Judging by her hull classification number, I'm betting they've got SEALs on board. We need to make them keep their distance. Let's use the dead guys."

"You'll have to remove his Redfire gear, cut off his fingers, scrape off any tattoos and pry out all their teeth," North said. "It's the only way to be sure they don't ever find out who they really are and what's really happening here."

"That's some serious butcher work," Holland said, swallowing hard.

"You and North made the mess," Barra said. "You two clean it up."

"I'm not doing it. It's your mission."

"Ah, hell. Like Hayger used to say, right, North? Something's wrong if something isn't wrong. It ain't a mission until things get all screwed up. You two," Barra said, pointing to two of his men. "Go field dress the bodies for dumping."

The two men left the bridge.

"We never took the masks off," North said. "Were those guys anyone I know?"

Barra shrugged. "Not anymore, bro."

4

"He's out cold," Martin said.

Meat was unconscious, his head leaning back and to the side, his face slimy with sweat. Yellow-pink pus leaked from the burn wounds on his thighs and torso. The washcloth gagging him was drenched with his saliva.

"Maybe he fakin', yo," Zack said.

Martin lifted each of Meat's eyelids.

"I don't think so. It's just as well. We could all use a rest."

He set the iron down on the bureau and sat on the bed, rubbing his eyes. Gwen was still standing in the corner, arms folded, her back to the room.

She turned around and spoke sharply.

"Notice he hasn't given you any useful information."

"Not yet," Martin said.

"Maybe he has none to give. Even assuming that he's one of them, maybe he just doesn't know where the bomb is."

"I refuse to argue about this anymore, dear."

"We should be getting off this boat, Martin, getting as far away as we can."

"It won't matter if it's a dirty bomb. We have to find a way to disarm it."

"Leave that to the professionals."

"If all you're going to do is complain, can you at least keep your voice down?"

Brittany whimpered. She was sitting on the edge of the bed, a blanket around her shoulders.

Zack reclined next to her, rubbing her back. "You all right, girl? Z here for you."

"Yeah," she said, "I'm okay. Better."

"How about some tube?" he said. "I'll dial up some toons for you."

He grabbed the remote from the bed stand and turned on the television. CNB News was on. The screen showed a vantage point high above the Sunset Mist.

"-activity now. I see movement," Fran Amaretto was saying.

"Oh, snap," Zack said. "We on the TV!"

"Turn it off," Gwen said. "Someone might hear us."

"My bad," Zack said, pressing mute on the remote.

"I thought I said turn it off."

"Can't hurt to learn what's going on," Martin said. "Turn the volume up just a little, Zack. It looks like something is happening on the top deck."

Zack did as told. They all leaned forward to hear.

"This is Fran Amaretto of CNB, live on the scene where four terrorists and two hostages have emerged from the bridge. The hostages are seated in deck chairs, covered from head to toe by bed sheets, their heads obscured by hoods. I can see some of their arms and legs. They appear to be two men, but of course I can't be sure. And it seems, yes, I believe the chairs have some kind of weight dangling from beneath, they look like gym barbells."

"Fran, we can't see from the studio, any chance the sniper on your helicopter will, ah, take action?"

"I don't want to guess what his orders are. Hussein has threatened numerous times that if any of his men are harmed, he will exact revenge on the hostages."

"What are they going to do to them?" Brittany asked.

"Turn your head," Gwen said. "Don't look."

The four masked men set down the two deck chairs. The covered bodies on them were motionless.

"As you can see," Amaretto continued, "a terrorist is standing behind each hostage, a pistol pointed to the back of each captive's head. The hostages are very still. Their bindings appear to be extremely tight, and of course with that covering, they can't see what's going on around them."

"Fran, are there new demands? Why this sudden display?"

"We can't let this happen!" Brittany cried. "Zack! Do something!"

"What, girl? What can I do?"

She looked around the room frantically.

"Turn it off!" Gwen said. "Shut it off or she's going to lose it!"

"The earpiece!" Brittany screamed.

Zack snatched it up and popped it in his ear.

Martin reached for him, yelling.

"Don't!"

* * *

The speakers on the Bonnie Jane bridge crackled.

"Yo, mic check, one two, one two! This word goes out to dem muddafukkas who wrecked my chill time. We got one of your homeys, aight? Don' touch those peeps or we ice your boy!"

"What the hell?" Goodkin said. He was watching the drama on the Sunset Mist top deck via the CNB television feed. "Are we picking up a radio station from the coast?"

"I think someone's telling the terrorists that he's captured one of them," Dunn said.

"But how?"

"Maybe the passengers got tired of waiting," Burnett said.

"It's a big boat," Dunn said. "Maybe they missed some people."

Burnett's earpiece blinked. He tapped it. "Burnett. Go."

Dunn tried to hear what the other captain was saying, but Burnett turned his back and cupped his hand over his mouth while whispering.

Goodkin grabbed the com as the terrorists held their position behind the restrained captives, guns pressed to the back of the covered people's heads.

"Hussein, don't do this!" Goodkin yelled. "Whoever that other person is speaking took your men, not me."

"Yo, bitch," the new voice said over the speakers, "don be tryna snitch on us. We on da inside, yo."

"Whoever you are, your actions are going to result in the deaths of two hostages!" Goodkin screamed. "Hello, Hussein. Answer me. Hussein, are you there?"

* * *

Holland, North, Sinclair and Barra watched from the bridge of the Sunset Mist. Sinclair sat in the captain's office, his head drooping forward as he nodded off.

Four of Barra's team carried the hooded corpses out onto the deck. They made a show of marching around the bodies and jabbing their weapons in the air.

"Pretty good theater," Holland said. "It looks real. I just hope no one notices how little the prisoners are moving."

The Sunset Mist's bridge speaker popped.

"Yo, mic check, one two, one two! This word goes out to dem muddafukkas who wrecked my chill time. We got one of your homeys, aight? Don' touch those peeps or we ice your boy!"

"Hussein, don't do this!" Goodkin yelled. "Whoever that other person is speaking took your men, not me."

"Yo, bitch, don be tryna snitch on us. We on da inside, yo."

"Whoever you are, your actions are going to result in the deaths of two hostages! Hello? Hello? Hussein, answer me. Hussein, are you there?"

Barra, Holland and North exchanged confused glances.

"Who's the wanna-be gangsta arguing with the negotiator?" North asked.

"Exactly what I was wondering," Barra said.

"Yo, we gon rise up," the new voice said. "Power to da people, takin this sucka back! So look da hell out, Z dawg is comin' for ya and you gon get blanked! Yo gimme dat back-"

The voice cut off abruptly.

"He's not one of yours?" Barra asked.

"No," North said, "only two of us boarded. Our sub pilot is M.I.A. and he sure as hell didn't talk like that."

"Think some kid got free?"

"Sounds like he did."

"Who does he have, then?" Barra said. "Counting the two you killed, my team is accounted for."

"It's obvious," Holland said, "he's making it up."

One of the men out on the bridge held his pistol high in one hand, then jammed the gun into the back of the head of one of the corpses bound to the deck chairs.

"The show must go on," Barra said.

* * *

Martin snatched the earpiece from Zack.

"Yo, gimme dat back," Zack said. "I was da great distraction."

Martin flicked the tiny switch on the earpiece, turning it off. "You need to be quiet," he said. "You were giving us away."

"I was tryna stop dis!" He pointed at the TV.

They watched silently as one of the terrorists rammed his pistol's barrel into the back of a hostage's head.

"Now dem bitches ain't listnin', G!"

Fran Amaretto narrated. "Oh, no. This is not good. I think he's-"

The terrorist pulled the trigger. The body's head snapped forward, black and red spraying through the hood, spitting gore on the ship's white deck and the bed linens covering the body.

"Oh, my God!" Amaretto yelled.

The TV audio cut off for several seconds, while the terrorists paraded around the covered body.

"Oh, shit!" Zack yelled. Brittany wailed. Gwen turned away. Martin clutched his gun to his chest, face grim. Meat stayed unconscious.

The TV audio popped back on. Amaretto cleared her throat. "Ahem, as you just saw, they did it. They killed a hostage." The corpse slumped forward, leaking blood.

"Now it appears, excuse me," she said, "that they are putting on a disgusting display of gloating."

The masked men took the American flag off the pole and wiped it under the hood, gathering blood to form an additional stripe, this one dark, ragged and lumpy. Two of the men lifted the corpse, still tied to the chair, barbells dangling underneath. After three swings they hurled the body off the ship. It sank before the splash subsided. The terrorists moved behind the second prisoner.

"Not again," Brittany whimpered, burying her face in her hands.

"Oh, my God," Amaretto said on the TV. "Back in the studio. I- I- I have no words. It looks like they're going to do it again. Oh, no. Please no."

The terrorists moved behind the second bound body.

"Fran," the studio reporter said. "Are you sure your sniper can't-"

The terrorist fired. The second body's head snapped forward, vomiting brain and bone like the first. The terrorists performed the same grisly ritual, rubbing the American flag underneath the hood, then carrying the weighted chair and body to the deck's edge and throwing it over.

Zack leapt off the bed and punched Meat in the face. The prisoner coughed awake.

"Oh, shit, muddafukka," Zack said. "You and your homeys gon pay for what you punks done. Tell us where the bomb is, or I shove that iron up your ass, lil bitch!"

Meat moaned through the gag and shook his head no.

Brittany had moved across the room and was crying onto Gwen's shoulder. The older woman hugged her and rubbed her back. "Enough," she said, grabbing the remote and shutting off the TV.

They were all quiet except for Brittany's whimpering.

Zack cocked back his fist.

"Zack, stop," Martin said.

"This punk got to pay!" Zack said, failing to hold back his tears.

"I agree."

The prisoner's eyes flew open, his muffled pleas muted as he looked past Zack.

Martin lunged forward with the iron, ramming it into the center of Meat's chest. Even with the gag in place, his screams filled the room.

"Tell us!" Martin yelled. "Tell us where the bomb is!"

"Make him suffer!" Brittany screamed, breaking loose from Gwen. "For what they did to those people! Hurt him!"

Martin pressed down harder on the iron, twisting it, burrowing it into flesh that melted away. Zack stood behind the prisoner, pushing him forward into the smoking iron. When Martin lifted it, a sizzling pink and yellow smear smoldered in the center of Meat's chest, burning through his black wetsuit. His eyes rolled back, his breath came and went with a quick and light mechanical rhythm. The room smelled like burnt bacon.

Zack smacked Meat. "Don't black out, lil bitch. You ain't gon like dat."

Martin held the pointed tip of iron near Meat's left eyeball.

"Yeah, do it! Do it!" Zack screamed.

Martin was blinking rapidly. His hand shook. He looked to Gwen. They held each other's gaze for a moment before she turned away.

Martin swallowed hard, turning back to Meat. "Now, will you tell me where the bomb is?"

The eye near the burning hot point of the iron was turning pink. Meat tried to turn away, but Zack grabbed the man's ears from behind and prevented his head from moving.

Meat said yes into his gag.

"Are you going to be quiet?"

Another yes.

"All right," Martin said, pulling back. "You lead the way, and you wear a gag. Try anything and this iron is going right through your eyeball, understand?"

Meat responded with a muffled, "Yes. Yes." He nodded his head up and down frantically.

Martin set down the iron, breathing heavily as if he had just finished a long jog. Zack released Meat's ears and smacked him roughly on the side of the head.

"Let's all take a moment before we set out," Martin said. "This is tiring." He sat down on the bed and held his head in his hands, gun on the covers beside him. Zack put his arm around Brittany.

Gwen remained standing. She was staring at Meat, her lips pressed together tightly.

"Honey?" Martin said, when he finally looked up. "Are you okay?"

She didn't respond immediately. She stared straight ahead for a moment before she turned.

"I want you back, Martin," she said her eyes filling with tears. "Please. I want you back. You're losing it. Please come back to me and let's just get off this boat."

He wrapped his arms around her and rubbed his hands up and down her back.

"Don't be afraid," he whispered. "Don't be scared."

She nuzzled her nose into his neck. "I just want you back, Martin. Please. Come back to me."

He shushed her with cooing noises and stroked her hair.

"It's going to be all right," he said. "We're going to be all right."

5

"Well, that's done," Barra said as his men returned to the bridge. "Carbuzzio and Schneider, rest in peace."

"What about that kid?" Holland said. "The one on the radio who listens to too much hip-hop. What do you make of him?"

Barra shrugged. "Not much. Counting the two we just dumped, everyone on my end is accounted for. Some kid got loose or it's a crazy trick by the negotiator. Either way, no worry."

"That's more or less what I thought."

"That reminds me," Barra said. "Hussein should be bragging."

Barra fitted his voice distorter box and picked up the com.

"Goodkin, you see what happens when you defy the Children of Kariqistan? There will be more! Many more bodies will feed the fish if you delay any longer."

"It's not me, Hussein," Goodkin said. "I didn't touch your men."

Barra laughed. "I believe you. My men have been found."

"Then why-"

"I killed those hostages because you talk too much. There is too much delay. Fulfill our demands soon or you will have more American blood on your hands."

"Hussein, wait-" Goodkin said.

Barra hung up the com and shifted his voice distortion box so he could talk normally.

"You're a little too good at that," North said.

"Hell, it's easy. I just say the same crap dudes said to you, me and Hayger before we wasted their dumb asses. It's nothing new. We hate you, you're a stinking dog, get my money. Not a lot to it, really. Weird thing is, it starts to make sense in a way, if you see it from their view."

"So you're a natural at being a dick," Holland said, smirking.

"That's what makes the big bucks," Barra shrugged.

He turned to the man he had assigned to monitor the television.

"How's the news treating us?"

"They're still showing footage of the fake executions," the other man said. "Good news is there's a definite increase in the talking heads now, trying to sell war or at least a strike. I'm mostly watching the crawl. Looks like there's an emergency meeting between some top senators, the president and the Secretary of Defense."

"Hell yeah," Barra said. "Declare war already. Shoot some missiles. It never seemed to take this long before."

"If they don't declare war," North said, "you still bail at 48 hours?"

"You got it, bro. Can't go into a mission with a backup plan. That's just stupid."

"Addison," North and Holland said to each other.

"Ideally, we get the war," Barra continued. "We're here to get as much violent and obnoxious imagery into the press as we can. Make Americans despise Kariqistanis. Make them want the war and not worry about who gets sent."

"So, how much longer to the goal?"

Barra glanced at his watch. "Crap. It feels like we should be along more, but I'm showing forty-one very long hours."

6

On the bridge of the Bonnie Jane, Burnett was whispering into his earpiece while Goodkin and Dunn talked.

"Damn," Goodkin said, watching where the two bodies had been dumped. "The probability of casualty-reduced event is approaching statistical zero."

"At least it's only two," Dunn said. "So far. That we know of."

"Including the three from the helicopter, it's a total five dead."

"Right," Dunn said. "Any thoughts on that kid who broke in on the com channel?"

"Please. He's either a deception attempt by the terrorists, or he's a passenger who got loose. Either way he's of no use to me. He just needs to shut up."

"I'm surprised you haven't heard from your little gadget there," Dunn said, pointing to Goodkin's tablet.

Goodkin tapped the screen.

"Good point. I'm still getting a signal, but it looks like they've gone dark."

He typed a quick message on the virtual keyboard, waited a minute, then raised the mic bud to his mouth.

"Hello? Hey, team. Where are you?"

He waited.

"Great. Now I'm all alone out here."

"Maybe it was lunch time," Dunn said, "or they were needed for a media appearance."

"Leave for lunch? That would be completely antithetical to the framework of our model's core concept. Someone should be in communication at all times. Some privacy, please, captain."

Goodkin hunched over his tablet, tapping away at it, muttering to himself.

Burnett was raising his voice as he spoke thru his earpiece. "I saw it. I know. What do you mean? What? You're kidding me. Already? It shouldn't be any! You're supposed to be the best!"

Goodkin was fiddling with his tablet as Burnett continued his argument. While both men were occupied, Dunn slipped his hand into a drawer near the ship's wheel. A small envelope was marked "Open only in case of extreme emergency." Dunn opened it, and pulled out the shot-sized bottle of rum. He downed the bottle in one gulp and returned it to the drawer. The other men never noticed.

Burnett tapped his earpiece to hang up. He paced the bridge.

Goodkin looked up from his tablet.

"Got something to say, Burnett? Don't you want to blame me for those two dead hostages, since I insisted on talking?"

"Come on, Goodkin," Dunn intervened, "Burnett's been keeping to himself lately. No need to start anything."

"No, sir, college boy," Burnett said, "I have nothing to say to you at this point. If anything, I was going to sympathize. This is a difficult situation."

"I'm proud of you, Burnett," Dunn said. "That's the first nice thing you've said to him all day."

"Yeah, well," Burnett stepped off the bridge.

"What's his problem?" Goodkin asked.

Dunn shrugged. "He must have gotten some bad news."

7

Martin looked over his wife's shoulder as he embraced her and rubbed her back. She was facing the curtained glass doors of their suite. He was facing inside, staring at their prisoner.

He kissed her. "Gwen, baby, I need you in this. All right? We need to be a team."

"And I need you back," she said, sniffling.

"I can't have you openly complaining in front of the prisoner, in front of these kids. We're committed to this now."

"Martin, we can always go. We can leave him here and swim, grab a raft, anything."

"Be my brave one, Gwen, like you always are." He tried to kiss her again. She shook her head and pushed away from him.

"I'd rather be your smart one."

Zack and Brittany were hugging each other on the far bed. They watched Martin as he trudged over to the steaming iron sitting on the bureau. He lifted it slowly and gazed at it thoughtfully. He held it close to Meat's face. The captive leaned away from it as far as he could while still bound to the chair.

"Meat," Martin said, "I'm going to remove your gag to ask you a few more specifics before we head out. If you scream, you're going to lose an eye. Got it?"

Meat nodded slowly.

Martin reached around the captive's head and loosened the gag, letting the soaked towel drop to the floor.

"Now, where exactly is the bomb?"

Meat looked down, and took several deep breaths before speaking.

"In the men's room," he mumbled, "the one nearest the bridge."

"Is it a dirty bomb?"

Meat, still staring at his feet, nodded yes.

"A dirty bomb?" Zack said. "What's up wit that?"

"It's packed with radioactive material," Martin said. "Cheaper and easier to make than a regular nuke, but still potent. It spreads radiation. Everyone not killed immediately in the blast zone dies a slow, painful death."

"I'm not buying it," Gwen said. "Why put the bomb up high? Why not put it low to blow a hole in the ship and sink it? Or put it near the engine?"

"If we blow the ship, it sinks," Meat said, head still bowed. "If we detonate a dirty bomb up high, the radiation spreads out and catches the surrounding ships."

"Then the peeps comin' to rescue would get infected too, right?"

"That's right," Meat said.

"Punk, you sick."

"Martin," Gwen said. "Please. I'm begging. Tie him down, gag him and let's get as far away as possible."

"You do that," Meat said, "and my team will shoot you in the back as you run. No one is allowed to escape."

"Can you defuse the bomb?" Martin said.

"It's actually easier than you think. We all had to learn it inside and out so no one was irreplaceable. In case we lost anyone."

"Look up when you're talking to me." Martin reached out, grabbed the prisoner's chin and lifted his head. Meat flinched.

His eyes were bloodshot. He was holding back tears, but the anger in his gaze shone through clearly.

"Listen," Martin said. "You're going to lead us to the bomb and then you're going to disable it. If you try anything, you're dead. Understand?"

"Yes."

"Martin," Gwen said. "What if this is a suicide mission and they just shoot him and all of us? Or they detonate the bomb? Or he says he's going to defuse it and he activates it?"

"Gwen, I know you're upset and scared, but you must stop questioning me. We have to get to that bomb or we're all going to die of radiation poisoning. They want us to run, so we have to attack."

"It's not a suicide mission," Meat said, turning his head to the side, trying to face Gwen. "We're freelancers. Mercenaries."

"So you got paid to do this?"

"I go where the money is."

Zack shook his head. "Filthy merc bitch."

"Go where the money is?" Gwen said. "Even if you're being paid to kill people?"

Meat bowed his head again.

"So what was your escape plan?"

"We've got a small submarine waiting for us. Once we're all on it and out of range, boom."

"A submarine," Gwen said, rolling her eyes.

"The plan isn't impossible," Martin said.

"Who hired you?"

"Gwen, we don't have time."

"Martin, why do you only believe what he says when it reinforces your paranoid fantasy, but you think he's lying when it doesn't? We have to get off this boat! Now!"

"We can't! He said his men would shoot us!"

"Oh, my God."

"Um, can we like, get going?" Brittany said. "I want to finish this and just go home."

"Me too," Martin said. "We can go after you gag him and after we defuse the bomb. Meat, you give directions by nodding your head."

Gwen didn't move.

Martin looked at her and said sternly, "Gwen."

She didn't respond.

"Gwen." Martin said, louder.

She didn't move.

"Gwen!" he yelled.

"I'll come with you, Martin, but I won't help."

"Fine. Then stay out of the way. Britt? Can you help out?"

Brittany glanced quickly at Gwen before moving to gag Meat with the washcloth. Zack helped her release him from the chair while tightening the electrical cord around his wrists. The cord binding his ankles was loosened so he would have enough mobility to take small steps.

Gwen stood in the corner with her arms folded.

Zack wrapped a third cord around Meat's neck and pulled it from behind.

"You on a short leash, bitch. Remember that."

Martin was peeking out the door.

He came back into the room. "The hall's clear. Everyone ready?"

Zack and Brittany nodded.

Martin pushed the door open and stepped out, gun pointing ahead of him.

Meat came next, the several vicious burns on his body oozed and made tiny squishing noises with each step. Brittany held onto his leash. Gwen followed.

Zack came last, his gun extended, watching their backs.

"Yo, yo," he said. "Game time."

8

"So, Barra," North said. "Have you contacted your sub?"

"We ping each other every hour. Why?"

"I was just thinking, if ours got taken out, maybe yours did, too."

"Relax, North."

"I'm just saying. Maybe they took each other out. Collided or something."

"Bro," Barra said, "no wonder the lobby security guys always say you're uptight."

"Hey, I'm concerned about your sub. The only way out for all of us now. So excuse me."

"Fine," Barra said, "I'll check in." He adjusted his headset and voice distorter. "Delta, come in. Delta, this is Alpha. Come in."

Everyone on the bridge watched Barra.

"Delta, this is Alpha. You there?"

Barra waited, then broke the connection.

"Now what?" North asked.

"Doesn't mean anything," Barra said, removing the voice box. "He's probably just laying low after taking out your sub."

"Can you guys keep it down?" Holland said. "We need to present a professional image for our customer."

"Who?" Barra said. "Oh you mean the old guy taking a nap?"

They all looked to the corner where Sinclair was sitting on a stool in the captain's office. His head drooped forward and he was lightly snoring.

"We need to talk about what to do with him when it's time to go." Holland said. "What's your plan? I know you're going to blow a hole in the bottom, but how? Can you give me specifics?"

"Well, I've got the bomb detonator right here." Barra reached into his wet-suit pocket and pulled out a small device that looked like a television remote control. He flicked up a metal guard, revealing a toggle switch beneath. He carefully replaced the guard and slid the detonator back into his pocket.

He continued. "We've also got some welding torches to prep the hull and make sure the opening will be big enough for us to swim through, but not too big. The blast will go just how we want it."

"I didn't see any welding gear."

"Because you were distracted by the bomb. All part of the plan. Hell, I should have been a movie director or something. Maybe a magician."

"So you have scuba equipment too?"

"Yep. Hidden with the welding stuff."

"What about the hostages?" North asked. "You going to let them drown?"

"Of course not. Take a look." Barra pointed to a cardboard box in the corner of the bridge. North opened it. It was full of scissors, knives and pliers.

"We're going to throw these to the people and tell them to cut themselves loose. That's why we didn't jettison the life rafts. So did I answer your question? We burn a hole out, then blow the ship and complete the only terrorist action in history with no casualties."

"No intentional ones," North said.

"Hey, that was you guys, not us."

"What about the news chopper?"

"Just some ambitious reporters. Can't say I'm upset."

"Look," Holland said, "I was only asking about your sub because I'm still trying to figure out a way to get our client out of here."

"We go on the sub," Barra said. "Sinclair can hang onto the outside."

"I heard that," Sinclair said from the captain's office, not bothering to open his eyes or lift his head.

"Go back to sleep," North said.

"It's not the fit that's the problem," Barra said. "It's the oxygen."

"So?" Holland said. "Surface earlier."

"And endanger two ops at once? No way."

"Why don't one of you mix in with the passengers?" Sinclair said, sitting up.

"Why don't you, old man?" Barra said.

"Because that's not what I paid for. I signed up for singular treatment, and that's what I'm going to get. Do you really think any of you are going to keep your jobs if you don't give me what I want?"

"If that bag of bones keeps rattling," Barra said, "I'm throwing it over."

"Come on, Barra," North said. "Don't make things harder on us. We have to start thinking about alternatives."

"Then do what the old guy says, North. You or your girlfriend merge in with the hostages."

Before anyone could answer, the bridge speakers popped. "Hussein, this is Goodkin. Hussein?"

"Duty calls," Barra said. "You guys have your own job and we've got two tickets out of here. You figure who should be odd man out."

"I'm leaving on that sub at the very least," Sinclair said. "And why hasn't someone gotten me a phone yet? You can't imagine how much money I'll lose if I don't tell my broker to go all-in on oil before this war gets started."

"Can you shut him up?" Barra said as he snapped his voice box into place. He grabbed the com.

9

On the Bonnie Jane, Goodkin leaned his head back and threw a pill into his mouth. He quickly stuffed the pill bottle in his pocket and swallowed hard, then activated the com.

"Hussein, this is Goodkin. Hussein?" He waited, tapping his fingers. "Hussein, are you there? I want to get us back on track."

"Yes," Hussein answered, "let us continue. Tell me the status of my demands."

"I have to say the fact that you shot those two people has limited my options. And you should note that even though you killed them, you didn't get what you wanted."

"So you suggest I kill more?"

"No, I'm pointing out that killing only works against you. And it makes you look like a monster. Soon you'll even run out of food and water. There has to be an end to this, so let's start talking about that. How does this end?"

"Who is the real barbarian, Goodkin? Consider this. The most wealthy nation on earth, the mighty United States, will not put forth a relatively small amount of money to save the lives of its citizens from Kariqistani savages, as you call us. You think that earns you respect? You think that makes me a savage?"

"Hussein, I don't want to play games. I want to start talking about options. What else can I give you in order to let those people go? Do you want safe passage back to Kariqistan? We can possibly do that. You get your freedom, and so do-"

"No. I want what I have asked for. Fifty million United States dollars. All multinationals and Western armies out of Muslim countries. If you will not give it to me, I will keep killing."

"Hussein, it is difficult enough now getting anyone to talk about concessions. Kill more and I won't be able to convince anyone to give you anything. Ask for something reasonable. I just offered you your freedom."

"That is not yours to give, Goodkin."

The speakers popped as Hussein disconnected.

* * *

On the Sunset Mist, Barra shut off the com and pulled off his voice distorter.

"This negotiator guy is a clown. If I were him, I'd have given the order to storm this ship long ago."

He turned to his men.

"You, keep trying to raise the sub. You, monitor the news. Keep an eye out for any official aggressive action from the U.S. toward Kariqistan. This job's getting as old and tiresome as Sinclair."

"I heard that."

10

In the CNB helicopter, Savant heard Burnett whispering in his earpiece.

"Savant? Come in, Savant. This is Captain Burnett. Come in, Savant."

Savant leaned away from his sniper rifle and pressed his finger in his ear. "Savant here, sir."

"Good. Now, listen up, the rest of your team is going to be applying pressure from the bottom, so expect the cork to pop off the top, understand? The first motherfucker that steps out on the top deck, you blow his fucking head off."

"Yes, sir."

"This circus has gone on long enough."

"Yes, sir."

"Burnett out."

"Who are you talking to?" Amaretto asked. "Did you just get an order?"

"Yes, ma'am." Savant pressed his eye to the sight.

"So, what was the order?" Amaretto said. "Come on. You can tell me."

"No, ma'am."

PART 7

DO IT YOURSELF

1

Martin reached back to signal the others to stop. He recoiled as he accidentally pushed his fingertips into the oozing wound in Meat's chest. Meat yelped into his gag.

"Quiet!" Martin whispered. "I hear something." He wiped his moist fingers on Meat's sleeve.

They waited at the base of the stairs, listening. They could hear talking, but the voices were too faint to make sense of the words. Martin and Zack pointed their guns up the staircase until the voices receded.

"Meat, are we close?" Martin whispered.

The prisoner nodded yes. He tilted his chin toward the guide sign on the wall.

"Plaza del Sol. The next level," Martin said quietly. "The bomb is in the men's room near the bridge. Right?"

Meat nodded yes again.

"Martin," Gwen said, "let's just leave him here. This is getting too dangerous."

"Gwen, we're committed now. There's no room for doubt anymore. We have to shut off that bomb. Everyone step lightly. These stairs might echo."

"We're heading right back to the ballroom. Where they kept us."

"Gwen, shut up. Now."

Gwen's nostrils flared and her eyes flung wide. She clamped her lips shut and said nothing.

Martin tiptoed up the stairs, aiming his gun down the long hallway that ran the length of the deck. Midway along the left side the double doors to the ballroom were closed. The corridor ended in a propped open door. Through it, he could see onto the bridge. The terrorists were moving about, talking without their voice boxes.

Past some smaller lounges on the right was a sign pointing toward the restrooms.

Martin turned back to the others.

"Quickly and quietly. Men's room is the first right. Everyone ready?"

2

Fran Amaretto directed her cameraman Phil as he filmed the top deck of the Sunset Mist.

"Make sure every shot has those gore stains in it," she said, "and the bloody flag."

"Naturally."

"Great. Any comment on that, Savant?" She pointed to the soiled American flag below.

"No, ma'am." He continued staring through his rifle scope.

"They desecrated your country's flag and you've got nothing to say?"

"No, ma'am."

"So you don't care at all?"

"No, ma'am."

"Did you know that anyone who answers this question with either 'no, ma'am' or 'yes, ma'am' is an asshole?"

Savant paused, then finally said, "No, ma'am."

"Gotcha," she said, smiling. "You know you could just say nothing, but those weren't your orders, were they? You were told to say 'yes, ma'am' or 'no, ma'am,' so that's what you do, follow orders to the letter, am I right?"

"Yes, ma'am."

"Look at that, Savant. We're getting to know each other. Isn't this great?"

"No, ma'am."

"Phil," she said.

"What's up?"

"This silence bites. A hostage situation shouldn't be boring. A news chopper is shot down, the terrorists just killed two people and now nothing." She yawned. "Any ideas?"

Her cell phone rang.

"Amaretto."

She listened.

"Well, we are in a bit of a lull. The terrorist and negotiator argue every now and then, but they're at an impasse. I secured a sniper on our chopper, but the guy doesn't talk." She raised her voice. "He's worthless."

Savant didn't react.

She paused for a second. "Sure, I don't mind waiting."

"Keep circling," she said to the pilot.

"No problem."

The chopper glided in a slow, wide oval path around the ship when her phone beeped. "Yeah," she said. "Why did you make me wait? Confirm what?" Her voice rose, "They did?"

She listened.

"No, I didn't know that," she said. "That will definitely make things interesting out here. I'll ask him. Are you sure? Really. You're sure? Positive? Verified? All right, I'm just checking. I'll run with it. Keep me posted."

She looked up recently received calls on her cell phone and dialed. Goodkin answered immediately.

"Miss Amaretto, I told you not to call."

"I just wanted to get your reaction to some recent news. Did you know that the President has ordered U.S. Navy warships to move within missile firing range of Kariqistan? Looks like they're getting ready for war. Or at least a strike."

Goodkin was silent. Finally, he said, "We'll have to talk about this later. I'm in the middle of negotiations."

"No you're not, it's quiet. I can hear, remember?"

"I can't comment."

"You didn't know, did you?"

"Goodbye."

"Or did you know and this was something you recommended. Is that it?"

The phone cut off. Amaretto turned in her seat.

"We're going to war, Savant. After this is all over you'll be shipped out. You'll have plenty more people to kill. Are you excited?"

"Yes, ma'am."

3

"You know," Sinclair said from the captain's office, fanning himself with a captain's hat, "instead of sitting here taunting the negotiator, you should be working on some way to get me off the ship."

"Bro, where did you find this guy?" Barra said to North, then to Sinclair, "There's no first-class on a vessel taken hostage."

"Barra, chill," Holland said. "He's a customer."

"Your customer. Not mine."

"Damn it!" Sinclair yelled. Startled, everyone on the bridge turned to face him. He was standing in the captain's office doorway, shaking, his fists clenched.

"You both work for the same company!" he said. "I'm a customer of you both! Once this debacle is concluded, I'm going to buy Redfire and burn it to the ground. Then I'm going to leave the destroyed husk of a building there for all to admire. Don't think I can't and don't think I won't. This is simply unacceptable. Your retirement program is gone once I'm through unless you get me off this ship. Right now."

Holland held her hands up defensively. "Sir, please, we're doing all we can. There's no practical way to get you clear unless you agree to go to the Coast Guard vessel."

"Doesn't anyone here have a phone? A way to communicate with your bosses?"

"Cell phones can be tracked and intercepted," North said. "That would compromise the secrecy and privacy of what we're all doing. Our bosses wouldn't even answer for that reason. It's what people like you pay us for."

"You confiscated all the cell phones when you took over the ship," Sinclair said. "What did you do with them?"

"We shoved them in a box, weighted it down and threw it overboard," Barra said.

"There has to be one lying around on the deck."

"We made sure there weren't."

"I'm going out there to look for one. You couldn't have gotten them all." He headed for the bridge door.

"Whoa. Whoa," Barra said, stepping in front of Sinclair. "What the hell?"

"Why don't you let us take him for a walk on the deck?" North said. "Get some fresh air. Help him calm down."

"I don't know about this," Holland said. "Mister Sinclair, the media will see you."

"Then give me one of your masks."

"And what will I tell the negotiator?" Barra said. "Damn, this is a pain in the ass. No wonder terrorists prefer to blow themselves up. It's easier."

"Tell them we're looking for a passenger's medicine," Sinclair said. "Do I have to do everything around here?"

"Well, you like to be the boss," North answered.

"Then what did I pay you clowns for?"

"All right," Barra said. "Everyone shut up. Hold on a second."

He slipped his voice box around his neck and picked up the com.

"Goodkin," he said, "are you still there?"

Goodkin replied quickly. "I'm here, Hussein. Let's continue-"

"Silence. One of our older guests has lost his medicine. We will be going outside to try to find it on deck."

"That must be a lot of trouble for you, Hussein. Why don't you let me take him off the boat? He's just one hostage. Show the world that Kariqistanis are not petty murderers."

Barra muted the com and pulled his voice box loose.

"What do you think?"

"No," Sinclair said. "I already told you. That is not what I paid for."

"It's a way off. A personalized trip."

"When you go to the jewelry store and you purchase a diamond ring, and they give you an aluminum band, do you accept it?"

Barra rolled his eyes, set his voice distorter back in place and lifted the com. "No, Goodkin. No deal. He is our captive until you act. I am warning you, if my men are harmed, your nightmares will be filled with the screams of dying Americans for the rest of your life."

"All right, Hussein. You have my word. We will take no aggression. But I will need-"

Barra hung up. He pulled off the voice box and hurled it against the console.

"Here," Holland said. She took off her ski mask and handed it to Sinclair. Hanging in the captain's office was a bright blue windbreaker with "Sunset Mist Crew" written in stencil on the breast. She held the jacket up behind Sinclair, helping him slip his arms into the sleeves.

"I need shades," he said.

Barra pulled open a drawer on the console, dug around among the small tools until he found a pair of sunglasses. "Here. And that's it. Don't ask for sunscreen."

Sinclair put on the glasses.

"Now, Sinclair," Barra said. "Since I'm letting you outside, no buying the company, burning it down and laying us off, okay? Tit for tat, right?"

"I'm not making any promises."

"You really don't have a sense of humor, do you?"

"I'm going out."

"Whoa," Barra said. "Wait up. North and I will go with you."

"I go where I please," Sinclair said loudly, "and I don't wait." He pushed the bridge door open and stepped out the door onto the deck.

4

"I go where I please and I don't wait."
A door slammed and the terrorists cursed.
Martin heard the voices clearly. They were speaking English. He stood beyond the hall intersection, where the way to the men's room branched off the main corridor. He knelt on one knee, using two hands to keep his gun aimed toward the bridge, covering the rest of the group as they pulled Meat along behind him, turning down the short hall to the right.
"Martin," Gwen whispered. "Come on!"
"They're talking. Maybe I can hear something."
"Who cares? Hurry!"
After some mumbling, the bridge door opened and closed again. Martin walked backwards towards the men's room as the others filed in.

5

Goodkin was on the outer walkway of the Bonnie Jane, talking on his mic, tablet in his left hand. He kept unplugging and reconnecting the mic cable, smacking the screen, as if the device had frozen.
Dunn and Burnett watched him from inside. Through the glass they could hear him repeating loudly, "Hello? Is anyone there? Hello? Is this working?"
Burnett's earpiece blinked. He tapped it. "Burnett. Go. You're in position? You're sure you've lost him? No word? None at all? But the other scout came back?"
He paused.
"But do you really think a terrorist would talk like some kind of rap star?"
He waited again.
"Yeah, I guess you're right. I always thought that German guy was a nut for what he said about culture, but maybe he was saying it's a lot like a weapon. Maybe he was reaching for his revolver as a means of

self-defense. Hm? Oh, never mind. I'm just thinking out loud. Keep advancing. Stop at nothing. We'll find your boy later. Kill some bad guys to make up for it and try to avoid collaterals. Godspeed."

Burnett tapped his earpiece. He noticed Captain Dunn was staring at him, eyebrows raised.

"Something you want to ask me, Dunn?" Burnett said.

"Oh, I want to," Dunn said, "but I'm smart enough not to."

6

The bridge door closed behind Sinclair. He stepped out onto the ship's upper deck and into the sun. He took a moment to adjust the ski mask he was wearing that Holland had loaned him. He looked up at the CNB helicopter, then with his hands trembling, he bent down and tossed aside a beach towel. He dug through a duffel bag.

Barra and North watched from the bridge.

"Damn it!" Barra said, "North, bro, this guy is a real prick."

"I noticed."

"Come with me. We'll help him look."

"He said he wanted to go out alone," Holland said.

"Are you crazy?" Barra said. "There's no telling what he'll do."

"Barra and I will go," North said to Holland. "That way you can stay on his good side. Work for you?"

She smiled. "Sure. And let's not forget I gave him my mask. As long as he isn't complaining about me when we get back, that's all I care about."

"That's what I figured," North said.

Barra and North adjusted their masks and stepped onto the deck. Sinclair had moved to a cluster of overturned chairs.

The deck glowed white from the blazing sun. Even wearing shades over their masks, North and Barra had to squint. They stepped among the chaotic remains of the interrupted beach party. The CNB helicopter buzzed overhead, angled so the cameraman in the rear could film through the window. A sniper muzzle poked out the other side.

"They're filming us," North said. "And they've got a sniper. But he's on a bad angle. They can easily come around, though."

"They won't shoot," Barra said. "They'll talk first and by the time they want to launch a raid we'll be gone. That's how we used to do it."

"Yeah, but that was a long time ago."

"Hey, you two," Sinclair said, left hand on the small of his back as he bent over to look through a purse. "Are you going to help me?"

"Oh, sure."

Barra and North half-heartedly pulled open some beach duffel bags and a cooler.

7

"What are they doing down there?" the pilot asked.

"Looking for an old guy's medicine," Amaretto said.

"Spin the chopper around," Savant said. "I can't see them."

"Oh, now you decide to say something," Amaretto said.

"Turn the chopper around. Now."

"Look at you, so talkative. How about I get some footage first and then we do what you want?"

"No, ma'am."

"Fine," she said to him. "Phil, keep rolling. Mark, keep flying as we are. Do not turn this chopper around."

"Fran, what's happening out there?" the studio asked.

"Apparently, one of the hostages needs medicine. Three of the terrorists are searching for it among all the possessions left on the upper deck."

8

Goodkin was still out on the deck alone when his tablet phone app rang.

He answered it yelling. "Finally! What the hell? Where have you been?"

"Nelson," the voice said. "It's me. I mean us. Your advisory team. We have you on speakerphone."

"You should!" Goodkin yelled. "We need to be in constant contact. That was one of the key tenets of the protocol design! You're my lifeline. The perpetrator has been stalling the last couple hours and I need you to help me establish some flexibility in his choice parameters. Then you go silent. You're also supposed to be distracting the media with the talking heads or the press conferences. I need help! I can't believe you idiots abandoned me!"

"We're sorry, buddy, we're all really sorry."

"Well, you should be, but we'll analyze it later. We have to get back to work."

"Back to work?"

"Yes! Back to work! You don't think I resolved an international crisis alone, do you? I think Hussein might be softening. He's got three of his team searching for an old hostage's medicine on the deck. And I just heard from the news reporter that warships are en route toward Kariqistan. It's probably just a rumor and she's just trying to get me to spill some info. Is it true?"

"You're still talking to Hussein?"

"Of course. Why wouldn't I?"

"Nelson, I'm sorry. We're all sorry."

"Sorry for what?"

"We need to apologize."

"Apologize? For what? For disappearing? For the warships?"

"I would have called sooner, but we all just spent the last couple hours getting chewed out by the boss."

"What are you talking about?"

"We talked to the higher ups. We were trying to secure your authority over the Navy guy for you, but instead we got spanked. They said if he's got a team of Navy SEALs with their hardware all ready to go, you should let him take command. We told them about the protocol we've developed and the danger to the hostages, but they said the SEALs are the best. Oh, and that bit about the warships? It's true."

"Wait. What are you saying? I don't have authority here?"

"Ah, no. You don't. We took it to the bosses and they took it to the Navy bosses and we all got slapped. The word from on high was that the Navy should be in command of the scene. Nobody told you? The Navy guy has been in control for a few hours now. How are you still giving orders?"

The color drained from Goodkin's face. "No one told me anything."

"Hell, then in addition to an apology, I need to tell you the decision of our bosses. As of a few hours ago, you're no longer incident commander. The Navy guy is. Captain Burnhard."

"Burnett," Goodkin growled.

"Yeah, him. He's in charge. You're not. Sorry. It's the Navy's problem now. Let the SEALs handle it. That comes from as high up our food chain as you can get. And I mean high up. The word came from you-know-who. We're out of the loop and so are you."

Goodkin turned to look at Burnett through the bridge windows. Burnett smiled with mock innocence. Goodkin tapped the tablet screen to hang up the phone before he entered the bridge. He let the door close behind him.

"How long have you known?" he said.

"Known what?" Burnett asked.

Goodkin shook. "You know what I'm talking about."

"I do. But I want to hear you say it. For the benefit of Captain Dunn as well."

"How long have you known… that you're in charge?"

"Well, I could say since the minute I got here, but officially, just a few hours."

"Damn it!" Goodkin kicked the ship's console. "Why didn't you tell me?"

"Same reason I don't tell the wife when I've been to the strip club. To avoid drama. Like the kind you're displaying right now."

"And your SEALs?"

"Advancing to the bridge as quickly as possible. Right now."

"They're already onboard? But how did they get there unseen?"

"That's why we call them the best."

"I swore on my children's lives that there was no one else on board! Hussein trusted me. Do you know what he'll do if he thinks I lied?"

"I don't give a crap what he thinks. And he won't do a damn thing. He's going to be dead soon."

Goodkin stepped off the bridge and pulled the cable from his ear. He hurled his tablet as far as he could into the sea, screaming as he did so. He leaned over the railing and looked up at the sky.

"Captain Dunn," Burnett said, "I know this is your vessel, and I respect that, but I might as well make it official. I'm in charge of this situation now."

"Aye, sir," Dunn said. "Makes no difference to me."

"Well, it will to some hostages waiting to be set free."

"Any orders, sir?"

"Just hold position. Sit back and watch to see how a real rescue operation is run. I'm going to give everyone, especially crybaby Goodkin out there, a lesson in exactly how to deal with bad guys."

9

North and Barra stayed a few paces distant from Sinclair as the older man pushed aside towels and rooted through bags, searching for a cell phone. Each time he bent over to search he took longer to stand up.

North and Barra barely gave any effort to the search.

"So, North," Barra said, "you ever think about Hayger?"

"Yeah. Sometimes."

"What do you think he'd say to this situation?"

"Something's wrong if something isn't wrong," they both said at the same time.

"You think he's looking down on us, right now? Laughing his ass off?"

"He's got to be sitting in a beach chair on a cloud, beer in one hand."

"A babe on his lap."

"Sunglasses on."

"Nine mil at his side."

"You think they allow guns in heaven?"

"Like they'd be able to stop him from bringing one in."

They both chuckled.

"It's good to laugh about it, but the way he went out," North paused, letting his voice trail off. "It still hurts. That's not the sort of world I want my son to grow up in."

Barra spat on the deck. "Told you not to have kids. It's a shitty world."

"But it's the only one we've got," North said. "All those missions we ran, what did they add up to? Seems like the only lasting thing we ever accomplished was getting Hayger killed. The world isn't a better place."

"Man, why do you have to be like that? All mopey. Everyone does what the boss wants. It's how things are."

"And the way it should be," Sinclair said as he leaned against the railing, holding his back before bending over to look in a cooler. "Now help me, you two."

North and Barra ignored him.

"Hayger's death," Barra said. "That really messed you up, didn't it? Get over it, bro. We're in the business of death. Naming your son after him was probably the worst thing you could have done."

"But don't you remember what he said, Barra? Why do we do this? So who comes next, meaning the kids, don't have to. He never met my son but he was already thinking about him. But now, this? Redfire? That's just for money."

"Isn't that making the world better for your son? What exactly is the problem?"

"That attitude. You're setting up a false flag here. Doing a great job of it. And we didn't even question it. But kids like the kids we were when we met Hayger are going to sign up for a war and get killed. Over a lie."

"What do you want me to do, bro? Refuse the job? Someone else would do it."

North didn't say anything, just kept walking and pushing aside the remains of the interrupted pool party.

Barra shook his head. "It's way past time for you to get out, bro."

They strolled along, tossing aside beach chairs, looking in bags. "Yeah," North said, "I've been thinking that, too. For a while."

"You want to know something, North? They didn't tell me the job, but they let me pick my team. They were surprised when I didn't pick you. Want to know why?"

North hesitated. "I'm sure you had your reasons."

"I did. Because after Hayger, you started taking it all too seriously."

Sinclair opened a cooler and shoved aside the beer bottles. "You guys sound like fairies."

"Shut the hell up," Barra said. "Who gets their own personal escort out of a hostage situation? What are you? Goddamn royalty?"

"Close enough," Sinclair said.

"Yeah, well, think about who you're looking to for help, jackass. All that money you got didn't do squat. We're both on the same boat. Pun intended."

Sinclair continued walking alongside the pool, moving toward the front of the cruise ship. The CNB news helicopter kept pace.

Sinclair stood up, chuckling, arching his back. "What a couple of pansies. I thought you ex-Special Forces were supposed to be tough."

"Shut up, old man," Barra said. "There's no phones out here. My team got them all, let's go back in."

"I'm not done yet." Sinclair stumbled over a soda can.

Neither North nor Barra reached out to help him regain his footing.

"We don't go in until I say," Sinclair said, turning his back and kicking aside a towel.

"Fine," Barra said.

10

Brittany held the door open for Meat as he hobbled into the men's room. The others filed in behind them. Martin, the last one in, closed the door behind him.

"So where it at, yo?" Zack asked. "Where da shaka-laka boom-boom?" He kicked open each of the stall doors.

Meat shuffled into the far corner next to a urinal and leaned his head against the wall.

"Wait a minute," Martin said, pressing his gun into Meat's back. "What are you trying to pull here? You'd better be careful."

He took the gag out, spun Meat around to face him, then rammed the barrel of his gun under Meat's chin.

"Talk."

"Thanks," Meat said. "That gag was bugging me." He leaned his head back and closed his eyes. He breathed deeply. Drops of dried blood trailed down his chest and thigh where Martin had burned him with the iron.

"Check the whole place," Martin said over his shoulder. "Zack, you watch the door." Brittany and Gwen looked in the cabinets, under the sinks and in the cleaning supplies closet.

"Nothing," Gwen said. "I told you. A complete waste of time."

"I don't see anything weird," Brittany said.

"Meat, what's going on? Is it behind some secret panel?" Martin asked. "Did you really hide the bomb in here?"

"No, I didn't," he said, his voice quivering. "I told you, I'm a Navy SEAL here to rescue you. I don't know anything about a bomb. As far as I know there is none."

"Oh, this is crazy," Gwen said. "We risked our lives to get here. Now we're in more danger! The terrorists are right down the hall! I told you!"

"Gwen, quiet!" Martin yelled. "Meat, what's your game? Where's the bomb?"

"My team's orders were to raid the bridge. My game is I wanted to be closer to them so they'll find me and get me away from you stupid yahoos."

"This is bullshit, yo," Zack said. "Fuck da bomb. Let's go show him to his terror homeys, threaten to take his ass out."

"You take me to the terrorists and they'll kill us all. You'll be walking right back into their arms after you escaped. Damn morons playing commando."

"Yo, punk, you watch it."

"Zack," Martin said, sternly. "Please."

He turned to face Meat. "We have no choice now but to use you as a bargaining chip. If you're a terrorist, we'll trade you for our freedom. If you're a Navy SEAL, we'll do the same. Ladies, grab a weapon. We're going to the bridge."

"A weapon? Against terrorists?" Gwen shrieked.

"Miss," Meat said to her, "please. You're the only one here with a brain. Can you talk him out of this?"

"I've been trying," she said.

"He's going to get us all killed."

"Martin," Gwen said, her eyes filling with tears, "he's telling the truth. He's right. We're going to die. You've been acting insane since he showed up."

"Hey, lady," Meat said, "don't make it sound like it's my fault."

"Shut up!" Martin shouted. Then to Gwen, "Don't talk to him. He's turning us against each other."

He turned to Meat. "One more word and you lose an eye."

Meat closed his lips tightly. He shrugged at Gwen.

"I'm sorry," she said, turning away.

Zack unscrewed the wooden handle from a mop and then snapped the wood over his thigh. He gave one end to Gwen and the other to Brittany.

"Girls got claws," he said.

"Oh, this will do great against a gun," Gwen said, looking at the improvised spear.

"Good thinking, son," Martin said. "Everyone form up behind our human shield here."

"The terrorists won't care if you offer me as a hostage," Meat said, his voice cracking. "As soon as they see me they'll shoot. Now, stop this. I'm American! I'm a Navy SEAL and there is no bomb!"

"Bullshit. The guys who took the rich man away said there was."

"What are you talking about? What rich man? Who took him away?"

"You're lying!"

"You don't know anything!"

"Gag him! Gwen, gag him."

"No, Martin. This has gone on enough. Let's leave him here. Whoever he is we should just go."

"Brittany," Martin interrupted. "Gag him."

She looked to Gwen and then to Zack.

"Come on, girl," Zack said. "Gag the punk, aight?"

"Help!" Meat screamed. "Help!"

Brittany slipped the gag in his mouth.

Zack elbowed Martin.

"Dawg, you gotta charm da ladies."

Martin grabbed Meat and pushed him out through the door, walking behind him.

11

"Turn this chopper around now," Savant said.

"You finally decide to talk, and you're giving orders?" Amaretto said. "I don't think so."

Savant's hand shot to his hip and came up with his pistol. He pressed the barrel against the temple of Mark, the pilot. Mark jolted and the chopper shook in tune with his movement.

Amaretto yelped.

"Okay! Okay!" Mark said, leaning away from the gun. "I'll do it. Relax, man. You don't need the gun."

"Now," Savant said.

"I'm doing it. I'm doing it." The chopper started to spin.

"Savant," Amaretto said. "Put the gun away. We'll do what you want."

"Do it now," he said, his monotone voice now tinted with an ominous edge.

"I am! I told you. Look outside," Mark said. "Please put the gun down."

"Not until we are positioned how I like."

Mark operated the control sticks with shaking hands. The CNB chopper rotated in the air.

"Fran," the studio newsreader said in Amaretto's headset. "What's going on out there? We've lost the video. All we can see is ocean now."

"We're having, um, uh, some local difficulties. I'll describe the scene. There are three terrorists still out on the deck, looking for a hostage's medicine. You aren't missing anything new."

"Can you send us the visuals?"

"Not now. We have a problem."

"Can you be more specific? What's going on out there?"

Savant shook his head no.

"Just some technical problems and, uh, some turbulence. That's all. We'll send video as soon as we can. This is Fran Amaretto for CNB News signing out."

She clicked off her microphone. Savant lowered his gun.

"Now what, Savant?"

He didn't answer her. Instead he looked at the pilot. "Keep us as steady as you can, right here."

"You got it."

"Good."

Savant yanked open the sliding side door of the helicopter and leaned out into the rushing wind. Half-in, half-out of the chopper, he rested one boot on the landing skid, aiming down the barrel toward the deck below.

12

"Come on geezer, time to go back," Barra said, stepping over a boom box.

"No thanks. I like the fresh air," Sinclair said, breathing deeply. He headed toward the fore of the boat. "Someday I'm going to bottle it up and sell it back to you. Make a fortune. Hell, it worked with water."

"Sir," North said. "Mr. Sinclair. We need to go in now. That would be best."

Sinclair chuckled. "Shut up. I could buy and sell you a thousand times. You don't tell me what's best. I tell you."

"Come on," Barra said. "There's no phones out here. Time to go back."

North and Barra were following behind him, pleading. Sinclair continued to the platform at the very front tip of the boat.

"Sir," North said, "your contract authorizes me to incapacitate you if I feel it necessary."

"And you're jeopardizing my mission," Barra said.

"Just do what you're told," Sinclair said. "That's my one rule for the help. Just do what you're told. It's so easy. Why can't you two handle it?"

"Sinclair, get back here," Barra said, reaching out to grab the older man. He slipped on a towel and fell to his knee. "Damn it!"

Sinclair stood out on the platform at the very tip of the ship's bow, high above the ocean.

"Sir," North said. "This is the last time I'll ask, then I'm coming for you."

"Oh, please. I own you," Sinclair said. "And if I wanted to, I could own this boat." Sinclair turned to face the front of the ship. He leaned his waist against the platform's railing and threw his arms out to either side like he was flying.

He leaned his head back, shouting, "I'm the king of the w-"

He never finished.

His head exploded, vomiting blood and spongy gore in all directions. The sound of the rifle shot from the helicopter above rang against the deck. Sinclair's body slumped over the railing and rested there, dribbling brains into the ocean below.

13

In the helicopter, Fran Amaretto screamed. "Oh, my God! You shot him!"

"Yes, ma'am," Savant said, as he yanked back a lever on his rifle, ejecting the smoking bullet cartridge.

"Captain's orders. Shoot the first motherfucker who steps out."

"Wow. But aren't they going to start killing hostages now?"

"No, ma'am."

Savant tracked the remaining two targets as they dropped low and sprinted for the bridge. They ran in a jagged, unpredictable pattern.

"Smart prey," Savant muttered.

The first target made it through the door, holding it open from inside the bridge. Savant aimed for the trailing terrorist's torso and fired. A red splotch smacked against the deck. The man tumbled onto the bridge, the door closing behind him.

Savant popped loose the spent cartridge and aimed again.

14

Barra skidded across the floor, his equipment breaking loose and flying about the bridge. He crashed hard into the control console, clutching at his belly. A streak of blood marked the path of his fall.

"I'm hit," he groaned through clenched teeth. His face tightened as he rolled onto his back. "Ah, damn it. God damn it."

North didn't hear him. His thought had disappeared into reflex.

He snatched Barra's AK-47 and crashed through the door, rolling across the deck. Another shot punched through the metal hull nearby.

North raised the AK and fired a quick burst back at the airborne shooter, hitting the side of the chopper with a ping that went soft as the bullets raked over the sniper, one catching him in the neck. Savant tumbled out of the chopper, hanging just below it from his safety line. His rifle fell spinning into the ocean.

The helicopter dove sharply, retreating from North's fire.

Savant's body snapped loose and dropped, disappearing past the side of the cruise ship. A small splash sounded from below.

For an instant North wasn't sure where he was. His pulse was booming inside his ears. He shook his head and jumped back inside the bridge.

15

From the vantage point of the Bonnie Jane the crew watched as sparks popped along the side of the CNB helicopter and Savant spilled out. He hung for a moment before his safety belt snapped and his corpse plunged into the sea.

Goodkin put his hand over his mouth. "Oh, my God."

Burnett clenched his teeth. "Shit. Savant was my best shot. How the hell did that terrorist get him?"

"I'm sorry, Burnett," Dunn said. "So sorry for your man."

"Well," Burnett said, "you have to admit that Kariqi got off a good one, taking him out like that. Hell of a shot," he rubbed his reddening eyes. "Give the bandit credit."

Goodkin's mouth dropped open. He looked at Dunn.

Dunn looked at his watch.

"God damn," he mumbled, "is this day over yet?"

PART 8

MAGIC BULLET

1

Martin pressed his gun into Meat's back and shoved him roughly down the hall. Gwen trudged after them, head bowed, looking up through her eyebrows at her husband, a scowl burned onto her face. Brittany stayed well behind her with Zack, who covered their rear.

"She looks possessed," Brittany whispered to him.

"Girl, she just angry. You get good 'n' scary when you mad, too."

"Maybe, but not like that."

"Up ahead, turn right," Martin said, shoving Meat forward. "Head straight for the bridge. Don't try a damn thing."

Meat had almost reached the intersection with the main hall when fingertips slipped over the back of Martin's hand and yanked the gun free with one quick motion. Martin fell against the wall as a thunderous bang exploded. A ragged hole erupted in Meat's back, gushing blood. He staggered forward.

Martin was stunned for a moment before he could turn to face the thief.

His wife was holding the gun in her shaking hand.

"Gwen!" he screamed. "What the hell?"

"I had to," she screeched back.

Meat was lurching toward the main hallway.

"You shot him!"

"I had to, Martin! I had to bring you back. With him around you've been acting crazy. Now he's gone and we have no choice. We can't defuse any non-existent bomb. We can't confront any terrorists. Let's get to the life rafts and go!"

Meat tumbled into the main hallway and lay there face down, the wound in his back pumping out blood.

"Dayyyyym," Zack said. "That was cold."

"Oh, my God," Brittany squealed. "That's like, so gross."

Gwen stood over Meat, kicking his corpse. A thin snake of smoke rose from the gun barrel.

"Now, for the last time, Martin," she beckoned frantically from the intersection. "Let's get off this damn ship!"

2

"Man down! One of ours!"

A voice barked to Gwen's right, down the hall in the opposite direction of the bridge. Armed men, dressed all in black and wearing ski masks, were standing at the top of the stairs.

"Honey! Get back!" Martin said, as he grabbed his wife's arm.

"Open fire!" the men in black yelled.

A barrage of bullets tore through the hallway intersection, catching Gwen in its deadly rain. She was yanked from Martin's grip and collapsed, the gun flying from her slack fingers.

* * *

"Gunshots! Down there!" Holland yelled, pointing toward the starboard doorway leading from the bridge. She stood at North's side as he ripped open Barra's wetsuit and began removing his bulletproof vest. Barra jolted and groaned. The bullet had slid in at his waistline, just under the protection, piercing his belly.

"Go earn your promotion," North said to Holland. "I've got him."

She swallowed hard. "Um, okay."

She took cover behind the bridge console and watched down the hall. A body in a black wetsuit was face down, blood bubbling from a gunshot to his back. A woman was kicking him.

"What the hell?" Holland said to one of Barra's men. "The down guy one of yours?"

"Nope."

"What about the woman?"

"No idea who she is."

Several armed men in appeared at the opposite end of the hall, rising to the top of the staircase beyond the corpse and the woman kicking it. Someone reached out from the intersecting hall to pull her back.

"Man down!" the newcomers yelled. Then they shot the woman. Her body lifted and then crashed to the floor near the prone man.

"Return fire!" Holland shouted. She knelt down and raised her gun over the console, blind-firing her pistol down the corridor.

* * *

"No! Gwen!" Martin yelled, as he watched his wife tumble to the floor, falling away from him. Her eyes were wide and lifeless at the same time.

"Goddamned terrorists!" Martin screamed.

He dove into the hallway, snatching up his gun. Standing between the prone bodies of Meat and Gwen, he gripped the gun with two hands, firing toward the black-clad commandos, his back to the bridge.

The attackers retreated, taking cover in the stairwell entrance.

"Martin," Gwen gasped. "Hold me."

Martin couldn't hear. His last instant of consciousness was a moment of surprise as he was struck in the back of the head by a bullet coming from the bridge.

He fell face down, dead.

"Martin," Gwen hissed with her last breath. "Please. Just be with me."

* * *

Holland peeked above her cover.

A man wearing the same pink polo and khaki shorts as the downed woman had stepped from the intersecting hallway into her line of fire. He caught Holland's bullet in the back of his head. Something about their clothes was familiar to her, but she didn't have time to think it over.

He had been firing at the newcomers, the same people she had been trying to hit.

"What a dumbass!" Holland yelled. "He stepped right in the way!"

She turned to Barra's man. "Who was that?"

"Doesn't matter now," he said, popping from cover and firing a burst from his AK-47 down the hall.

Holland peeked around the console. No one else was emerging from the intersecting hall. She waited until one of the commandos stuck his head out from cover. She fired. He ducked back, her shot sparking off the wall near him.

* * *

Zack charged into the hall as it filled with gun smoke. With his left hand he grabbed Martin's shirt, trying to pull him out of the crossfire. With his right, he shot at the bridge.

"You bitches gon' pay for wastin' my homey!"

* * *

Barra's man, the one nearest to Holland, peeked out.

"Cease fire!" he yelled as the others took positions around the doorway, preparing to defend the bridge.

"Don't shoot! It's a kid-"

He never finished. A small black hole appeared on his forehead, dribbling dark blood as he fell over.

Another of Barra's men sighted down his pistol at Zack and fired. The boy fell backwards, his blood from a chest wound spurting across the wall.

The rest of Barra's men were taking cover all around Holland. The black-clad attackers were advancing down the hall, ducking into the doorways for cover.

"Who are those idiots that keep jumping out of that side hallway?" Holland yelled.

No one answered.

* * *

Brittany watched Zack fall, adding his body to the pile at the hall intersection. First Meat, then Gwen, then Martin, now Zack. She was the only one left.

"No!" she wailed. "Zack!"

"Shots from the bridge," voices barked to her left. "Return fire!"

"Zack!" Brittany screamed, leaping out into the hallway to grab his falling body.

"No, wait, hold your fire!" she heard from behind her. "Civilian!"

The warning was too late. A bullet pierced her back. She staggered against the wall. With all her remaining strength, she hurled the sharpened broomstick in the direction of the bridge, where the bullets that had killed Zack had come from.

"Bastards," she gasped.

She fell forward to die alongside her boyfriend.

* * *

Holland peeked over the console just in time for a javelin to tear through the gun smoke and pierce her eye, stopping only as it scraped against the back of her skull.

She stood up, confused, looking down the long object obstructing her one remaining eye's vision. She took a step and collapsed, falling onto something small and hard.

A boom rattled the ship.

She turned on her side, lifting off the angular object digging into her ribcage. She brushed it out from under her and held it up to her good eye.

Her vision was fading fast, but she could see it was Barra's detonator, damaged from the gunshot and fall he had taken. Her weight had crushed through what was left of the switch guard and activated it.

"Oops," she gasped.

Then everything went black.

3

A shudder rumbled through the entire Sunset Mist. The floor tilted slightly, but enough that everyone on board could feel it.

"Hull breach!" signs lit up and flashed all around bridge. A man's pre-recorded voice repeated the words calmly in a robotic cadence.

"Hull. Breach. Hull. Breach."

Barra was pale, his face coated with a lacquer of sweat. He clenched and released his fists over and over.

"God damn," he groaned, gasping. "It hurts."

"Throwing smoke!" one of the SEALs yelled from down the hall. A grenade bounced onto the bridge, an unnatural and dense fog billowing from the cylinder.

"Cover both entrances," one of Barra's men yelled.

Two of them ran to the port door. The spitting sound of silencer gunfire echoed around the bridge as Barra's team tried to hold off the advancing SEALs.

"What- What-" Barra choked.

"Don't worry," North said. "Stay with me, buddy." He pulled aside Barra's body armor to expose his torso. Blood was pumping from a gaping wound in his abdomen. North could see the edges of torn intestines through the ragged hole.

"I- hear- shots," Barra grumbled.

"Your team has it handled," North said, pressing his palm over the hole in Barra's side. The force of the blood trying to escape was strong, forming a knob of pressure. It reminded North of putting his palm over a garden hose nozzle.

While pushing against the wound with his left hand, North yanked open a nearby cabinet with his right, snatching two white beach towels embroidered with "Sunset Mist" written in script.

Smoke from the grenade filled the bridge. Barra's men were yelling, shooting down the halls on either side of the ship. The attacking SEALs had split their force and were returning fire on both entrances to the bridge as well.

"These will help," North said, pressing one towel against the wound. He rolled up the second and lifted Barra up, then let him rest on it to block the exit wound. Both towels were immediately drenched with blood.

"I'm done," Barra gasped. "I can feel it. I can see it in your face."

"No way," North said. He grabbed Barra's hand and guided it to the towel. "Press here."

Barra moaned, his hand sliding loose.

"Ah, shit," North said.

"Leave me."

"No."

"I'm. Done. Bro." He took a sucking, shallow breath. "Just leave."

The CNB helicopter bobbed into view, rising above the deck.

"Hull. Breach. Hull. Breach," the ship's pre-recorded voice said.

North shook his head. Barra's facial muscles were relaxing, his eyes losing focus. His blood was all over the deck, mingling with the blood from Holland and his dying team.

"So. Tired," Barra said. He closed his eyes.

"Stay with me, buddy," North said. "We've got a shot at this."

He crashed through the bridge door onto the deck, waving his arms frantically at the CNB helicopter.

4

"What the hell was that?" Goodkin asked.

Form the bridge of the Bonnie Jane, they saw the Sunset Mist shudder and the water at her rear begin to foam and bubble violently.

"Looks like an explosion," Burnett said. "Damn rag-heads."

Captain Dunn slammed a lever on the steering console. The Bonnie Jane's motor roared as the ship lurched backward.

Dunn yelled into the intercom. "Hold on, crew, we're clearing the area!"

"What the hell?" Goodkin yelled. "What's happening?"

"Captain Dunn? What are you doing?" Burnett yelled. "I didn't give any order."

"That cruise ship's hull has been punctured in a big way," Dunn said. "That foam is just the start. She's going under and I'm getting us clear."

Dunn spoke into the intercom again, urgent but calm. "All crew prepare for search and rescue. Make sure you are clearly identified as unarmed."

"If the ship is sinking," Goodkin said, "why isn't anyone going for the life rafts?"

"Because they're in a gunfight," Dunn said. "They can't turn their backs. Or the terrorists blew the ship and are keeping everyone pinned down. Does it really matter? Besides you're the one who told me not to speculate."

"You waited too long, college boy," Burnett said. "You see what happens when you let them push you around?"

"Your caveman approach made them blow the bomb!" Goodkin yelled back.

"Don't talk to me like that!"

"Why not? You're in charge now, sailor!"

"I should kick your ass."

"Why, because I'm right?"

"Shut up, both of you!" Dunn bellowed.

Goodkin and Burnett were stunned silent.

"I've listened to you two idiots for too long," Dunn said. "This is no longer a hostage situation, or a combat operation. This is a rescue mission, so I'm in charge. Now both of you get the hell off my bridge!"

PART 9

THE THOUGHT THAT COUNTS

1

Amaretto was screaming into her microphone.

"There's a lot happening here! Are you seeing this back in the studio?"

The studio newsreaders responded. "Some of it, Fran. The smoke pouring from the bridge is very thick. Please keep describing what you see and please be safe. What's happening? Have there been any more shots fired at you?"

"No. I think they just wanted to kill the Navy sniper. As you can see and hear now, there's gunfire inside the ship. Gray smoke is pouring out of the upper deck and bridge. The ship is listing and the aft appears to be going under."

"Please be careful out there, Fran."

"I have to talk with my pilot a second, cutting off my mic."

She flicked a switch.

"Phil, keep filming. Film everything!"

"Doing it."

She elbowed the pilot. "Mark, is that someone flagging us for help?"

Mark moved his head from side to side, looking through the smoke. "Looks like it. One of the terrorists. Let him drown."

"No! Pick him up."

"Are you kidding?"

"Bring us lower. Get him."

"Down into the smoke? I can barely see. And there's gunfire."

"That's all inside!"

"He's a terrorist! And he just shot a guy clean out of our helicopter!"

"If he wanted to shoot at us, he'd have done it already. He's waving for our help."

"You do realize the ship is sinking, don't you? You do realize this could be a trick."

"A terrorist who happens to be a chopper pilot? What are the odds? He doesn't have any weapons out. My gut tells me to go for it. When has my gut ever steered you wrong?"

Mark paused.

Fran smiled wildly. "Get low enough so he can jump on. I'll throw him the emergency ladder."

"Oh crap," Mark growled. "This is nuts."

The helicopter descended slowly, blowing aside the smoke now pouring off the bridge in huge, dark, churning clouds. Towels and beach chairs flew about, caught in the rotor's whirlwind.

"What the hell?" the pilot said. "He's running back onto the bridge."

"Stay down here," Amaretto said, preparing the emergency ladder. "Show him we're welcoming."

Mark looked in all directions; the smoke was all around them. The chopper's rotor carved a cone of grey through the gray clouds. "This is crazy."

"Phil, keep filming, but not the terrorist. He might not want to be seen."

"The guy's wearing a mask."

"Just do it."

"Fine."

She turned back to Mark.

"Perfect. Hold us right here. I knew you could do it."

"Remind me again why I work with you."

"Because of times like these." She punched his arm. "I bring out your best."

* * *

The ship's incline was increasing with every second as the aft went under. North half-ran, half-slid down the deck and back onto the bridge. Barra was resting against the bridge control console, still and pale. Holland and several of Barra's men were dead. The survivors were firing into the smoke, throwing grenades.

"We have to retreat!" one of them yelled, leaping from cover to run. A bullet caught him in the back and he fell.

"We need to surrender!"

"They're shooting to kill!"

"Pop a gas grenade so they can't get breathe. If I'm going to die, I'm taking them with me."

"You're crazy."

"Hey, buddy! North! Help us out!"

North ignored them as he dragged Barra off the bridge.

"Come on, Barra," North said. "Don't die on me."

* * *

The helicopter rose away from the deck.

"What are you doing?" Amaretto screamed.

"Time's up," the pilot Mark said. "This is too risky."

"Why? The ship isn't going to jump up and grab us. Look! Here he comes!"

"I can't see!"

"There!" she pointed.

With his right hand on the ship's railing, North dragged Barra with his left, working his way toward the helicopter. He screamed with each painful effort of the ascent.

Drag. Pull. Scream. Drag. Pull. Scream.

Barra's blood left a faint pink trail, marking their progress.

North's bulky arms shook as he moved up the tilting deck into the helicopter's artificial tornado. Amaretto leaned out the window.

She held up one finger and yelled, exaggerating her words so he could read her lips.

"Only you!" she shouted. "Only one."

"Take him!" North yelled back, nodding his head toward Barra.

Scream. Drag. Pull.

Through the cockpit's domed window, North could see the pilot shake his head no. He and Amaretto appeared to be arguing.

She leaned out of the cockpit again. "Only you!"

"Just him!" North yelled up.

The pilot turned to Amaretto shook his head no again.

She yelled back to North.

"Just you!"

* * *

North clung to Barra. The ship's incline was adding up. Every second, Barra's dead weight pulled harder on his muscles. He could feel the burn in his arms. He coughed with each breath, the smoke scratching his already taxed breathing.

"Damn it, Barra," North yelled. "God damn it!"

He let loose a primal scream into the smoke.

The helicopter bobbed above him.

Amaretto leaned out the window.

"Now or never!"

Scream.

Drag.

Pull.

Amaretto was shaking her head violently behind the bubble of the chopper's window as North got closer.

"No! Only you!" she kept mouthing, holding up one finger.

North stopped. His arms shook.

"I'm sorry," he said aloud.

He bent his right arm around one of the ship's railing supports and kneeled next to Barra's prone body.

"I tried," he gasped.

He kissed Barra's forehead.

"Sorry, bro."

He let the dead weight go.

Barra's body slid down the deck, gathering speed, tumbling, and finally disappearing into huge clouds rolling from inside the bridge. All gunfire had stopped. Flames were leaping out now. There was no indication anyone from the bridge or attacking it was still alive.

"Visibility is almost nothing," the pilot yelled. "Gotta go now!"

The small chain-link emergency ladder hung down about twenty feet.

North put one foot on the ship's railing and leapt up out over the sea through the smoke to grab the ladder. He ascended to the cabin as the helicopter lifted. The cameraman helped him into the back seat.

By the time they cleared the smoke, North was inside.

* * *

He collapsed onto the rear bench of the helicopter.

"How fast can this thing go?" Amaretto asked her pilot.

"Damn fast," he said.

"Impress me."

The helicopter tilted forward and shot away from the doomed Sunset Mist. They roared past the competing news network choppers that were heading in the opposite direction to film the last moments of the sinking ship.

By the time North gathered his breath and looked back, the Sunset Mist was nearly vertical and diving fast. A tilted funnel of black smoke reached to the sky.

Coast Guard rafts and a rescue helicopter circled the drowning vessel.

"Are we out of range of the Navy's guns?" Amaretto asked.

"Hell yeah," the pilot said. "They can't chase us in that thing. This crap is over."

North settled in his seat and leaned his head against the window.

The studio producer spoke in Fran's headset. "Fran? What's going on out there? We stopped getting video and we haven't heard from you. Are you all right?"

"Just chasing a story, like always."

"The other networks are showing the ship sinking."

"I've got something better. I'll call you back."

"But Fran-"

She clicked off her radio, turned around and stuck out her hand. "I'm Fran Amaretto for the CNB Network. And who are you? Do you speak English?"

"I'm not talking," North said. He stared out the window, refusing to look at her. She pulled her hand back.

"You don't sound Kariqistani."

"I'm not."

"Well, that requires some explanation, don't you think?"

"I said I'm not talking."

"Not talking? But we just saved your life."

"I need to think," North said, shifting in his seat. He tugged at his mask to align its eye holes with his vision.

"Can you think out loud?"

"Just take me back." North coughed violently, pushing the last of the smoke from his lungs.

"Back where? This isn't a limo service. We're going to our studios where I'm going to call the FBI to collect you, unless you choose to talk."

North stared out the window.

"You sound American," Amaretto said. "Are you a mercenary?"

Phil lifted his camera. North cupped his huge hand over the lens. "No pictures."

"Sure thing," the cameraman said, setting down the camera.

North pointed to a red light on the camera. "No audio either."

Phil shrugged, hit a switch and the light went out.

"All right, then," Amaretto said, "talk to me. Why did you think taking over the cruise ship would help the Children of Kariqistan?"

North said nothing.

"Why did you shoot the sniper we had in our helicopter?"

"Because he killed my friend."

"That man you tried to save?"

North's hand dropped to his hip and came up with his pistol. He pressed the barrel against Amaretto's face, just below her right eye. The cameraman squeezed himself into his seat, using the camera as a shield.

Amaretto swallowed hard.

"You're not going to live for the next few seconds," North said, "unless you start doing what I say, and making sure your pilot does, too."

"I'll do whatever you want, buddy," the pilot said. "No need for the gun, okay? Just put it down, all right?"

"Come on," Amaretto said, her voice shaking as she slowly raised her hands. "I just want to talk."

"No talking. I just need to be dropped off where I want. If I'm not, then everyone in this helicopter dies. Starting with you."

Amaretto leaned backwards away from North's gun. "Where do you want to go?"

"I need to think. Head back to the coast for now."

"You got it," the pilot said.

"Don't try anything cute," North said, lowering his gun. "Or I start killing."

2

Five rescue rafts from the Bonnie Jane circled the large area of foam and bubbles that marked where the Sunset Mist had gone down. The Coast Guard rescuers scanned beneath the water, choking on the thin mist left over from the gunfight.

Occasionally a diver would surface. All eyes would turn to him with anticipation. Inevitably, the diver shook his head no and went under again.

* * *

On the deck of the Bonnie Jane, Burnett tapped his earpiece. "Burnett. Go."

"Captain, the two other news helicopters are moving in."

"Let them. There's nothing left to see here." Burnett paused. "Any word from the away team?"

"Only the sub. It's still down there, waiting in case the team needs it. Should I call him back?"

"Patch me through."

"Aye, sir."

Burnett waited a moment before static burst in his ear.

"Captain Burnett, sir? Sub pilot is on the line."

"Pilot, tell me exactly what happened from your perspective."

"Aye, Captain. I felt the shockwave. Appears to have been some kind of massive detonation in the engine room. Blew a nice big hole in the hull."

"What can you see now?"

"The ship is still going down, deeper than where I can chase and dropping fast."

"Any survivors? Is anyone trying to get out?"

"Doesn't appear so, sir. Wait! Wait. Trouble seeing because of all the bubbles. Yes! I think I see a body floating up. Looks like a woman. Might be moving, but maybe that's just the current. Looks like she's bound by hand and foot."

"All right, sub. Return to the Gunfish. The Coasties will get her. Gunfish?"

"Yes, Captain?"

"Be discreet. And once you get the sub, get me off this sorry excuse for a boat."

"Aye, sir."

Burnett rested his hands on the Bonnie Jane's railing and bowed his head.

* * *

Among the rafts, a head popped up, hair soaked over the face. The person spat and sputtered.

"Over there!" a rescuer yelled, pointing. "Survivor!"

The woman rolled on her back, coughing. Two divers swam to her immediately. They each supported her from underneath, one on either side.

"We've got you."

"I can't move," the woman coughed. "My hands and feet are tied!"

One diver went under and cut loose her bindings with his knife.

"Oh, that's good," the woman said. "Feels so good to be free."

At the back of the closest raft, two rescuers were talking.

"Those huge fake tits worked just like water wings."

"Shut up, dude. You're an idiot."

The crew grabbed the woman by her arms and dragged her onto the life raft. She rolled on her back, choking. Her soaked shirt stuck to her large breasts as her chest heaved with each labored gasp.

"What's your name, miss?"

"Windstorm," she spat. "Yvonne Windstorm."

"All right, Yvonne, we're going to-"

"I'm a singer. An actress. Haven't you heard of me?"

The rescuers exchanged looks and shrugged.

"Miss, I'm a doctor, I need to give you a checkup, all right? Does anything-" he closed in on her with his stethoscope.

"Wait," she said, shoving him back.

The two remaining helicopters from ACB and MCSBN were hovering overhead. Windstorm arched her back, pressing her black bikini top against her wet white shirt. She tossed her head, whipping her wet hair across her face, pouting her lips up to the helicopters for several seconds before collapsing.

She turned her head to the side and coughed violently before vomiting up a ball of green phlegm.

"Okay," she gasped. "I'm ready for my checkup now."

* * *

On the deck of the Bonnie Jane, the television was showing a map of the Arabian sea, a row of battleship icons lining the coast. Cartoon rockets arched over Pakistan and Afghanistan into the cluster of ex-Soviet territories west of China.

The TV newsreader spoke briskly. "We are receiving confirmed reports that American warships have launched several cruise missile strikes against terrorist training camps in Kariqistan. Keep it tuned here for all the details."

"Captain Dunn," the intercom barked. "We've got a survivor. Only one so far."

"Well," Dunn said, "I guess that's better than none."

Dunn noticed the television images were looking down on his own ship from above.

"Breaking news! This just in! It appears the earlier rumors were true. Yvonne Windstorm, the singer and actress, was on the doomed cruise vessel the Sunset Mist. We have footage of her here."

The television showed Yvonne Windstorm on the rescue boat, her back arched, shaking the water from her hair as if she was emerging from a shower.

"Hm," Dunn said, keeping one hand on the steering while with the other he adjusted his pants.

3

The wind roared against the bubble of the CNB helicopter window. North could see nothing but sea and sky in every direction. Only the water rushing by underneath them proved that they were moving, and moving fast.

"You know," Amaretto said, turning to North.

"Shut up," he growled, still staring outside.

"You'll want to hear this," she continued. "We have footage of you. That camera Phil's holding transmits automatically back to the station. It's so we don't lose anything if the camera is destroyed. Bottom line, they know what you look like."

"Are you saying once we land I should kill you all since you've seen me up close? You're as good a negotiator as that guy the feds sent."

"I'm trying to help you. If you tell me your story, I can demand the studio keep you off the air. I can keep you anonymous because then I'm protecting my source. That's journalistic integrity, protected by law. If all I do is help you escape, then I'm aiding a criminal. The people back at the studio have video of you right now. They'll air it unless I tell them not to. The point is, are you going to be my source or are you going to let them show your face all over TV?"

North turned his gun toward Phil, pressing the barrel against the cameraman's chest.

"Is she bluffing? Does it really work like that?"

Phil slowly lifted his hands.

"Um. Yeah, I, um. It saves memory, too. Camera can't keep hours stored on its internal drive. Could it?"

"I'm not sure I believe you."

North spun back to the front, jabbing his gun against the pilot's seat.

"Whoa, buddy," Mark said. The helicopter tilted slightly as his hand jolted the control stick. "I'm doing what you asked. Flying back to the coast. As fast as possible."

North withdrew his gun. "Good. Keep it up." He turned to Amaretto. "Just say I held a gun to your head. You wouldn't be lying."

"Sure. But then you're on the run. If we work together, I can help you."

They flew on for several minutes, only the sound of the rushing wind around them.

"I don't have many choices, do I?" North said. "And the longer I wait, the better the chance they show my face."

"Help us help you," Amaretto said, reaching her hand out slowly, "Mister…?"

North looked at her hand, then back out the window. He holstered his gun and folded his arms.

"North. Rod North."

"Nice to meet you, Mister North. My name is Fran Amaretto."

"Now what? Do I get something from you that says you promise not to tell anyone who I am?"

"I give you my word."

"Oh. Well, that's a comfort."

"I'm sure you understand if I betray you, no one will ever tell me anything again. It'll ruin my career."

"But I'll already be screwed. I want something in writing."

"Fine," she said. She dug around in the pouch next to her seat and pulled out a wrinkled form covered with small legal text, poorly photocopied on an angle.

"This is our confidentiality agreement," she filled in her name, signed it, then handed the papers and a pen to North. "I won't show your face, I won't use your name. We'll even distort your voice. Your employers will never be able to prove it was you."

Her cell phone rang. She ignored it.

"And," North said, "you fly me where I want."

"Sure. Keeping your picture off? No problem. Flying you somewhere within reason, no problem."

North signed the paper and handed it back to her. "I'll need a copy," he said.

They each signed a second one. Her phone rang again and she ignored it again.

"Okay," Amaretto said, "now that we've settled that, tell me what this is all about. Start at the beginning. How did you end up on the ship?"

Her phone rang again. This time it was a text message.

She glanced at the screen, the text read, "Ansr yr fkn fon!"

"Excuse me a minute."

She pressed a button on her phone. "Yes. I've got the story. The only survivor of the ship. Exclusive. I was just getting-"

She paused.

"Another survivor?"

Her mouth dropped open.

"The singer?"

She paused.

"Well, I've got something better. One of the terrorists." She turned and winked at North. "We picked him up when the boat was going down. We're working out the details now. He wants confidentiality. I was just going to call you. Hold all that footage we sent after the boat sank. I know. Right. Yes. Yes. Trust me, okay?"

She hung up the phone and turned back to her cameraman. "Hey, Phil, can you tune in to one of our rivals? Seems they picked up a survivor. No one else made it."

She watched North as she spoke. He simply looked back at her, his eyes betraying nothing. Her eyes fell to the necklace showing through the tear in his suit. North raised his hand to cover it.

Phil fiddled with the knobs under a screen built into the wall of the helicopter. He switched the channel between their major network competitors. All of them showed Yvonne Windstorm arching her back as she was rescued. The Coast Guard rescuers around her kept lifting a blanket over her shoulders and she kept lowering it around her upper arms so it looked like a fur stole accenting her cleavage. She tossed her head to the side, whipping her wet hair.

Two microphones were in her face, from ACB and MCSBN.

"Well, they beat us to the celebrity angle," Amaretto said, "but we've still got the hard news."

"I just want to say," Yvonne Windstorm said, shivering, "thank you to all my fans. When I was drowning, when I was hopeless, when I lost… lost my Danny…" she made sobbing sounds.

"Those tears are as fake as her tits," Amaretto said.

"When I lost him and I was in the darkness, it would have been so easy to just let go, but I knew I would be letting my fans down. It was only their faith that saved my life. I was lifted up by their love."

"If you weren't seasick yet, you are now," Amaretto said. "Turn it off."

"It's crap," Phil the cameraman said, "but it will score."

"We'll outscore them. Wait, let's see what's next."

The text crawl at the bottom of the screen read "Emergency session of U.S. Congress votes unanimously to declare war on Kariqistan."

An old, chubby man with a shock of white hair blowing over the bald sections of his head shook, his scalp turning red. He stood behind a forest of microphones on the concrete steps of Congress.

"Kariqistan is a nation of barbarism, as we've seen from the vicious attack on the Sunset Mist. Those savages are sitting on top of precious natural resources the global community needs. As a moral nation, we must act to secure justice and democracy. Remember the Sunset Mist! We're all cruise tourists today!"

"Enough," Amaretto said.

Phil shut off the television.

"All right, Mister North, let's begin. Phil?"

Phil hefted the camera onto his shoulder. He focused the image tight on Amaretto's and North's faces.

North pushed the camera away. "I don't want my face shown."

"We'll black it out."

North hesitated. He looked down at the locket with the photo at his chest. Toby and Mister Duck-Duck stared back at him.

"Fine," he said, and pulled off his mask.

Amaretto looked to Phil then back at North.

"State your name," she said.

"Rod North."

"Nice to meet you, Rod North. Relax and tell me everything. From the beginning. How did you end up on that ship, the Sunset Mist? Are you Kariqistani? How did you become involved?"

"I'm an American citizen. An employee of Redfire Advanced Security Solutions. I was on the ship looking for Danforth Percy Sinclair."

"The billionaire? The husband of Yvonne Windstorm?"

"Yes."

"Why were you looking for him?"

"Mister Sinclair has a contract with Redfire."

"Redfire is a security and military contractor. Correct?"

"That's the one."

"What does that have to do with Sinclair?"

"He's a customer. He has a private rescue contract with them. Also called a Katrina contract."

"And what is that?"

"It's an agreement that says Redfire will extract the customer from anywhere at any time under any circumstance. After Hurricane Katrina wiped out New Orleans in 2005, it was clear that public rescue service wasn't reliable. Those who can afford it hire their own private rescue."

"So it's like a personal, worldwide, subscription-only 9-1-1?"

"Exactly. We'll go in if there's a natural disaster, or the client is caught in a war zone or if he just doesn't feel like waiting. He doesn't have to hang around for a public rescue, he gets his very own private one."

"So Sinclair was taken hostage and you had to fulfill your employer's obligation to him for his private rescue, his Katrina contract."

"That's right."

"Are you violating your confidentiality agreements with Redfire by talking about it?"

"Definitely, but this pain-in-the-ass reporter lady blackmailed me and said she would hand my pictures over to the police if I didn't play ball. Hopefully Redfire will understand and be able to recover. A company like that, you know they've got the best public relations people money can buy."

"And the press is much easier to control than law enforcement?"

"I'm pretty sure."

Amaretto smiled. "We'll see about that."

"Hopefully not. For your sake."

Her smiled faded slightly. "Moving on. So you had nothing to do with the terrorists?"

"No. I was there to rescue Mr. Sinclair."

Amaretto paused and squinted at him. "You weren't part of the terrorist group?"

"No."

"Oh," she looked to Phil. "I'm not getting a good feeling here."

"He's still got quite a story," Phil said from behind his camera. "Maybe we make the angle on this the Katrina contract. It's the first time I'm hearing about it. I didn't know they existed, but it's not surprising. Seems obvious, really."

"Yeah," Amaretto said, "I'm just worried it's too nuanced."

"It's all we've got."

"Thus, my worry."

"Thus?" Phil said.

Amaretto turned to North, "All right, Mister North. Rod. So what other contracts does Redfire offer?"

"Any security-related or military-related task. I work in their corporate headquarters, but I'm on call for any type of contract that needs fulfillment."

"When you say anything military-related, do you mean, including, say, infiltrating another country? Sabotaging the factory of a competitor? Assassination?"

North paused.

"You said you would tell everything," Amaretto said.

"I never went on one of those assignments."

"But you acknowledge they exist?"

"I don't know. Everything is secret. Extremely confidential."

"But if ordered, you would have to do them, or you would be in violation of the terms of your employment, correct?"

Phil gave her a thumbs-up.

"I don't know the specifics," North said. "But probably. That was my understanding."

"How do I know you're telling the truth?"

"You'd probably have to check with Redfire. I was on the Sunset Mist for one thing. To get Sinclair out."

"What about the other passengers?"

"They were on their own."

"But if you were there, why not help them?"

"Helping them is not what I was paid to do. That would only slow us down from reaching our customer. Damn," North turned his head and looked out the window, up at the sky. "I'm starting to sound like Holland. Or Barra."

"Who is Holland? Or Barra? Are they also Redfire employees?"

"Yes."

"So they were trying to find Sinclair too?"

"No. Well, Holland was. Barra had a different assignment."

"What? Then what was he doing there?"

North paused.

"He was one of the terrorists."

"I thought you said he was a Redfire employee."

"He was."

"You're implying that one of the terrorists was a Redfire employee."

"I'm stating it outright."

"Wait. You're saying Redfire employees were among the terrorists?"

"No. They were the terrorists. All of them. It was another Redfire contract."

Amaretto smiled widely. "Now we've got a story. Phil, are you getting this?"

"I am," Phil said. "Great stuff. Yvonne Windstorm can kiss my ass."

"All right," Amaretto said, "so let me summarize. You were attempting to rescue one Redfire customer from a staged hijacking paid for by another Redfire customer?"

"Exactly."

Amaretto leaned back.

Phil whistled.

"Holy crap, this is getting good."

Amaretto winked at him.

North went on. "All the contracts are of extreme secrecy and have different handlers. There's no way either group would have known about the other."

"This is crazy."

"You've never heard of false flag operations?"

"Oh, I'm sure they've happened, but..."

"They've been around since Ancient China. Sun Tzu wrote about them. We're talking way back, as in B.C. That's how old the idea is."

"Sure. But war? Paid for by a private entity?"

"Why not?"

"Who, then? Who paid for this event in the hopes it would start a war?"

"I don't know. An oil company? Arms manufacturers? A neighboring country of Kariqistan? A bitter and wealthy Kariqistani exile? Who knows? Whoever benefits from Kariqistan being taken over by so-called civilized countries. Whoever can afford it."

"You actually expect me to believe that a company based in the United States was hired by persons unknown to stage a terrorist attack in order to persuade American citizens to be fully in favor of a war against Kariqistan?"

"I don't know what you'll believe but that sums it up."

"That's breathtaking." She clapped. "I love it!"

"Well, good for you because it's the truth. The only thing that went wrong was Barra caught up to us. That slick bastard."

North sighed heavily and turned to stare out the window as he kept talking. "He and I were the last of our unit after Hayger died. Now it's just me."

Amaretto shook her head. "This is crazy."

North didn't answer.

She went on.

"I mean, I just can't believe this part about Redfire. It's just crazy. It's too insane to be true."

"That's their defense," North said. "You can't even accuse them without sounding insane. They wouldn't attempt something that was easy to believe. Anyway, isn't your job as a journalist to confirm things?"

"There would have to be a money trail. From Sinclair to Redfire is the obvious one. For the false flag, not so much."

"Good place to start."

"But these are people with the resources and knowledge to keep money in clean channels. Even if a crime was committed."

"True."

Amaretto shook her head, as if trying to wake up. "All right, let's stop here. I have to call my producer. This is either the story of the century, or you're one hell of a storyteller."

"I failed Literature," North said.

"Phil, cut."

Phil rested the camera on his lap.

"Oh, my God," he said. "This is nuts."

Amaretto dialed her cell. "Hey, it's me. This story? If this checks out, save some space on your bookshelf for an award. Hell yeah, I'm serious… "

She dropped her voice low. North couldn't make out what she was saying.

"Hey, buddy," the pilot said. "While she's talking, tell me where we're headed. Is there a high school or a park near where you want to go?"

"A community college. They're on spring break."

"They have soccer fields?"

"Yeah."

"Perfect."

* * *

North stepped from the helicopter out onto the grassy field wearing a CNB windbreaker.

"I'll be in touch," Amaretto yelled out to him.

He ran in a crouch, away from the rotor wash.

The helicopter ascended, disappeared over the tree line, and was gone.

North sat on the bleachers, disassembled his gun and threw the parts and bullets in separate trash cans.

Inside a nearby convenience store, he claimed his car had broken down and asked the clerk to call him a cab.

Using the house key hidden under a fake rock in the front garden, he let himself in and returned to pay the driver, offering enough for him to wait.

North came out of his townhome an hour later, showered and dressed in casual clothes. He got into the cab.

"Thanks for waiting," North said.

"Hey, no problem," the driver said. "Thanks for the easy fare. Where to next?"

"I need to rent a car."

As they drove, the driver flipped through the radio channels. All the music had been interrupted with news of the sinking of the Sunset Mist, the strikes on Kariqistan and impending war.

"-senator said in a statement, 'Let this be a warning to terrorists the world over.' At the end of his announcement that U.S. warships have begun firing cruise missiles at selected targets within Kariqi-"

The driver changed the channel.

"-military recruitment lines are around the block. Every young man and even many young women that we have spoken with are outraged and looking for payback. You, can you tell us why you're-"

"Can you turn that off?" Rod asked the driver.

"Sure, buddy."

They drove on in silence.

4

Rod parked his rental car around the corner, out of sight of Carol's home.

His ex-wife's car was parked in the driveway along with another car. Rod took in the details of the second car: tinted windows, black with silver trim, chic, expensive.

"Addison," North mumbled.

North approached the front door. It was unlocked.

He tiptoed down the main hall as the television in the living room murmured.

"-officials say the first troops will be on the ground before the end of the week. The sinking of the Sunset Mist and the death of her passengers has ignited patriotism in this country like I haven't seen since-"

Rod crept toward the kitchen in the back of the house, where Carol and Addison were both seated around the small table.

"Your husband was a good man, Mrs. North."

"He was all right. Had his flaws, though, that's for sure."

"Even so, he will be missed. All of us at Redfire express our regret."

"Yeah," she sniffled. "Okay, well, I'm sort of sad, but sort of... just lots of mixed feelings. Never mind. Where do I sign?"

Rod was peeking around the doorway. They hadn't seen him yet. Carol leaned forward, pen in hand.

Someone crashed into North from the side. He twisted and grabbed, ready to hurl his attacker to the floor.

Toby squealed.

"Daddy's here!"

Rod aborted his throwing motion, holding his son in one arm and balancing himself against the wall with his other. They staggered together into the kitchen. Over Toby's shoulder, Rod saw Carol's pen come down on a stack of papers, but Addison pulled the packet back before she could sign, leaving a blue gash across the top sheet.

Toby was climbing on Rod's back. North stood up, his son clambering over him.

"North!" Addison said. "I thought you were dead."

"You hoped. What's that you're signing, Carol?"

"R-R-Rod," she stammered. "He told me you were gone. That whole hijacking thing everyone's talking about. The cruise ship. He said you were there to help and you didn't make it."

"Well, I did. Bummer, huh?"

"Daddy's here!" Toby yelled.

Rod clutched his son's legs tightly.

"The document," he said, extending his free hand and stepping toward Addison.

"Just a non-disclosure," Addison said, rising from his chair. "The terms of your separation from Redfire and the life insurance going to Carol."

Rod glanced at his ex-wife. She smiled and shrugged. There were some tears in her eyes. He had to give her some credit for that at least.

"Obviously, things have changed," Addison continued. "So, are you going to tell me how you got back, but the other two didn't?"

"Maybe."

"It doesn't matter," Addison said. "Since you're here, I can have you sign it instead."

"Terms of separation? I'm not going anywhere."

"Yes. You are."

Rod bowed his head, and nodded yes. "Failure is unacceptable," he said.

"You'll get a portion of your retirement pay," Addison said. "We just want you to be quiet about your mission. You get everything you want, but if you say anything to the press, you lose custody."

Rod clutched Toby closer. "You can't guarantee that."

"You betray Redfire and they won't just make life miserable for you financially." Addison said. He pointed to Carol. "You want to go up against her with financial and legal backing from Redfire? After you were terminated from your employment for poor performance? For a job that takes you away from home regularly?"

"Fine," Rod said. "I quit."

"You can't," Addison said. "I already told you. You're fired. Sign the papers."

"I don't think so."

"These are terms you've already agreed to. We're just reminding you. No discussion about the Katrina contract."

"But I can say what I want about anything else?"

"What do you mean anything else?"

"You don't know, do you?" Rod said, tilting his head as a thought occurred to him. "You don't know everything that happened out there."

"Everything what? I know some terrorists took over a vessel, you were sent to fulfill a Katrina contract, and you failed. That's all," Addison said.

Rod stared at him. Addison's face revealed nothing.

"What's so funny?" Addison asked.

"Nothing."

"Well, good. I just need you to sign this and I'll be on my way."

"If I've already agreed to the terms, no need to sign again."

"True. You know I like to get multiple signatures, but no matter." Addison picked up his briefcase.

"Daddy?" Toby said.

"Hush, Toby. Go in the other room," Carol said. "Watch TV."

"No," Rod said to Carol.

Then he turned to Toby. "What is it, buddy? What do you want to say?"

"I just want to say thank you."

"What for?"

"What you told me on the phone. For making the world a better place."

Rod felt Toby's tiny weight grow even lighter, as if the boy were a balloon lifting his feet from the floor. He felt his back straighten and grow stronger. He felt his arms turn to steel. His heart seemed to pulse with more force.

Addison smirked. Carol rolled her eyes.

Rod didn't notice.

"Thanks, buddy," he said to his son. "Thanks a lot."

"Well, I'll be on my way," Addison said. "Remember, North. Nothing in the press, no talking to the media, nothing about Katrina contracts or Sinclair."

"You're a good kid, Toby," he continued, speaking about Toby but still facing Rod. "A son any father would be glad to have."

"Get out," North growled.

"On my way," Addison said. He didn't bother to pull the door closed.

"Daddy," Toby said, "can we still have pizza tonight?"

"Sure, buddy."

"Great!"

Carol was looking at her cell phone. "So, um, you can take care of him?" she asked, furiously texting. "I can probably catch up with the girls."

"Yeah, I got him," Rod said, not looking away from his boy's beautiful face.

5

Squeak!

"Daddy?" Toby said. "Daddy, are you okay?"

Rod woke up slowly. The first thing he saw was the pale grey glow of the television. He didn't notice the picture. What caught his attention were the huge red letters across the top: "Going To War."

Rod felt something fall from his hand. An empty bottle of vodka bounced off the floor.

"Daddy? Are you all right?" Toby asked, stepping backwards, clutching Mister Duck-Duck to his chest.

"Yeah, buddy. Daddy just fell asleep, that's all."

Toby wrinkled his nose at the vodka bottle. "That smells stinky."

"It's a grown-up drink."

Rod's mind slowly came to. Toby was wearing pajamas.

"What time is it?"

"I don't know. It's morning."

"Oh. Well, go get ready for your bath."

"I was. I was waiting for you. That's why I came down here."

Squeak!

Rod's mind was still full of cotton. He squinted out the window and rubbed his head. The horizon was glowing, the sun about to break.

The clock read six a.m.

Squeak!

"Can you stop that noise?"

Rod rubbed his eyes, put the vodka bottle away and shut off the television. He followed Toby up the stairs.

Squeak!

"I said stop it!" Rod snapped.

Toby bowed his head and trudged up the stairs slowly, holding Mister Duck-Duck out before him with his palms up.

"Hey, buddy, I'm sorry," Rod said.

Toby continued up the stairs without responding.

* * *

Sitting beside the bathtub, Rod scrubbed Toby's back.

Toby aimlessly pushed Mister Duck-Duck across the surface of the soapy water.

"Hey, buddy," Rod said, "I have a question for you."

"Okay."

"Let's pretend you have to make a choice between helping someone and not helping someone."

"I should help them. That's what you always say."

"What if you didn't know what to do?"

"Ask a grown-up. You or Mrs. Kincaid. Or Mommy."

"Mrs. Kincaid? Oh, your teacher, right?"

"Yeah."

"But suppose some bad people said, if you say anything to your parents or your teacher, we're going to hurt Mister Duck-Duck. You'll never see him again."

"Why would they do that?"

"Because they're not nice."

Toby stared down into the water, thinking.

"But why?"

"Because they're bad, okay? Bad people."

"Okay."

"But you can stop them. Maybe."

"Daddy, I don't like this pretend."

"Just please. Play along."

"Okay."

"So what do you do?"

"I don't know."

"The bad people say if you help those people, we'll take away Mister Duck-Duck and you'll never see him again."

"I don't know."

"Look, Toby. You have to answer this, okay? It's important."

"But why?"

"It's a game."

"It's not fun."

"Well, you need to play it. It's like your homework. You have to do it. You have to. Either you help people and they take away Mister

Duck-Duck, or you don't help them and you get to keep Mister Duck-Duck."

Toby tilted his head from side to side, humming to himself. Finally he said, "Does everyone have a daddy?"

"Huh? Yeah. Of course."

"So Mister Duck-Duck has a daddy."

"Yeah, I guess so. You're Mister Duck-Duck's daddy. Why?"

"Because I know my Daddy won't ever let anyone take me away from him. And he always does the right thing."

Rod dropped the sponge in the water. He rested his elbow on the tub's edge and held his forehead with his dry hand.

Toby looked over his shoulder.

"Daddy, why are you crying?"

Rod sniffled his tears back. "Because you make me happy."

"But people cry when they're sad, not when they're happy."

"Adults are silly, buddy. We don't always make sense."

"Yeah." He paused, pushing Mister Duck-Duck across the water. "I know."

* * *

After taking a long, hot shower, Rod picked up Fran Amaretto's business card on his dresser. He ran his finger over the embossed CNB network logo, put the card down and walked away to check on Toby. He surrounded his son with toys in the living room and returned to his bedroom.

He checked his answering machine. Even though the digital display showed zero, he pushed the button anyway.

"You have no new messages," the robotic voice said.

"That's weird," Rod said to himself.

He grabbed the card and sat at his desk in the den.

He laid a pen and pad before him. He could hear Toby talking to himself as he played in front of the television.

Rod looked at the photo on his bookshelf. It was the same photo from his Redfire locker, the six men in Rod's Green Beret unit, of which he was now the only living member. The others were long gone. Hayger was gone.

Now Barra was gone.

He waited in the near quiet, just breathing.

He pushed the photograph face-down and dialed.

"CNB network. This is Amaretto," the voice answered.

"Hello, Miss Amaretto, it's Rod North. I hadn't heard from you. I'm ready to talk more, tell you the full story of what happened, you know, out there."

"Oh, Mister North. I'm glad you called. Sort of."

"I wanted to discuss when and where we could meet. I'm ready to tell you everything."

"That won't be necessary. I've been talking with my producer and a few of the higher-ups here. Everyone agrees that we need to back-burner your story."

"But I thought you said-"

"Have you been watching the news? The whole country can't wait until we bomb the living crap out of Kariqistan. People want revenge for those killed on the Sunset Mist. We're not going to put ourselves in front of the bloodthirsty mob and say, you're wrong! No way. Who's going to listen? Then who's going to believe? Maybe in a few years, but right now, that would be suicide for our ratings. We'd lose all our advertisers overnight. Even if your insane story checks out. Which I have some doubts about."

"But Miss Amar-"

"Oh, and don't worry," Amaretto went on. "I'm not showing anyone your picture. You kept your end of the deal. I'll keep mine. I might want to ask you something if I think it involves Redfire in the future."

"They fired me."

"Fired you? Well, that's great. Now I have nothing. Absolutely nothing. I don't get the inside source on a terrorist attack, and I don't even get a background on these Kathleen contracts."

"Katrina contracts."

Amaretto didn't seem to hear him, she just kept talking. "I got nothing from the biggest event of the decade and I was right there. My career is sinking faster than the Sunset Mist."

"I'm trying to do the right thing," North said.

"That's why no one wants to talk to you."

Rod stared at the ceiling.

"But you tried," Amaretto said. "Your conscience is clean."

"What about yours?"

"What conscience?" she chuckled. "I serve the market."

"Why do I feel like I'm the only one who is taking this seriously?"

"Because you are. Everyone else is setting up slogans and graphics, moving to make a profit or cover their ass. Sure there may be a few isolated sad families here and there if some servicemen get killed, but nothing will interfere with the daily life of most people."

Rod sighed and stared at the wall. He held the phone away from his ear for a moment.

"But this is outrageous. I need your help. People are going to die."

"Right. No matter what we do."

Rod stared at the wall, silent for a while.

Amaretto continued. "On some level I agree with you, North. It would be great if this could be stopped. But now I've got to go. You had good intentions, that's got to be worth something. Somewhere."

"Yeah. I tried to do the right thing."

"And you failed."

Rod could hear the bitterness in his voice. "But it's the thought that counts, right?"

"Not really. No one cares if you know a secret, only if you talk about it. Look, I have to run. Have a nice life, Mr. North."

Rod hung up without returning the sentiment.

* * *

Rod sat staring at the phone and the face-down photo of Hayger and Barra for a long time. The house was unusually quiet except for the TV's mumbling.

Rod felt suddenly tense.

"Toby?" he called out.

No answer.

"Toby!"

Rod bolted downstairs. The television was playing a commercial. Toby's toys were strewn about the floor.

Rod saw his boy in the back yard, playing.

He inhaled deeply, closing his eyes, trying to slow his racing heart.

Squeak!

Rod leapt, startled, landing in crouched fighting stance.

He felt a lump under his right foot. He lifted his leg and Mister Duck-Duck tumbled out from beneath his sneaker.

"That's it!" Rod said, grabbing the toy and dropping it in the sink. He jammed it down the drain with a wooden spoon then flicked on the garbage disposal switch. Mister Duck-Duck emitted one last airy squeak that was quickly drowned by the roar of the motor.

Rod let the disposal run until the sound of rattling plastic pieces stopped and the blades were slicing through air. He shut the disposal off.

"Toby!" he yelled through the open window.

The boy turned around.

"Get in here."

"Why?"

"Come on inside, buddy. Let's watch TV."

Rod sat on the couch with his son on his lap. The news had interrupted the children's shows. A woman was crying into the camera. Text on the screen read, "Military Recruitment at an all-time high."

"My sons enlisted," the woman sobbed. "All three of them. I'm so proud of them, but so scared. I'm just terrified. Worried they'll never come back."

"Daddy? Why is that lady crying?"

Rod switched the channel to some cartoons.

"Daddy?"

"Yes."

"Where's Mister Duck-Duck?"

"Don't worry about it, kid," Rod said. "Don't worry about anything at all."

*** THE END ***

THANKS

I would like to extend an ocean-sized thank you to Jeffrey Baumgard, STG2(SW) Ret. for answering my many questions about the Navy, the Coast Guard, and their customs. Any errors or fabrications about naval conduct are my own.

Thanks very much to Tom Demi for proofreading. Any remaining errors are mine.

Thanks also to the feedback crew: Heather, Ted and Bob.

LN

# # #

A NOTE TO READERS

Dear Reader,

Thank you so much for taking the time to read *The Katrina Contract*. If you have a moment, you can help independent publishing by leaving a fair and honest review on Amazon.com or your favorite reading website. Reviews help authors reach more readers and assist those authors in improving their craft.

So thanks again for reading *The Katrina Contract*. I hope you found it time well spent. All the best to you.

Larry Nocella

ABOUT THE AUTHOR

Larry Nocella sold his first article at age fourteen, and has been writing ever since. He lives in the USA. Visit www.LarryNocella.com.

OTHER WORKS BY LARRY NOCELLA
AVAILABLE ON AMAZON.COM

Loser's Memorial - a novel

Loser's Memorial takes readers on a dark journey through the surreal and sinister world where war and profit mix. Written with a masterful blend of brutality, humanity and demented humor, the madness of this gruesome thrill ride stays with you right up to the shocking finish.

Told from alternating perspectives between a Moroccan boy falsely accused of being a terrorist, and a down-on-his luck American who ends up in jail, *Loser's Memorial* follows both as they descend into the surreal and self-perpetuating world of war for profit.

Together the two young men descend into the lawless world of unsupervised military contractors and secret prisons, where the surreal becomes horrifyingly real.

Both end up fighting a losing battle to retain their humanity as they learn that sometimes the only hope of escaping a twisted situation is to become more twisted.

Where Did This Come From? - a novel

Based in the fictional South American nation of Palagua, the novel *Where Did This Come From?* follows the Huapi tribe's desperate struggle for survival. When American tourist Joe Vera saves the life of the Huapi chief, he is rewarded with a rare and beautiful crystal unknown to the outside world.

Back in America, Joe gives the crystal as a gift to the terminally-ill son of his ex-girlfriend, but it isn't long before the crystal attracts the interest of a leading U.S. toy manufacturer, MajorCo Toys. In an instant, Joe is rich and the crystal is selling like crazy. MajorCo stock is skyrocketing, just before the Christmas shopping season.

The news from Palagua is much more grim. Mining operations are tearing apart the Huapi land. Civil war erupts as factions battle for control of the huge wealth suddenly found in this once-poor nation.

The Huapi find themselves and the jungle that supports them on the brink of annihilation. Joe struggles to stem the forces of desire he has unleashed. How do you fight want? How do you fight greed?

Can Joe and the Huapi hope to resist the hunger of those who never bother to care *Where Did This Come From?*

It Never Goes Away (short story)

Author Larry Nocella terrifies readers with a suspenseful struggle for survival in the short story ***It Never Goes Away***. The lone survivor of a mysterious catastrophe awakes to find himself buried alive in the ruins of his home. Every attempt to escape only buries him deeper. Facing starvation, thirst, and a lack of air, his odds of survival diminish with each passing second. As he pieces together the true nature of the disaster, it seems beyond imagining. Will he live long enough to find out the truth?

Includes an essay by the author about the story's real-life inspiration.